STRIPPED

STRIPPED

Tori St. Claire

HEAT | NEW YORK

THE BERKLEY PUBLISHING GROUP
Published by the Penguin Group
Penguin Group (USA) Inc.
375 Hudson Street, New York, New York 10014, USA
Penguin Group (Canada), 90 Eglinton Avenue East, Suite 700, Toronto, Ontario M4P 2Y3, Canada
(a division of Pearson Penguin Canada Inc.)
Penguin Books Ltd., 80 Strand, London WC2R 0RL, England
Penguin Group Ireland, 25 St. Stephen's Green, Dublin 2, Ireland (a division of Penguin Books Ltd.)
Penguin Group (Australia), 250 Camberwell Road, Camberwell, Victoria 3124, Australia
(a division of Pearson Australia Group Pty. Ltd.)
Penguin Books India Pvt. Ltd., 11 Community Centre, Panchsheel Park, New Delhi—110 017, India
Penguin Group (NZ), 67 Apollo Drive, Rosedale, Auckland 0632, New Zealand
(a division of Pearson New Zealand Ltd.)
Penguin Books (South Africa) (Pty.) Ltd., 24 Sturdee Avenue, Rosebank, Johannesburg 2196,
South Africa

Penguin Books Ltd., Registered Offices: 80 Strand, London WC2R 0RL, England

This book is an original publication of The Berkley Publishing Group.

PUBLISHING HISTORY
Heat trade paperback edition / January 2012

Library of Congress Cataloging-in-Publication Data

Claire, Tori St.
    Stripped / Tori St. Claire. — Heat trade paperback ed.
      p. cm.
    ISBN 978-0-425-24677-1
    1. Women intelligence officers—Fiction.   2. United States. Central Intelligence Agency—Fiction.
3. Undercover operations—Fiction.   4. Human trafficking—Fiction.   5. Stripteasers—Fiction.
6. Las Vegas (Nev.)—Fiction.   I. Title.
    PS3619.T235S77   2012
    813'.6—dc22
                                2011028165

PRINTED IN THE UNITED STATES OF AMERICA

10 9 8 7 6 5 4 3 2 1

To Yuriy. Though the dream was different, your lessons taught me how to rise above obstacles and believe in the gold. They will always be part of me. I love you, my friend.

Acknowledgments

To my agent, Jewelann Cone, and my editor, Leis Pederson: this book would not have been possible without either of you. Literally. The both of you made it all come together and gave me a dream come true by opening a door I didn't even see. I don't have words to express my gratitude.

To Alexis Walker, who gave me the courage to go where limits didn't apply, thank you so much.

Alta Durrant, when everyone was buried under deadlines, yourself included, you pushed me to create, to see the story through. Your brainstorming sessions made this work, and your enthusiasm kept me going.

Dyann Love Barr, your belief in me helped me knock down barricades. You've been there through the best of times and the worst, and I value your friendship, your support, and your wisdom so very much. Thank you for everything. (And give Dennis a hug!)

Mom, thank you for the time you've invested and the sacrifices you've made. I love you very much.

Garrett and Pierce, thank you for your patience, your love, and the joy you bring to my life. You make my days brighter and my heart light, even when you're bathing in the mud.

Matt, you encouraged me from the beginning and remain steadfast. I wouldn't have embarked on this path without your support.

Jackie Bannon, from writing to nursing crying jags with margaritas, you've been there. Thank you so much.

Thank you, Linda Kage, for the time you put forth and the ideas you spurred, as well as your constant support and encouragement.

Cathy Morrison, Judy Ridgely, Goldie Edwards, Alicia Dean, Kimberly, and Diana Coyle, thank you for all the time you've dedicated to reading, commenting, and advising, both in this project and a multitude of others. I sincerely appreciate your insight and the time you've given me.

Jason, the support you give and the time you invest is priceless. You were willing to learn with me, to ask necessary questions, and whittle away at the Victorian. Thank you for being you, a man I respect, and a hero I admire.

They exist only in shadow. An elite team of deadly operatives created to satisfy increasing international threats. Their world is the dark underground, where sin and pleasure dominate and lies are second nature. To those who cross them, they are professional killers. Within the CIA, they are the rare Black Opals. . . .

One

The woman Natalya Trubachev would escort to hell lay beneath a halo of murky light, trembling in fear. Her long blonde hair was clumped in an unruly mass of tangles around her slender shoulders. Her clothes were hardly decent, let alone useful covering against the cold cement floor. She shivered, proving the point.

Natalya shivered with her. This part was the worst. Three years of soothing the women should have made her immune. At one time, she *had* been disconnected from them. But now, each pale face, each quivering lip, curled her stomach and left her questioning things she didn't dare consider. Things like her purpose. The state of her soul. Like why she'd ever become a Black Opal, an elite, deadly, and highly undocumented CIA operative.

Beyond the reinforced square pane of glass, the blonde shivered again. She tucked her hands between her knees and curled her shoulders.

Natalya braced an open palm on the soundproof door and pushed it open. *Soon you won't remember.* Well, she'd remember, but she wouldn't *care.* Not once the barbiturates invaded the woman's veins and she woke up in Dubai. By then, a prisoner to her tranquilized state, she'd already be dependent on daily heroin injections. She'd agree to anything as long as she got her fix.

Natalya dismissed unwelcome visions of that illicit place of sin and opulence and rolled a syringe against her palm. *She's just a job. One step closer.* No different from any other job Natalya had performed in any other place under any other cover. Problem was, this one Natalya knew well. She knew them all. That's why she was here. She gained their trust, used it against them, and led them straight to hell.

All for the sake of national security. Only nowadays, it felt more like for the sake of Dmitri Gavrikov's sick pleasure than any act of protecting the United States. God, she had to get out of here. Had to get this job over with before she lost her mind and her ability to function as a Black Opal. Three years in one place was too long.

At the sound of Natalya's heels against the hard floor, the blonde turned her head. Hope filled her wide blue eyes. "Natalya?" Her voice was a hoarse whisper. *"Pomogite mne."*

Help me. Natalya tightened her fingers around the syringe she held. If only she could.

Blocking unwanted emotion, she found a confident smile. She walked with more purpose. Flawless Russian tumbled off her lips along with a light laugh. "Help you, Tatiana? Don't be silly. There's not a soul here who'd hurt you."

Not here. No one would dare mar Tatiana's porcelain skin with bruises. That would mean delivering damaged goods to Sheikh Amir in Dubai. Natalya refused to think about what would happen to Tatiana there. But the sheikh's wealthy clients wouldn't be at all pleased to find their treasures waiting in silk-clad beds and covered with purple welts.

She knelt at Tatiana's side and helped her upright. "I'm sorry Alexei scared you. Didn't he tell you I'd be back to keep you company before your big date?"

Tatiana wiped a dust-streaked hand across her cheek as she shook her head. "He said nothing."

Rolling her eyes, Natalya let out another false laugh. "Men." She gave Tatiana's arm a gentle pinch. "Well, he was supposed to. Now I guess we'll have to get you to a shower before the party starts. You can't very well dance covered in dirt—even if you are taking off your clothes." With a conspiratorial wink, she grinned.

A sigh of relief escaped Tatiana's pale lips, and a hesitant smile drifted over her mouth. "I'm still entertaining the businessmen tonight? I'll need something to wear."

"Of course. I've got the perfect thing in mind. In a couple hours, they'll walk out of here with their cocks harder than they've ever thought possible and their money stuffed in your thong."

Tatiana wrinkled her nose with an amused giggle. "It's how it always is, no? Show a bit of skin, twist your hips just so, and they eat out of your palm."

Literally, as Natalya had witnessed from behind the stage at Dmitri's many strip clubs throughout Moscow—where Tatiana and the other women had all come from. They were chosen for their exceptional beauty and their equally exceptional ability to seduce through dance.

She hoisted Tatiana to her feet. "Let's get you cleaned up. We don't have much time."

Tatiana's grateful gaze found Natalya's. "Thank you. I was afraid you'd told me stories."

Guilt punched Natalya in the gut. She forced her smile to widen over a threatening grimace. Following ingrained routine, she wrapped her arms around the woman's dirty shoulders and gave Tatiana a hug.

As waif-thin arms slipped around Natalya's waist to return the affectionate gesture, Natalya turned her wrist and pressed the needle into Tatiana's jugular. As she pushed the barbiturate into her bloodstream, Tatiana jerked back. Cornflower blue eyes filled with shock. Pale pink lips parted with a question that would never escape. Then she slumped forward, her slight weight barely rocking Natalya.

With a heavy sigh, Natalya eased her onto the floor. She dropped the syringe and turned to the door, where Dmitri waited with a proud smile. In his hand, he held a box of chocolate-covered cherries.

Natalya startled. Dmitri wasn't supposed to be back until tomorrow night.

He spread his arms in welcome. *"Moya lyubov'."*

My love.

Natalya's smile brightened as a shadow crossed over her soul, chilling her from the inside out. She hurried across the small space between them, accepted the box of candy, and threw herself into his arms. He clasped her against his hard chest. Broad palms slid up the back of her cashmere sweater. Warm, soft lips found hers, but though the stroke of his tongue was ardent, no heat crept into her veins. It never had. What he was, what he believed in, turned his handsome face and well-maintained body into a cold, lifeless statue. He was every bit as soulless too.

He dropped his hands to her waist and leaned back to look at her. His soft brown eyes sparkled with genuine affection. If Dmitri Gavrikov, merciless leader of the *Solntsevskaya Bratva*, had ever cared for anything, or anyone, it most assuredly was her.

He pushed her hair away from her face. "Did you miss me?"

"Yes." She wriggled closer. "It's miserable when you go away."

"It was necessary." He brushed his mouth against the top of her head as he caught her by the hand.

It always was. Someone needed to learn a lesson. A buyer demanded his time. A seller offered the right price on black-market arms. Dmitri always had a necessary reason for leaving. And in his wake, would always be a body. No one would ever find it, but someone forfeited their life when Dmitri's meetings required more than an hour or two to complete.

This time he'd been gone almost a week. Tomorrow, she'd get a full report from her partner, Sergei. Maybe he'd had luck. Maybe he'd finally made the connection that would allow them to shut this whole ring down. The drugs, the arms . . .

Natalya glanced over her shoulder as Dmitri pulled the door shut on Tatiana's unconscious form.

The human trafficking.

"I bring news, *czarina*."

"Oh?" Natalya followed at his side while he led her down the hall to their bedroom. Inside, she set the chocolates on a marble-topped table.

"We're going to marry in America. Las Vegas." He released her hand and moved to the brass-embellished liquor cabinet. Glass tinkled as he pulled down two snifters along with his favorite Armagnac. Though his hands poured steadily, fury gave his voice a sharp edge. "The idiots who work for me can't seem to keep from killing our precious American cargo. I need you to handle the girls—you do such a wonderful job here. The trail of bodies is causing Yakov problems."

Natalya's heart skipped a beat. *Yakov.* One of the contacts in America she couldn't identify. His codename symbolized his duty—the one who took Dmitri's place. He worked with Iskatel´, codename for *the finder.* Like she did with the girls in Moscow, Yakov and Iskatel´ hand-selected the best strippers Vegas had to offer and shipped them overseas to satisfy the appetites of powerful men hungry for a bit of classy, American pussy—or what they could delude themselves into believing was classy. Now Dmitri intended to send her right into Yakov's nest? She stifled a smile.

"Must I leave?" Dipping her chin, she looked up through her eyelashes. "You've just returned."

Dmitri turned with her glass extended in offering. His gaze roved appreciatively over her body. Desire sparked in his eyes. Dark and intense, his was a look meant to leave her wet and wanting. On any other woman it might have worked.

Boldly holding his gaze, Natalya accepted the oaken-flavored drink. "I hate the idea of another night alone."

"Ah, *czarina*, I do not deserve you." His hand settled on her hip, his thumb stroking the flesh beneath her sweater's short hem. He lowered his voice to an intimate whisper. "Forgive me." A sultry smile crossed his mouth. "Tonight I'll make up for the time away. In two weeks, I'll give you all I possess when I give you my name." He tugged at her waist, urging her hips into his. Firm, hard arousal pressed against her abdomen. "You *will* forgive me, won't you?"

Natalya teased with a slow roll of her hips. "It might take some convincing."

Chuckling, Dmitri released her. He nodded at her dresser. "Wear the green for me tonight?"

She hated the green. Maybe because he liked it too much. Maybe because it made her eyes stand out unnaturally and that drove Dmitri to abandon. Whatever the case, she hated the green. But for him, for her *duty* to her country and the hope that somehow, by sacrificing every last damn moral she possessed, those women would find freedom, she'd not refuse.

Leaning forward, she dusted her lips over his. "Tell me more while I undress." Before his hand could catch and hold her close, she twisted out of his reach and went to the small table that held her jewelry box. She plucked off one gold hoop earring. "I'm to do the same things I do here? Befriend them and lead them to . . . ?" *Who, Dmitri?*

"To Yakov, yes." The bed creaked as he reclined against the pillows.

Through the mirror, she watched as he stretched out his muscular legs and braced his arms behind his head. Damn. Yakov again. What the hell was the man's name?

"Iskatel′ has already chosen the next girl."

"Oh?" Natalya took off the matching earring and dropped both into the case. Reaching behind her, she pulled her pistol from the waist of her fitted skirt and laid it on the tabletop.

"Yes. You'll be working at Fantasia, next door to the St. Petersburg casino. My contacts there are creating a position for you as we speak. Your first project is Katerina Slater."

Natalya's hand froze over the Sig's matte black barrel. Her throat inched closed. She'd misheard him. Kate wasn't stripping. She had a little boy to raise. She wouldn't expose him to that kind of lifestyle.

Aware Dmitri watched through the mirror, Natalya forced a casual smile. "I'm sorry, I didn't hear you, love."

"Katerina Slater. I hear she's commanding Fantasia's stage." His low chuckle rasped through the room. "You should bond easily. She's an Ivanov, of all ironies. Born in an Old Believer Russian village in Alaska. Her parents immigrated from St. Petersburg. You can tell her about Mother Russia."

Kate! By God, she hadn't heard him wrong.

It took every bit of Natalya's willpower to pull her hand away from the Sig and reach behind her neck to unfasten her pearl necklace. As she laid it in the jewelry box, she willed her hands not to shake. Though they cooperated, her stomach rebelled with a vicious upside-down-sideways twist.

There were only so many wrongs she could commit in the name of US Intelligence. Turning her fraternal twin into a rich bastard's heroin-addicted whore wasn't one of them. She'd put a bullet between Dmitri's eyes and willfully blow her cover before she'd risk a single hair on Kate's head.

With a sugary-sweet smile, Natalia pulled her sweater over her head and caught Dmitri's smoldering gaze. "When do I leave, darling?"

As Natalya approached the bed, the sway of her full pert breasts obliterated all thoughts of whether she wore green or blue or even purple. Need launched through Dmitri. All he could think about was how good she would feel around him. How nothing in this world compared to how she felt in his arms. He rose to his knees, interrupting her path to her dresser for the negligee he'd requested. One hand latched on to her narrow wrist. One tug brought her to her knees on the bed.

"Tomorrow. You leave tomorrow." He caught her hair in his hand, tugged her mouth to his, and drank from the softness of her full lips. The slide of her tongue against his was enough to strip a man to the bone. A shudder rolled through his body, the week he'd spent away from her a torture unto itself.

The sudden violent need to possess her completely had him dragging her closer. With his free hand he cupped her bottom, urged her hips hard against his erection, and let out a hoarse groan. What he would give to indulge in all the things he *really* wanted to do to her—his belt would serve nicely tonight. Latch it around her wrists, fasten those delightful hands to the headboard, and take her from behind—ride her hard into oblivion. Thrust inside her glorious ass where she would be even tighter. *Ah, fucking heaven.*

But Natalya didn't know the meaning of submit, and Dmitri had witnessed her expertise with her gun one too many times to push. Though he trusted her implicitly, a tiny, almost insignificant part of his soul feared what might happen if his beautiful fiancée lost control.

Instead of following through with his fantasies, he tore his mouth from hers to stare into her eyes. "Tonight, though, I will make sure you cannot help but miss me."

Indeed, he would take her so many times that when she boarded the plane tomorrow, she could still smell him on her skin.

Her shiver unraveled him. Unable to form any conscious thought beyond how desperately he needed the feel of her, how he yearned for this closeness they alone shared, he withdrew and kicked free of his trousers. Her soft laughter danced over his skin, pleasantly scraping raw nerve endings as she aided in the removal of his shirt.

He gave in to a smile. How he had missed fucking her. Missed the love that radiated through the pressure of her hands. "Tell me what you want, *czarina*."

"You," she murmured.

For this he could deal with the idiots who failed him. For this he would tolerate the fact her duties required her to flirt a line of seduction to make the contacts she would require in America.

This singular moment, where the two of them knew no greater paradise than the pleasure of their bodies, was more priceless to Dmitri than any wealth, any power. Struck by momentary tenderness, he lifted up to brush his lips against hers. *"Moya lyubov',"* he whispered.

Yes, love her—the only woman he had ever loved. For that matter, the only *thing.* What he would do without her, he didn't know. She made the duties he must carry out possible, and the next few days apart, after so many already past, would be impossible. Yet it was necessary. She alone could teach Iskatel´ how to smoothly make the women subservient. But if Iskatel´ didn't cooperate with Natalya, or Iskatel´'s ineptitude put her in harm's way, Iskatel´ would join the murdered women in the grave.

For Natalya, Dmitri would kill even his own *Bratva* family.

He sealed his lips to hers and reclined into the pillows, taking her with him.

TWO

Three brand-new, state-of-the-art, boxed cell phones toppled onto the bar, along with three Bluetooth earpieces and a trio of identical black protective cases. Lieutenant Brandon Moretti pushed the jumbled stack across the polished oak and grinned at his gathered team. "I don't want to hear anymore bitching about outdated technology."

Two pairs of hands shot forward to snatch up the high-tech toys. Cardboard ripped open, instructions fluttered to the floor, and the dim light brightened as LCD touch screens lit up.

Brandon avoided looking at the untouched packages. A pair of feminine hands should be digging in as well. The fact they weren't stirred twelve years of undercover instincts and made his gut shift with unease.

"Shit, Moretti, what the hell am I going to do with this?" Aaron Mayer dangled the earpiece between his thumb and forefinger.

Brandon gave him a one-shoulder shrug. "You wanted the damned things, you figure it out." He'd been lucky enough to figure out how to turn his on. A plain-Jane flip phone suited his needs perfectly. But the team had a point—they couldn't integrate with their new upscale clientele without upgrading. Fantasia was a far cry from Sadie's, where they'd been for the last year.

And their new assignment, stopping a serial killer, was a far cry from busting drug rings. The phones weren't all that needed upgrading—the whole team had adjustments to make.

He glanced back at the untouched boxes. Where the hell was

Rachel? He'd even stopped by her house, only to find it as cluttered as it had been two nights before when they'd all celebrated his acceptance as Fantasia's manager with too much beer and bad pizza.

Looking up, Brandon caught Rory Neal's unblinking stare. Behind a day's worth of dark stubble, a muscle in Rory's jaw ticked. Gray eyes hardened, then dropped to the untouched phone and accessories. Scarred knuckles drummed on the bar's mirror-smooth top.

Brandon expelled a harsh breath. They all worried. No one would mention it, least of all Rory, but the question loomed in all their minds: *What had happened to her?* Ten years of exemplary service. Eight spent with the team. And out of the blue she'd failed to show last night, their first night on the job in their new club. With a serial killer on the loose, targeting women who matched Rachel's blonde hair and china-fair skin, the warnings screamed like sirens.

"Well." Brandon pushed away from the bar. *Focus them on work. Keep their minds from drifting to the possibilities.* "Let's go over this again. Mayer, what's the pattern?"

Aaron hands stilled over his cell phone's display. "Every two weeks. Cyclical through the clubs. Unless he changes up, Fantasia's next, and he'll hit on the twenty-fourth. Always a Friday. Always a blonde. Always the best dancer of the bunch."

"Christ," Rory muttered.

Brandon's gaze slanted to where the lanky detective sat. Worried fingers shoved through cropped hair, then grazed down his forgotten whiskers.

He needed to say something. That's what friends did—looked to the positive even when all factors pointed to disaster. Brandon pulled in a deep breath. Beyond friendship, he was their lieutenant, and he had to keep his team focused. "Rachel didn't dance. She doesn't match the profile."

Which made her unexplained disappearance more odd. If Brandon's suspicions were correct, her boyfriend was sitting at the bar in front of him right now. Her family lived in Vegas—if there'd been an emergency she'd have let her team know. Rachel wouldn't just bail on a murderer *she'd* linked to the drug ring they'd been investigating for two years.

Rory answered with a jerk of his head that could almost be considered a nod.

Keep 'em focused.

Brandon cleared his throat. "Rory, I want you behind the bar. You've got four guys who've been slinging drinks here for over a year. Use them. Get a feel for the regulars." He shifted his attention to Mayer. "You've got security. No one goes in or out of the VIP rooms without you knowing." He rounded the bar to retreat into the quiet of his office. At the corner, the frown he'd been fighting all morning wrinkled his brow. He turned it on Mayer. "Stick to Kate Slater like her fucking shadow. She's got a kid. I'm not letting that bastard touch her."

Aaron flashed Brandon a cocky grin. "Got it, boss. That was the plan."

"Right." Brandon tapped a fist on the brass rail. "We open in four hours. I've gotta interview this dancer. She'll be here any minute."

The last thing he wanted to do was interview another girl. But Kate had referred her, and Kate knew how to pick dancers that drew crowds. Crowds meant money. If Brandon intended to keep his position as manager long enough to find a killer, he couldn't lose sight of the club's bottom line.

With a little luck, this girl wouldn't show up with blonde hair.

He pushed through his office door and dropped into his leather chair with a harassed sigh. This was Rachel's job—the hiring, firing, and general needs of the girls. As housemom, she knew the right questions to ask. Where the hell was she?

Pulling his phone off his hip pocket, he tapped the screen to try her apartment again. He dialed from memory, having not yet figured out how to set up his address book.

Her voice mail answered. "This is Rach! Leave a message!"

"Where the fuck are you, Rach?" He tossed the phone on the desk with another muttered oath.

Before the last syllable escaped, a bright electronic tune issued from his phone. He snatched it up, not bothering to look at the display. "Rach! Where are you? Are you okay?"

"Hey, Moretti." Captain Joe Cavelli's whiskey-roughened voice drifted through the line. "I'm sending a car out. They're going to ask you about your liquor license. You're not going to be able to find it. I need you downtown."

The hair on the back of Brandon's neck lifted. He leaned forward and crumpled a sheet of paper in his fist. "What's up?"

Cavelli paused. The silence stretched out, mingling with the rustling of paper before concluding on a harsh sigh. "I think you better come in."

"I think you better tell me. What's wrong?" Brandon asked, but he already knew. The answer blared in his head. Twisted painful knots behind his ribs.

"It's Rachel. Park ranger found her body up near the Canyon around eight this morning. Same MO as your guy."

Brandon closed his eyes to block the sudden onslaught of grief. His team. She was his responsibility. He'd done everything according to protocol. Followed his own edicts, made sure she had an escort, and didn't take her expert marksmanship for granted. Still, he'd failed her.

"Don't send the car," he murmured as he terminated the call.

The phone clattered against his desktop, and he dropped his head into his hands. Dead. What the hell was he supposed to say to Rory now? Or Aaron—Rachel was like his sister. Hell, she was like Brandon's for that matter. A replacement for the one he'd also failed fifteen years ago. And now, like that biological sister, Rachel was just as dead.

"Fuck!" He slammed his palm against his desk, sending his chair rocketing backward. Bolting to his feet, he swiped his phone off and stuffed it into his pocket.

"I'm sorry, I guess this is a bad time?"

The husky feminine voice, heavily laden with a European flavor, drew Brandon to an abrupt halt. His head snapped up. His gaze zeroed in on an auburn-haired beauty standing in his doorway.

She offered him a hesitant smile that turned up the corners of jade green eyes. One delicate hand pointed over her shoulder. "They said you were in here. Told me to come on back."

His dancer. Brandon groaned inwardly. He quickly pulled himself together and struggled for a welcoming, professional, smile. "No, it's fine, come in." With a sweep of his hand, he invited her to sit in the chair across from his. "You're Kate's friend?"

Impossibly long legs moved across his carpet with a queen's grace. She seated herself, draped one lithe thigh across the other, and bounced a black stiletto. "Natalya Trubachev." She reached across his desk to shake his hand.

Brandon fitted his palm into hers. In one sweeping glance, he took her in from head to toe. What he could see of her anyway. And what the desk didn't hide tripped his system into unexpected awareness. A V-neck white blouse exposed creamy skin and the high swell of full breasts. Narrow hips barely took up half of the chair. But her smile . . .

Her smile robbed him of the ability to breathe.

Kate had said he'd be pleased. Hell, there wasn't a man on earth who *wouldn't* be pleased. From the tiny gold bangles in her ears, to the perfect white crescents on the end of her long nails, she radiated class. The crisp lines of her clothing hinted at designer names Brandon couldn't hope to recognize. Yet he saw them daily amongst the elite crowds that circulated the back rooms of Vegas nightlife. Women who had more money than they knew what to do with—so they spent it on larks, voyeuristic escapades, and sometimes not-so-hands-off entertainment.

Why was a woman like this interviewing to strip?

"Brandon Moretti." He pumped her hand, then resumed his chair. "Kate says you want to dance?" Sifting through the clutter on his desk, he searched for her application that Kate had brought in the day before.

"Yeah. I'm in between jobs right now and could use the cash."

Her faint accent caressed his ears like fingertips might stroke his skin. The effect wasn't all that different either. His flesh prickled, a jolt of energy thrummed down his spine. Blood raced to his groin. Just like that he was rock hard.

Shit! Appalled by his body's unexpected reaction, Brandon cleared his throat and shifted his weight to make a little room behind his fly. For God's sake, Rachel was dead. What was the matter with him?

He shuffled through another stack of papers. Where had he put the damn thing? It was here somewhere . . . "I'm sorry. I can't seem to find the application Kate brought in. Can you tell me if you have experience?" Looking up, he met her gaze. Mistake. His chest constricted, and for a moment, he forgot what she was doing here. Visions of pulling her out of that chair and bending her over his desk, those breasts cupped in his hands, creamy butt cheeks begging him to slide his tongue over their sloping curves, invaded all rational thought.

"I danced with Kate in college. Didn't she tell you?"

Her light laugh jerked him out of fantasy. Kate had told him that. Rachel's disappearance, however, erased most of the memory of that conversation. Now she was dead . . .

A wave of sadness flooded him. Before it could root in, he shook off the news he had yet to share with his team. He couldn't dwell on Rachel now. Couldn't grieve until he finished business.

The flash of sorrow behind Brandon's tawny eyes strained Natalya's smile. Worse, it threatened to break through the wall around her emotions. That pile of rock and mortar had been crumbling for the last three days. First Tatiana. Then Kate. Now grief over a loss Natalya's employment necessitated. If she didn't get this infernal sympathy under control, she'd get herself killed.

"I'm sorry. It's been a very . . . long . . . day." There it was again.

A softening of his gaze that wound her insides together tighter than iron mesh. Lieutenant Brandon Moretti grieved for his team member.

Dmitri and his hooligans didn't know they'd offed a cop. Natalya, however, had made a few discreet phone calls once she and Sergei hit stateside. Though Moretti's captain had embedded him impeccably, the CIA records easily identified the four Vegas Vice members. And this man wasn't taking the news of Rachel Kensington's death well at all.

Natalya cringed inwardly. Why would he? He didn't suffer the same insensitivity that she'd become accustomed to. Softening her voice, Natalya reached for the compassion she'd left behind long ago. "I could come back later tonight. Tomorrow."

"No." Sitting forward, Brandon folded his hands on the stack of papers atop his desk. "You worked with Kate. That was when? Ten years ago? Have you danced since then?"

"Fifteen, and no. But I'm quite capable." Only because Dmitri made her dance for him. She supposed she could consider that a benefit. If he hadn't insisted on private pole dances, her body would have forgotten how.

The reproachful arch of a dark eyebrow hinted at doubt. "What makes you certain you can compete with the girls who've been doing this for years?" His gaze dropped to her breasts, then slid slowly back up to lock with hers. "Beyond the obvious."

Natalya's body flushed with heat. She crossed the opposite leg over her opposite knee, unsettled by the blatant appreciation in those tawny eyes. How many times had Dmitri looked at her with the same suggestion in his gaze?

How long had it been since she'd *liked* being stripped bare with a mere glance?

The sudden tingling of her skin disturbed her. Moretti could very well be one of Dmitri's faithful—he had more than one cop on the take. While Dmitri understood her job required a bit of . . . feminine finesse . . . he'd only grant her so much leeway. If she gave him a reason to suspect her allegiance, he'd slice her throat before she could see the knife glint. And the way her body was warming beneath Brandon's heated stare spelled trouble.

Determined to ignore his blatantly sexual gaze, she focused on the small white scar across Moretti's chin and dredged up every reason she could think of to convince him into giving her the job. "I danced well. Was the crowd favorite for a while. I held the job all through college, and two years in, the girls were coming to me for dance suggestions, costuming, on-the-spot fixes for breakdowns. Advice on how to handle the more exuberant customers." She took a breath and began counting items off her fingers. "I hired. I fired. I kept the drugs out of the dressing rooms. I trained the girls on the pole— Kate said you needed someone strong with the pole. My core body strength—"

"You're hired."

Natalya snapped her mouth shut. Slowly, she blinked. "What?"

"You're hired." Moretti stood, stretching out his muscular thighs that even his loose denim jeans couldn't disguise. He shoved his left hand into his hip pocket. Against her will, Natalya's gaze dropped to his crotch. Her breath caught at the tightening of his fly, the hard ridge that evidenced arousal.

When she yanked her gaze back to Brandon's, his eyes flashed dark gold, telling her he knew exactly where she'd been looking. His voice, however, belied his awareness. "We open in three hours. I'll need you here early to help get the girls settled in."

"The girls?"

He fished a set of keys out of the top right desk drawer and held his fist over her hand. "These are to the dressing rooms. I have a copy, you have a copy. No one else. Kate's our star. She goes on at ten, and every two hours after. Jill follows. Beyond that, you'll have to talk to the girls."

Natalya moved her hand beneath his, palm up, waiting for the keys. "And me?"

"I need a housemom more than I need a dancer." His fingers brushed the base of her wrist.

Ignoring the chill that raced to her shoulder, she blinked again. "A housemom?" He had to be kidding! She needed to be onstage. Scoping out the crowd. Looking for Iskatel´, as he was bound to be looking for potential targets.

Brandon lifted his hand a fraction. "A housemom."

Or the job wasn't hers. The hard line of his chiseled jaw voiced what he didn't.

Hell, not if she had anything to say about it. She was here to crack a case, and she couldn't do that locked away in the back of the house.

Throwing Brandon a sultry smile, she slowly eased to her feet. As she rounded the corner of his desk, she slid her fingertips from beneath his, around his wrist, and let them rest against the back of his hand. Her gaze held his, offering promises she wouldn't let tumble off her tongue. She dropped her voice deliberately, assuming the same husky tones she used to appease Dmitri. "You sure that's the only use you have for me?"

To her delight, Brandon's gaze darkened again. Chips of molten brass fringed the tawny browns and sent another damning shiver down her spine. The man had simply gorgeous eyes.

Her shiver intensified as those breathtaking eyes trailed down the length of her body, slowly wandered up her legs, lingered at her waist, and came to a dead stop at the deep V in her blouse. Appreciation glinted like hot embers. "I'm not sure I grasp your meaning."

Oh, yes he did—the sudden gravel that roughened his voice told her loud and clear he understood her implication. She gave him another slow, sexual smile and trailed one nail up his forearm to the bend in his elbow. "I'm just saying it would be a waste of talent to keep me backstage."

He dropped his arm, the keys jangling in the heavy tension that settled around them. Turning, he faced her fully. Natalya took a bold step forward, close enough she could catch the hard fall of his breath, see the sudden bounding of his pulse in the thick vein that ran alongside his neck.

"Oh? That convinced of your . . . talent . . . are you?"

Deliberately she bit her top teeth into her lower lip and took another step forward. She didn't realize the error in her judgment until it was too late. His body heat assaulted her. The scent of spice, blended with something sweet she couldn't describe tempted her to close her eyes, breathe in, and let the warmth in her veins take over.

As a gnawing ache stirred between her legs, she blinked and forced the uncomfortable sensations aside. This wasn't about pleasure. This was about a job. A job she needed to land to get the hell away from Dmitri's dark world.

Natalya traced the thick strip of leather around his waist with one fingertip. She felt him stiffen, recognized the instantaneous tension that lodged into his spine. "Yeah." Keeping her smile at one corner of her mouth, she closed the remaining distance between them and flattened her palm against the firm ridge of his cock. "I would be . . ."

Holy crap—Brandon Moretti hit her like a landslide, completely eradicating her ability to form words. His cock was hard as stone beneath her palm. Searingly hot even through the denim. It wasn't the first time she'd used seduction to get her way—hell, she manipulated Dmitri daily. But it was the first time an aroused man had rendered her thoughtless.

She swallowed, tipped her head up to look at his face, and struggled to remember what she was saying. But she'd moved too close. Too far into the powerful, intimidating frame of his muscular body. His mouth hovered near hers. His breath stirred the fine hairs alongside her temple. Chills rolled through her. Beneath her lightweight blouse, her nipples beaded. Forget remembering what she intended to say— she was having a hard enough time remembering to breathe.

If she were smart, she'd back away. Fast. But she couldn't bring herself to move beyond sliding her palm over his swollen erection. Visions of that weighty flesh in her bare hands, the smooth head moistening as she bent to run her tongue across it, flared to life. Steel . . . silk . . .

"You would be what?" Brandon's lips barely touched hers, the flutter almost inconsequential, yet agonizing all the same. In a heartbeat, the aching need to taste him, to explore that sensual mouth sent moisture rushing through her pussy.

She swallowed hard. This was madness. He was a man. Nothing special, and likely someone tied into Dmitri's sick designs. She had no business being aroused by Brandon Moretti.

Speech came back to her in a rush. "Worth it."

A slow, lazy smile settled into the corner's of Brandon's eyes. Whether it touched his mouth, she couldn't decipher—she stood too close. But if it had, she was certain it would be amused, definitely cocky.

He set both hands on her waist, the press of his fingers torture to her oversensitized nerves. But instead of pulling her close for the kiss she anticipated—the kiss she'd twist free of before his mouth ever planted on hers—he pushed her back, distancing their bodies until her hand no longer rested on his crotch.

"I'm sure you would be, Natalya. But I need a housemom. And I'm not changing my mind."

Annoyance flickered through her, and she narrowed her gaze at his outstretched hand. The keys dangled between his thumb and forefinger. One dark eyebrow arched—*Do you want the job?*

Fine. If seduction wouldn't get her what she wanted, she'd have to play by Brandon's rules—for now. Dmitri might have been able to create the opening for her to move into the club by killing Rachel, but he could only intervene so far without calling attention to the *Bratva* connections. A link the Nevada Gaming Commission would devour. Then they'd spit out the St. Petersburg casino, along with Fantasia, like the bad meat it was.

Hell for that matter, if Brandon worked for Dmitri, this was exactly what she should have expected. Her fiancé would never let her strip in public. And Brandon's steely resistance to her attempts to convince him otherwise only reinforced her suspicions.

"Fine."

Brandon dropped the keys into her palm. As she closed her fingers, they caught his. His gaze jumped to hers, hot and full of promises she didn't dare consider. She swallowed again to relieve the sudden dryness of her throat and politely pulled her hand away. Her legs felt jittery nonetheless.

"We aren't attached to the casino, so you don't need a gaming license, and you can use St. Petersburg as you want. We'll talk payroll later."

"Okay." She flashed him a coolly detached smile. "I'll run home and change. See you soon, Moretti."

"Brandon."

She stopped at the door, fingers resting on the brass handle. Not Brandon. First names were too personal. He was a job. Part of a bigger scheme. His eyes might convey invitation to a world of intimate splendor, but she couldn't give in to the strange, unexpected desire that had infiltrated her composure and let him become familiar.

Glancing over her shoulder, she opened the door. "Boss."

One corner of his mouth pulled with a satisfied smirk. "Welcome aboard, Natalya."

Aboard—if he only knew.

She squelched a brimming laugh and sauntered into the darkened bar where Sergei waited at the door.

Three

Brandon's gaze followed the gentle swish of Natalya's long auburn ponytail as she walked away. It grazed the top of her hips, accenting a waist he had easily captured between his hands. Long, confident strides carried her across the floor, the height of her heels as insignificant as if she walked barefoot.

That woman was trouble—he had the evidence in his jeans. He was so fucking hard walking was near impossible. If it hadn't been for his gut-deep suspicion her tactics were merely a ruse, he'd have had her splayed out on his desk. He'd have had her on the damn floor. But he hadn't survived twelve years of vice work by being naive. Natalya was playing him.

She also hadn't been entirely immune to her little game. The flush in her cheeks, the catch in her voice, the way her eyelashes weighed closer to her cheekbones—he'd almost given in then. Almost surrendered to the blistering heat in his veins. Somehow, though, he understood that allowing Natalya to strip would scar in him ways even bullets couldn't. He couldn't take that risk. Sticking her behind the stage to deal with the unending needs of thirty strippers would mean he'd never have to face the torment of watching those damnable legs strut across his stage. Nor would he have to confront the unexplainable urge to possess her that had invaded his common sense when she cupped his cock in her sweet little palm.

Brandon came to an abrupt halt as the front doors swung open and Natalya slid an arm around a man's waist. A few inches taller than her five-nine-ish height, the man cut an imposing figure. The way he bent his head to kiss the top of hers sent a bout of unexpected fire swirling through Brandon's gut. Seconds ago, she'd had her hand on his dick, toying with him like she meant business. Now she sauntered casually into another man's embrace as if holding on to his cock was an everyday routine.

Yeah, he'd made a good decision, both in keeping her clothed and keeping her backstage. The last thing he needed was a boyfriend causing trouble.

Boyfriend.

The word held a bitter taste that he damn sure couldn't explain. He didn't *want* her. Well, not beyond the idle fantasy of what it would be like to bend her over his desk. He didn't want anyone. Women were meant for the moment. Clearly, Natalya was not *his* moment. Didn't bother him—one less headache to deal with and one more reminder he didn't do strippers. Not after Jill.

He'd made the mistake of dallying with Jill a couple months back. A few nights, a few intense orgasms, and she'd glued herself to his side. Back then, she'd been reasonably safe. She worked here. He worked at Sadie's. Now though, it was all he could do to keep her at arms' distance. Literally.

Definitely not a situation he wanted to duplicate.

"That, my friend, is one perfect piece of art," Aaron commented at Brandon's left.

Brandon pinched a frown. "With one perfect piece of boyfriend." He gave his best friend a stiff smack between the shoulder blades. "Wake up, Mayer. Your dick's staring at a *keep out* sign."

"Nothing it hasn't stared at before." The same self-assured, cocky grin spread over Aaron's boyish face. Despite his twenty-nine years, his face had failed to mature. It drew the women, but made his sparse goatee look like a high school teen's.

"Shave that thing off."

Aaron stroked the wispy hairs on his chin. "I'm getting around to it." He jerked his head toward the closed entrance doors. "You didn't put her onstage. We were looking forward to it."

The grim reminder of why he had hired Natalya thumped Brandon in the chest. His good humor drained out through his toes, and he gritted his teeth. "She's not dancing."

Aaron's jaw dropped. Recovering from momentary stupor, he blinked twice and exclaimed, "Why the hell not?"

"Yeah, why not? I could've gone for a bit of entertainment." Rory stabbed a thumb over his shoulder, indicating the mirrored wall behind the main bar. "Beats the hell out of counting these bottles."

Rory's voice sent Rachel crashing through Brandon's thoughts. He braced both hands on the table in front of him, bent over, and sucked in a deep, fortifying breath. He'd lost a teammate once before. But there was something drastically different about losing a buddy who owned a pair of testicles, than a woman who, despite her competence, he felt compelled to protect.

He'd also never had to stand before someone's significant other and break the news he'd never see her again.

"Moretti, spit it out," Aaron ordered in a low rumble.

"It's Rachel. She's . . ." *Dead.* The word lingered on his tongue, but his throat closed. He couldn't say it. If he voiced the truth, his heart couldn't stay in denial.

"Fucking bastard!" Rory's explosion shattered the stillness.

Before Brandon could turn around, the bottle of Scotch Rory had been holding hurtled across the room. It smashed into the wall, raining shards of crystal onto the carpeting.

From the entrance, a feminine squeak chorused the tinkling of glass. As Brandon whipped toward the doors, Rory shouldered past a wide-eyed Jill, nearly knocking her on her ass.

She threw a scalding glare at Rory's back. "What's his problem?"

Brandon shoved his fingers through his hair. He couldn't hide. Duty dictated he stand up and face his faults. He beckoned Jill to join

Aaron at the table. He couldn't tell her about Rachel's death, but he'd have to explain why Natalya had suddenly assumed Rachel's duties.

With more calm to his voice than he'd ever believed possible, he answered, "There've been some . . . changes, Jill."

The vibration in Dmitri's pants pocket drew him from the comfort of his couch and to his feet. Pulling his phone out, he checked the display, recognizing the number. He dipped his chin at the men who had gathered to renegotiate the terms of their involvement with Sheik Amir and the Dubai Project. "I must take this call."

As he shouldered through the heavy mahogany doors that barred his household from his private meeting room, he answered, "Dmitri."

"She's hired."

Iskatel″'s brittle American attempt at Russian made Dmitri cringe. The words were right. The accent all wrong. Nothing like the melody of Natalya's sweet words or the way the mother tongue should be spoken.

He moved to the window and stared at his manicured front lawn, now in full fall color. "She's safe?"

"Yes. As beautiful as ever."

As a vision of Natalya's green eyes leapt to life in his mind, Dmitri couldn't help but smile. He ran a hand down the curtains, fabric she'd chosen when he'd invited her to move in. Then, he had never imagined he could come to care so much for a woman who'd once been no more than a hired gun. But her eyes, like the heavy silk between his fingers, made him think of summer, of happiness. Of life. Not the death that surrounded him.

Now, he wondered how he'd ever believed she could be just a temporary pleasure. Though he possessed many diamonds, she was the flawless gem amidst uncountable imperfections.

"You'll keep her that way." He glanced at the billowing white clouds in the sky. "If you don't, I will personally escort you to your grave."

"Don't worry. I won't let her out of my sight."

"And the girl? This Kate Slater? Nothing has changed there?"

"No. Twelve days. Yakov has the papers in order. Once the boat's returned, we're ready to go."

Dmitri nodded absently. "You'll find Natalya invaluable. I hope you'll learn from her. I don't intend to move to Las Vegas to ensure your incompetency doesn't become an issue again."

A pause drifted through the line, punctuated with an unsteady laugh. "No. That won't be necessary. I'll learn. I won't disappoint you again."

Deference. *Good*. It was more than Dmitri had expected. They were making progress already. "Very well. I believe our business is finished for now."

"I'll keep you updated."

Dmitri closed his phone and stared out at a pair of swans circling the pond. Forgetting the men in the other room, he conjured the memory of the last night he'd spent with his fiancée and closed his eyes to the tightening of his body. *"Moya lyubov'."*

Natalya sat on the edge of her sister's secondhand couch, grateful for the strong arm Sergei had looped around her shoulders. Not more than ten feet away, the nephew she hadn't seen since the day he'd been born played with a fire truck on the kitchen floor. To say he resembled his father, the love of Kate's life, was an understatement. Looking at Derek Slater was like staring at Erik's ghost.

She couldn't take her eyes off the adorable little boy. Each laugh that interrupted their conversation tugged the same string that had knotted around her stomach when Brandon Moretti's tawny brown eyes filled with sadness.

Too much unwanted, *unexpected*, emotion for one day. For that matter, a lifetime. Between the sympathy he managed to wrench from her and the shocking way her body responded to his, if she survived the next handful of days without cracking it would be a miracle. When this was all over, she intended to take some serious R&R on a desolate island where she could regroup with uncomplicated trees. Maybe she'd coerce her partner in Russia, Alexei, into joining her. Spend a little frustrated sexual energy with a guy who actually did something for her. Someone she didn't have to fake it with.

Like Brandon Moretti.

Natalya blinked as the wayward thought flitted across her brain. With it came the fantasy of Brandon's mouth settling over hers, the heat of his body enveloping her. An uncomfortable ache stirred between her legs. Before the fleeting image could take root and balloon into the train wreck it promised, she jerked her gaze off Derek and honed in on the way her sister's hands fidgeted with her wire-rimmed glasses.

A telltale habit that warned Kate was nearing the end of her emotional rope.

"Calm down, Kate." Natalya's gaze flicked over her sister's drawn features. Despite the heavy makeup that gave her a cat-eyed appearance, Kate was still as pretty as she'd always been. Why she felt the need to hide her features with so much paint, Natalya had never been able to understand. It couldn't even hide the fear shimmering behind those long false eyelashes.

"Calm down?" Kate cried. She glanced over her shoulder at her son and lowered her voice to a hushed whisper. "When I'm supposed to be abducted in less than two weeks? Are you *insane?*"

Removing the arm he'd wrapped around Natalya's shoulders, Sergei reached across the coffee table that separated the identical plaid couches and clasped one of Kate's restless hands. "Kate, you must trust us. We won't allow it to happen."

Hearing Sergei speak English was as foreign to Natalya's ears as the idea that Dmitri would ever speak it. Though she knew he'd been born and raised in the States, they'd spent so much time embedded with the *Bratva*, she expected his thick Russian. And while his English held the heavy accent required to maintain his cover, the very words jarred her focus.

She stared at him, certain he'd sprouted two heads.

He ignored her with fluency equal to his foreign languages.

"I can't get a position inside the club," he continued, his thumb stroking the back of Kate's hand. "I asked around, and Aaron has locked down security. But I won't be far from you or Natalya."

"That's so comforting." Kate rolled her eyes. "I'm supposed to just sit back and wait for whatever's supposed to happen to . . . happen?"

"No," Natalya rushed to answer. "I'll find a way to get Sergei hired if it makes you feel better." She slid a sideways glance at her partner. "Though I'm a better shot than he is."

"God!" Kate tossed both hands in the air. The pile of drooping curls atop her head threatened to topple down her shoulders. "You're so cavalier about this!"

Natalya's sigh stirred the loose tendrils of hair that had escaped her ponytail. She swiped them out of her face and frowned at her twin. "It's what I do, Kate. If you panic, you make mistakes. Errors that inevitably lead to death. You're just going to have to accept that we know what we're doing, and as Sergei said, trust us."

Kate sank into the couch in defeat. "I want to. But this isn't just about me." Her troubled gaze sought out her son.

"That's exactly why you must have faith." Sergei left his perch at Natalya's side, moved to sit next to Kate, and settled a reassuring hand on her thigh. "You face no threat until the night of the twenty-fourth. The risk is mine and Natalya's. You're free to do all you do normally. The only exception is you must not reveal your relationship to Natalya. To anyone."

"To my friends. I have to lie to them all. Pretend I know nothing. I can't do that!"

Frustrated with Kate's lack of cooperation, Natalia reclined with a groan. "I don't get it, Kate. We went over this last night. Why didn't you freak out then? Why now, Katey?"

"Don't call me Katey." She thrust her glasses back onto her face.

A glimmer of Kate's inner strength crept out in the warning flash of her eyes. Natalya grabbed on to it with a pit bull's determination. "Why, it'll piss you off? Get mad. Maybe then something will click into place."

As Kate's scowl narrowed to a mere slit of green light, Natalya challenged her stare. Their gazes warred. Long moments of tense silence passed before Kate blew out a breath that mirrored Natalya's earlier exhale, and her expression went blank. She looked out the window. "I can't lie to Brandon, and I don't understand why I have to. I've known him for a year. He's a *cop*, according to what you said last night. All the management from Sadie's is."

Unease trickled down Natalya's spine as she studied Kate's faraway expression and the touch of sorrow that pulled at the corners of her mouth. Kate had mentioned Moretti spent time with Derek. Was there more to their relationship?

"Are you in love with him?" she asked quietly. Why she cared, she couldn't answer. But the idea that Kate might have experienced Brandon's hard body first hand tightened Natalya's stomach into a knot.

Kate's gaze swung back to Natalya. "With who?"

"Moretti."

"Good Lord, no!" She let out a laugh that quickly evolved into amused chuckles. "Brandon? Are you kidding? He's too . . . big." She swept her hand to a framed picture of Erik and her on their honeymoon. "Erik was normal. Just your average guy. Incredible in his own way, but unobtrusive. Brandon walks into a room, and he's *there*. You can't miss him."

A fact Natalya had deliberately tried not to acknowledge. When he'd stood behind his desk, he dominated the room. Not just in size, but in presence. Confidence and power radiated off shoulders that easily filled the doorframe. Emanated through the soft light in his eyes.

Crept into her veins at the slight touch of his hand.

Her cheeks warmed. Brandon was big otherwise too . . . The man had a package that put every other lover she'd had to shame, and she hadn't even seen him out of his jeans.

"Oh, my God, you like him." Kate exhaled. She shrugged off Sergei's hand and leaned forward to peer at Natalya. "You're blushing."

Perturbed by her twin's too-keen observance, Natalya frowned. "He's not to be trusted, Kate. Dmitri has connections in the force. How do you think the St. Petersburg casino manages to fly just under the radar?"

Always the voice of reason, Sergei leveled Natalya with a look of unmistakable warning. "There are eyes everywhere. Ears as well. Both of you can't forget that."

As Natalya opened her mouth to remind him she was more than aware of Dmitri's connections, her phone chirped inside her purse. She fished it out and glanced at the display. Her stomach slowly turned over.

"It's Dmitri, I've got to take this."

Crossing the room and heading for Kate's bedroom, she answered in her fiancé's native tongue, "Hello, darling."

As Kate left the couch in her sister's wake and disappeared into the kitchen, Sergei watched Derek mimic fighting a fire with the hoses on his toy truck. His thoughts drifted to Natalya's proclamation that she'd get him a job inside the club. He had no doubt she'd arrange it. But coming face-to-face with Brandon Moretti posed more problems than the blush that had infused her cheeks at the mention of Brandon's build.

The possibility that Brandon would recognize him, though he'd been eighteen when he'd last spoken to his brother, could destroy the entire mission.

Worse, Sergei would have to explain what happened to Stefan Moretti. How the FBI agent that had placed their family in witness protection had pulled him out of work that fateful day, less than thirty minutes before their mother and sister, and the agent, perished in their home's explosion.

He'd have to explain to Brandon why he'd never let him know he'd survived. How, for a while, he hated himself for surviving and how he'd blamed his brother for causing the explosion. How, by the time he made peace with his inner demons, he'd been so wrapped up in the CIA he couldn't contact the brother he'd once looked up to.

A year after the day their family shattered, Sergei had learned the truth. Brandon had nothing to do with the bomb. If anyone could be blamed, it was Carmina Moretti. When the FBI had ushered her off to Texas with a new last name, they'd never stopped to consider how a native Sicilian would blend into the landscape. They claimed they couldn't send them to an Italian sector because Angelo Mancuso had too many connections—a fact Sergei now understood as true. But Texas? She didn't have a chance. *They* didn't have a chance.

When Angelo got word of her whereabouts, he extracted revenge. Twelve years of separation had hardened his love for his children—if he'd ever possessed any—and he issued the order to exterminate them all. Brandon escaped because he'd gone to college. If it hadn't been for that FBI agent, who caught word of the plan, Sergei would have perished alongside his twelve-year-old sister and his mother.

But now . . . So much time had passed. So many memories had been put to rest. Sergei had no way of guaranteeing Brandon wouldn't recognize him, even with his longer hair and adult size. And while he felt certain his brother would never align himself with the mafia, any mafia, he couldn't chance exposure. He'd spent too many years gaining Dmitri's trust. If Natalya's plan failed, his role as Dmitri's most trusted bodyguard must stay secure.

Yet, he saw no way around the necessity to be as close to both Kate and Natalya as possible. He couldn't protect either one of them from a distance. He couldn't confide in Natalya either. Too much chance remained that she *would* fail, and somehow, through the inevitable torture Dmitri would exact upon her betrayal, she'd say too much. In doing so, she not only risked Sergei's life, but the only living family he could claim. While years stood between him and his brother, that love ran too deep. Too fierce.

Four

Natalya approached Fantasia alone. Behind her, Sergei watched from within a nondescript four-door sedan. He'd remain there until the club closed at four in the morning. Kate would arrive on her own sometime in the next fifteen minutes. For now, the less time she spent with her twin in public, the better the chances no one would notice their similarities, despite their outwardly different appearances.

She pushed open the door and stepped into the cool darkness. The surreal sensation she'd walked into the wrong place settled around her. Where incandescent light had given the club a sense of ordinary earlier in the afternoon, black lights, high spots, and strategically placed colorful LEDs gave Fantasia justification for its name.

Wispy fog rolled beneath heavy black curtains and cascaded off the stage where a petite Asian woman practiced a sequence. The tables were clean, upholstered chairs tucked in, brass ashtrays polished and waiting. Cocktail waitresses—identified by sequined miniskirts and skin-tight midriff shirts—laughed near the mirrored bar. An edgy pop beat filled the speakers.

Natalya smiled. Too many years had passed since she'd felt the pulsing bass and smelled the overtones of sex. She'd missed this. Missed the freedom of simply being a woman. The no-strings-attached enticement of standing beneath those bright lights and letting go. The carnal power of being comfortable with her body and not having to hide behind intricate lies.

"Try it again, Eddie. I can't get this right," the raven-haired woman onstage called.

From the glass-enclosed DJ booth a man replied, "Okay, Jill. Backing it up."

A moment of silence passed, and then the music began again, spurring Natalya deeper into the club. She fished the keys Brandon had given her earlier out of her purse and cut a course through the tables to the door near the stage. A man she didn't recognize from her brief interview stood beside it, arms folded over a boulder-sized chest. His cropped hair accented his sharp features and deep-set eyes. On observing her approach, he moved to block the door.

She lifted her keys, indicating her right to enter.

"Sorry, miss, waitresses aren't allowed back here."

So Moretti hadn't seen fit to inform his security he'd hired her. Perfect. Just what she needed to deal with on her first night. She summoned a smile and jangled her keys once more. "I'm Natalya. The new housemom."

Confusion pulled his thick eyebrows closer together. The hollow beneath his cheekbones deepened as he cocked his head and studied her. But when his expression cleared, and Natalya became convinced he was about to step aside and let her through, his deep baritone rumbled over the music. "Brandon!"

Natalya followed the turn of the man's head and traced his gaze to the far end of the bar where Moretti leaned on one elbow, conversing with one of the men she'd seen that afternoon. He lifted his dark head, looked to the man in front of Natalya, then lowered his gaze to her.

A charge of excitement spiked up her spine. In the smoky light, he was more imposing. Larger than life, as Kate had said. And way too *there*. The square line of his jaw sharpened. The glint in his eyes darkened. Intense. Dangerous.

To her absolute horror her nipples tightened into hard little beads. Good Lord, the man was more intimidating than Dmitri's entire arsenal of hit men. She'd bet all the bullets in her Sig's magazine Brandon would be formidable in the bedroom. A force to be reckoned with.

As if he sensed the live current that tingled through her womb, he abruptly straightened. A frown settled on his brow. "She's good," he called before he turned.

The guard in front of her offered a sheepish smile. He thrust out a meaty hand. "Scott."

Doing her best to pretend Brandon's stare hadn't just singed her from the inside out, Natalya shook Scott's hand. "A pleasure. If you'll excuse me, I need to see to the girls."

He stepped out of her way, allowing her to unlock the door and escape into the brighter, more active, back rooms. As she regrouped with a deep breath, the door swung open again. Kate burst through, pulling at her white fishnet stockings with one hand, adjusting a glittery shoulder strap with the other.

With all the falseness of a trained professional, she blinked at Natalya, then squinted. "Who are you?"

Good job, Katey.

"Natalya. Moretti hired me today. I'm your new housemom."

"Oh." Kate shrugged and readjusted her drooping strap. "I'm Kate, and I'm late. Gotta go." She waggled her fingers, then disappeared into a lounge area where three other women wearing short kimono wraps sat on leather couches.

Natalya followed her sister's path. As she stepped into the lounge, Jill entered from the opposite direction. She came to an abrupt halt, pushed her thick dark hair over one shoulder, and sized Natalya up with one head-to-toe glance.

"You must be Natalya."

At best, her greeting was chilly. The frostiness in her voice set Natalya's instincts on red alert. Rivalry? For what—the position? Or just meant to mark territory? Returning the woman's cool detachment, Natalya replied, "Yes. Brandon hired—"

Jill pushed past her to flounce into an easy chair. "Your office is there." She pointed through the open doorway to a closed door across a narrow hall. "Costumes are next door. Candy goes on in twenty minutes. She's in there with Becca. Her bikini clasp broke, and Becca's trying to fix it." Picking up a bottle of lotion, she extended a leg and smoothed a dollop down her shin. "Angie's period caught her off guard, and we're out of tampons. She goes on second. The props for her set aren't up here yet either. You'll want to find Harvey about that."

Natalya blinked. So much for chilliness—Jill was downright frigid. All too anxious to be relieved of her company, she strode for her office. "I'll get started then."

"Oh, and by the way . . . ," Jill called after her.

Halfway into the hall, Natalya looked over her shoulder, eyebrows lifted.

"Chablis called in and quit. She follows me after ten o'clock."

Quit. Natalya latched on to the solitary word, tuning out all else. If a dancer had quit, that meant an opening. A slot she could fill. Moretti couldn't keep her off the stage after all.

Feeling much better about how the night would play out, Natalya proceeded to her office, dropped her purse inside, and made for the costume room. As she wandered down the hall, three burly men wheeled a dolly of equipment boxes past her. Confused, she twisted to watch where they were going.

They stopped at the stage wing, popped open a box, and withdrew several armloads of gauze-covered metal tresses. While she looked on, they fitted the pieces together, indifferent to the scantily-clad bodies that strolled through the corridors. Bit by bit, a ten-foot-tall archway took shape.

What in the hell?

A hand fell on her shoulder, startling her. She jumped, turning to find Kate at her side. Siren red lips struggled to hold back a grin. "You better hurry," she urged in a near whisper. "Candy's about to panic."

"Who are they?" Natalya pointed at the three men, now busily fitting together a bundle of dark brown odds and ends. "And what are they doing?"

The amusement Kate had worked so hard to stifle broke free with a smirk. Leaning close to Natalya's ear she whispered, "Do better research next time. Fantasia makes dreams come true. We don't just dance here. We perform."

Perform?

Kate was gone before Natalya could inquire.

Three hours later, Natalya stood in the wings wearing a midnight blue robe in preparation for her intended dance and watching the blonde onstage. She finally understood Kate's meaning. The heavy curtains she'd observed earlier shielded an elaborate set of backdrops, moveable platforms and balconies, and props suitable for a Hollywood production. The arch she'd witnessed contributed to a fantasy setting. The dancer who used it—Becca—didn't just waltz onstage scantily clad. With the aid of light tricks, fog machines, and her gauze-covered arch, she emerged as an ethereal innocent. Her act quickly turned her into an experienced seductress.

They performed. Not just danced. True, they all ended up center stage dressed down to thongs and pasties, but each girl who took the floor had a story to tell. Each act re-created a broad range of fantasy. The props turned each song into Broadway shorts with a darkly sexual flair.

Natalya tapped her toe in time with the thrumming drums as Becca sashayed around a chrome-embellished Harley. Thirty minutes from now, she'd be out there. Gyrating around the pole with an expertise even Kate couldn't match. While Natalya worked, she'd scan the crowd for a face she recognized as one of Dmitri's men.

Iskatel′ was out there assessing the six blondes Fantasia employed for the next target. She could feel it. Though several months would pass as he cycled through the other clubs, he'd come back for someone else. He always did.

Only this time, Iskatel´ was playing chess with an opponent who had mastered the game. She knew the tricks. Understood the silent signals.

She *would* find him, and three years of Russian undercover operations would see fruition with the total exposure of Dmitri's underground. Alexei would blow the top off the Dubai involvements. Sergei would uncover the arms filtering into terrorist nations. And she would spend the rest of her life looking over her shoulder for personally betraying Dmitri and collapsing his deviant ring of sexual indulgence.

If she spent the rest of her life on the run, she'd make sure every woman that had been hauled into that pit of sin came home. Somehow, she'd make it happen. Or die trying.

Stepping away from the curtain, Natalya retreated down the corridor into her closet-sized office. The girls were settled. Time to get dressed.

She refused to think about the lies she'd have to concoct if Dmitri got word of her stage escapade. Furious wouldn't describe his reaction. He'd be more like a raging volcano. But, if she said the right things, used the soft voice that crumpled him, he'd forgive. By the time he arrived here, she'd be long gone, and his anger wouldn't matter.

Bending over, she picked up a pair of sequined, black, four-inch heels. As she straightened, she pulled the pins from her hair and studied the full-length bodysuit hanging on the wall behind her door. Tonight she would be a shadow.

Brandon let himself backstage, intending to make amends for the abrupt way he'd treated Natalya when she arrived. He'd known then he was being an ass. But hell, one look at her hair all piled up in a bun, her neat and tidy, *appropriate*, black suit skirt, and her equally appropriate white button-down blouse, and he'd been thrown right back to that moment in his office when all he could think about was her on his desk, her skirt around her waist, and his dick rooted firmly inside her.

He'd been struck speechless to see the same glow of arousal in her eyes, despite the dim light and the distance that separated them. Even from across the room he couldn't miss the tightening of her breasts the longer he held her gaze. And those aroused peaks had wreaked havoc on his system. It had required sheer willpower to remind himself that not only did she have a boyfriend, but he didn't mix business with pleasure.

Now that he was prepared for Miss Prim and Proper, he intended to apologize for not only failing to introduce her, but also failing to give her a heads-up that she'd have to jostle around the dance schedule and accommodate Chablis' absence. The least he could have done was give her a little forewarning about which girls were crowd favorites.

He avoided the handful of girls lounging on the couches. Though in truth, they gave him a wide berth as well. Most of them had heard through the grapevine he didn't mix business with pleasure. Especially in-house business. They worked for him, and in turn, he was their boss. Exclusively.

From the corner of his eye, he caught Jill rounding the bathroom hallway and quickened his pace.

Except for her.

One slip, under the belief a girl from another club wouldn't cause trouble, and damned if he could escape it.

Natalya's office door stood half open, and he stiffened. A thrill of anticipation bubbled through his blood as the fleeting notion crossed his mind that it would be too damn easy to shut that door, trap the both of them inside, and live out that brief fantasy of desks and skirts and mind-numbing sex—business aside.

Kate's voice, drifting out from beyond the partially open door, had the effect of a bucket of cold water on his head. Thank God. He wouldn't have to face Natalya and her never-ending legs alone. If that door happened to shut, there'd be no chance in hell he'd find that desk tempting. Unlike his best friend, Mayer, Brandon didn't do threesomes. He preferred to devote his attentions to one woman at a time. Prove that while she was in his arms, she was the *only* thing on his mind. Even if it was just for a night, it was *her* night alone.

He raised his hand to knock, but the soundless brush of his knuckles swung the door inward. The scene beyond froze him in place. Kate perched on the edge of a leather armchair, straightening out a string bikini top with beaded fringe. In front of her, her back to the doorway, Natalya stood with one foot propped on the seat of her office chair. Slender fingers pulled a black garter up a shapely calf, all the way to one smooth, muscular thigh.

His cock jumped to attention as his heart ground to a stop.

Christ Almighty, she could kill a man with those legs.

To hell with business. He couldn't explain what idiocy had descended on him, or why this woman lit him up like a firecracker, but he was done with denying he wanted anything else but her. Naked. Legs wrapped around his waist. His cock buried so far inside her she'd never forget he was there.

Fuck!

What the hell was the matter with him? Countless girls, wearing far less than what Natalya Trubachev wore now, had paraded in front of him over the last several years. It hadn't been *that* long since he'd had a woman—and it wasn't like he had to look far to find one. So why was he reacting to this redhead like one of the raunchy bastards who frequented the strip?

Brandon ground his teeth together and focused his scowl on the exposed skin at the back of Natalya's neck. "What do you think you're doing?"

Both women's heads snapped his way. Kate let out a squeak. Natalya stumbled as she attempted to put her lifted foot on the floor. She caught herself on the back of the chair. Jade green eyes widened. "What do you mean?"

"I think I'll . . . er . . . I need . . ." Kate stood, her gaze alternating between Brandon and Natalya. She readjusted her glasses. "I've got to go."

No! The protest exploded from the depths of his mind. He needed Kate to stay. Needed a viable, tangible, reason not to drag Natalya across the handful of feet that separated them and discover if her mouth held the same flavor of wine that the deep burgundy of her lips professed.

Kate edged past him before he could develop a rational objection.

"This," Brandon gritted out through clenched teeth. He gestured at Natalya's short robe.

"This what?" Affronted, Natalya straightened her shoulders. The act made the deep V down the front of her kimono gap. Creamy skin peeked out, along with a glimpse of black lace. His gaze pulled to the cleft between her breasts. Under the weight of his stare, the silk that covered those full breasts puckered as her nipples stiffened. A flush spread across her skin.

Brandon choked down a groan. He dragged his gaze back to her eyes. "You damn well know what."

Her eyes flashed before she presented him with her back and picked up the black bodysuit slung across the rise of her chair. "We're a dancer down, Moretti. I'm taking the slot."

Dance? All that long, lithe body exposed for the entire club to enjoy before he could get his hands on it? Over his dead body.

One swift stride brought him up behind her. "Like hell." He grabbed her elbow and twisted her around. She caught her heel on the chair and stumbled into the desk, the back of her thighs supporting her against the wood surface. Their close proximity forced her to arch her back in order to look him in the eyes. Her breasts thrust forward to rub against his chest, and Brandon's blood warmed to the scent of flowers. Heat spread deliciously through his veins to pool in his cock. He thickened in a heartbeat. Holy God, under no circumstances had he prepared for Natalya on this level.

Annoyance dissipated at the catch in her breathing, the way her beautiful eyes glazed over with the same arousal that flooded through his body. He shoved the voice of reason aside and stepped closer, in between her parted knees. Her thighs framed his, her robe draped open revealing more of that taunting black lace—but not everything. No, even her robe wouldn't defy the elegance that was Natalya by gaping open and revealing all her hidden treasures.

Her eyes flickered with something he couldn't describe, and the tip of her tongue swept out to moisten her lips. His stare riveted on parted lips, the call of her mouth overriding all common sense. He set his hands on her knees, slowly, hesitantly skimmed his fingers up her thighs to the band of her stockings. Smooth skin. Toned muscle.

Hell, what was he doing? Why wasn't she fighting him off?

She shivered, and he no longer cared. She was feeling this too. And whatever it was felt *damn* good. Every nerve ending in his body had awakened, and he couldn't tear his eyes off her dewy lips, off the way her throat worked as she swallowed.

He traced the lacy edge of her stocking, skated his fingertips higher, barely touching her as he worked his way to her hips so he could hold her still while he claimed that taunting mouth.

"What are you doing, Moretti?" Her voice rasped over his cheek. The tremor in her words sent another shock of desire surging through his body.

He was going to fuck her, that's what he was doing. Right here. Right now. Right after he got drunk on the tangle of her tongue—if he wasn't already drunk. Damn, he couldn't remember a time that it had been so impossible to put words together, let alone *think*.

"I think you know," he managed through his tightening throat.

Natalya's long eyelashes fluttered shut. Powerless against the unspoken invitation, Brandon dipped his head. Their breaths mingled, and the sweet aroma of cherry beckoned him to sample the sultry heat. He ran the tip of his tongue over her upper lip. The satiny feel of her mouth sent a shock of raw lust ripping down his spine. *Oh, yeah . . . this was going to be good.*

When she pressed her palm against his chest and her nails curled into his pecs, he fought off the sudden need to drag her hips flush with his and bury his aching cock in her softness. Not yet. They'd get there, but first he wanted to enjoy the silken stroke of her tongue. Wanted to draw her into the same sexual frenzy that threatened to overtake his body.

"Let me on the stage, boss," she whispered against his mouth.

It took a moment for her words to sink through the haze of desire and infiltrate Brandon's mind. When they did, the full meaning of what was happening slammed into him. Her stumble might have been accidental, but the rest—they were back to Natalya's games. Son of a bitch—she'd almost hooked him too.

He thrust her hand away and stepped out of the mesmerizing field of her nearly naked body. Grinding his teeth, he took a moment to let anger balm the ache of desire. He met her wide-eyed gaze with a snort. "I hired you as a housemom, not a dancer. That floor's about money. I'm not wasting it on someone who hasn't danced in fifteen years."

He took another step backward, grateful for the distance that separated them. Anger flashed behind those shards of jade, but the pinkening of her cheeks told him her elevated breathing had little to do with temper.

Jesus, she was just as aroused as he was. Maybe this wasn't all pure games. Yet, even if she was as turned on as he, that could only spell trouble. Her boyfriend aside, Brandon needed to stay focused on the case. Committed to protecting Kate. For all he knew, Natalya could have something to do with the string of murders on the strip.

Using that bit of logic to find the strength to walk away, he turned for the hall. "Put Becca on after Jill."

He slammed the door on any objection she might have tried.

Five

Natalya's body quaked in Brandon's wake. She dragged in one deep breath after another. Her breasts felt heavy and full, her nipples sharp enough to cut glass. Another heaviness settled into her womb, adding to the dampness between her legs. She bit the inside of her cheek to silence a moan.

The force of her reaction to Brandon Moretti stunned her. She wasn't innocent. Not by a long shot. But sex with Dmitri was no different than the rest of her life—a lie. She faked it like a master actress. The two brief excursions with Alexei had been nothing more than a product of loneliness. Even he though, with his fantastically thick blond hair and deep-set dimples, hadn't awakened such fierce longing. One touch hadn't left her skin tingling as it did now where Brandon's fingers had scalded into her thighs.

No one had ever treated her with such disregard for her abilities. As a Black Opal, her talents placed her in the middle of danger. Nerves of steel sent her across the world in search of targets that quietly disappeared. Threats she'd exterminated without a moment's hesitation. Three years with Dmitri saw her as first a hired hit man, then his lover. His cronies, to the very people on the street in Moscow, gave her deferential treatment. Regardless of assignment, of location, those she interacted with—or in some cases hunted—respected her capabilities.

Brandon's ignorance of her capabilities exposed her to something completely unfamiliar. Something that thrilled her more than any chase.

He treated her like a normal human being. Like a woman he was capable of overpowering.

The effect was stifling. More than a little terrifying.

She pulled in another short breath and straightened her robe. What the hell was happening to her? He'd touched her, and her carefully maintained network of reflexes and sixth senses fled out the window. Under any other circumstance, she'd have turned the tables. Claimed power with a strategically placed knee or a twist of a wrist. But no. He'd put his hands on her, and she'd drowned in the intoxicating aroma of clean-shaven, agitated, *aroused* male.

Unacceptable.

Natalya jerked open the door and made a sharp left turn toward the emergency exit at the end of the hall. A shove sent the door flying against the concrete exterior. Cool night air rushed through the thin silk of her robe. She stepped out onto the fire escape, breathing in the scents of the city. Horns beeped. Voices carried up from the street below. All around, neon lights infused the Strip with a magical glow.

Arms braced on the iron rail, she gazed up at the stars and willed her body into submission. Normal didn't play a part of her everyday life. She couldn't bathe in the luxury. Couldn't afford to become distracted. While they could easily remove Kate from danger, doing so would tip off Dmitri. They'd lose their advantage, and three years of hell would amount to nothing.

She must keep her mind focused on finding Iskatel´, not Brandon and the way he set off her yearnings. Which meant she had to find a way to convince him to let her onstage and Sergei inside the club.

The door snicked open behind her. She glanced over her shoulder as one of the men she'd seen earlier that afternoon stepped out. He greeted her with a cordial smile. "Hey. Don't think Brandon introduced us yet. I'm Aaron Mayer. In charge of security." He thrust out his hand. "And you're violating that security by being out here."

Natalya stiffened, but as she opened her mouth to tell him what he could do with his security, she caught the playful twinkle in his dark eyes. Tension fled from her shoulders. She shook his hand. "Natalya Trubachev."

An amicable grin spanned across his face as he leaned his rangy body against the rail. "So I saw the boss come storming out of the back room. Before I could count to thirty, I heard the buzz on the back door go off. I'm guessing you two didn't see eye to eye?"

Oh, they'd seen eye to eye well enough. His had been dark and stormy. His body had been hot. . . .

She banished the memory with a silent oath. "We had words."

Aaron gave a quiet chuckle. "Don't take it personally. It's all part of the Brandon Moretti hiring strategy."

Despite the restlessness in her veins, Natalya couldn't keep from grinning. "Beat us into submission?" *Seduce us into submission?* If he were Iskatel', Brandon's tactics fit right in line with the methods she employed against the dancers.

"Something like that." Aaron pushed away from the railing and stuffed his hands into his pockets. His gaze drifted to the horizon. "All kidding aside, he lost a friend today. He's in a bit of a funk."

Rachel.

Natalya closed her eyes and swallowed a damnable lump of remorse. She'd tried to convince Dmitri that murdering that woman wasn't necessary. But in the end, Dmitri had his way—as always. He'd ordered Iskatel' to inject Rachel with a fatal dose of barbiturates.

"Yeah." A strange roughness infiltrated her voice. She cleared her throat. "I'll keep that in mind."

Aaron's gaze shifted to her, full of friendly openness. Hard not to like a face like Aaron's. Thankfully, unlike Brandon's, his good looks didn't tease her mind with thoughts of all the things she'd like to do to the handsome lieutenant. Or let him do to her.

Her smile broke free as the encounter in her office took a backseat to the more pressing demands of why she'd flown across the world. This was the man she'd need to sway into hiring Sergei. At the very least, she needed him in her court so he could sway his partner. She tucked her robe around her body more tightly and folded her arms across her chest. "So tell me, what's a girl gotta do to get on that stage?"

The light in Aaron's eyes glittered, his amusement increasing. "You could always try walking into his office and dropping your clothes."

"Right." She rolled her eyes. "I was thinking something more subtle."

Aaron passed a hand over his chin, drawing her attention to the bare skin that had sported a wiry goatee earlier. "Brandon's not much for subtle. He's not going to take a risk unless you give him good reason."

Good reason meaning flash a little skin. Make it worth his while. The bottom line in stripping was a body, and if she wanted Brandon to put her on the stage, she'd need to prove herself first. He'd said he wouldn't sacrifice the money on a girl he didn't know could dance.

Damn it. To obtain what she most needed, she'd have to dance for him.

Stripping onstage in front of a crowd was one thing. A private showing for Brandon could be deadly in a way that went far beyond the risk of betraying Dmitri. The man had power over her. The kind of power that could destroy her on levels she couldn't begin to name.

"You better come inside." Aaron slipped an arm around her shoulders and steered her to the door. "He's already pissed off. Let's not give him reason to make all our lives hell by standing outside where it's not safe."

Natalya quizzed him with a narrowed gaze. What was that supposed to mean? The fire escape's ladder couldn't be manipulated by anyone below. "Not safe?"

He gave her an indifferent shrug. "You've seen the papers. Girls have been disappearing. Better not tempt the fates."

It took an amazing amount of self-control to stop the laugh that brimmed and not tell him she could take care of herself. Instead, she flashed him a demure smile. "Probably right."

Inside the dressing room corridor, she slowed to a stop. "I'd like to ask you a favor."

"Anything you want, babe." Aaron's wink gave her another glimpse of his good-natured temperament.

"I have a friend who needs a job. Sergei Khitrovo."

As if she'd suddenly struck territory that interested him, Aaron's expression morphed into stoic quiet. He cocked his head and gave her an encouraging nod.

"His background's in security. He's been on private hire to some celebrities in Hollywood recently, but his stint's over and now he's in between jobs."

"And you're thinking he'd be good here?"

In perfect timing to her request, another group of men from the props department exited the elevator ten feet away and hustled down the corridor. She gestured at their retreating backs. "They come and go whenever. I haven't seen anyone looking over them. With all the disappearances, wouldn't it be a good idea to have someone backstage with the girls? Sergei's discreet."

He answered with the objection she had expected any good undercover cop would use. "I can't take someone off the street and put them in the back."

Aaron rubbed his chin again. His eyes lost focus, his thoughts turned inward, considering her request. After several moments of tense silence, where Natalya began to question how she'd ever thought she might be able to sway a man who'd spent almost ten years undercover, he finally nodded his head.

"I'll see what Brandon thinks. I'll let you know before we head out tonight."

Natalya groaned inwardly. She hadn't seen that coming. Her research indicated the two operated on equal footing with Aaron managing his own scope of control and Brandon operating as a senior, but equal, partner. Fat chance Brandon would honor anything she requested.

Unless he happened to recognize Sergei's name, make the connection between her and Dmitri, and recognize they were players in the Dubai Project.

She bobbed her head, acknowledging Aaron's efforts, and hurried past him to the dressing room where Becca had already donned her jeans in expectation of an early night off. "Becca."

"Oh, hi! I was wondering where you'd gone. I wanted to thank you again for helping me earlier."

Natalya dismissed the thanks with a wave of her hand. "That's what I'm here for. But I've got a directive from the boss."

"Oh?"

"He wants you on in Chablis' place."

Elation turned Becca's otherwise pretty features into a mask of startling beauty. "Oh, my God! He's giving me her slot?"

Convinced she would somehow land the opening onstage, Natalya schooled her expression into serene compassion and gently delivered the news that would crush a dancer hungry for promotion. "It's only temporary. But it's yours for tonight."

A short nod confirmed Becca's dismay. With far less enthusiasm, she bent over to pick up her sweatshirt. "Could you ask Harvey to bring up the jungle props?"

"Sure thing."

Mark down another girl who'd treat her to Jill's same icy demeanor. When Becca discovered Natalya had manipulated her out of the slot, she'd be six kinds of hateful. Natalya sighed and shook her head. What these girls thought of her shouldn't matter. She wasn't here to make friends. She was here to protect Kate, and in the process, protect the rest of them. When she accomplished that, she wouldn't be here to care what the girls thought of her.

Maybe then, Becca could claim her coveted slot.

As Natalya returned to her office, she glimpsed Brandon and Aaron standing in the stage wings. Arms folded across his chest, Brandon didn't look at all pleased. His gaze flicked over Aaron's shoulder and landed on her, halting her forward progress for a tremulous heartbeat. A chill skittered over her flesh. Goose bumps followed in its wake.

When Aaron turned to investigate what had drawn Brandon's

attention, a knowing grin broke across his face. Natalya hustled into her office. Small wonder Aaron had smirked. The whole damn hallway could have felt the tension that crackled between her and Brandon.

Maybe stripping for Brandon wouldn't be the best idea she'd ever had.

Then again, she couldn't deny a small part of her reveled in the possibility of what might happen when she did exactly as Aaron suggested and dropped her clothes in front of Brandon Moretti. She liked the way he made her feel.

Moreover, she had elicited more than one secret between the sheets, and Brandon put a whole new meaning on the term *undercover operative*.

She shook herself. What was she thinking? If Moretti worked for Dmitri and she yielded to his smoldering stare, she'd sign her death wish. He'd tell Dmitri everything.

No, under no circumstance could she entertain the idea of what it might feel like to have Brandon's hands on her breasts, his lips following the stroke of his fingers. But dear God, the very thought lit her up brighter than the neon lights outside.

For the third time in easily as many weeks, she found herself wondering what had ever compelled her to join the Black Opals. She could have worked in foreign policy. Translated for government leaders. But no, all that had been too . . . normal.

Now, she barely remembered what normal was like.

Go on. Get out of here." Natalya released Kate from her impromptu hug and unlocked her office door. "Sergei will follow you home."

Kate's face paled to the color of fine porcelain, and her eyes widened to twice their normal size. She adjusted her glasses, glanced nervously over her shoulder. "What about you?"

"Me?" Natalya blinked. How long had it been since someone had legitimately worried about her safety? Five years? Ten? She'd spent so long with a gun tucked into her waistband that she'd forgotten other people didn't share the same confidence.

She shook her head to ward off the sudden discomfort and used her toe to point to her purse. "Don't worry about me. I've got all the protection I need in there."

That coupled with an upcoming wedding to the world's most powerful mafia boss—a girl couldn't ask for safer passage through dark alleys. Sure as her gun was loaded, there'd be eyes following her home tonight. Keeping her safe. Never questioning her unfaltering loyalty.

As long as she kept it that way, she didn't need to worry about anything.

"Go," she urged. "We'll sneak out for lunch tomorrow and talk then."

Kate stopped in the doorway. "I hate this."

"I know." Unceremoniously, Natalya shut the door, pushing Kate out of the way.

She sank into her chair feeling more drained than she had in the last year as Dmitri's go-to girl. One full day had passed, and they were no closer to identifying Iskatel´, much less Yakov, than they'd been in Russia. She knew nothing more about Fantasia's employees than what she'd discovered in the CIA records. Other than the fact that Jill made it imminently clear she considered Brandon her personal property.

Which could be legitimate possessiveness, or it could be a front to keep Yakov disguised. Hell, Natalya had played Iskatel´'s part in Russia—why shouldn't it be a woman in America?

Because it made sense for Iskatel´ to be a guy. Women trusted men easier, for the most part. In strip clubs cattiness abounded, and she'd only succeeded in gaining the victims' trust because she *didn't* dance. Jill danced. Jill made it known she wanted top billing.

Besides, Brandon and his team had taken three management positions in three years. It could be no coincidence that he took over at Fantasia less than two weeks before the next job.

A light rap on Natalya's door brought her upright and dragged her from her thoughts. "It's open."

Brandon's voice rumbled through the metal barrier. "We're done. It's time to close up."

"Hey!" She jumped up and jerked open the door. Sticking her head out, she found him halfway down the hall. "Boss! I want to ask you something."

He'd have to be deaf to not hear her bellow, but he kept walking, head down, fists clenched at his sides. Unbidden, her gaze skimmed over his backside. Broad shoulders tapered into a trim waist set on strong, but narrow, hips. The slight swing in his step added to the confidence that poured off him. She looked lower and sucked in a sharp breath at the firm buttocks that his dress pants accented. Perfect for a pair of feminine hands to grip and squeeze. To curl her nails into as she urged him to push deeper . . .

Her blood warmed as she watched him walk away. The man was incredible. Not an ounce of softness anywhere, except on occasion in his mesmerizing eyes. And if she didn't get her body under control, along with her all-too-suddenly vivid imagination, she'd do more than ensure her swift demise. She'd escort Kate straight to a hotel in Dubai.

Natalya closed her office door to block out Brandon and discarded her robe in favor of her suit skirt. Brandon Moretti was strictly business.

When she had her blouse buttoned, she fished her gun from her purse and stuffed it into her waistband. To hide it, she slipped into the lightweight jacket she'd brought along in preparation for the cooler Nevada nights. Tonight she'd walk to Dmitri's luxury condominium on the north end of the Strip. The chilly air would do her faltering sense some good.

First though, she needed to track down Aaron and discover the verdict on hiring Sergei. With luck on her side, tomorrow night they'd make some progress.

She wandered through the girls' lounge and into the brightly lit club. Unlike the rundown bars in Russia, this place screamed wealth. She hadn't particularly noticed it before, but now, after spending a full night behind the scenes and witnessing the sheer fortune invested in stage props, the front room's luxury became unmistakable. What she'd thought were ordinary velour chairs revealed themselves as velvet on closer inspection. She ran a hand down the edge of the stage, noting it wasn't just painted wood, but a Formica-like substance that had been polished to a mirrored sheen. She'd stake her life on the presumption the overhead chandeliers were lead crystal as well.

Glancing around, she searched for Brandon. When she couldn't find him, she relaxed. The last thing she needed was one more encounter before she retired for the night. As it was, her nightly hot bath would do little to keep the wicked fantasies at bay.

A tall figure on the far side of the room identified Aaron. She quickened her step to catch him before he disappeared into the manager's office, where she presumed Brandon waited. "Aaron."

He turned, treating her again to his warm, welcoming smile. "Hey."

"Any word?"

His mouth pursed, and he let out a quiet grunt.

"That bad, huh?"

"Not bad. Not good. I can't get a straight answer."

The door behind Aaron opened, and Brandon exited, head down, attention elsewhere. Looking up at the last minute, he came to an abrupt halt, inches from his partner's back. His scowl was immediate and fierce, and centered straight on her.

With a lift of her shoulders, Natalya steeled herself against his silent attack. Did he think she liked this any more than he did? The way her heart stuttered each time those tawny eyes locked with hers annoyed the piss out of her. That she couldn't control it bothered her more than the reaction itself.

"Did you need something, Natalya?"

If Aaron couldn't pin him down for an answer, maybe she could. "I wanted to ask if—"

"No."

Before she could stutter out anything further, he sidestepped around them and strode toward the main doors. Natalya exchanged a dumbfounded look with Aaron, then started after him, determined. She caught him at the entrance, keys in hand, locking up. "Wait just a damn second. I want to have a conversation with you. Boss. Employee. You know, that sort of thing?"

He glanced sideways, the already tight line to his jaw hardening. "I already told you, no. You're not dancing." With one more twist of his wrist, he latched the last door and stalked off in the direction of the main bar.

Oh, for God's sake, that again. She nearly rolled her eyes, but checked the gut reaction. No sense furthering his anger with blatant disrespect. Not that he could see it. But she wouldn't put it past him to sense she had.

She did an about face and fell into pursuit, dogging his heels as he weaved around the chairs and the remaining waitresses. "It's about a job, Moretti. If you'd just stand still and hear me out—"

"Go home, Natalya."

Three quick strides distanced him completely. She scowled at his broad, retreating shoulders. For a fleeting moment, she considered how satisfying it would be to fire a shot into the back of his calf and stop his retreat. Or maybe through the back of his head.

Expelling a frustrated mutter, she fisted her hands on her hips. She couldn't shoot him, but she'd be damned if she let him dismiss her so easily. There was one surefire way to make him listen.

Inhaling deeply, she bellowed across the room, "The back rooms aren't safe, Moretti!"

Brandon skidded to a halt at the edge of the bar. He felt, rather than saw, his employees' heads swing his way and stare at the back of his skull. Fury filtered into his blood, overriding the sexual awareness brought on by one glimpse of Miss Prim and Proper. Heat rushed up his neck, burned in his cheeks. He slowly clenched a fist and turned around to glower at Natalya.

Christ. He had a murderer running around, and here she stood, hollering at the top of her lungs about the lack of security in his dressing rooms. She might as well stand at the door and invite the bastard inside.

He stalked toward her, bent on wringing her delicate neck. To his surprise, the closer he came, the straighter she stood. Her eyes warred with his. The set of her jaw mirrored the tightness in his face. When he invaded her space, she tipped her chin up. Stubborn defiance glinted in her jade green eyes.

A little voice of warning screamed he couldn't strangle her in the middle of the club's main room. Nor could he spew the multitude of ways he wanted to tell her to go to hell—right after he told her in no uncertain terms all the things he wanted to do to her. Lay her on the bar. Push her up against the wall. Peel off that blouse, hoist up that skirt and . . . damn!

He grabbed her by the upper arm, wheeled her around, and propelled her inside his office. With one swift kick of his heel, he sent the door crashing shut. "What do you think you're doing?"

Her voice didn't so much as quiver as she answered, "Having a necessary conversation."

"No. I'll tell you what you're doing." He grabbed her other arm and squeezed as he gave her a little shake. "You don't throw out accusations about the safety of my girls. Unless you want to be out of a job. Immediately."

Anger flashed behind her eyes. Quick. Brief. Deadly. "Take your hands off me."

"Not until you get it through your head, Natalya, I'm your boss. You don't get to call the shots here." He took another step into her space, forcing her to back up. "And you don't, *don't*, give the dancers any more reason to worry about coming into work. Or leaving when the night's through."

"Maybe you should act like my boss then."

He blinked, certain he'd heard her incorrectly. When her expression didn't change, and the defiance lingered in her unblinking stare, he knew he hadn't misinterpreted. He stepped forward once more, infuriated by her inability to grasp the full meaning of what her bellow could have produced. If the killer was on his staff, he now knew the back rooms were weak. Something Brandon had intended to rectify by the end of his first week on the job. But to have it thrown out so publically—he couldn't stomach the thought someone else might suffer Rachel's fate.

"This isn't a game, Natalya." Her back came into contact with the wall, forbidding her further retreat. He closed the insignificant distance between them. "There are lives at stake. You've read the headlines, I'm sure. And you just invited a murderer to take advantage."

"Three minutes of your time—that's all I wanted." She paused long enough to lick her lips and swallow. The flash of rosy pink ripped through Brandon's awareness like she'd pressed hot coals into his skin. He ground his teeth together.

"Enough to point that out to you privately and ask you to consider hiring Sergei."

He should turn her loose. Step back before he forgot what they were doing against the wall. Forgot that moments ago he'd wanted to throttle her for exposing Fantasia's weakest link. But damned if he could get his fingers to do anything more than relax enough to give her room to twist free.

She stayed motionless, her gaze traveling over his face, dipping to his mouth. It jerked back to his eyes, and her cheeks colored a pretty pink. "His references are excellent."

As she shifted position, lifting her back away from the wall to relieve some unseen pinch, he caught a whiff of her lilac perfume. He reeled under the heady fragrance. Sweet. Innocent. Goddamn enticing. His cock seconded the observation.

Fuck. He was in trouble and he knew it. She stood too close. He caught the catch of her breath, the sudden darkening of her eyes. The heat of their bodies ebbed between them, and his pulse skyrocketed. He no longer cared if the spark in her gaze came from anger or desire. Didn't care if she was playing him. Nor did he give a damn about the conversation she'd been so intent on having. The only thought that drummed in his head was of seeing that same flash of dark color in her gaze as he slid home between her legs and pushed her over the edge into orgasm.

He released his grip intending to step away. Instead, his hands slid down the flimsy material of her blouse to her wrists, then against his better judgment, worked their way back up to the firm muscle of her biceps. "Let me get this straight," he murmured, all too aware of the hoarseness of his voice. "You want me to hire someone on your word alone. A new girl. Who I hired because someone I trust referred her. When I haven't even had the chance to check out *your* references?"

"Yeah." She exhaled. Her next deep breath brought her breasts against his chest. Hardened nipples stabbed into his overwarm skin. Her gaze flickered again. Long lashes lowered to veil the brilliant hue of her eyes. "Something like that."

"Why? Is he your boyfriend? Put him on the floor, and you on the stage?" He leaned in close, knowing he tread a thin line between sanity and madness. His hips flattened against hers, and the throbbing of his cock became unbearable. Her stomach quivered against his abdomen. "Would that heat things up between you two?"

If she said yes, he'd die. Why, he didn't know. But the idea that Natalya Trubachev would dance before her lover, and then go home and fuck until the sun rose, was enough to torment him the rest of the night. Enough for him to realize he would never, in a hundred years, hire this Sergei.

Right now, though, he didn't intend to break the bubble of bliss that the press of her soft full breasts wrapped around him by informing her he'd already come to a decision.

"Things don't need . . ." Her breathless whisper hitched. She swallowed visibly, then licked her lips once more. "Any more heating up."

His awareness honed in on the strong beat of her pulse against the side of her neck, and he had the sudden feeling they'd switched gears. This conversation was no longer about hiring anyone. "No, they don't, do they?" he murmured.

Reaching between them, he caught a shank of her long auburn hair and wrapped it loosely around his hand. It slid through his palm like silk. She turned her face aside, exposing the full length of her delicate throat. He lowered his head, the need to feel that fierce pulse against his tongue eradicating all other thoughts.

Her sweet perfume filled his nose as his lips hovered over her jugular. He dusted his mouth across her fragile skin, a featherlight touch he couldn't know for certain whether she felt, or he imagined. But her surrendering sigh filled his ears. She sagged into the wall.

Ah, hell, this wasn't a game. That little sound was as real as the heat pressing against his stiff cock. She wanted him.

Brandon braced one hand on the wall above her shoulder. Using the other, he pushed her jacket aside and drew the back of his hand along the deep collar of her blouse. Where his knuckles brushed, her skin pebbled with goose bumps. The dark lace showing through the translucent fabric beckoned, and he slowly twisted free the first button on her blouse. His gaze remained locked on her face. Her eyes closed, her lips parted.

He popped another button. Let his knuckles kiss her skin as he moved to the next. One by one the little pearls gave free all the way to her waist and exposed that black lace he'd only glimpsed earlier. The contrast of ebony against her creamy skin made him suck in a sharp breath. Rosy nipples strained against the delicate lace, beckoning to his fingers. He gave in and cupped one weighty breast.

"Brandon." Her voice was unsteady.

He rolled his thumb across her nipple, his own breathing shallow. He didn't know what he wanted most—the certain sweetness of her mouth or that hard little bud against his tongue. Silence or needy whimpers. He took a moment to close his eyes and gave her breast a soft squeeze. Perfect. She fit against his palm like they'd been designed to match.

As if she could feel the torment of his indecision, Natalya dropped the back of her head against the wall, and a quiet mewl of pleasure slipped off her parted lips. The sound shot straight to his cock, answering his dilemma. More—he needed more of those delightful little noises.

He eased his body away from hers just enough he could dip his head and trail his tongue over the line of dark lace where it met her skin. Her back arched, thrusting her nipple forward, silently commanding him to close his mouth over it. Brandon complied without hesitation.

The feel of lace against his tongue was strangely pleasant. But the way she lifted one hand and dug her nails into his scalp defied pleasure by leaps and bounds. It was fucking out of this world. His body threatened to surge into hers, his swollen erection demanding satisfaction. He closed his eyes to the faint scent of flowers that drifted off her skin.

He nipped and teased until Natalya let out another quiet moan. Her hold on his hair tightened, pressed him closer to her breast. He inched his free hand between their bodies and tugged at the lace covering her opposite breast. When he covered her exposed flesh with his palm, she wriggled into his fingertips.

"Brandon. God . . ."

Yeah, he was feeling it too. Just teasing her was driving him out of his mind, something that was wholly unfamiliar to him. With all the lovers he'd had before, not one had managed to make him this hard, this excited, this quickly. He could draw this out a little longer, but when he got her naked—and he was going to—he wasn't going to last long. Damn . . . he wanted to savor Natalya Trubachev, not devour her in seconds.

Willing himself into patience, he shifted his mouth, dusted kisses across the lace-clad swell of her breast to drag his tongue through the deep valley between. She shivered beneath his hands. Her other hand found his hair, and she urged him closer to her uncovered nipple. Brandon opened his eyes to admire the pert little bud. He flicked his thumb over the turgid nub and smiled when she gasped.

"Pretty. So pretty," he murmured absently.

He closed his lips around the dusky peak and sucked it into his mouth. Her flesh was warm, soft as the satin robe she'd worn earlier tonight. Natalya cried out as he drew on her firmly. Her hips thrust forward, and she rubbed against his aching cock. Sensation rocketed through him, pulling at his balls, threatening to send him over the edge right there. He dropped his hand from her breast to her hip to hold her still.

The door banged open, yanking Brandon out of the haze of desire. He jerked away from Natalya, and rationality slammed into him. Holy fuck. What the *hell* was he doing?

Natalya gasped at the same time she turned her back to the door. Her hands fluttered furiously at her blouse. Her long hair hid the blush that had hit her cheeks the instant the *thud* jarred them apart.

Brandon swiveled to confront the intruder. Regardless of what had cross-fired in his brain and what he was doing, he'd shut the door. No one had the right to walk in unannounced . . .

Except Mayer.

Brandon avoided Aaron's bemused smirk. "What do you need, Mayer?"

Aaron glanced between the both of them, silent laughter dancing in his eyes. "After the way you dragged her out of the club, I figured I better come referee."

Brandon sank down into his chair, stretching out his legs to accommodate the tightness in his groin. Damn, he couldn't remember a time when he'd wanted a woman more. He looked to Natalya, surprised to find her blush absent, her countenance unshaken. Undisturbed. Nodding at her, he held her quiet stare. "We were just discussing this friend she wants me to hire."

"I think it's a great idea." Aaron dropped into the chair across from Brandon and tossed his boots on the desk. Ankles crossed, he reclined. "We could use an extra guy on the floor. She's right—the back room needs to be beefed up. You said so yesterday."

Beneath the desk, Brandon once again clenched his fist. For the love of all that was holy, he hadn't expected his best friend to override his decision. His *partner* would never dream of it. Unless . . .

He shifted his glower to Natalya.

Unless she'd used her tricks to get under Mayer's skin as well. Damn it all! They didn't know anything about her, or her friends.

But with his own words revealed, he could hardly refuse. He'd look like an ass. Worse, he didn't have a single justifiable reason to not hire someone who came with impeccable recommendations, like she claimed. And with Kate as Natalya's reference, one of the few people he considered a friend, he risked the very real possibility of insulting his lead dancer.

"Fine," he gritted out through clenched teeth.

Natalya took a dignified step toward the door. The unmistakable gleam of victory shone behind her eyes, and her mouth pulled with the beginning of a self-satisfied smile. "I'll tell him to come in with me tomorrow."

"Natalya."

She stopped, the door half closed. "Yes?"

"You didn't answer my question."

Lingering in the doorway, she held his gaze for several never-ending seconds. They both knew what he meant—the only question he'd asked was whether this Sergei character was her boyfriend. He didn't have an explanation for why he pressed the question now. The moment was over. The need to know, insignificant. When she walked out that door, they'd once again be employer and employee. Come morning, he'd be back in control of himself, the events of today locked away in a corner of his mind where he could forget them.

She surprised him with a bright smile. "I don't intend to."

The door closed. Like a pop can shaken too much, his frustration bottlenecked. He slammed an open palm against the top of his desk, releasing the building explosion with a violent oath.

"Problems?" Aaron asked, laughter lurking in his voice.

"Get the fuck out, Mayer."

Seven

Brandon raked his hands through his hair and dropped his head against the back of his chair. Still uncomfortably aroused from the close encounter with Natalya, he concentrated on evening out his blood pressure. She was long gone, but she filled his senses to such insanity, he'd swear she sat right next to him. What the hell had come over him?

He didn't like the answer that rose. *Courage.* That woman, for all her lithe beauty, had more spine than any woman he'd ever met. She hadn't uttered a single squeak, even when he'd been acting like a rabid dog, and he wouldn't be surprised if his fingers had dug into her arms so tightly that tomorrow she sported bruises.

He couldn't defeat her. Couldn't burst her confident bubble or temper her persistence. Not to mention he was powerless against the pull she had over his body. He didn't know what to do with that. Natalya infuriated him while she simultaneously filled his head with visions of spreading those shapely thighs and burying his head between her legs.

One thing was certain, he'd accomplished nothing since she'd waltzed into his office. He had intended to spend the night scoping the crowd, getting to know the regulars. Instead, he'd spent the whole damn evening dwelling on Natalya Trubachev and her too-sexy accent.

Shoving away from his desk, he straightened out his pants with a shake of his ankle. His dick still hadn't fully recovered from that intimate brush with Natalya's body, and the scrape of his trousers sent a shudder rolling down his spine. He flinched, uncomfortable with the way she lingered in his office, though she'd physically departed almost an hour ago.

A glance at the clock above the door revealed the time as ten to five. He should be home, fast asleep, priming for an early morning with the case files. Rachel's death changed things. She didn't fit the MO at all, not beyond the autopsy findings that she'd died from an overdose of injected barbiturates. Which meant they'd missed something, or the killer had altered his pattern. Although the chances of his changing his preferences after so many neatly matched deaths was slim. Maybe if there'd only been one or two blondes. But seven? With another four missing? Not likely.

Had Rachel stumbled onto their man?

Too exhausted to consider all the angles, Brandon flipped off the light, tucked his gun into his back pocket, and locked up the office. Tomorrow, he'd run everything by Rory and Aaron. Maybe they'd discovered something useful tonight.

As he turned for the rear exit, his brain registered misplaced light. Glancing over his shoulder, he mumbled an inward curse that some-one had neglected to turn off the main bar's overhead rack. Tempted to leave the damn thing on, he changed his mind at the sight of a shadow tossing back a drink.

Brandon's gut turned in on itself as he made the connection. *Rory.* Strong, always positive, Rory was back there drinking himself into oblivion. Christ! The bottom of a bottle never held answers. Brandon should know. He'd spent the better part of a year staring at that convex glass after his family's murder. Sure it helped temporarily. But when it wore off, when the hangover set in, nothing changed. The aches still ached. The emptiness inside only deepened.

Seeing entirely too much of himself in his teammate's silhouette, Brandon palmed his keys and approached the bar. Rory looked up. Behind his eyes, pain flashed. He gave Brandon a stiff nod.

Brandon gestured at the bottle of whiskey in Rory's hands. Wordlessly, a shot appeared before him. He picked it up and stared into the amber liquid. "How long, man?"

"Huh?" Rory's features scrunched into a tight, unreadable line.

Tossing the drink back, Brandon swirled it over his tongue before swallowing. He grimaced at the burn as the alcohol rolled down his throat. God, he hated whiskey. His father had loved it . . .

Brandon shoved the thought aside with force. Another reason why he avoided whiskey—it always made him think of Dear Old Dad. The very same bastard who had blown up his wife and two youngest children, leaving his eldest, Brandon, to clean up the mess.

He studied Rory's distant stare, recognizing the hollow vacancy reflected in his eyes. "How long have you been more than partners?"

Rory recoiled like he'd been slugged. His gaze shifted to the bar, to his feet, the ceiling overhead—anywhere but Brandon's face. "It's not—"

"Bullshit." Brandon gestured for another drink. Obligingly, Rory filled his glass. This time, Brandon sipped his shot like a mixed drink. "If you think I give a rat's ass that you violated protocol, you've misjudged nine years of friendship. Now cut the crap, Neal, and answer my question."

"Four months." The answer came in a rough whisper.

Longer than Brandon had suspected. Long enough to forge something much deeper than a good-time roll between the sheets.

"It just kinda happened. One night we were talking casework. The next morning I woke up in her bed."

Sensing Rory needed to talk, Brandon remained silent, sipping on his shot and pretending he liked the pungent flavor.

"I met her folks. We got a dog—" His voice cracked as he dropped his head into one hand. On a shuddering inhale, he dragged his fingers down his face and looked beyond Brandon to the empty stage. "I'm gonna kill that bastard, Bran. Swear to God, you better hope you find him before I do."

In that moment, Brandon realized he'd lost a team member. He could keep Rory on the case—hell, his drive would probably push them closer than they'd ever been. But his all-over-the-place emotions posed a risk they couldn't afford. One wrong word spoken by the wrong person, and Rory's need to avenge Rachel's death could drive them all down the wrong path.

Maybe it was a good thing he'd agreed to hire Sergei after all.

Brandon reached into his back pocket, pulled out his wallet, and withdrew the money he kept on hand in case he found himself in a position to hob-nob with Fantasia's wealthy elite. He fanned five hundred-dollar bills on the bar and pushed them at Rory. "I can't let you do that, bud. Go home. Go see your mom. Didn't she break her hip?"

"Fuck that." Rory's head snapped up, his eyes blazing. "You think I'm gonna sit back and do nothing? Fuck you. I was going to marry Rachel. She's *dead*, because of that sick bastard."

Keeping his voice level, Brandon chose his words carefully. "I know she is, and I hurt too. But she worked too hard on this case to take any chances. She'd tell you the same thing, Rory." He tapped his finger on the money, never taking his eyes off Rory's. "Let me take you home. I'll keep you in the loop, but I'm not *asking* you to visit your mother."

Rory's knuckles whitened as he curled his fingers around his glass. His arm tensed, along with the hardening of his jaw. Brandon counted to ten, waiting for the inevitable explosion.

It came with an anguished cry, and the glass shot past Brandon's ear. Behind him, it shattered against a tabletop. Rory crumpled against the bar, giving over to grief he'd rather die than yield to. Ugly, pitiful sobs choked out of his throat. His shoulders heaved.

Inside, Brandon grieved with his friend. He didn't know which was worse—losing a partner he considered a sister, or watching one of the toughest guys he knew crack into pieces. A fine sheen of moisture filled his own eyes, and he rapidly blinked back the unwelcome tears. Rachel deserved a better end. Deserved a whole hell of a lot more than what her short, twenty-nine years provided. They'd find the bastard—he wouldn't quit until he dragged the sack of shit into the station and turned the key on his cell. If he had to, he'd spend the rest of his life hunting this monster.

He swallowed hard and made his way around the bar to set a supportive hand on Rory's shoulder. "C'mon, let's get you home."

Rory swiped the back of one hand over his eyes. He grabbed the money and stuffed it into his pocket. A short nod expressed both willingness and unspoken gratitude.

"You want company tonight?" Brandon asked as they walked to the exit.

"No. I'll be fine."

Right. As fine as a guppy with a shark on its tail. But there was no need to call Rory on the falsehood. They both knew it was a lie.

Just like Brandon lied each time he swore off Natalya. Brevity necessary to survive.

The short drive to Rory's small house on the east side of Las Vegas passed in silence. Brandon didn't know what to say any more than Rory knew how to voice all the chaos in his head. Sometimes silence comforted more than any words, and Brandon allowed it to flow unimpeded. Rory would talk when he needed to, when he was ready to confront inevitable loss.

He pulled into the narrow driveway and idled while Rory hauled himself out of the passenger seat. "If you need anything . . ."

Rory answered with a vacant nod.

"I'll call in a couple of days and brief you."

He dipped his chin, then punctuated his good-bye with a firm tap on the Shelby's roof and shut the door. Feeling helpless for the first time since he'd been twenty and received the news his family had been killed, Brandon watched his friend trudge lifelessly up the dark porch steps and let himself inside an even darker house.

I should have pulled his piece.

He shook his head. No. Taking a cop's weapon was the ultimate blow to his pride. Rory wasn't the kind who'd consider suicide. He'd rally, in time. Find the strength that made him the decorated officer who'd devoted ten years to the force. He wouldn't turn vigilante. He knew when to respect an order, when to sidestep around the unnecessary. Rory didn't need to be knocked down another round by confiscating his gun.

As Brandon backed out of the driveway, a light flicked on inside Rory's house. He expelled a worried breath he hadn't realized he'd been holding. Convinced he'd made the right decision to respect Rory's wish to be alone, he navigated for home. While he drove, his thoughts meandered between the case and Natalya.

Gut instincts lumped the two together. Something about her didn't fit. The accent, her immaculate attire, her insistence to dance. The way she played the consummate professional one minute, and the next, experienced seductress. All the while, she cloaked a tigress' spirit. Hid a woman who wouldn't back down when common sense said she ought to.

He'd allowed himself to be swayed into hiring her boyfriend. A man who's references came only through words—just like Natalya's. Two mistakes in one day. He hadn't run either one of their records, a practice he'd made habit long, long ago.

Angry with his foolishness, he pulled his cell phone off his hip and punched in Aaron's number. A groggy, sleep-laden voice answered on the fourth ring. "You sent me home. Now you want to talk? It's almost dawn, man."

"I took Rory off the case."

"Huh?" Wakefulness crept into Aaron's response. "What for?"

"He can't cope. He was planning on asking her to marry him, Mayer."

"Shit." The whisper drifted through the phone, a ghostly echo of Brandon's equal upset. Several moments of quiet passed through the line before Aaron let out a heavy sigh. "I'm sorry, I didn't realize."

"Nothing to realize. I didn't know it had been going on this long either. He's grieving. He'll pull through. I sent him to his mom's."

"Probably best."

"I need you to look into some things first thing in the morning."

As if he welcomed the subject change, Aaron answered with more strength. "Sure. Whatcha need?"

Brandon turned the corner and pulled into his own quiet neighborhood. He drove past the houses, taking strange comfort in the porch lights that burned through the night. His glowed like the rest of them, a solitary lantern to illuminate brick steps and a small front porch. Hitting the button for his garage door, he nosed into his driveway. "Get Natalya's file from my desk. Run everything you can on her. Find out where she picked up that accent. Find out the link between her and this Sergei guy. Hell, I don't even know his last name."

"Not a problem, boss. Will do."

"Thanks. Let me know what you find out. My ass is sleeping in. I'm beat." Pushed beyond all reasonable limitations, thanks to one feline-esque redhead and her never-ending legs.

He strangled the visual of Natalya sliding on her garter before it could fully erupt from his memory. Not going there. He needed rest, not several more hours of torment.

"Will do. Can I go back to sleep now?"

"Yeah." Brandon shut off the car, punched the garage door opener again, and climbed out. "One more thing, Mayer."

A hint of annoyance accompanied the solitary response. "Yeah?"

"If you ever override me like that in front of someone—"

To Brandon's absolute frustration, laughter erupted in his ear. "Get over it, Moretti."

Still chuckling, Aaron terminated the call. Brandon stared at the silent cell phone in his hand, debating whether or not to redial and tell his best friend exactly where he could put his amusement. Deciding to reevaluate the situation in the morning, he let himself inside his house, tossed his phone on the table by the door, and wandered down the hall to his bedroom. There, he belly-flopped onto his bed, not even bothering with the chore of undressing.

The instant he shut his eyes, long auburn hair danced against his eyelids and tickled the inside of his palm. The sound of her soft cry as he suckled at her breast filled his ears.

Eight

As the sun broke over the horizon and cast a warm pink glow on the tops of the monstrous casinos, Natalya jogged down the wide sidewalk. Though she kept a steady enough pace that perspiration dampened her brow, inside she felt sluggish. Out of sorts. Like someone had strung her up by the ankles, spun her around three times, and then left her swaying, blindfolded, in the wind.

All thanks to one Brandon Moretti who refused to give her a moment's peace, even in sleep.

In dreams, she allowed him all the wickedness his smoldering eyes and adept mouth promised. Fantasy Brandon knew every sweet spot on her body and had discovered a few she hadn't realized she possessed. Masterful hands left her aching for fulfillment each time she opened her eyes to toss the covers off her overheated skin. Shortly before dawn, she gave up the idea of rest and sought relief from the pent-up tension on her own. It had worked . . . to a degree. She'd come fast and hard, but the restlessness remained. Burning in her belly, weighting down her limbs.

Jogging became a necessity. If for no other reason than to spend the energy accumulating in her veins. When Sergei had called, asking her to meet him, she'd leapt at the opportunity to burn off a little steam.

Sighting the tall towers of the MGM Grand Signature, where the CIA had arranged a separate working residence for she and Sergei, she quickened her pace. Too many eyes and ears filled the properties Dmitri owned to chance meeting in either one of their condominiums.

While she doubted Dmitri would bug her place, the possibility remained that someone would see Sergei enter, stay longer than a bodyguard should, and questions would arise. Though Dmitri understood Sergei was posing as her boyfriend, they didn't need the resulting interrogation. Or people looking to prove the cover-up wrong.

She rounded the corner onto Harmon, feeling the burn in her thighs. Sweat trickled between her breasts, and her breath came in controlled measurements. At the Signature's gated entrance, she stopped, tightened her ponytail, and fished into her back pocket for her ID. She passed it to the guard. "Sergei Khitrovo is expecting me."

He inspected the laminated plastic, then glanced at her. "Morning, Ms. Trubachev. Hope you enjoyed your run." As he spoke, the gates soundlessly opened. "Next time, I won't forget. I'm good with faces."

Natalya reclaimed her ID and jogged up the walk to the spacious front entry. Inside, following the marbled floor, she made her way down a narrow hallway to the elevators. She rode to the twenty-sixth floor.

Sergei answered seconds after she knocked. Looking well-rested and alert, he flashed a bright smile. "Morning."

"How do you do that?" As she entered, she swept a hand down the length of his body, indicating his immaculate jeans and crisp white T-shirt. "I know what time you got in last night."

Chuckling, he ushered her onto a stool at the granite-topped bar between the dining area and the kitchen. "Magic."

"Inhuman."

He pushed a tall mug of black coffee under her nose. "Have some caffeine."

One thing could be said for her partnership with Sergei—he always knew how to use coffee to his advantage. She drank deeply, savoring the rich dark roast.

"Want a cinnamon roll?"

Natalya raised an eyebrow. "From the bakery? Or did you cook them?"

With a shake of his head, he scoffed. "Why buy when I have an entire kitchen at my disposal?"

Another thing about her partnership that she treasured—Sergei could cook better than Dmitri's personal chef. Her stomach growled at the prospect of a hot, buttery, home-cooked cinnamon roll. "Sure."

As he busied himself with preparing her breakfast, she glanced around the luxury suite, admiring the wood trim, the crisp retro furniture, and the glass accents that added elegance to what would otherwise be harsh angles and lines. Modern. Exceedingly upscale.

"HQ really put themselves out this time, didn't they."

Standing in front of the stove with his back to her, he shrugged. "I told 'em you'd become accustomed to the wealthy life."

"Uh-huh. You're in a mood. Why so chipper?"

"Why are you so crabby?"

A vivid image of Brandon's dark head moving across her breasts, his tongue searing over her nipple flashed through her memory. In less time than it took to furiously blink the vision away, the uncomfortable ache between her legs returned. She crossed them against the deep throb. "Strange bed. I didn't sleep so well."

Sergei answered the microwave's bell and slid a piping-hot roll in front of her. Cinnamon permeated her awareness, momentarily erasing Brandon from her mind. She picked up her fork, speared it into the doughy corkscrew, and took a bite. "Mm. Tell me again why we aren't married?"

His laughter rumbled low as he dished out one for himself. "Because marriage requires sexual attraction."

"I don't know about that." She pointed her fork at her plate. "I could give up sex for good food."

As Sergei pulled up a stool beside her, he gave her thigh a pat. "I have needs, babe."

"I have needs too. Good food. Good wine. Laughter—that's important also." Good sex certainly hadn't been a part of her life. At least not until Brandon filled her head with possibilities.

She cringed inwardly, the unbidden thought spoiling her attempt at good humor. "So why am I here at the crack of dawn?"

He pulled off a hunk of roll and stuffed it into his mouth. Speaking around his food, he answered, "Because we have a case to work on. Or did you forget why we're here?"

"I didn't forget. *I* worked last night. You, on the other hand, had a whole night off."

In typical form, Sergei ignored her attempt to rattle his easy-going demeanor. He slid off the stool, retrieved an opaque plastic bag from the corner of the kitchen entry, and plopped it on the countertop between them. Taking his seat once more, he dumped the contents out. A handful of ballpoint pens and thumbnail-sized electronic gadgets spilled free. "Wrong. I spent last night with a few of our buddies."

Excitement thrummed through Natalya. Audio transmitters. Sometimes her partner proved useful outside of the kitchen. She flashed him a mischievous grin and picked up one of the pens. "Voice activated?"

"You betcha. Scatter some of those around the club. Other Opals are set up to monitor the various channels."

"Won't they override with so many?"

"Nope. There's ten pens. Ten channels. Ten Opals monitoring."

Holy shit. That was more resources than they'd ever been allotted. The full reality of her situation hit home as she stared at the transmitters. They'd moved beyond the child's play of Russia. Vegas was life and death. Hers specifically. Kate's had never been in question. But Natalya stood the very real possibility of never waking to see another morning. And anyone associated with her—like Sergei—stared down a loaded weapon far more deadly than the 9mm on the counter beside the stove.

One wrong move, and they'd cease to exist. As Dmitri disposed of their bodies, the CIA would erase every footstep they'd taken on this earth.

Natalya shivered. For the first time in her life, she considered running. She could hide Kate and Derek in a remote corner of the world where Dmitri would never find them and give up the lies, the subterfuge.

An unbidden memory of Tatiana crumpled on the cold concrete floor in the confinement room surfaced, and Natalya swallowed hard. If she ran, all the women she'd hurt meant nothing. They'd never find freedom. Never again would they know what it was like to wake each morning with a clear head and spend each night as they chose. They'd never see the families they left behind. Families *she'd* forced them to leave.

No. Running was out of the question. Failure wasn't an option.

She picked up one of the circular transmitters. "And these?"

"I want you to put one of those on the main bar, one in Moretti's office, and one backstage."

A pang of regret pulled at her stomach. Closing her eyes, she set the transmitter back on the bar. If Sergei wanted Brandon's office monitored, he must suspect him as well. It made sense, as much as she might wish it otherwise. Brandon had access to Kate. By her own words they'd become close. If he coerced her into an after-hours excursion, or offered her a gig at a private club where she'd make three times what one night at Fantasia brought in, she'd never question his motives.

Not wanting to hear Sergei's response, she quietly asked, "You think he's Iskatel´?"

Sergei barked a short laugh. "Not a chance in hell."

His response so stunned her, she could do nothing more than blink. Half of her had wanted to hear Brandon topped the list of Sergei's suspects. It would make it easier to distance herself from the handsome lieutenant. The other half, however, jumped up and danced at the decisiveness in Sergei's response. It was that half that left her unable to stutter more than a surprised, "W-Why not?"

"He's a cop, babe. A dedicated, *honorable* cop."

"But he fits perfectly." She couldn't believe him. If she did, she'd never survive the next encounter with Brandon Moretti. The possibility he might work for Dmitri, no matter how small it might be, was the safety net between her and the unexplainable desire that flared between them.

Sergei shook his head. "I did some asking around. He's got marks on his record. He's been known to side-step protocol to see an investigation closed. But he's clean."

"That doesn't mean anything. *We're* clean on paper."

Swiveling on his stool, Sergei fixed her with a hard look. "His father was Angelo Mancuso, a hit man for the mafia in Kansas City. Angelo didn't take too kindly to having his wife turn him over to the feds. When she blew her witness protection, Angelo ordered the murder of his family. Moretti lived." Sergei paused, chewed on the inside of his cheek. With a frown he continued, "He was put on narcotics undercover because he's too eager to find his father's men. This is his first homicide stint. He's not going to fuck it up and lose a chance at getting a transfer he wants."

Murdered? By his own father? A lance of sympathy sliced through her chest. Uncomfortable emotion that only complicated things further. She *shouldn't* care. If she opened herself to that tug of feeling, all the rest that she'd blocked away would come crashing through. She stuffed another bite of cinnamon roll in her mouth, the flavor now dull. "He hawks over Kate."

Long dark hair tumbled over Sergei's face as he cocked his head and arched a scoundrel's eyebrow. "Really? Not according to what she told me last night. Way I hear it, he hawked over you."

Like bolts snapping into heavy doors, Natalya barred the warmth that flickered in her veins from spreading. She sat up straighter, chewed with more determination. "He did not."

Sergei's laughter echoed throughout the room. Shaking his head, he stood, gathered both their empty plates, and took them to the sink. "Give it up, babe. Your reaction yesterday, when Kate brought him up, says you're done for." He turned around and braced his elbows on the counter behind him. The amusement faded from his eyes. His smile gradually disappeared. "Use it to your advantage if you must. But get those transmitters passed out."

In no mood to be presented with reasons why she *could* indulge in Brandon, Natalya abruptly stood. She hastily gulped down the rest of her coffee. "You can do it when you show up for work tonight. I got you the job. You're on the floor in the main house. Brandon won't let me onstage—I need you there. We've got to find out who perks up when Kate takes the stage."

For one suspended heartbeat, she'd have sworn Sergei stiffened. But by the time she'd blinked, he was lounging against the countertop, ankles crossed, and looking every bit the casual Vegas vacationer in his rental kitchen. She dismissed his ramrod straight posture as a figment of her imagination and went to the door.

"Natalya?"

His quiet voice brought her to a stop. Warily, she looked over her shoulder. "Yes?"

"What if it doesn't happen? What if we *don't* make the connection before the twenty-fourth?"

Icy fingers scraped down her spine. One hand on the doorknob, she stilled, her chest suddenly too tight to draw in a normal breath. "I won't let him take her, Sergei."

"So we pull her out?"

As her throat inched closed, she swallowed down a rising lump that threatened to choke off her already scant air. What he didn't say boomed louder than his words: *And blow everything we've worked toward for the last three years?*

"She's my sister. Dmitri will *not* have her." Unwilling to consider the ramifications, she yanked the door open and fled. One way or the other, she'd see Kate and Derek to safety.

Failure is not an option.

Nine

*S*tefan Moretti.

Sergei silently tried the name on to see how it fit. He'd been Alec for a handful of years as an agency rookie. Spent another few months in Colombia as Javier. But for more years than he could count, he'd considered himself Sergei Khitrovo, and he'd never stopped to consider what might come next.

The name he'd grown his skin in had certainly never crossed his mind. Stefan Moretti brought memories of trucks, wide Texan star-filled skies, girls in cheerleading skirts, and innocence. He was so far removed from that simple life that even considering acknowledging who he really was felt like fraud. Stefan Moretti, the boy who'd known how to navigate under a car hood better than he knew how to drive, died fifteen years ago. He should stay in the grave.

Tonight, though, he just might rise from the dead. Summoned, unbidden, like a demon from the otherworld conjured by some voodoo priestess.

A priestess known as Natalya, who couldn't begin to comprehend the layers of dirt she'd pulled him through by finagling him a job.

He'd known from the day the case file landed in his lap that he might be exposed. But when he learned Aaron Mayer had locked down hiring, with the exception of the girls, Sergei had grown comfortable with the idea of staying in the shadows, outside the club, and doing things like what he'd done the night before—meet with operatives, ask a few questions on the underground, sit in dark clubs, and do no more than listen.

Be there for his partner, the only friend he could claim. But never stand face-to-face with the brother he longed to embrace.

Pushing away from the countertop, he picked up his Glock and wandered to the living room couch, where he placed the weapon on the glass table and proceeded to take it apart. Like working with engines had served as an outlet for pent-up teenage angst, cleaning his gun gave him an outlet for adulthood frustration. The motion of his fingers stopped the unrelenting chaos in his head and allowed him to think more slowly.

Things were bad. He wouldn't try to delude himself into believing this Dubai Project was a bed of roses with only a few thorns to navigate. The agent who'd spent too many years killing people for Dmitri Gavrikov knew pulling Natalya would be the safest way to protect both her, her sister, and the case. The man, the friend who sometimes knew his partner better than she knew herself, couldn't deny her the satisfaction of seeing a job completed.

Working on autopilot, he maneuvered the slide back in place, then methodically took everything apart again.

Sergei didn't doubt Natalya knew the risks. But twice now, she'd clammed up tighter than an oyster when Brandon became the topic of discussion. Unfortunately, Sergei knew that silence too well. She rarely dropped her guard, even in front of him, but when she did, he could read her cover to cover and everything in between. She'd taken risks with Alexei in Russia. Sergei could hardly blame her for that—hell, he couldn't imagine tying himself down to someone he *liked* for three years, let alone someone he despised. Natalya was bound to crave a little human affection.

But she hadn't worked side by side with Alexei. Their brief liaisons occurred on the rare times Dmitri was out of town. A few hours stolen in the house, under the guise of negotiating the next contact. Passing information between the two key players of the Russian equation. They'd passed more than information. But they parted and stayed apart. No close confines for someone to observe a heated glance. No possibility a casual touch could slip into an intimate brush of hands.

Not that either one of them would have allowed those risks. Still, distance and detached wisdom prevented disaster.

This, however . . .

While Sergei's memories of Brandon came from youth, and undoubtedly his brother had changed—grown up more specifically—Brandon had never been the sort of guy to let something go when he wanted it. The red pickup he'd set his eye on at sixteen became his after an intense summer of doing every lawn job he could get his hands on. When he'd decided the captain of the cheerleading squad would be his date for the senior prom, the fact she'd been steady with someone else hadn't even entered his brain. He'd set off after her like a hound dog on a thick trail, and a month later, that prom date was in the bag.

Sergei had made the mistake of flirting with one of Brandon's girls too. He'd done it out of spite, with no real interest in the pretty girl. It hadn't worked—she'd laughed at his feeble attempt at mimicking big brother's moves and patted him on the head. Brandon, however, had walked in, seen his girlfriend's hand in his little brother's hair, and an hour later, when their mother came home from work, Brandon was no where to be found and she'd had to call the neighbor to pry off the thick boards nailed across Sergei's bedroom door. Hammered in place to keep him, and his black eye, inside.

What Brandon wanted, Brandon got.

At least back then.

And from what Kate had said, all signs indicated Brandon's sights were fixed on Natalya. The one woman on this earth who could, quite literally, kill him.

Worse, where Natalya *should* be contemplating the many ways she could exact said death if Brandon was indeed coming on to her, her reactions screamed the opposite. For the first time Sergei could remember, Natalya lost her cool at the very mention of Brandon's name. Her composure cracked. She avoided the subject worse than she avoided talking about what she'd done to the girls. For God's sake, she'd *blushed*.

If he were any other man, or just a simple physical attraction, she wouldn't have hesitated to confess she envisioned orgasms and sweat. Sex for Natalya was just that—enjoyment meant to relieve a little stress. She played the game like a man. Here for a little while, there a little while longer, then gone. *Excursions*, she called them. She even referred to them like a man.

Blushing was entirely too feminine. Natalya couldn't afford feminine reactions when it came to Brandon.

Sergei fitted his Glock's loaded magazine back into place with an authoritative *snick*, then laid the gun on the glass.

The Natalya/Brandon factor was like adding kerosene to a pile of smoldering wood. Why then, hadn't he allowed her to believe Brandon might be Iskatel'? He could have fed her suspicions and steered her away. But he hadn't. He'd fostered an amicable perception of his brother.

His gut twisted uncomfortably. Maybe because the pink in Natalya's cheeks reminded him a little bit too much of a freckle-faced girl who'd come home gushing to her brothers about a boy after a sixth-grade dance. Maybe because, despite the hell that existed around them, Natalya might have a chance at the joy their sister had been denied.

Brandon downed his second cup of coffee in the hour since he'd rolled out of bed. The caffeine hit his bloodstream, rattling his already jittery nerves. But he held on to the hope that if he drank enough Joe, he might erase the sluggishness inside his head.

He ran a hand over his bristly cheek and stared out the window overlooking his backyard and the wooden play set the former owners left behind. In the late-morning breeze, a swing swayed. Rory had intended to marry Rachel. She'd have, no doubt, resigned from the force. A year or so later, Rory would have taken a desk job. Then they'd be the ones standing at their window, looking at kids playing on swing sets.

Good thing he didn't intend to ever marry. Or produce children.

It wasn't that he had anything against kids. He liked them well enough. Hell, Derek, Kate's boy, filled a void Brandon hadn't realized he'd possessed until he met the bright-eyed toddler last year. Once a week, he indulged in the role of father figure and spent the afternoon with Derek. They both needed the time together—Derek because he'd lost his father, and Brandon because he could pretend the world wasn't such a dark place.

But intimacy wasn't his thing. A wife, a girlfriend, a child, only gave Angelo Mancuso and the mob a target. Beyond that, women didn't take too kindly to having their safety constantly in question. And most women he knew, or would consider getting involved with, didn't carry guns in their back pocket. Not that he'd considered getting involved.

Nope. It was much smarter to keep things casual. No complications to divide his time. No one waiting at home to worry about. He chose his partners carefully, made sure they understood—and agreed to— the boundaries. When things cooled off, they parted with pleasant words and promises to keep in touch that never happened. Women passed through his life without leaving so much as a fingerprint behind. As he did through theirs.

So why, *why*, couldn't he get Natalya Trubachev off his mind? Why had he awakened, so damnably aware of her that he could have sworn she lay beside him in his bed? His *bed*, of all places! He let no woman near his bed. It was his safe harbor. The one place in this world he could count on to provide comfort, along with escape.

But sure as shooting, he'd opened his eyes to a rock-hard erection and had instinctively rolled over in search of the source and the necessary relief.

Damn it, she was worse than a hangover. He could cure that—down a bottle of Gatorade, eat some Saltines, down a second bottle, and he was good to go. He couldn't, however, banish her out of his head. Or the suspicion that she would taste every bit as sweet as her lilac perfume.

Maybe it was lotion. *Yeah.* He smiled to himself. Lotion she slathered over those long legs. Massaged around rosy pink nipples while . . . *Shit!*

He set his coffee mug down with force. He didn't have time for this, and somehow he had to make his dick understand what the smarter head knew—catching a serial killer who'd murdered Rachel was more important than fucking and orgasms.

Tugging at his cotton pajama pants, he relieved the sudden tension at his waist with a grimace and strode to the dining room table-turned workstation. He opened the case file, methodically spreading out data sheets, notes he'd collected, and the autopsy findings on all the girls. Mentally, he recited what he knew by heart: *Blonde hair. Between 5'7" and 5'9". Fair skin, no fake tan. No bruising, no signs of struggle. All dead from a lethal injection of barbiturates. All dumped in remote places near the Grand Canyon, clothes intact. Sexual assault—negative.*

They'd known their attacker. That had been the first piece of evidence that stood out to everyone. So who did Rachel share in common with them?

He groaned as he sunk his head into his hands and speared his fingers through his hair. He might as well ask who she didn't know. Years on narcotics connected Rachel with every slime ball who frequented the Strip. The regulars were like family. Black sheep maybe, but family all the same.

Why Rachel?

She must have made the connection. Must have IDed him somehow. There couldn't be any other explanation for a serial killer to deviate so drastically from his MO.

He dragged his hands down his unshaven face and looked out the window once more. *Who is it, Rach?*

On a sigh, he resigned himself to the uselessness of reviewing the file. Everything he could ever hope to know he'd already memorized. Now he had to find the missing pieces, and the only unusual circumstances came with Natalya and this Sergei guy. He needed their files. Maybe in them he'd find a link. A little fragment that put them in Vegas around the time of the murders.

No, that didn't make sense either. Not entirely. At a time when dancers were hard to come by, she begged for a job. It was only natural she'd want someone she trusted close at all times. She wouldn't understand that a good killer—and this one certainly fit that description— would find a way around boyfriends. He'd already done it twice. Sable from Treasures had been living with one of the security guards there. Mercury from Sapphire never went anywhere without her body-building fiancé. But like clockwork, they ended up on the Grand Canyon rim.

Which all led back to the glaring fact—the killer knew the girls.

Maybe he should let Natalya dance. Her naked body would wreck havoc on his system, but if the killer approached her . . . No, she didn't have blonde hair.

He could get her a wig.

The idea had merit, much as he hated to admit. New girl in town wouldn't have the established friendships the killer claimed. The murderer would have to work at building that relationship, and he couldn't accomplish that under Brandon's nose without Brandon noticing.

Brandon let out a grunt and shoved the file aside. No more risks. If something happened to Natalya because he'd been desperate enough to use her as bait, he'd never pull himself out of the darkness that threatened to engulf him daily. He'd find another way.

Closing his eyes, he leaned back in his chair and stretched out his cramped legs.

Natalya's soft, perfect breasts burst from the recesses of his mind. Tired of fighting the incredible pull of his body, he let the vision take shape. It couldn't hurt. As long as he didn't allow fantasy to go to his head, a dose of morning erotica might be just the cure for the itchy feeling beneath his skin.

She swung that lean, muscular leg off the chair, slipped slender fingers beneath the tight lace garter, and stalked toward him, a sultry smile on her lips. Her other hand wound into his shirt, dragged him closer. Soft honeyed lips touched his. Before his mind could control what she'd do next, he sat in her office chair and her firm bottom gyrated against his lap. Where their clothes had gone to, he didn't know. But they were missing, and she was naked, and her pussy slicked against his cock, hot, wet, and coaxing. Slowly he lifted his hips. Slowly she slid down. He could hear the slap of their skin, feel the tightness of her sheath as she snugged him close and took him deep. Up, down . . . Up, down . . . Fucking him slowly. Then harder . . . faster . . . as those intoxicating mewls tumbled, one after the other, from her parted lips.

With a frustrated oath, Brandon bolted upright in his chair. Behind the tight constraints of his pants, his skin felt damp. He took himself in hand, the need for release something he could no longer control. One firm pump pushed him over the edge, and he tucked the head of his cock against his palm to control his ejaculation. He let out a throaty groan, coaxed himself through orgasm until the last pulse seeped from his body and left him panting. Sinking into the chair he lay still, too sensitized to move.

Wrong move, Moretti.

Several mind-numbing moments later, his gaze caught the distant picture he'd taken with him to college so many years ago. His mother, his brother, his sister smiled back. Behind them, colorful hot air balloons littered the sky. Drawn to the memory, he rose from his chair, wiped his hand off with his shirt, and picked up the framed photograph. They'd all been so happy then. Scared that Angelo might find them, but happy. Family. The only one he'd ever known, and he had nothing but one picture to hold on to.

Sighing, he set the photo down. Natalya be damned. He would not allow this crazy attraction to destroy the only chance he had at putting his father's thugs behind bars.

Ten

Natalya glanced up from her iced tea as a shadow descended on her table. Kate, looking tense and weary, plopped into the chair opposite and set her oversize purse on the table. "Sorry I'm late."

Natalya's shrugged her shoulders and looked around her sister for her adorable nephew. "Where's Derek?"

"With his sitter."

A puzzled frown tugged at Natalya's forehead. After yesterday, she'd looked forward to spending some time with Kate's son. She'd missed every Christmas, and every major event in Derek's life—all but his first birthday. While she and Kate had agreed not to tell Derek that Natalya was his aunt, she'd hoped to sneak in a few priceless memories when she could. It surprised her how his absence darkened her mood.

"Why? He could have joined us. I wouldn't mind, you know."

"No. He can't."

At the harshness in her sister's voice, Natalya drew back. Suspicion reared its head. Warning bells tolled. Kate's frazzled look didn't bode well. What had her agitated now? Cautiously, Natalya asked, "Why not?"

Using her menu as a shield, Kate leaned across the table and lowered her voice to a barely audible whisper. "Because you're a killer."

"I am not!" Natalya slapped her napkin onto the tabletop, jarring her tea. Ice cubes rattled, mixing with the clank of silverware.

"No?" Leaning back, Kate laid her menu across her waiting plate.

"I could've sworn that's what you've been telling me the last couple of days."

The bitter truth jammed into Natalya's gut. Sure, she could claim a dozen justifiable reasons, or more, to explain why she'd taken lives. They all sounded right on paper: dispose of the leader of a terrorist sect in Jordan, make a known threat on the president quietly disappear, terminate an arms shipment and if someone got caught in the crossfire . . .

She sighed. When it all boiled down to outside perception, black-and-white fact couldn't necessarily override national security. Still, the accusation stung. A great deal of difference separated her from the thugs on the street. "It's not like that."

"It's close enough Derek doesn't need to be around it."

Indignation arced through Natalya. For God's sake, it wasn't like she intended to start taking out marks in front of a four-year-old little boy. On a rare occasion, she'd even left her gun in her car, just in case her nephew happened to get his hands on her purse. She scowled at her righteous twin. "I suppose it's perfectly okay for him to be around what his mother does?"

Her barb hit the mark, and Kate's overblushed cheeks darkened with anger. She pursed her lips, returning Natalya's scowl. Three years away from each other, and they could still fight like they had when they were teens.

"I do what I have to do because I have no choice," Kate ground out through gritted teeth. "You *chose* your path."

"Oh, come off it, Kate." Natalya gave a sad shake of her head. "I may have been gone most of your marriage, but I remember Erik. He had a good job. A damn good career. And he looked out for you better than Mom and Dad. You expect me to believe he left you *nothing?*"

Behind her glasses, Kate's face washed white. The fire in her eyes disappeared. Like some heavy weight had just been dropped on her shoulders, she slumped in her seat. "He tried."

Feeling a modicum of guilt over her uncalled-for attack, Natalya softened her voice. "What do you mean he *tried*?"

Kate's teeth dug into her lower lip. The motion of her shoulders suggested she wrung her hands beneath the white tablecloth. In her far-away gaze, tears collected. "You're right. He did have a damn good job. I loved it a lot. It got the house of my dreams, paid for years of infertility treatments, and I got to see a good portion of the world each summer."

So what was the problem now? If they could spend like that, they surely had invested. Natalya lifted an eyebrow, asking for more.

"We lived like the rest of the world." Kate shrugged one shoulder, but her teeth worked at her lip harder. "Paycheck to paycheck. He spoiled me something silly. Derek, too, that first year." She expelled a harsh breath that scattered the undisciplined blonde hair framing her face. "We weren't in debt, but without his paycheck . . ."

They'd lost everything. Natalya flinched. "Surely he had some sort of life insurance policy?"

Kate shook her head. "He worked a lot. Seventy- or eighty-hour weeks most of the year. Which meant I handled everything else. Bills, meals, shopping, cleaning." A deep gulp confessed embarrassment. "I forgot to renew his policy."

In that moment, Natalya knew sympathy like never before. She reached across the table and squeezed her sister's hand. "I'm sorry, Katey."

She also knew that before this case spiraled any further, she'd pass word to her superiors and set Kate as her beneficiary. Whatever it took to help her sister out of this mess. If she'd been closer . . .

Natalya shoved the surfacing guilt aside. She couldn't change the past. All she could do was move forward and try to make up for being out of contact and inadvertently pushing her sister back to stripping. Which meant focusing on the reason she'd asked to have lunch together.

She withdrew her hand and beckoned the waitress over. "Two mango-spinach salads, please." Her gaze slid to Kate, checking for approval.

A more enthusiastic nod agreed.

"And two strawberry daiquiris."

At that, Kate cracked a smile. She pulled off her glasses and overly long eyelashes blinked rapidly in attempts to rid her unshed tears without smearing her makeup.

Their fight over, tension rolled off Natalya's shoulders. With a nod, the waitress retreated to the bar at the end of the sidewalk café.

"Tell me about Brandon Moretti."

Kate choked on her ice water. She dabbed at her mouth with her napkin, her eyes dancing with riotous laughter. "I thought you weren't interested?"

"I'm not." Natalya fixed her with a frown meant to eradicate the thought from Kate's brain. She was not, would not be, *could* not be, interested in Brandon Moretti. It was just a physical thing. A bit of . . . sport.

Right. If she kept saying it, maybe she could will it to happen.

"He's the strongest suspect I have for Iskatel'."

Again came Kate's laughter. She shook her head. "Don't be silly. I've known him a year. I bet I could even vouch for his whereabouts on a few occasions. And the man's crazy about Derek."

Crazy about kids didn't fit with Natalya's impression of Brandon Moretti. In fact, she'd place kids dead last on that arrogant man's list of interests. Yet, for some strange reason, the thought he might be crazy about her nephew set off Natalya's pulse. She did her best to convince herself the stuttering beat in her veins was anxiety.

She grasped at a fleeting possibility like it was the last life raft out of a choppy sea. "That could all be a guise. We know how Iskatel' operates. He befriends the girls. Brandon has the connections."

Kate shook her head more emphatically. "There's nothing you can tell me that's going to make me believe my boss killed seven women. Jeez, Natalya, the guy changes lightbulbs. Does the dishes."

More information she didn't want to know about Moretti. Natalya fidgeted in her seat.

"And if you ask me, sis, my boss has it bad for you."

Now *that* wasn't a subject Natalya intended to go near. The brief reminder of Brandon's scalding touch and the fabulous pull of his mouth was enough to stir warmth in her veins as it was. No way in hell would she give desire room to bloom. "Lightbulbs and dishes don't mean anything, Kate. *Why* can't I get you to understand you *know* this person?"

"I get it." She rolled her eyes on a frustrated sigh. "Just not Brandon. I don't think I've ever seen him look at someone the way he looked at you—and I've seen him with plenty of women."

Great. So Moretti was a player too. That ought to put her mind at ease. If he didn't get involved, it meant what brewed between them wouldn't come with complications. A quick tumble in the sheets. An even quicker good-bye . . .

Exactly what she wanted.

So why did the thought that Moretti strolled through women the way she might stroll through shoes, make Natalya's stomach bunch?

"Someone you know, Kate. Tell me about Jill. She cut you a couple of looks meant to kill last night."

"Jill?" The amusement drained from Kate's expression. Her mouth turned down, along with her brows, and she studied her plate.

"Yes, Jill."

Interrupting insight Natalya craved, the waitress appeared with their order. "Anything else, ladies?"

"No, that's all." Natalya lifted her daiquiri and sipped from the straw. Frosty sweetness soothed the agitation fluttering around in her stomach. More seeped out as she sighed in mock bliss. "I've missed rum."

"Jill's been around forever," Kate murmured once the waitress walked away. "I don't know how old she is, but she's got some guy who keeps her in plastic surgery."

Her quiet disclosure drew Natalya forward in her seat. She pushed her salad aside, set her elbows on the table, and focused on her sister's expression. Kate's gaze reflected inward, concentrating on something that clearly disturbed her.

"She's done everything she can to land the lead dancer's spot. Her body's good. She's got the moves. But it's like men can sense her personality's no better than a porcupine's."

Keep talking, Katey.

"They don't ask for her. She's hated me since I walked in the door, pretty much."

That or she'd already chosen her for a target and distanced herself before her job required she get close. Maybe that's how she coped with the guilt—kept herself detached until the absolute last minute necessary. Maybe that's also why so many girls became problematic.

"There's something between her and Brandon. Old business, I think. I've never asked, but when he and I became friends, and I'd pop in at his bar for an after-hours drink, it became evident, pretty fast, she didn't like me hanging around."

Natalya hadn't cared to have Alexei's girls hanging around either. It complicated things. More than once, uninformed observers had accused her of jealousy. Only when the news about her engagement to Dmitri circulated did the eyebrows cease to lift and the whispered comments died off.

"Has she made a point of buddying up to you lately?"

Kate's features scrunched together with a touch of disgust. "I think Brandon might have said something to her. She hasn't been *friendly*, but she's been . . . better."

Natalya's stomach took a nosedive to her feet. Nothing could put the pair in Iskatel´ and Yakov's shoes better than Kate's words. It all stacked up. Black and white, there for her to pin up on a wall and take aim. Brandon was the elusive Yakov, the supplantor; Jill the fiendish Iskatel´, the finder.

Shit.

She'd hoped. Had almost believed Sergei's adamant insistence that Brandon couldn't be Dmitri's go-to guy. Lord knew she wanted to. All she needed was one solid excuse to yield to the press of his body. The insistent heat in his gaze.

One night.

Well that would never happen now. She stuffed her dismay down so deep it didn't have a prayer of surfacing. At least she'd found out before Brandon lured her into bed and Dmitri learned she'd been unfaithful.

Damn it all!

She stabbed her fork into her salad and forced down a bite. The same uncomfortable silence gripped her sister, who pushed her spinach around the bowl as she had when they'd been kids and something bothered her. Natalya caught the habit and lowered her fork. "Is something wrong?"

Kate's gaze slowly lifted to Natalya's face. "Didn't it bother you?"

A little voice told Natalya she didn't want to ask for an explanation. But curiosity overwhelmed sense, and before she could stop the question, she heard herself say, "Didn't what bother me?"

"The girls." Kate lowered her voice. Her eyes took on a pleading quality. "You took away their freedom. Then you lay in the same bed with the man who *sold* them to a sheikh."

Okay. Way too much self-reflection for a hot Vegas afternoon. Natalya choked down the lump of spinach that had wedged itself in her throat. How the hell did she answer that?

Did she start by telling her twin all the times she'd contemplated killing Dmitri in his sleep? Maybe she should tell Kate how sometimes just looking in the mirror made her want to turn her gun on herself. Would Kate understand if she confessed that she'd considered killing the girls outright to save them from the hell they'd meet across the ocean?

She blinked. What if Iskatel' had failed intentionally? Her pulse ratcheted up a notch. If Iskatel' *were* Jill, a woman would be subject to the same gut-wrenching emotions Natalya had suffered. Maybe she'd cracked.

Only one way to find out. Jill's reaction to Brandon, when he wasn't within arms' distance, would speak volumes.

Natalya bolted out of her chair. "I've got to go. I've got to convince Brandon to put me onstage before we open tonight." Tossing a handful of bills onto the table, she snatched up her purse and jogged out of the café.

Eleven

The rap on Brandon's office door smoothed the scowl that had etched itself on his face the minute he arrived at Fantasia. He leaned back in his chair, answering with a rough, "Yeah."

Mayer stuck his head in, looked from side to side, then flashed a devilish grin. "Thought I better check."

In no mood for his partner's teasing, Brandon grunted. Tonight was already lining up as hell with two cocktail waitresses calling in sick, Rory gone, and Jill sulking about the housemom job she didn't get. All he needed was for Natalya to waltz through the door to solidify the coming disaster.

Four hours, a nap, *and* a lukewarm shower hadn't banished her from his thoughts. Now he waited on edge, torn between barring his door to keep her at a distance and locking her inside.

"I called a former CIA buddy and got those files you wanted." Aaron tossed one thick manila folder and a smaller, narrower twin, on Brandon's desk, then flopped into the chair.

Wanted. A very operative word. Brandon didn't *want* to learn anything more about that damnable redhead for fear it would just draw him to her more. But necessity demanded he discover all he could.

He sat forward and beckoned for the files. "Let me see Sergei's first." He'd told himself he put Natalya's off because if he found anything incriminating he could move right on to interrogating her.

To Brandon's surprise, Aaron passed him the thicker folder.

Brandon double-checked the name, certain his partner had grabbed the wrong one. *Sergei Khitrovo* adorned the right corner tab.

Well damn. He hadn't expected a security guard with impeccable credentials to have a file. Not anything significant at least.

"You've read through them?" Brandon eyed Aaron over the folder's edge.

"Yeah." Folding his arms behind his head, Aaron reclined.

What lay inside the two inches of papers was a collective report of Sergei Khitrovo's early adulthood life. Immigration papers marked him as arriving in America at the age of eighteen. Parental history, unknown. In his early twenties, he'd run with a rough crowd in the streets of East Los Angeles, collecting an assortment of misdemeanor drug charges. Possession. Possession with intent to sell. DUI. Nothing that stuck or warranted jail time.

He'd done enough college to obtain an associates degree in construction. His job history in that field spanned four years. No terminations. And his run-ins with the law disappeared. He'd obviously cleaned himself up. Pretty commendable.

Brandon scanned a list of female involvements. A couple long-term stints with women whose names didn't trigger alarms. Then, a name jumped off the page: Amanda Colestetter. Daughter of the Silicon Valley mogul Harrison Colestetter.

Sergei had spent a year legitimately employed as a private Colestetter guard. From there, his work history contained some of the most reputable names in private security. A year at Black and Munroe—known to work exclusively with international diplomats. Another two years with Hoffman and Brandt, the premiere outfit used for political events. They answered only to the Secret Service and staffed things like presidential town meetings, senatorial rallies, and other national governmental affairs.

Last but not least, as Natalya had mentioned, he'd come off a job three weeks ago in Hollywood, working private detail for the young starlet Lynn Reede. Behind all the documentation, Brandon discovered letters of reference, obviously supplied by the person Aaron had contacted to obtain the background check.

Son of a bitch! The guy was flawless. What hopes Brandon had nurtured about discovering a reason to not hire Sergei Khitrovo scattered like ashes on a strong wind. He couldn't turn away someone with Sergei's credentials when they were in need of a good eye and a strong conscience.

He grumbled to himself as he tossed Sergei's file back onto his desk and flipped open Natalya's.

In the first few lines, he identified her accent. He'd thought it was Ukrainian, but she'd been born in Moscow, raised with a foster family after her parents' early death, and the summer of her seventeenth year she had come across the ocean to attend Southern California University, where she presumably met Kate.

She graduated four years later. She'd evidently returned to Moscow shortly thereafter—the records dropped off after a listed departure. Then, two years ago, she returned with green card in hand. Passed her immigration tests six months later, while holding down a secretarial job for a law firm in LA, where she'd remained employed until two months ago.

That certainly explained her impeccable taste in fashion.

Huh. She had a cat. Or did have at one time, according to the slow-pay annotation on her very brief credit statement and the accompanying copy of the veterinarian's bill. A nine-hundred-dollar cat.

He hated cats.

Brandon scowled. Whether he hated cats or not made no difference.

"She's clean," Aaron commented as he spun Sergei's report back in front of him. "They both are."

Clean, but . . .

Flipping through the papers once more, Brandon searched for an explanation to why his criminal alert began to buzz. There was something very strange about this report, and something very familiar.

"Too clean," Aaron murmured.

Brandon's focus narrowed on her criminal history. "Not even a damn speeding ticket." He flipped back to her school records and ran his finger down her transcript. Bs, Cs. Not one single A. No area of expertise. Completely average.

As if someone tried to blend her in.

The hair on the back of his neck prickled as the familiarity registered. If Aaron had pulled his record, the one witness protection fabricated for him, they'd be staring at a near mirror image.

Aaron reached across the desk and tugged the folder from Brandon's hands. He flipped it open to Natalya's personal background and stabbed his index finger on the blank page. "Someone's been dicking with her file. Who lives in America for six years with *no* personal involvements?"

Brandon's gaze locked on the line below Aaron's fingertip: *No known personal involvements or political affiliations.* His heart kicked into his ribs.

Ignoring the forceful pang, he lifted his gaze to Aaron's. "This came from the CIA?"

A smirk tugged at the corner of Mayer's mouth. "In a roundabout sorta way."

Which meant the file didn't technically exist. Whoever Aaron had contacted would deny everything. Still, the data couldn't be argued. Amazing what the government kept track of, especially since 9-11. He shuddered to think what the government had on him.

No doubt his *real* file would triple Sergei's, particularly with his father's mafia connections.

He closed the folder, braced his elbows on his desk, and steepled his fingers. Secrets shouldn't exist between partners. But Brandon had learned the hard way what happened when he said too much. One drunk frat night at A&M where he vaguely remembered telling a girl that he was in witness protection had exposed his family. He'd been paying the price ever since. Nothing, or no one, would prompt him into suggesting to Aaron that Natalya might be part of the same program.

If she were, she had a damned good reason.

Yet the lack of evidence in her file did nothing to further his investigation. He knew no more about her than he had before. Sergei's name didn't even make an appearance in that tidy little file. And he *knew* they shared some involvement. Hell, Kate's name didn't even make an appearance in Natalya's record, and if the government knew Sergei shared an apartment in 1995 with a Michael Saunders, they damn well would know Natalya's college roommate.

The sudden closing of his office door jerked him out of his thoughts with so much force he reached for the gun atop his desk. He glanced up as his fingers closed around the grip. Aaron whipped around to face the intruder, his hand creeping toward the piece tucked into the back of his jeans.

Natalya stood stock still in the doorway. Her gaze dropped to Brandon's curled fingers, then lifted to his face. She took a confident step forward, and a dazzling smile spread across her face. "I've been thinking about what you said last night." Door open, she proceeded across the room, never once taking a wobbly step despite her four-inch black heels.

"This isn't a good time, Natalya," Brandon muttered as he pulled his hand away. Not now. Not in his office. Not ever again.

She blew right past his argument, lifted a slender hand to her dark green suit jacket, and popped the solitary button. The fabric that had stretched across her breasts fell open, giving him the most exquisite view of a low-cut, red lace bra. One slow roll of her shoulders sent the jacket tumbling to the floor. "And I decided I'd just have to prove my ability."

Holy fuck! Brandon's gut clamped down like a vise as what was about to happen hammered into his head. He sent Aaron a beseeching glance, hoping like hell his friend would step up and ask the redheaded she-devil to leave.

Instead, Aaron jumped out of his chair, nearly knocking it over as he scrambled toward the door. "Maybe not so clean after all," he quipped from the doorway before he vanished into the club, leaving the door firmly closed in his wake.

Brandon's gaze flicked back to Natalya and locked in place. In the time it took Aaron to rocket out of the room, she'd lost her skirt as well. She stood before him in a bra that could hardly be called decent and matching thong panties.

She made a slow pirouette, and his eyes swept down, all the way down, those never-ending legs. From the tops of muscular thighs, to shapely knees and toned calves, down to anklebones so delicate they looked like a doll's and bright, pink-tipped toenails. Slowly, he made his way back up her body, across a flat, sloping waist, to her full, pert breasts, then higher, stopping at her parted pink lips.

His entire body tightened. His pulse beat so fast it buzzed in his ears. Good fucking Lord, he'd known seeing Natalya naked would be a mistake of the worst kind. Shielded behind her fastidious suits lay a seductress's body. A man's playground guaranteed to keep him entertained for hours. And yet, somehow, she retained her elegance. The confidence in her step as she rounded the corner of his desk and approached his chair could only be described as class.

His own personal fantasy come true.

Christ!

He ground his teeth together and clenched his hands into fists. And he couldn't touch her. Well . . . shouldn't. The reasons were too numerous to count.

To his abject horror, she evidently intended to do the touching for him. Her slender hands swept slowly up her waist, cupped her breasts, and pushed them together. The soft swell of flesh that rose above the edge of her bra made his fingers twitch. His throat felt dry, the air in the room too stifling hot to breathe.

He watched, not daring to move for fear he'd come out of his chair and back her against the wall where he'd had her yesterday. Her hands skimmed higher, climbing the delicate lines of her neck to the back of her hair. She pulled out a simple ballpoint pen, dropped it on his desk, and with one shake of her head, sent her glorious auburn hair tumbling to her waist.

Brandon checked a groan. Not the wall. His desk. Where those fire-kissed lengths would fan out behind her head. A she-devil's halo. Blood raced to his groin. Bittersweet agony, a product of wanting her beyond all reason, and knowing he dared not cross that line.

As she dragged the backs of her knuckles down her sides, she tipped her head, listening to the music that drifted through his closed door. Her toe began to tap. Sloping hips soon followed, subtly undulating. "That'll do," she murmured. Flashing him a sultry smile, she rotated her hips in one slow circle as she bent over and ran her hands down her legs in a cat-like stretch. Looking up through her eyelashes, she asked, "So where do you want me, boss? On the desk or in your lap?"

Their gazes locked, the tension in the room suddenly palpable. His nostrils flared at the faint scent of lilacs that wafted off her smooth skin.

Definitely lotion.

The irrational thought drifted through his mind seconds before Natalya sent his world careening sideways as her body assumed the muffled tempo, and she reached behind her back for the clasp of her bra.

The scrap of lace fell away to land on his lap. Although minimal, the contact against his straining erection was enough to make him gasp. Her breasts swayed with the music, full and free, and beckoning him to touch.

"Are there rules here, Brandon?" she asked as she worked her way closer to his knees. "It's been a while since I've danced in Vegas, you know."

He found his voice, hoarse as it was. "No."

"That's what I thought." A coy smile drifted over her lips. "Maybe we should establish a few." She hooked a leg over his thigh and dropped her body down. Close enough he dug his fingers into the arm of his chair and prepared for the shock of her weight.

It didn't come.

Instead, she rolled her hips forward, mimicking the action they both knew their entendres referred to. He visualized slipping inside her waiting feminine warmth. Felt the heat of her moist pussy gloving his straining cock. Brandon clenched his hands tighter and ordered his body not to respond.

The undulation rolled up her body, a gentle arc that pushed rosy nipples close to his face, and he caught another intoxicating whiff of flowers. He closed his eyes to temper the fierce desire that shot through his veins. When he opened them again, she'd retreated, standing once more with her legs spread wide around his and her hands roaming over the curves he ached to caress.

"No touching above the belly button or below the waist," she whispered, the hitch in her voice unmistakable.

Brandon swallowed to wet his suddenly dry throat. "That pretty much eliminates everywhere."

"Exactly." A wink followed a husky laugh.

Catching on to her game, he released his death grip on the chair and reached a hand between their bodies to trail one finger horizontally cross her tight midriff. "Except here."

"Except there." Natalya's eyes sparked with dark color. Her confident smile faltered for a millisecond. But before she completely stumbled, she gyrated in a slow circle, presenting him with a mind-boggling view of firm buttocks and the delicate hollow of her spine. As she bent forward, undulating that perfect bottom in his face, his hand accidentally slipped down one taut curve.

She sucked in a sharp breath. Goose bumps broke out over her flesh. He hadn't meant to violate her rules, but Brandon was damn glad for that unintentional slip. It proved, beyond all measure, she wasn't as immune to him as she'd like him to believe.

He kept his finger on her skin as she worked a slow circle and eased her way around to face him once more. His hand rested on her upper thigh. Her gaze dropped to where he touched her. Belligerence drove him to draw a lazy circle over her skin.

Natalya rewarded his forbidden caress by setting her hands on his desk, leaning back, and in perfect time with the music, placing her foot in his chest and pushing him away. A wicked grin pulled at her full lips. "No touching, boss."

"Right," he murmured. Her shove sent him back into his chair, but as she lowered her leg, he observed the faint sheen of moisture on her inner thigh. His gut ground into a tight ball, and his balls pulled into his body.

To hell with her rules. If she didn't stop now, he was going to have his hands all over her. It took every bit of willpower he possessed to resist the call of her body, as it was. And he possessed little patience for this game. He was about to come in his pants, and before he allowed that to happen, Natalya would be on her back, screaming his name.

She set her foot between his legs, her toes brushing the base of his confined erection. One deliberate lowering of her heel stroked his swollen length, and his cock pulsed. He grabbed her ankle, imprisoning that malicious foot. "Natalya."

"Hm?" Bending forward, she set her elbow on her knee and leaned her weight on the leg he held. Her long lashes lowered, then lifted over heavy-lidded eyes.

Against his better judgment, he gave in to the urge to explore and slid his hand up the back of her calf, over the back of her knee, and came to a stop where he'd witnessed the garter hug her muscular leg the night before. "What do you want?"

"The stage." Her foot now free, she stroked his cock with her toe once more. "I think I've proved I'm good enough."

Good enough to surpass Kate, but he'd be damned if he told her that. After this little show, he was more convinced than ever that she'd never take the stage. She'd have every guy in the house on the verge of spontaneous ejaculation. As long as she looked at him like she did now, pupils dilated, lips parted against the heavy fall of her breath, he wouldn't allow her to creep into any other man's fantasy.

"No," he argued, his voice thick. "All you've proved is that I want to fuck you."

She didn't even flinch as a laugh rumbled in the back of her throat. Her gaze slid down to where his fingers compressed her skin. "You're violating the rules, boss."

Nuh-huh. She wasn't getting out of this so easily. She'd started it, but he intended to finish it. Before she walked out of this room, he'd have her admission that she wanted the same. He was done with the games.

Holding her gaze so he could witness her reaction, he inched his hand up her thigh. The back of his knuckles brushed against the damp scrap of her panties, and Natalya's bold stare flickered with a flash of bright desire.

Brandon rubbed his knuckle over her moist folds, stroking the hardened nub of her clitoris. "On my desk, or in my lap?" If he hadn't been watching her so intently, he'd have never noticed the moment of hesitation as she bit down on her lower lip. But he felt the tremor roll through her body.

"I want the stage." Her voice lacked her usual confidence. The waver in her words only proved the falseness of her claim.

In a surprisingly bold move, even for him, Brandon nudged that worthless scrap of silk aside, and pushed his finger inside her. Her gasp ricocheted through him with more force than a discharging gun. Her thighs parted, and her hips crept forward. Around his finger, her wet flesh clamped down hard.

"I think you want me too." At her silence, he pushed in again. Deeper. Slower. Drawing out the friction as he pressed the base of his palm against her aroused clit.

Natalya teetered on her heels.

Twelve

Pleasure thrummed through Natalya's body. She closed her eyes and concentrated on breathing to keep from crumpling into Brandon's hand. Every instinct for self-preservation she possessed demanded she clamp her legs together and step away from the fantastic intrusion of Brandon's thick finger. She should deny his observation and give him a scathing lecture on violating her privacy.

But it would be a lie. One she couldn't hide from. The proof lay in the quivering of her abdomen, the way her body glided in time with his slow, steady thrusts. And dear God, she didn't want to.

She was sick of the lies. Sick of hiding behind masks and personalities that imprisoned her worse than any bars or chains.

Just once, she wanted to bask in the truth, no matter how insignificant or fleeting it might be. What difference would it make? If he worked for Dmitri, he'd already elicited all the information he needed to prove she didn't care for the man she was supposed to marry in two weeks. That she'd even allowed Brandon to touch her, when she sensed his intentions—and he'd made little attempt to hide them—revealed her fickle loyalties. All Brandon needed to do was relay what had happened.

So why wasn't he stopping?

She opened her eyes to find his lethal gaze locked on her face. Tawny eyes burned into her skin. Hot color raced to her cheeks as a wave of heat flooded through her veins. Her pussy contracted around his finger, and she tottered again.

Damn, he felt good. And he'd feel so much better with his weight pressed on top of her, his cock gliding in and out of her body, not his hand.

A soft moan slipped from her throat.

Brandon nudged her foot out of the chair and eased to his feet. One arm came around her waist, fingers splayed across the small of her back. The other stayed between her legs, languorous strokes edging her closer to inevitable climax.

"Tell me what you want, beautiful." His breath rasped over her cheek. Featherlight kisses accompanied the whisper, trailing across her skin in a taunting path toward her mouth.

Kiss me. She turned her head in search of lips she instinctively knew would be warm, the words on the tip of her tongue. *Kiss me until I don't care whether I live or die.*

Honesty. Just once.

He caught her lower lip with his teeth, the nip nowhere near gentle. But the lazy stroke of his tongue soothed the stinging bite. She parted her lips, dipped her tongue out to touch his.

Brandon's body tightened like a whip. The pressure in her lower back increased as his fingers curled into her skin. Their breaths mingled. The tips of their tongues met in a slow, sensual dance. As another spasm of ecstasy threatened to send her tumbling into his solid chest, she braced her hands on his shoulders.

And then Brandon was gone, the magic of his fingers disappearing as he stepped back and set both hands on her waist. His gaze scorched in to flood her body with tingles. He waited, his question unspoken, but hanging between them.

Tell me what you want.

Clearly he intended to make her admit she wanted to feel him deep inside her. Wanted to experience the slide of his bare skin against hers. And God, how she wanted to kiss him. To taste the desire that burned in his gaze and the indescribable flavor of hot, aroused man.

Confessing might lead her to an early grave, but for once, her conscience would be clear. She swallowed hard and dug deep for the courage that had kept her alive these last three years. His gaze followed the sweep of her tongue as she moistened her lips.

"Kiss me." Her senses honed in on her whisper, amplifying it and the ragged fall of their mutual breathing. She became aware of every minuscule sound as she waited for Brandon to either dip his head and honor her request, or shove her aside with a wicked sneer.

He took a step closer, bringing their bodies in contact from chest to toes. One arm wrapped around her waist, then slid up her back to offer support between her shoulder blades. The other tangled in her hair, tipping her head back. Putting her where he wanted her—subtle dominance that thrilled her in places she hadn't known existed. Her womb clamped hard, sending another rush of moisture through her pussy.

His mouth descended. Warm lips played against hers, drawing her into the spell his body wove. Pulling her in so deep she struggled for air.

The sudden, brassy ring of her cell phone jolted her out of hazy desire. She froze. With Kate and Sergei due to arrive at Fantasia any minute, there could only be one other person calling at this time of day—Dmitri. It would be almost one in the morning in Moscow. The time Dmitri put aside his work and crawled into bed. He'd want to talk before he slept.

"Don't answer that," Brandon whispered against her mouth.

Damn if those lips weren't compelling. She'd had his mouth on her breast, knew the incredible magic his tongue could create there, but had yet to experience the tantalizing slide of his tongue against hers. The need to feel his mouth on hers, to get lost in his potent masculinity pressed her to ignore the ringing tones.

Duty, however, rose up screaming. If she didn't answer, Dmitri would get suspicious.

"I have to." Natalya shoved out of Brandon's embrace and darted across the room for her phone. As she hurtled around the desk, she snatched up her jacket, thrust her arms inside, and caught her cell as the fourth ring began to dwindle. She punched the button and slipped into Dmitri's native language. "Hello, darling."

As she buttoned her jacket, she tossed an apologetic look over her shoulder before yanking on her skirt.

"How are you, my love? Are you enjoying Vegas?"

"Yes, absolutely." A little too much. Aware of the heavy weight of Brandon's annoyed scowl, she hurried to the door and let herself outside.

Dmitri's chuckle drifted through the line, robust and warm. An almost pleasant sound, if she didn't intimately know his darker nature. "Spending my money at craps?"

"No, nothing like that. I did go shopping." Laughing, she headed for her office.

"Tell me you bought something green for me. Something naughty."

"Of course." Never in a hundred years.

"Tell me what it looks like so I can picture it while I'm jacking off in our bed and thinking of fucking you."

She fought back a shudder, the imagery of Dmitri bringing himself to pleasure with her as his chosen bit of erotica made her want to puke. But like the good actress she was, she let out another laugh. "It's a surprise."

A feeling so foreign he couldn't find words to describe it crept into Brandon's veins as Natalya's laughter drifted through his door. He couldn't name it, but he didn't like it. It made him feel confined. Restrained. And the only thought that consumed his brain was shoving his fist through Sergei Khitrovo's face.

It didn't take a rocket scientist to put their homelands together, add

in Natalya's accent along with the way she lowered it to intimate familiarity, and come up with lovers. Maybe the government didn't have
record of a personal association, but give her a few more months and
they would.

He swiveled around and shoved his chair into his desk. "Fuck!"

If he hadn't been so adamant about hearing her tell him she wanted
him, that phone call would have gone unanswered. She'd still be here.
And he'd be riding out the orgasm that had threatened to break loose
against his palm.

Like a caged man with no outlet, he stalked the length of his office.
For the dozenth time, he questioned what the hell was the matter with
him. Since when had words mattered? Her body told him plain as day
what she wanted. He could still smell her on his hand.

Why the hell did he care who she was murmuring sweet nothings
to? She wasn't his. He didn't want to keep her. He just wanted to screw
her silly.

Which he very well could be doing if he hadn't decided he needed
to hear her confession and eek out one slight degree of control with
that simple victory.

He came to a standstill as what she'd said echoed distantly in his
brain.

Kiss me.

Not some blatant sexual request, like he had expected. Not a brash,
fuck me, as he'd been wholly prepared to hear. No, she'd wanted something simpler. Something . . .

A chill wafted across his heated body.

Innocent.

And that touch of innocence tumbling off her lips spoke to him
more profoundly than any coarse confession of physical desire.

Where did it come from? Natalya Trubachev was not innocent. Not
by a long shot. He'd bet his entire career she knew her way around a
man's body, and her striptease illustrated her comfort with her own

skin. Hell, she hadn't backed down the last two times they'd been alone. In his experience, women like her didn't hesitate to tell a man what they wanted, and often *how* they wanted it.

Yet all she'd asked for, when he obviously would have honored any request, was a simple kiss.

He shook his head. No, not so simple. Those two whispered words had collided in his brain like train engines crashing nose to nose at full speed. They'd stopped him in his tracks, ripped his breath from his lungs, and rendered him dysfunctional for a fleeting moment. He'd been . . . touched, damn it.

Affected enough that when he'd reclaimed control over his body, and the fist around his lungs let go, allowing him to breathe, all thoughts of fucking her senseless vanished under the single desire to find absolute fulfillment in the softness of her mouth.

By the time he'd managed to recover from the shock of realizing all he *wanted* was that sweet kiss and had touched his lips to hers, once again, he'd been too goddamn late.

A kiss.

A goddamned kiss had stripped him senseless.

How the hell was that possible?

It wasn't. His reaction came from too many hours of pent-up desire. In the last twenty-four, he'd experienced enough sexual frustration that he'd take whatever he could get, and if she wanted a kiss, well, it was a far cry better than walking away completely unsatisfied.

Uh-huh. Keep telling yourself that, buddy.

If Rachel were alive and had overheard the nonsense going on inside his skull, she'd smack her shoe over his head.

No, however ridiculous it sounded, the more he thought about it, the more he realized he'd wanted that kiss more than he had ever wanted anything. Sure, he craved where that kiss would inevitably lead, but in that moment, kissing Natalya became more important than experiencing the divinity of her pussy squeezing around his cock.

And that emasculating discovery shook him to the core.

He sat down before his shaky legs could give out and embarrass him further.

What kind of killer asked for a kiss?

He plowed his fingers through his hair. This nonsense had to stop. Tonight. Before he completely lost his mind. She wanted rules; he'd give her some. Right. Fucking. Now.

Shoving out of his chair, he stalked into the club. The bang of his office door barely registered, along with the handful of heads that swiveled his way as he stomped toward backstage. The door clanged open with his forceful shove, nearly knocking the half-dressed dancer standing behind it on her ass.

He spared her an annoyed glance and marched toward Natalya's office. When he banged on her door, Jill answered.

"Hi, baby." Sidling up to his chest, she petted his pectorals, then glided her land lower, to his still swollen cock.

Brandon clenched his jaw. He wrapped punishing fingers around Jill's wrist and pulled her hand off his body. Looking over her head, he scanned Natalya's office, only to find it empty. "Where's Natalya?"

Jill's brown eyes widened for a nanosecond before a frown crept across her forehead. "I haven't seen her. What's the problem? Anything I can help with? You know she was late yesterday. A housemom needs to be on time." Oblivious to the anger that ebbed off him in waves, she crept into his side once more and ran a fingernail down the length of his chest. She came to a stop at the waistband of his jeans.

He lifted his gaze to the ceiling, praying for patience as he slowly counted to ten. In his present mood, he didn't trust himself not to fire Jill on the spot. Once again, he grabbed her wrist and deliberately extricated himself from her pawing hands. "When you see her, tell her I want to talk to her. Immediately."

Brandon stopped in the doorway with a puzzled frown. Wait just a damn second. . . He looked over his shoulder at Jill. "What are *you* doing in *her* office?"

"Me?" False innocence spread across her pert features, and an unnatural laugh burst free.

"Yes, you."

"I, ah . . . was looking for . . ." Her gaze darted wildly around the room. When it landed in the corner, her worried expression brightened. She hurried to a lump of clothing piled high on a folding metal chair and dangled a pair of opaque white stockings close to her chin. "A pair of these. Mine ripped on my garter last night."

She hadn't worn white stockings last night. Her first routine included fishnets, and her second dance involved nothing. While she'd circulated the clubhouse, she'd worn bare skin too. She was up to something. But his foul mood wouldn't allow him to dissect it further. He'd pin her down for the truth when he cooled off.

He pushed the door open wide and thumbed her toward the hall. "Out."

Jill demurely lowered her chin, batting her eyelashes as she pranced past his outstretched arm. "Sorry, baby, I didn't think you'd mind."

Another reason he'd distanced himself from her. Cute, she might be. But the woman didn't have the faintest concept of what pleased, or didn't please him. She took liberties—like spreading it around the Strip that they were sleeping together—that surpassed her position.

Thank God he hadn't been obsessed with the notion of kissing her.

Brandon groaned aloud. As he pulled Natalya's office door shut, he reminded himself that as soon as he set boundaries with Natalya sanity would return. He pushed on the heavy steel to ensure the door had locked behind him, then pivoted on his heel to resume his search for the vixen who'd wiggled her bare ass in his face and pushed him over the edge into madness.

Thirteen

Natalya lowered her phone to her lap with a shaking hand. Clutching it tight, she squeezed her eyes shut and forced herself to draw in deep breaths that did nothing to lessen her trembling.

The insanely erotic encounter with Brandon had been enough to leave her shaken. Having to fake a conversation with Dmitri while her body still cried out for satisfaction had pushed her normally steadfast composure to the brink of total fragmentation. She ached in places that had long been neglected, and Dmitri's unwanted affection grated on her nerves. To the point she'd had to stop herself from snapping at him at least twice.

This had moved beyond ridiculous. Somehow, she must gain control over what she was allowing to happen to her good sense. Not to mention all the other things that were happening to her body.

Her phone buzzed against her palm. She snapped up straight in the chair, eyes wide, breath lodged in her throat. Where she was, what she was doing, filtered through her conscious. She glanced down at her clenched hands and observed the illuminated LCD. Sergei's name stamped an incoming text message: **I'm here. Where are you? Answer your phone.**

Gathering her composure as much possible, Natalya quickly replied: **On my way. Meet you out front.** She checked her hastily wrapped bun, pushed a jeweled hairpin deeper, and abandoned her chair. The walk from the restroom passed in a blur, and her heartbeat picked up once more. Sergei's arrival meant another encounter with Brandon.

He'd been angry when she jetted out of his office; he wouldn't be happy to see her now.

Her stomach knotted so tight she doubted she'd ever fit another morsel of food into her belly. *Stupid, stupid!* She'd deliberately toyed with Brandon. She'd witnessed that dark spark of desire glint in his tawny eyes and strove to manipulate it to her advantage. A plan that had backfired in triplicate. Who knew when one of Dmitri's goons would step around a corner, pistol ready, aimed at the center of her forehead?

She had obliterated the understood boundaries Dmitri accepted. It was a matter of minutes, a matter of days—if her suspicions were correct—she could bank on a deadly shadow appearing. Lord knew she'd done it enough times to know what happened next.

The thick tinting on the main doors purpled the world beyond. But when she swung them open, the splash of late-afternoon sunlight warmed away some of the iciness in her veins. Her stomach unclamped by several degrees as Sergei entered the club.

She latched on to his arm, drawing comfort from his constant, unfaltering, self-assuredness. "Come backstage. We'll find Brandon in a few minutes." Not nearly enough time to bring the racket in her head under control, but hopefully long enough she could quiet the trembling under her skin.

The collective murmur of appreciation that drifted through the girls' lounge as Sergei followed her to her office shaved off a few more layers of tension. Natalya suppressed a grin and flashed her partner a conspiratorial wink. In complete contrast to his usual cool, a touch of embarrassed color crept into his cheeks. It amused her to see him rattled.

"What's the matter? Too many at once?" she asked as she eased her office door shut.

He shot her a warning look. "Why didn't you answer your phone?"

Tables turned, Natalya's discomfort returned with a vengeance. Visions of the wanton way she'd stood in front of Brandon, gyrating against his hand, on the verge of melting into a puddle at his feet, set off the tremors once again. On the heels of that splendid memory, Dmitri's raspy voice pummeled through her head. The combination discombobulated her enough she felt dizzy and nauseous all at once.

She turned her back on Sergei and took her chair before her legs gave out. Drawing in a deep breath, she held it and waited for her stomach to stop pitching. But a glance in the mirror revealed the full effect of her mixed-up emotions. Fear, excitement, revulsion, and arousal turned her face a pasty shade of gray.

"Hey. You okay?" Sergei appeared at her side, one hand on her shoulder.

Unable to find words, she bit down on her lower lip as a shock of moisture touched her eyes. She shook her head, clamping her teeth until pain lanced through her lip and the coppery tang of blood touched her tongue.

She couldn't remember when she'd last cried. Definitely not since her arrival in Russia. Absolutely never in front of Sergei. Mortification drove her to cover her face with her hands. He'd laugh—as he should. She'd laugh, if her insides didn't feel like she'd been ripped in half.

"Hey," Sergei murmured. His arm slid around her shoulder, and he drew her snug against his side. One large hand rubbed her arm, a comforting motion that helped ebb the unexpected rush of feeling.

She turned her face into his belly, wrapped her arms around his waist, and inhaled the clean, fresh scent of laundry detergent. If this display wasn't enough to prove she'd lost complete control, she didn't know what would be. She'd cracked. Ten years of flawless performance, and two days in Vegas had pummeled through her constructed defenses. Forced her to confront things she'd buried deep and eradicated her ability to remain unfeeling.

As if Sergei sensed words would only humiliate her further, he said nothing. He merely brought his other arm around her and held her close, languidly stroking her back. No lectures. No sympathy. Just silent understanding.

The door thumped open, startling her out of the protective bubble of Sergei's embrace. Nearly falling out of her chair, she twisted around, praying that the only person who'd seen her fall apart was Kate.

Brandon stood in the doorway, his stormy expression darker than any thundercloud she'd ever witnessed. His jaw worked, the angle harsh, his mouth tight.

The last thing Brandon had expected to encounter when he flung open Natalya's office door was her cuddled up to another man. Shock roiled through his system. In its wake, anger surfaced. Less than an hour ago, she'd moaned at the press of his fingertips. Yet, he'd barged in to find her face inches away from another man's dick.

He ignored the very obvious fact that if he'd bothered to knock he wouldn't have been confronted with the startling scene. He also ignored the irony that he'd been coming here to establish rules, the first one being, no more private encounters in his office. Bottom line— she'd been putty in his hands and his primal animal instinct refused to accept he could be so easily dismissed.

His scowl slanted toward the stranger at her side. The man didn't flinch. He held Brandon's gaze with all the arrogance of a man who had nothing to hide. His hand slid down Natalya's shoulder as she eased to her feet.

"Brandon." A nervous hand pushed the tendrils of hair that had escaped her bun behind her ear. "This is Sergei Khitrovo." She gave Sergei a tentative smile. "Sergei, Brandon Moretti."

Brandon's gut dropped to his toes. The notorious Sergei. She'd fled his office to answer *his* call. No wonder he stood at her side like he belonged there. He did. Brandon was the unwanted party. The interloper who'd intruded on a private moment between two lovers. Christ!

Fine. So be it. The guy might be big and sturdy, but a paycheck said he wasn't man enough for Natalya. Not if she'd needed to find a little outside stimulation.

Wanting nothing else but to demand the man's immediate departure, Brandon reluctantly accepted Sergei's offered hand. He'd agreed
to hire him. He might be a lot of things, but he never went back on his
word.

"Pleased to meet you, Moretti."

Sergei's accent slammed into Brandon. He didn't know what he'd
expected, but hearing the thick Russian accent drove another fist into
Brandon's already bruised ego. It sounded too much like Natalya's,
marking a bond between them that he could never claim.

Mystified and uncomfortable by the thorny sensations prickling
at his subconscious, his frown deepened. Damn, what was wrong with
him? In thirty-five years he'd never cared to carve out a place just for
him in a woman's life. But as he stood before these two, feeling every
bit the ass he was acting, a sudden sense of loss snuck over him. Yeah.
He'd lost her. Only he hadn't even known he was trying to win.

He shook off the nonsensical thought. Lost? Hell, she hadn't been
available for the taking.

And that was all he wanted, he told himself. Take her. Enjoy her.
Fuck her senseless and move on when they both got tired of the same
routine. He certainly wasn't considering getting involved with the pri-
mary suspect in his case.

Still, he couldn't stop the burn that surfaced at the thought Sergei
had heard that soft, throaty moan.

Brandon gritted his teeth. Much as he didn't want to, he needed to
meet with his newest employee. And he needed to introduce Aaron to
the latest man on his staff. Business called. Given his experience, Sergei might just be the best asset Fantasia possessed. Brandon took a step
backward through the door and stared hard at Natalya's lover.

Those light brown eyes looked familiar. The way they issued quiet
challenge, the chin that held just a touch of a square line. Brandon
cocked his head and studied Sergei's impassive expression. Yeah,
they'd met. He felt certain of it. Too many faces filled the clubs for him
to remember where, exactly. "Have we met before?"

"Don't think so."

Brandon shrugged. No, maybe not. He'd remember that accent. Not too many Russians frequented Vegas. "Meet me in front of the stage in ten minutes. You're working the front of the house."

"Brandon?" Natalya asked quietly.

He didn't want to look at her. Wouldn't. He'd already revealed too much of himself by storming into her office.

His gaze slipped in disobedience and leveled with hers. That same dark color flickered in her eyes, drilling holes in his composure. In one heavy heartbeat the need to stalk across the room, yank her away from Sergei, and kiss her senseless consumed him. His dick reminded him they shared unfinished business, and his body was all too willing to finish it now. He silently swore.

"About that dance . . ." She gave him a coy smile.

"Forget it." *Not in a hundred years.* "You're a housemom, not a dancer."

As he turned to leave, he caught the way Natalya flashed her lover a soft, intimate smile. The brightness on her face set off the boiling in his blood, and he clenched one hand into a tight fist. Glancing over his shoulder, he met her cool green stare. "No personal calls on my dime. And when you're here, it's my damn dime."

Her mouth dropped, but whatever protest she intended to try, he squelched by closing her door.

Sergei released a long, slow breath. Almost resurrected. How long would it take before Brandon put the similarities together with memory and discovered Stefan? It would happen—he didn't try to hold on to the hope it wouldn't. When it did, he better have his explanations lined up, ready to fire.

Coming clean might be better in the long run. The conversation would suck. Digging through the past and confessing all the sordid things he'd not only done, but thought . . . He'd rather stand in front of a firing squad. But with the truth exposed, he could focus his energy on the case, as opposed to worrying about keeping his cover intact.

Brandon was a cop. A damn good cop. He'd worked the beat for twelve years almost all of which he'd spent deep undercover. He understood the necessity of keeping identities intact. And frankly, Brandon might have information they could use.

Still, the chance remained, no matter how dismal, that mannerisms would change. As opposed to treating Sergei like an employee, or even punishing him for standing too close to the woman Brandon wanted—like he'd just done—could fade into awkwardness, or worse, companionship. It might not even be Brandon's slip. *Sergei* couldn't fathom the idea of not kicking back a few beers with his brother once the truth came out. He might very well make the fatal slip that cracked their cover.

Then there was the matter of Natalya. She'd sense something was off-kilter. Until he knew for certain Dmitri couldn't, or wouldn't, harm her, he refused to clue her in. Beyond all the logical agency reasons he shouldn't, she had more than enough on her mind. Not the least of which was, evidently, Brandon.

Sergei swallowed a chuckle, but his mouth twisted with wry humor. Some things never changed. Brandon still didn't know the meaning of defeat. Or for that matter, compromise. He set his sights, and if anything stood in his way, he barreled right through, bent on obtaining what he wanted.

Problem being, at twenty, Brandon hadn't been much more than the boy Sergei was. Competitiveness was all part of growing up, learning the game, testing out the waters. They won. They lost. They won some more. In the end it didn't really matter. But the brother who had stormed through that door a minute ago had taken one look at Natalya and reacted with a man's fury.

A man who knew exactly what he wanted and no longer had to play the game. He chose. And clearly, he'd chosen her. No holds barred, he'd fight to the death to win this prize.

Brandon might not know it yet, but any other guy within ten feet of his angry gaze would have recognized all the warning signs.

"Yoo-hoo, Sergei? Are you in there?" Natalya rapped a light fist on his chest.

Blinking, he glanced down at her and realized she'd been talking to him. Waiting for his response. He took one look at the door and switched languages, doubting anyone in the building—save for Dmitri's hired guns—would understand his words. "He's not Iskatel'."

She drew back, frowning. "What?"

"Moretti's not Iskatel'."

"I told you earlier about my conversation with Kate. You can't just dismiss the possibility."

Completely exasperated by her refusal to see what stood right beneath her nose, he reached across her body to her desk and picked up her phone. He slapped it into her palm. "Think about it. If he were Iskatel', he'd know you're engaged to Dmitri, yes?"

She nodded.

"Then tell me why the hell Dmitri's puppet would refuse you personal calls?"

Her green eyes turned as wide as saucers, and he knew he'd made one point she couldn't argue.

Fourteen

Brandon chewed on the inside of his cheek as he weaved his way through the club toward Aaron's post at the end of the bar. He'd swear he knew that face, accent or not. Maybe it was a case of the "everyone has a twin syndrome," because he damn sure had never met a *Sergei* in his life. But, man. The name sat on the tip of his tongue.

He sidestepped around a waitress and gave her a cordial nod. Forty minutes to showtime. Eleven days until the asshole made his move on Kate. Brandon had pissed away two by allowing Natalya to fog his mind. Rachel's murderer hovered right beneath their noses, and by the end of tonight, he intended to be one step closer to hauling the bastard to jail.

He'd start with putting his new man to use. Give him a minor information-gathering job and feel out his dependability. If he botched it, Brandon won the ability to send him packing. If he proved trustworthy . . .

Brandon didn't intend to think about that.

A swathe of long blond hair coming through the front door caught his attention. He stopped to give Kate the first genuinely warm smile he'd felt all day. Sweet Kate. Why couldn't his dick have become obsessed with her? She was smart. Funny. Kind-hearted. And she had the best damn kid known to mankind.

Her smile didn't hold the same brightness it usually did. As she approached, he noticed the dark circles beneath her eyes that her false eyelashes and electric blue eye shadow failed to disguise. Tight creases framed her dainty mouth. Suspicion clouded over him. Had the killer approached her?

He intercepted her path to the backstage dressing rooms. "You all right?"

She pushed her hair over her shoulder, stood taller in her casual sandals, and attempted her usual good cheer. "Yeah, why?"

Not working. She might be sweet and kind, but she couldn't lie for shit. Thank God. In two days' time, he'd had more circular conversations to last a lifetime. He arched a disbelieving eyebrow and cupped her cheek in his palm. His thumb brushed over the swollen tissue beneath her right eye. "What's keeping you up at night?"

Her laugh was forced. She twisted out of his reach and shook her head. With one fingertip, she nudged her glasses up the bridge of her nose. "Just stress. Derek's been full of it this week."

Another lie. But whatever she was hiding, she didn't intend to reveal. Brandon's frown returned.

Before he could press her for answers, she took a step backward. "I've got to hurry. I'm running late."

A sly glance at the clock behind the bar proved yet again, she spoke false. Four thirty on the money. Just like every night. He let it slide. He'd dig deeper tomorrow when he stopped by to pick up Derek. "We'll burn off some of his steam tomorrow. I talked to my buddy over at MGM, she's going to let Derek help feed the lions." At the sudden paling of her face, he hurried to add, "Not in the habitat, Kate. He's going to help the trainers prep. And then, after the official feeding's over, they're going to let him go back and bottle feed a cub."

Relief restored the color to her face. "You about gave me a heart attack."

"I'm not stupid enough to let a child get in with lions. In case I get caught up here tonight, I'll be by around ten."

She glanced sideways with a distracted nod. "I'll have him ready." The forced smile returned as she backed up another step. "Gotta get dressed."

Strange. Damned strange. Kate didn't usually clam up when something bothered her. He watched her walk to the dressing room. Sergei and Natalya exited as Kate entered. One foot still in the doorway, Natalya looped her arms around his neck and gave him a tight hug.

Brandon's gaze narrowed, and his jaw tightened. That man was asking for a fist between his teeth. He'd been three kinds of a fool to hire him, knowing Natalya spent her nights in Sergei's bed. He might be the best damn guard they could hope to find, but Fantasia didn't have room for both of them.

One night. See how it goes. He's Aaron's responsibility.

Yeah. Aaron's responsibility. He'd introduce Sergei to Aaron, tell him what he wanted accomplished, and be done with the buffoon. Khitrovo might be his employee, but a job didn't equate to friendship.

He straightened as Sergei headed directly for him. Deciding he'd rather not walk the short distance to the bar in the man's company, Brandon struck off alone. He pulled up a stool beside Mayer and dropped one hip on the leather cushion. "There's your new man." He inclined his head toward the advancing Russian.

"I figured." Aaron's gaze slid to Brandon's, bright with unspent laughter. "How'd the show go?"

The look Brandon shot his best friend had cowed criminals who considered guns natural extensions of their hands.

"That good?"

"Knock it off, Mayer."

Luckily, Aaron couldn't say any more; Sergei reached his destination. He thrust out a hand, which Aaron heartily clasped. "Welcome aboard, Khitrovo."

"Good to be here."

The thick accent scraped Brandon's nerves. He motioned to the bartender, signaling for his usual, start-of-the-night, rum and Coke.

"I want you on the wall, there." Aaron pointed to the left-hand corner nearest the stage. "If anyone sticks so much as a finger on that floor, you haul 'em back."

Sergei nodded as Brandon's drink slid in front of him. Brandon downed it in one deep gulp, savoring the pleasant burn that spread through his belly. The ice cubes, however, only reminded him a long night waited ahead. A night that would eventually end with one Natalya Trubachev leaving with her Russian lover.

He signaled for another and swiveled on his stool, putting his back to Sergei.

"You get three breaks. Eight, eleven, and two. Spend them how you want, but if I catch you with a one of our girls on the clock, you're outta here."

"Not a problem."

Of course it wasn't a problem. He got his own private show nightly. Brandon grumbled low. Christ, he was jealous! Thirty-five years, and for the first time in his life he was experiencing that malignant cancer. How pathetic.

Determined to beat the green beast back into its corner, he twisted around to look Sergei in the eye. "There's something I want you to do tonight."

With a nod, Sergei accepted unhesitatingly.

"I want a full report of who pays for a lap dance in that section and who gets multiples. I want to know the girls—description's fine—and the guys." That ought to choke him up. Brandon wasn't certain he could even keep the tally for the entire night. He could observe and notice trends, or oddities, but track *all* the girls for twelve hours? If Sergei could pull it off, he deserved the job.

"Understood."

Aaron slid off his stool as Brandon's second drink arrived. He urged Brandon to the office with a jerk of his head. "I need to see you before we open."

Thank God for small miracles. If they weren't working this damn case, he'd spend the rest of the night behind that office door. Collecting himself—not sulking. Absolutely not licking his wounds and nursing a battered ego. He jumped off his seat and strode two steps away.

"A word with you, Moretti?"

The no-nonsense tone to Sergei's question stopped Brandon in his tracks. He bristled. Here it came. The conversation where Sergei warned him away from the pretty girl and Brandon had to inform him to piss off. He knew it would happen, he just hadn't expected it to occur before the night even began.

Slowly, he turned around.

Aaron clapped him on the shoulder. "I'll meet you there."

Sergei's emotionless stare held Brandon's. "I'm only going to say this once, and then it's not going to be an issue between us again."

Brandon felt his entire body slowly tighten. From his toes all the way up to the base of his skull, his muscles cinched together. One wrong word, and they'd all snap. "Spit it out," he ground out tightly.

"I'm not, have not ever, and never will be, fucking Natalya."

The statement nearly knocked Brandon sideways. Stunned speechless, he could do no more than open his mouth, shut it, and blink. He'd made an ass out of himself. A monumental ass. For what?

Nothing.

Fuck.

Wordlessly, he pivoted and left Sergei to assume his duties.

Eating crow was something entirely new to him. On some deep level, he knew he owed both Sergei and Natalya an apology. But on an even deeper level, he recognized that apologizing would acknowledge that his interest in Natalya went further than a casual romp through the sheets. He could try to tell himself otherwise all day long. When it all boiled down to cold hard fact, if he wanted one solitary night with the auburn-haired beauty, he wouldn't have fixated on a kiss.

He wasn't quite ready to admit that to himself, let alone a man he'd just hired, and certainly not *her.*

Nope. He wouldn't touch that subject. Because the other cold hard fact he couldn't avoid was that he didn't know a damn thing about Natalya, and she remained a key person of interest in his current investigation.

His head began to pound. He squeezed his temples between thumb and middle finger and pushed open his office door. Right about now, he'd give everything he owned for ten minutes of peace.

Aaron's grim expression said he wouldn't find it now.

Sighing, Brandon dropped into his chair, slugged back his second drink, and crossed his right ankle over his left knee. "What's up?"

"I called Rory to see how he was doing this afternoon. He's pretty beat up."

Brandon waited. Aaron hadn't dragged him into his office to discuss their partner's emotional meltdown. No, this was lead-in to something bigger. Something that pricked the hairs on the back of Brandon's neck and laced his lungs closer together.

"We got to chatting about the case." Aaron passed a hand over his chin, his expression thoughtful. "We overlooked something major, man."

The prickling at the back of Brandon's neck inched down his spine. He dropped his foot to the floor and leaned his forearms on his desk. "And that would be?"

"Well, I can't say we really overlooked it. We just didn't see it. Rory did while we were talking. It may be insignificant—you know the turnover with dancers is high."

"Spit it out, Mayer."

He scratched the back of his head, took a deep breath. "Each club hired a new dancer two weeks before a body turned up on the Rim."

"Son of a bitch," Brandon exhaled.

"It could be coincidence, Bran."

"Coincidence my ass. Do we have names? Descriptions? Anything?"

"I'm working on it."

Brandon's gut rolled over. He should have listened to his instincts. Instead, he'd invited a stranger into the tidy circle he intimately understood. Two strangers. One with a suspiciously clear file. He might as well have tied Kate to the street corner with a sign that read FREE.

"Listen. We don't know for sure. I know there's . . . something between . . . you and Natalya."

Unwilling to hear any more, Brandon lifted his hand to beg his partner off.

Aaron delved ahead, oblivious to his silent request. "You've done undercover a long time. Play it. Get close to her. Find out what she knows." He paused on an indifferent shrug. "Can't hurt. If you find out she's clean, all the better."

If she were clean. A big *if*, considering the alarms buzzing in his head. If she weren't . . .

Brandon shut the thought down before it could solidify. That promised to be a calamity. One he couldn't guarantee he'd walk away from unscathed.

"You're the only one who can," Aaron continued in his matter-of-fact, good-observant-cop tone. "None of us are gonna get close to her, that's for damn sure. Not if she's waltzing into your office and peeling off her clothes."

Against Brandon's will, his gaze pulled to the corner of his desk where she'd stood, her body trembling, her lips less than a breath away from his. The memory of how good she felt against his hand, the tight way her wet pussy had squeezed as she edged closer to orgasm engulfed him. Her soft moan filled his ears.

Kiss me.

A new tightness invaded his body, this one far more uncomfortable than the compression of anger. With it came a hollowing in his gut, a void aching to be filled. By her. With her.

"I don't think that's a good idea, Aaron." Meritable, but he couldn't ensure he possessed the ability to remain objective. He wanted Natalya too damn much. With Kate's life on the line, and Rachel begging to be laid to rest, he couldn't risk an inability to see in black and white.

Aaron shook his head. "It's a damn good idea, Moretti. It's the only solid lead we have."

Falling against the back of his chair, Brandon raked both hands through his hair. No matter how much he wanted to protest, Aaron was right. With eleven days left, and no more information than they'd possessed when they left Sadie's, they didn't have many other options.

He expelled a heavy sigh. "I'll think about it."

Fifteen

Brandon worked the floor for the next several hours, schmoozing with the regulars and attending to a stream of issues that were all designed to keep him distracted from what he really needed to be doing—monitoring the crowd from a distance, where he could observe subtleties he couldn't up close.

Between the waitresses dropping orders, bartenders pouring too heavy, and Jill doing her damndest to distract him every time he found a moment to stand in a corner alone, he hadn't had time to think about the conversation with Aaron. Not really. It hummed around inside his head like an angry hornet in hot pursuit, but he kept a careful distance from that agonizing stinger.

Jill's knee drifted between his thighs as she wiggled closer to his side. Her palm rested on his chest, petting him like he were a puppy she'd picked up at the pound. "C'mon, baby, it's been so long. You know Kate can't be as dirty as I can be." Her fingers wandered down his chest to slide over his indifferent cock.

Giving her a perturbed frown, he plucked her hand off his dick and stepped around her intruding leg. "I'm sure you're right. But—" As he forcibly guided her to arms' distance, a flash of auburn in the corner of his eyes cut him off. He turned his head to find Natalya standing at the backstage door, hair tumbling around her shoulders as she bent over to pick up a towel she'd dropped.

His heart thumped hard, shooting a 3-D image to his brain of the way she'd bent over in front of him, hips gyrating, breasts swaying.

She stood, and their eyes locked over the crowd. His reaction was instantaneous and powerful. Blood surged to his groin. His cock stirred to attention, and his pulse ratcheted up three degrees.

Cozy up to her. What could it hurt?

Jill made some cooing noise that reminded him he'd been saying something. For a moment, he struggled to recall the conversation. It came back as she pushed at his arm to creep back into his personal space.

"I'm not sleeping with Kate." He barely registered the swivel of her head and the angry color that filled her cheeks as he extracted himself from her clawing fingers and made a beeline for Natalya.

It could hurt a lot of things, but he'd never shirked risk before. He'd never been afraid to take chances other guys would run from. His sometimes-daredevil approach, while not always in line with department policy, landed him this investigation and took him out of the dung heap of narcotics. If he had to cozy up to a killer to close this case, Natalya wouldn't be the first. She just put a whole new definition on the meaning of *cozy*.

So what if he liked it? So what if he *wanted* to know what made her tick and every hidden erogenous zone on her body?

So what if she scarred him in the process?

Natalya hadn't moved. As if she understood the boundaries had suddenly shifted, she stood in front of the door, watching him stalk across the room, daring him to turn tail and run.

No deal. He was done with running. All he'd needed was motive to pursue. Aaron had handed it over.

"C'mon, sugar, I've been begging for a week. I just want to take you on the town. Show you a good time. Whatcha say? I'll wait outside. Have the car running."

The gravelly male voice invaded Brandon's ears and dragged him to a stop. He tore his eyes off Natalya and cocked his head as he turned toward the sound.

"Ben, you know I can't do that," Becca answered with a laugh.

Standing over a middle-aged dark-haired man in an expensive Italian suit, she shimmied up his body, wagging her crotch in his face. "I'm too tired after work." Her hands glided over her thighs, then dipped between her legs as she pantomimed sliding down on his cock.

The man hissed. His hands inched toward her hips.

Becca noticed the flutter of movement, gave him a sultry smile, and batted his hands away. "Now, Benny Boy, I don't like men who break the rules," she purred as she bent forward, bringing her rather large breasts beneath his nose.

"Then come with me where there aren't any. The other girls haven't complained."

Brandon's instincts stood at attention. The other girls. How *many* other girls? Eleven maybe? He memorized the face. Hawk-like nose, deep-set beady eyes, salon haircut. A lift of a tailored cuff exposed a Rolex. Money, yes. Not just nice clothes.

"I'll make you feel good, Becca." Ben grabbed her ivory ass and squeezed. "Real fucking good."

Before Brandon could step in and remind *Benny Boy* that if the girls didn't want to be touched then hands stayed off the goods, Becca smacked Ben's hand hard enough the *slap* echoed over the music. She threw her leg over his knees, gave him one saucy wag of her ass, then sauntered away, leaving Ben grumbling and rubbing the back of his wrist.

Brandon backed into the shadows. As much as he wanted to continue on his path to Natalya, he couldn't. Ben might be put off enough he'd leave, and Brandon needed Aaron to do some fishing. He went to the bar; Aaron's preferred station was the stool closest to the door.

Aaron took one look at Brandon's face, set down his beer, and slid to his feet. "Who?"

"Guy at table twelve. Dark hair. Nice suit. Name's Ben. Why don't you offer him some VIP benefits and see what you can find out. He's hot to trot over Becca."

Becca, who fit the physical description and whose talents onstage made her the next candidate to fill Kate's time slots, should Kate disappear. They'd already figured out the killer marked his targets well in advance. The strategy made it possible to rotate methodically through the clubs. Another several months, and Becca just might rise to the top of the bastard's list.

"On it." Aaron drained his bottle, grabbed another that he'd nurse for the next couple of hours, and meandered toward Ben's table.

Feeling like he'd finally accomplished something worthwhile, Brandon gave himself permission to indulge in Natalya. Anticipation buzzed through his blood. He took a deep breath and wove through the crowd, murmuring silent prayers she'd returned to her office and he wouldn't have to hunt her down.

Hungry.

It was the only way Natalya could describe how Brandon had looked at her when she'd taken a few minutes to herself and decided to survey the crowd. The harsh lines on his face that she'd become accustomed to had disappeared. The intensity in his eyes was feral and breathtaking. She'd stood frozen in place, captivated by the realization he looked at her, while simultaneously wanting to run.

Run far and fast, because she knew where that look led.

She hadn't though. Not until his attention had diverted and she could flee without looking like a coward.

Natalya pushed away from her office door and sank into her chair. The low sensual bass thumped through the walls, seeping into her veins and filling her with the same restless energy that ebbed off the men gathered before the stage. Anticipation.

It made her twitchy.

Although the when eluded her, she knew what was coming. One way or the other, what had begun in Brandon's office *would* find satisfaction. The primitive part of her composition, that animalistic remnant of early mankind buried in her soul, shared the same hunger that burned in Brandon's eyes. It begged her to submit. To spread her legs and let him mount and rut until the ache subsided and they collapsed together panting.

The woman who'd spent the majority of her life fighting to survive, however, knew the danger of yielding to Brandon. The assignment. Her life. Kate's. His. She'd seen, and brought, enough death she didn't often consider consequence. Work was work. The casualties—insignificant. This time, the stakes were higher. Casualties weren't names she could unlearn or faces she could forget. Kate was her only living family, and Kate had a child who needed his mother. Not to mention, if Brandon didn't work for Dmitri, she exposed him to danger all of his years of undercover work couldn't prepare him for.

Precisely why all of her lovers had been operatives. Men who understood the risk and made choices knowing guilt killed good agents. They never looked back. Never assigned blame. And if they happened to meet again on the barrel end of the other's gun, sex was sex, but duty came first. *Sayonara*—may the best shot win.

Brandon Moretti might have run in the trenches with scumbags and cutthroats, but if she allowed herself to believe what Sergei wanted her to, he was still a good man. He lived. He breathed. He felt. He existed.

She didn't. Physically, maybe. But one press of a DELETE key, and who she was today vanished. With the next assignment she became someone else. She assumed another role and embraced the reality everything could end at any given moment.

In good conscious, she couldn't drag Brandon into that world.

Bemused, Natalya chuckled. In good conscious—since when had that ever mattered?

A knock issued from her door. She dragged herself out of her thoughts, plastered a smile on her face, and called, "It's open."

Jill sauntered inside, her disheveled hair and askew robe announcing she'd just returned from the front of the house. She closed the door behind her and perched on the edge of Natalya's desk.

Too close for Natalya's comfort. She rolled her chair back a couple of feet. "What can I help you with, Jill?"

Twirling a thick lock of black hair around her index finger, Jill studied Natalya's face. She shifted her weight, changing the tilt of her head. "You know, you're not a half-bad housemom."

The compliment took Natalya by surprise. Since when had Jill decided to be friendly?

"I'd be careful though, if I were you."

Maybe not so friendly. Natalya resisted the urge to roll her eyes. "Why's that?"

"There's a lot of things that can happen if a girl makes too many enemies on the Strip."

Definitely malicious. Just the kind of discussion Natalya wanted to have with an inevitable confrontation with Brandon looming in her near future. She sifted through the possible ways she could cut the conversation short, then decided the least likely way to send Jill into a tailspin of ranting would be to pretend interest. She lifted her eyebrows. "Oh?"

"Yeah, take Kate for instance." Jill rocked her slight weight onto her other hip, tipping her head back to its original slant. "There's a lot of girls here who can't stand the bitch. She prances around like she owns the place. I'll be glad when she's gone."

An icy chill crept into Natalya's blood. Was that a signal? Some sort of attempt at contact to tell her she worked for Dmitri? Frankly, that Iskatel´ hadn't made contact surprised Natalya. Alexei never hesitated to keep the line of communication open when he prepared to ship a girl off to Dubai. Was this Jill's icebreaker?

She tested the waters, hoping a small reveal would grant her something more definite. "I heard she might be leaving. I suppose when she moves on someone will be glad."

Jill shrugged and flipped her hair behind her shoulder. "I guess. One man's trash, another's treasure, and all that BS."

So much for definites. Natalya held in a sigh.

Sliding off the edge of the desk, Jill flashed a smile. She righted her robe, smoothed the back of it over her butt. "Since you're new, I guess I better clue you in on something else."

"And that would be?"

"There's a loyalty that runs through here. Through St. Petersburg, for that matter. We're all kinda a family."

Natalya flinched inwardly. Didn't she know it. If the Gaming Commission had any idea how many people were linked to Dmitri, St. Petersburg's doors would be closed and barred in a heartbeat.

"We don't take too kindly to sticks being dipped where they don't belong. Tends to lead to . . . problems with the management, if you get my meaning." With a saucy wink, she reached for the doorknob. "There are eyes everywhere. Don't make the mistake of thinking things go unnoticed."

As Natalya's skin pricked with goose bumps, Jill sauntered into the hall. The door closed with a foreboding *snick*.

Clearer than any warning she'd ever heard, Jill's veiled remarks sent Natalya's pulse into a staccato beat. Despite the fact that the only public exchanges Natalya and Brandon had shared were those of professional disagreement, Jill knew. She might as well have said, *Keep it up, and I'll tell.*

Fine. Warning understood. Point taken. No more Brandon. Period.

Before Natalya could fully thaw the blood running in her veins, another knock sounded on her door. She cleared her voice to rid the cobwebs from her throat and answered in a shaky voice, "Come in."

The door burst open on a pitiful wail. Tears streaming down her face, Nightingale held up a shredded veil. "It got caught on the hanger! I can't wear it, and Summer and Kitty are dressed and ready."

The harem routine—one of the crowd's favorites, if last night was any indicator. Natalya glanced at the veil Nightingale held in one hand, and the mask it was supposed to attach to that she held in the other.

Metallic coins on Nightingale's belly chain clinked as she let out another hysterical sob.

"Here, let me see it." Natalya reached for the sheer scrap of nylon. "How long do we have?"

Swiping at a fresh rush of tears, Nightingale sniffled. "Ten minutes, max."

Sixteen

Brandon's steps slowed as the sound of female sobbing drifted to his ears. In the dressing room off the girls' lounge, two women argued, presumably about whatever had reduced the third to tears. He frowned, perturbed. Strippers could be so damn touchy. Strike that. Women in general could be damn touchy.

As he took another step closer to Natalya's open door and realized the crying came from within, he questioned the logic of intruding. Tears didn't bother him—he'd grown rather immune after hauling junkie moms away from their neglected children. But Rachel had never been very good with hysterical dancers. Like a sponge, she soaked up their upset, channeled it into annoyance, and spit out crankiness at anyone who bothered her post-crises.

Sounded like a good enough reason to see how Natalya navigated hysterics, to him. He crossed the hall and leaned a shoulder against the doorjamb.

The scene within stunned him.

Nightingale sat cross-legged on the floor, a box of Kleenex propped in her lap and several wadded tissues scattered beside her. She sniffled and dabbed like she'd lost a body part, typical drama for the rather plain, rather flat-chested brunette. For her, everything was the end of the world. *Everything.* Brandon could recall at least six occasions where she'd broken down in tears when she'd stopped into Sadie's for after-hours drinks. A spilled drink on her skirt, a broken fingernail she'd just spent too much to have pierced, a girl accused her of flirting with a boyfriend—the reasons spanned the gamut.

No, the hysterics didn't surprise him. What had him cocking an eyebrow was the way Natalya applied needle and thread to Nightingale's malfunctioning veil. Pocket-sized scissors grasped in her teeth, she bent over the fabric, her fingers moving fluidly.

He'd never pictured her as the sewing sort of Home Ec girl. Strange how such a simple thing gave legitimacy to her tailored black suit. Like he'd discovered a tiny piece of her that suddenly made sense. Something that filled a gap in the puzzle she was.

A *natural* aspect of the overconfident seductress who seemed bent on pushing him to the ends of his limits.

She glanced up, and their gazes met. A pleasant burn rippled through Brandon's body. He caught himself smiling.

Natalya turned back to her mending, a similar upturn gracing her mouth. She pulled the needle through again, this time drawing it fast and tight. Then she spit out the scissors, lifted the whole thing to her mouth, and put her teeth to the string, neatly gnawing it off. Swiveling her chair to face Nightingale, she extended the repaired veil. "All finished. All better. Right?"

As Nightingale gingerly accepted her costume piece, another sob broke from her throat.

With astounding patience Brandon had only ever witnessed when Kate tended to Derek, Natalya plucked a Kleenex out of the box and dabbed it against Nightingale's wet cheeks. "It's not the end of the world," she encouraged. "You're all fixed up, good as new. Now dry your eyes before you make a bigger mess of your makeup."

In the same way Derek obeyed his mother, Nightingale eerily followed Natalya's directive. She took the tissue from Natalya's hands, blew her nose like a man, and nodded.

"Here." Spinning back toward her desk, Natalya picked up a clear plastic shoebox. She set it on her lap, opened the top, and rummaged through a collection of cosmetics that could have easily taken up a full shelf at Walmart. She passed Nightingale a tube of mascara and a circular compact. "Fix your eyes, then you'd better finish dressing."

"Thank you," the dancer sniveled.

Natalya slid out of her chair and helped Nightingale to her feet.

Another smile spread across Natalya's full mouth, lighting up her entire face. Brandon's breath caught. He'd swear the woman who offered comfort to a high-maintenance dancer was a completely different woman than the one who'd waltzed into his office and taunted him with a striptease that would make any man beg. He'd never dreamed she possessed such a beautiful smile, nor had he ever imagined she nurtured such . . . motherly . . . instincts.

His eyes raked down her slender shoulders, along the elegant line of her waist, and down the gentle slope of her hips to the legs she wielded to her advantage. Slowly he took her in as he lifted his gaze back to her face. Savored the picture.

She wore suits like a Wall Street exec. Anyone who hadn't experienced the comfortable way she wore her skin would never guess mere hours ago she'd straddled his lap and pushed her breasts into his face. That she'd slid those elegant hands, with those perfectly manicured nails and their half-moon white polish, all over her body, knowing full well she had him hard as a rock, straining against the urge to bend her over and slam so deep inside her that she screamed his name for the whole club to hear.

They'd never believe Miss Prim and Proper had almost come against his palm.

His body tightened uncomfortably. He gritted his teeth. He didn't want to be aroused. He simply wanted to observe this new, surprising facet of her personality.

While Nightingale reapplied her mascara, Natalya tucked loose wisps of hair into the dancer's thigh-length braid. They finished the chore of re-outfitting together, and amazing Brandon further, briefly embraced.

"Go make some money," Natalya encouraged.

With a shy dip of her head, Nightingale slipped out of the room, leaving Brandon alone with Natalya. He reached behind him, shut the door, and turned the lock. Not because he intended anything he didn't want another pair of eyes observing, but because he wanted these few minutes for himself alone.

"You must have kids." The remark slipped off his lips before he could stop it. Mentally, he kicked himself. Getting personal crossed boundaries. And yet, he couldn't stop this insatiable need to know where the woman he just witnessed had come from. What made her tick? Which one was she really—nurturer or vixen?

Natalya blinked, the remark taking her with equal surprise. "Um. No. Why?"

What can it hurt?

Nothing. It did absolutely no damage to learn a little bit about her, or to let her learn a little bit about him. "You were pretty good with those tears. I just assumed . . ."

Her smile returned with the shake of her head. "I think you're the first person who's ever used *mother* and *me* in the same sentence."

A thread of unexplainable disappointment pulled through him. "Kids aren't your thing, huh?" He shrugged off the foreign sensation with the reminder he didn't care. Kids weren't his thing either. Derek was the closest he'd ever allow himself to parenthood.

"Well, no . . ." She resumed her seat and plucked at the hem of her skirt. "I just don't have much occasion to be around them." Smoothing her already-smooth skirt, she tried for another smile. It pulled thin. "I'm busy. Work . . . and work . . . and . . . Well, you know how it goes."

"Haven't met the right person?" Damn. Why was he pushing? What difference did it make whether she'd given children consideration, or what stopped her from entertaining the notion? She obviously didn't want to talk about it. He should back off, before this conversation became any more awkward.

Just say, I know the feeling, man, and let it go.

"You could say that."

"Right person wrong time, or wrong person all the way around?"

Natalya lifted her eyes to his, and in that moment Brandon knew whatever image she presented outwardly, a far different person lived beneath the shell. He stared into the clearest, greenest eyes he could ever recall seeing, and for an endless passing of mere seconds, he witnessed fragile, unguarded, truth.

"I've never been in a position to consider having children." In a blink, her confidence returned. She folded her hands in her lap and crossed her left leg over the right. "What about you?"

"Right time, I'm the wrong guy." He clamped his mouth closed, having not even realized that he'd reached that point in his life where he felt his mortality and the need to leave a piece of himself behind.

He supposed it was true enough—why else did he gravitate to Derek? The little boy filled that void. But he'd never given his attachment to Kate's son consideration long enough to reach the obvious conclusion.

"Oh, I don't know," Natalya said with a laugh. "I've met worse prospects for repopulating the world."

"Wrong guy, trust me."

"Kate says you're good with Derek."

"One day a week."

"Well, that's a start." .

"Let's change the subject." He gave her a grin. "Tell me about Russia."

Again, he caught her off guard, evidenced by her blinking and the quick way her face paled. Not a good subject, evidently. Well, he'd do his best to keep it comfortable. "Did you meet Sergei there or here?"

"Here. When I worked at the . . . law firm." Her expression shifted, as if she grasped at memories. Or maybe stories. "In Los Angeles." She chuckled and switched one crossed leg for the other. "You did background checks on us, I take it?"

"Any smart employer does. What happened to your folks?"

Jesus, Moretti, chill. This isn't an interrogation.

He cleared his throat to soften the abrupt question. "I'm sorry. That didn't come out like I meant it to."

Shaking her head, she lifted a palm to fend off his apology. "No, it's okay. I don't remember them. Not my real ones. I imagine they were wonderful people. They were killed in 1976 when their plane crashed. They were going to visit my dying grandmother. I'd have been on the plane, but at the last minute, they decided not to take me with them and hired a nanny."

"I'm sorry."

"It's all right, really. I don't remember them at all."

She combed her fingers through her hair, then smoothed her skirt again. He was making her uncomfortable, damn it.

"My adoptive parents were more interested in the allotment from the government and a free pair of hands to mind the store than in me. They call now and then, like last night, hands out and begging. Reminding me what I *owe* them for feeding and clothing me through childhood."

At that, he flinched. No wonder she'd fled Moscow as soon as she turned seventeen. With no family to keep her there, America must have been tempting.

But why'd she go back?

He decided to wait for those answers. He'd come here to accomplish something more important.

Crossing the distance between them, he stopped at her chair and caught her hands in his. With a gentle tug, he pulled her to her feet. The close proximity of her body hit him full on, filling his blood with the heat that ebbed off her skin. Her sweet lilac perfume drifted to his nose. Her breasts brushed against his chest. At the light scrape of her erect nipples, his cock stirred against his thigh.

Holy God, he'd been crazy to think he could remain relatively immune. She was like a magnet, and he iron filings. Or maybe they were both slivers of metal standing too close to the same magnetic rod. Hell, he didn't know. But, Christ, he wanted her, and the unnatural hitch in her breathing told him she fought the same fierce desire that stormed through his body.

He slid one hand up the length of her arm to her hair and captured a thick shank of auburn. Rubbing the silken strands between his thumb and forefinger, he watched the golden highlights glint in the low light of her solitary lamp. Natural. Like every other fantastic inch of her body. He pushed the long length behind her shoulder and gently traced the delicate line of her jaw with his knuckles.

She closed her eyes. Drew in an unsteady breath.

"You asked me for something earlier," he murmured, his own breathing becoming heavier.

Her hand moved against his thigh. He braced for the push that would distance her beyond reach. Waited for the brutal announcement she'd changed her mind.

Instead, her fingers settled on his waist. Tightened. Urged him a hairsbreadth closer.

Sirens screamed in his head. He wanted this too much. If he crossed this line, he was heading straight for catastrophe.

Screw it. He'd survived worse.

He lowered his mouth to hers.

Brandon's mouth captured Natalya's lower lip, the gentle tug drawing her deeper into the protective envelope of his powerful presence. His teeth grazed the sensitive skin, his warm breath brushed over her cheek. Her own breath caught, raggedly escaping a heartbeat later, and a shiver rolled from her shoulders down to her toes. As if he sensed her need to stop the world from falling away beneath her feet, his free hand wound around her waist, fingers splaying at the base of her spine, guiding her body into his.

The slide of his tongue across the seam of her mouth urged her to open to him. She parted her lips, caught his, suckled at his upper lip. His fingers moved from the side of her face to twine through the hair at the nape of her neck. With an impatient grunt, he angled her head where he wanted it and deepened the kiss. Rich, masculine flavor assaulted her senses.

Slow possessive strokes of his tongue threatened to draw her straight out of her skin. Every nerve ending in her body rose on end, charged by some unfamiliar electric current in desperate need of grounding. She fanned her hands over his hard pectorals, soaking up the heat of his body. His heart drummed hard beneath her palm, a mirror of the pounding behind her ribs. The fabric of his shirt scraped against her fingertips as her senses sharpened to a fine point, and she began to feel him in a way she'd never felt any other man.

He dominated her body as he dominated her mouth. Thick arms imprisoned her in a delightful paradise. Even thicker thighs framed her unsteady legs. She couldn't have moved if she'd wanted to, and dear God, she *didn't* want to. Desire stirred in the depths of her womb, spreading a slow-burning ache through her lower body and moistening the flesh between her legs. She wanted to be closer, though she was already as close as their clothing would allow. She wanted more. Whatever he would give.

A mewl bubbled to the back of her throat, part protest, part plea.

Brandon swallowed the sound, and if it were possible, his arm around her tightened more. His own husky sound of satisfaction vibrated against her lips. The hard evidence of his shared arousal pressed against the tops of her thighs, taunting her with the pleasure his hands had granted earlier in the day. Visions of how he would slide into her body, in the same slow, thorough way his tongue slid against hers, rose behind her closed eyelids.

The combined effect of heat beneath her hands, restless agitation in her veins, and the languid caress of his tongue pushed her into sensory overload. Too much at once. *Not enough.* Oh, Lord, she needed to breathe.

Natalya tore her mouth away and turned her face aside, gasping for air. His equally hard breath stirred her hair. He brought his hand to the crown of her head and guided her cheek to his shoulder. For several moments they stood unmoving, the only sound, their jagged breathing.

Brandon broke the silence first. "You know where we're going, Natalya." His hand skimmed around her ribs to fit between their bodies and cover her breast. Her lips parted on a silent gasp as he flicked his thumb over her aroused nipple. "You know how this ends, and you want it too."

Yes, she did, and she couldn't remember a time when she'd wanted a man the way she wanted Brandon Moretti. But the easy way he reduced her to warmed honey unnerved her more than the fierce desire that clamped her womb into a knot. She didn't know how to just surrender to pleasure, to yield the control, and Brandon wrested that control out of her hands effortlessly.

Naturally.

She couldn't allow that to happen. Couldn't lose herself that far.

She stepped back, intending to extract herself from the magic of his fingers and escape. When she could discipline her body and mind, she could entertain Brandon's suggestion. "Yes, but—"

He followed her retreat, forbidding her to flee as he cupped her other breast in his free hand. His fingers gently worked the soft flesh, his gaze never breaking from hers. The burn in that tawny stare sent rivulets of excitement thrumming through her blood. He knew what he wanted, and damned if she was going to stop him.

Brandon took a puckered nipple between his thumb and forefinger and squeezed. Natalya felt the pinch all the way through her womb, and her pussy contracted with need. Her thong was damp, the ache between her legs crying out for the stroke of his hands, the intrusion of his cock.

"But?" His voice was husky against the backdrop of reverberating bass. "But what?" He released her breasts to slide one large palm down her side, over the curve of her hip, and along her thigh. Gathering her skirt in his fingers, he exposed her bare leg at the same time he popped the solitary button of her dark green suit jacket. His gaze seared through the red lace that covered her breasts, warming her skin.

"I don't—I mean, I'm—"

"Wet," he murmured as his fingers crept beneath the curve of her bottom and slipped between her legs. He ran a solitary knuckle over the damp scrap of cloth that covered her pussy. "So very wet."

A gasp sliced through her as Brandon nudged the worthless shield aside and stroked one thick finger through her slickened folds. At the sound, his eyes snapped back to hers. "You would be heaven on my tongue."

Images flashed through her mind—her ankles hooked at his shoulders, his tongue spearing through her folds, swirling over her clit, edging into her opening. The vivid snapshots combined with the riot of sensation his fingers produced and arced sensation through her from head to toe. She had never given one man complete freedom with her body, but she wanted to now. With Brandon. Here. Tonight.

Reaching for him, she moved to her toes in search of his mouth. He gave it to her briefly, tugging her lower lip between his teeth and then easing the sting of his bite with a slow sweep of his tongue. Then his mouth dusted over the corner of hers, inched across her cheek, and dipped to the super-sensitive spot beneath the hollow of her ear. The gentle scrape of his teeth pulled another gasp from her constricted lungs.

She hadn't realized they were moving until her thighs touched the edge of her desk and she came to an abrupt stop. When she did, Brandon eased his hand from between her legs and used both to push her jacket off her shoulders. He drew the sleeves down her arms slowly, his lips following the path of revealed skin and dusting warm kisses over her goose-pimpled flesh. He teased the inside of her elbow with the tip of his tongue, nipped at the delicate bones of her wrist.

When he had removed the garment completely, he dropped it behind her back on the desk, then picked up her hands one by one and planted a lingering kiss inside each palm. His lips still hovering over the base of her wrist, he looked up at her through thick, dark eyelashes. "Tell me what you want, Natalya," he whispered.

What she wanted—the rehearsed answer rose instinctively. "Fu—" *No.* She wasn't going to say it. Those words were reserved for Dmitri. She swallowed to gain control over her throat. "You," she murmured. "I want you, deep inside me."

A slow, wicked smile spread over his mouth as satisfaction glinted in Brandon's eyes. But with that self-satisfied smirk, something darker, something more potent, glinted in those tawny depths. Natalya didn't know what it was, but the gleam awakened a soul-deep hunger. She wanted far more than Brandon's cock inside her. What, exactly, she couldn't define. But the promised orgasm didn't seem like nearly enough.

She laced her fingertips in his hair and tugged his mouth to hers. His kiss was feral and wild, and it stoked the fire in her veins until she thought she might burn in his arms. Her body melted into his, her pussy aligning with the hard ridge of his erection, and she rubbed herself against that hot, confined length.

As if he shared the same wild need, his hands gripped her bottom and ground her against his cock. Like he needed her every bit as immediately as she needed him. Like he too fought to hold on to some semblance of control.

He dragged his mouth away from hers, panting. "Fuck." Loosening his grip on her buttocks, he closed his eyes and sucked in a deep breath. "Slow down, sweetheart, or it's going to be over before we get started."

"No." She shook her head as she tugged at his belt. Not slow. Slow would let her think, and right now she didn't want one bit of logic interfering with the incredible pleasure building in her veins.

Brandon batted at her hands and let out a light chuckle. "Natalya. We have—"

The rest of whatever he'd intended to say died off on a hiss as she dodged his swatting hands, freed his jutting cock from his pants, and took him into her hand. His hips thrust forward, sliding himself deeper into her firm grip. She ran her thumb over the smooth, engorged head, thrilling when a drop of moisture beaded on the tip. Not slow—not slow at all.

"Christ," he muttered as he jerked out of her hand. "You've got me on the edge."

Just where she wanted him. But if he wasn't going to let her take the lead, she'd give him the illusion of control. Flashing him a soft smile, she whispered, "What do *you* want, Brandon?"

His eyes flashed dangerously. His jaw morphed into a tight line. Annoyance? No . . . not annoyance, she realized as he tucked his fingers into the waistband of her skirt and hauled her closer. Unraveled.

He set his hands on her shoulders and guided her around in a half circle. "Turn around. I've wanted you on the desk since you walked into my office."

Excitement bubbled through her, even as uncertainty flickered at the base of her skull. She'd held on to the power by giving him the choice, but what he chose exposed her beyond simple nakedness.

Brandon didn't give her mind time to form objections. In a heartbeat's passing he'd stripped her of her skirt and released the clasp of her bra. His big, warm hands wound around her body to lift her breasts, gathering them together. As he ran his thumbs over her distended nipples, his body pressed against her back, strong, firm, and bare. The panels of his shirt brushed against her sides, but his muscular chest was warm and smooth against her spine. His heart drummed into her shoulder blade. His thick cock nestled between her buttocks.

"I'm sorry," he murmured against the side of her neck.

"For what?" It took all of Natalya's energy to focus on making words, not the incredible pleasure of feeling his thick erection slide forward through her folds to rub against her clitoris. Enticed by that tantalizing heat, she levered her hips, pushing back into his body, urging the wide head of him closer to her slickened opening. She needed him now. All of him. Firmly rooted inside her and rubbing away the ache that had become almost painful. "Oh, Brandon . . ."

His weight pressed into her shoulders, guiding her upper body to the desk. Natalya went willingly, bending over until her breasts pressed against cluttered papers and her cheek laid on her jacket. He spanned his hands over her buttocks, gently rubbed the firm flesh as he drew himself through her folds again, teasing her pussy, making her vagina clench in want.

"You have the prettiest ass." He gave her buttocks a squeeze. "So perfect." One hand molded around her waist, lifting her off the desk and closer to the edge. The other ran down the indentation between her cheeks, his middle finger slipping over the tight, tiny anterior hole before he rolled his wrist and pressed his fingertip to her clitoris. Shocks of pleasure coursed up her spine. She dug her hands into her jacket, desperate for something to hold on to before bliss carried her into oblivion.

"Brandon, don't . . . tease," she breathed as another jolt of ecstasy tripped through her body. She rocked against his hand, letting out a low moan.

"Can't . . . tease . . ." His voice had taken on a brittle edge that matched the tension in his thighs where they flattened next to hers. "Shit. Natalya, I'm sorry." A brief rustle of foil, and an instant of separation, told her he'd donned a condom.

In the next heartbeat, Natalya cried out as Brandon's cock slid into her, filling her up, stretching her painfully. She hadn't wanted slow, and got anything but. In one swift thrust, he embedded himself fully. The feel of him obliterated fantasy. Buried deep inside her, she felt the throb of his flesh, the tiny pulses that rippled through the length of his wide erection.

He gripped her waist with both hands, tilting her hips as he withdrew, his rhythm steady but deliberate. She closed her eyes, lost to the building sensation, the need that had lived inside her veins but had gone forgotten for too many years to count. His powerful hands dominated her body. His muscular thighs held her legs apart. She relaxed her hips, allowing him to guide her at the pace he desired, and pleasure built.

"Ah, Natalya, you are . . ." Brandon's breath caught. Against her back, she felt the shudder roll through his torso. "Ah, *God.*"

Urgency possessed him, his strokes becoming harder, more demanding. She reared back, lifting to her elbows to brace against the fierce thrusts. Her new position, however, opened her to even more pleasure as Brandon wound an arm around her waist and his fingers delved between her legs. As he drove into her, high and hard, he pressed his fingertip to her clit. Pleasure poured through her, pounded into her senses. She moved against him wildly, chasing the friction of his cock and the mind-numbing flick of his finger, uncertain which she needed more. Uncaring about the moans of pleasure that slid from her throat.

Brandon's teeth pricked her shoulder, and it was too much. Orgasm crashed through her, carrying her up to a dizzying height she felt certain she would fall from and crash to her death. Distantly, she heard his hoarse groan, felt the spasm of his cock deep inside her pussy as he filled the condom with his release.

Then, his body blanketed hers, pressing her gently into the desk, where they lay together gasping for breath. After several drawn out seconds, Brandon pushed her damp hair off her neck and his lips fluttered against her skin. "I owe you more than this. We close in a half hour. Come to my place?"

Go home with him. Spend the night giving herself to this man who defined pleasure. She almost said yes . . . until a voice in the hall reminded her they were in the middle of Fantasia, Dmitri's American paradise, and someone had very likely heard them fucking.

"I can't get involved with you," she whispered.

His body tightened like a whip. The same tension edged his

words. "I'm not playing any more games, Natalya. We're already fuck-ing involved."

Before she could craft something to say that would soothe his brim-ming anger, he blew out a hard breath and the tight muscles against her back relaxed. "How about a late-night breakfast? No pressure."

Natalya stared at the crinkled fabric around his bicep as reason warred with yearning. Sergei was absolutely convinced Brandon didn't work for Dmitri, and her reasons for suspecting him were rapidly dwindling. No hired goon would *think* of putting limits on what she could, or could not do, much less deny her phone calls with Dmitri half a world away. Dmitri would choke the life out of the first idiot who tried.

Which took her right back to the danger *she* posed to Brandon. Jill made it perfectly clear they were watching her. That she'd seen enough to, at the very least, raise her suspicions. What Brandon wanted, what Natalya wanted—forbidden fruit. They'd already gone too far. This had to stop now.

"Natalya?" he murmured as his fingers pulled through her hair.

A smile played at her mouth as another thought occurred. She wanted to know more about Brandon Moretti. Wanted to bask in his dominating, masculine presence a little longer. As long as a table sepa-rated them, if questions arose, she could always claim it was a working dinner. Part of her efforts to keep her true intentions—as Dmitri knew them—hidden from her employer. Breakfast was safe. The casino had eyes, but those eyes would look elsewhere if she didn't give them rea-son to pry. Reasons like being locked in her office, bent over the desk, Brandon's cock buried in her body as he worked her into a frenzy.

She turned her head to meet his sated gaze. Her nod consented. Her words, however, set boundaries. "I don't think it's wise if we're seen leaving together. There are . . . people . . . here who wouldn't ap-preciate it."

"Fine," Brandon grumbled. Backing off her, he eased himself out of her and bent over to pull up his pants. In seconds, he was dressed, that fantastic body cloaked from view. "Meet me at the roulette table near the Simple Kitchen."

Natalya eased upright and hastily buttoned her shirt. As she grabbed for her skirt, Brandon stopped at the door. The profile of his jaw worked for a handful of seconds while he chewed a thought. "I'm not into sharing. If there's someone else . . ."

Though he couldn't see with his back to her, she shook her head. "There's no one else." Not anyone who mattered. Not in her heart. By the time Dmitri arrived, she'd be gone anyway.

A short jerk of his head closed the subject. "I'll have Aaron lock up for me. Head out when Kate takes the stage."

The door closed behind him. She shut her eyes and sucked in a shallow breath. If he only knew the irony of choosing roulette.

Seventeen

As Kate glided past Natalya's office, Natalya wiped her perspiring palms on her skirt and left her sanctuary. Thirty minutes had never passed so slowly. Each second that ticked by hiked her nerves into overdrive. Breakfast might have been the cover, but she knew she was going to give herself to Brandon—again. She couldn't wait to feel his body sliding against hers. Although what she was about to do filled her with an emotion she'd forgotten. *Fear.*

Pushing open the clubhouse door, she stepped into the dark, smoky lounge. Excitement ran beneath her anxiety, amping up her heartbeat to a tempo that matched the rhythm of Kate's undulating hips. She stopped for a minute, admiring Kate's seductive rhythm. She still had the moves. But a sliver of sadness pricked Natalya as she watched Kate spread her knees, lean back, and dry hump the air. Katey was a mom. She shouldn't be here.

If I'd only known . . .

She shook her head. She knew now. When this was all over, Kate would never again set foot on a stripper's stage. Derek and she would live the life Erik had intended for them—a comfortable home, good schools, security.

Spying Sergei against the wall, Natalya sidestepped around Nightingale, whose costume adjustments had evidently served her well—the man she straddled certainly looked pleased enough.

"How's it going? Notice anything?" She glanced surreptitiously over her shoulder.

Sergei grimaced. "Haven't seen shit. Moretti's got me tallying lap dances."

A roving glance down the length of his body revealed he hadn't remained entirely immune to the floor's display. Smirking, she patted him square in the center of his chest. "Poor thing."

He shot her a glare.

"I'm going to head out early tonight."

"Early?"

With a shrug she hoped came off as indifferent, she nodded. "I'm hungry. Brandon won't let me onstage—he'd probably have a fit if he caught me out here talking to you. I'll see you in the morning."

She turned to leave. That had gone smoother than planned. At least she completely hadn't lost her talent for lying. Now to scurry into the casino before Jill's VIP show came to an end.

Sergei's hand locked around her elbow. "Not so fast." He dragged her backward a step and swiveled her around. His frown penetrated through her confidence. "One of these days you're going to realize you can't hide things from me. What are you up to?"

Damn. She would have to have the most observant partner known to mankind.

Natalya muttered beneath her breath. "I'm just having breakfast."

His gaze narrowed. "With Moretti." It wasn't a question.

When she found sudden fascination with the neon pink light above Sergei's head, the grip on her arm tightened. "You're playing with a loaded gun, Natalya."

She freed her arm with a sharp twist. "I do that daily. Since when did it become your job to baby-sit?"

He lifted both eyebrows and looked down his nose in meaning. She knew the reference—Dmitri sent him along to keep her safe. Right now, she chose to overlook that insignificant detail. A matter of semantics, really, given the role had nothing more to do with Sergei's true assignment than her position as Dmitri's fiancée.

Sergei leaned in close and lowered his voice. "Iskatel´ is here. I can feel it. And you're going to walk out of here with Moretti on your heels? You're going to get yourself killed."

Her temper flared, and her gaze constricted to match his. To prevent the trio of men that had moved behind her from hearing, she slipped into Russian. "Don't you dare treat me like a rookie, Sergei Khitrovo. I've been doing this for ten years—you think I don't know the risks? Stick to your own job and let me do mine."

Joining her Russian, he shot back, "You aren't doing your *job*. You're scratching an itch."

"So what if I am?" Her voice rose to a furious whisper. "Three years I've pretended to feel. It isn't fake this time. If I want to have breakfast, hell if I want to *be* breakfast, that's my choice."

Sergei's eyes blazed with fire. He snatched her by the upper arm and dragged her close with such force she stumbled into his chest. His head dipped near her ear, his low whisper harsh and scathing. "Your pussy's booby-trapped. That's *his* choice, not yours."

She went utterly still, her voice deadly calm as she wedged her arm between them and laid it over his. "Turn me loose or I'll break it."

One finger at a time, Sergei released her. She straightened the hem of her suit jacket with a jerk and lifted her gaze to amber eyes that gleamed with equal rage. "I won't forget that."

The widening of his eyes told her he'd received the deeper message that he'd just crossed a line he couldn't easily retreat across. Brief regret passed over his face, then quickly disappeared behind a mask of indifference. He dropped his hands to his sides and quietly held her stare.

"I'm going to breakfast now." With a tight smile, she spun on her spiked heels and stalked through the sea of drunk and horny men.

As she rounded the last set of tables, the casino exit a mere fifteen feet away, one overstimulated man made the fatal mistake of reaching out and sliding his hand up the back of her skirt to give her bottom a squeeze. She whirled on him like a cyclone, his face millimeters away from her breasts. Before she could unleash all the rage Sergei had ignited and tell the stranger how many ways he could go to hell, he dipped his nose into her cleavage and rubbed his cheeks side to side.

For a moment, she allowed the indulgence. Smiling, she even slipped her fingers through his hair, rumpling it, drawing him closer, before she dropped her hands to his shoulders and pursed her lips. With every bit of strength her veteran body possessed, she cocked her knee and drove it into his chest.

The resulting *crack* granted bone-deep satisfaction.

Fuck you, Dmitri.

His yowl, however, said she'd gone too far. Before his buddies could recover from their openmouthed gaping, she turned her back on the man's wheezing cough . . . and ran straight into the solid wall of Brandon's chest.

He looked to her, to the doubled-over man, back to her. One dark eyebrow arched in reproach.

Natalya shrugged. "He put his hands on me." Twisting to bypass Brandon's wide shoulders, she maneuvered around his too powerful body and marched to the doors. One violent shove sent them clanging into the wall. Without so much as a backward glance, she abandoned the pumping bass and the rapidly gathering crowd, slowed her pace, and headed for the roulette table.

Breakfast alone didn't hold the same appeal. But the chances of Brandon joining her, or that he'd be anything less than enraged by her uncalled-for assault, pretty much spoiled all hope of companionship.

Oh, well. Breakfast alone was still breakfast, and she could use a good meal. Besides, Sergei was right—she was booby-trapped. The best thing Brandon Moretti could do was stay away. Far, far away.

In twelve years on the force, Brandon had seen chest kicks knock the wind out of many people. He'd witnessed a punch stop a man's heart—granted, that man had been on a pacemaker. He'd even seen roundhouse kicks crack ribs. But he had never seen someone break a man's sternum with one strategically placed knee.

He passed a hand through his hair as he watched the paramedics wheel the businessman out of the club. He didn't know whether to be impressed, or whether he should fire Natalya on the spot.

He *wanted* to fire her. If Fantasia didn't end up in the middle of a lawsuit over that stunt, it'd be a miracle. But the street-hardened cop that walked the edge of the law and tended to shirk policy more often than not, couldn't stop chuckling. The sound stayed locked inside, despite the tickle in his lungs.

Damned impressive. He'd have to ask her where she learned that move.

Glancing at his watch, he cursed. If he didn't hurry, he wouldn't be asking her anything. She'd left forty minutes ago. By now, she probably assumed he didn't intend to show.

She couldn't have been more wrong. After that little display, a hurricane wouldn't have kept him away from breakfast with the fascinating, sinfully sexy, Natalya Trubachev. Not to mention, seeing her manhandle the client had twisted his libido into overdrive. Although he'd had her less than an hour ago, his cock wanted more of that sweet treat.

He stamped down a rush of anxious energy, reminding himself he was investigating a possible killer. Despite his current inability to control his arousal, each moment he spent with her, he became more convinced she was hiding something that pertained to his case. Breakfast had been part of his plan to draw her out. Coax her into conversation, grill her about Russia, and hopefully, find a few links.

If he couldn't find those links, he'd have to dig deeper. Pry her open a little more. His cock twinged at the thought. *Yeah . . . pry her open . . .*

He scowled, perturbed with his body's one-track course. Meeting up with her now had nothing to do with really wanting to get to know her better. Her body—fuck yes. The rest of it? Emotional baggage he couldn't afford. He'd already exposed too much of himself in her office.

No, for the next several hours, assuming she hadn't left the casino, he'd keep her talking. When they finished talking, he'd fuck her out of his system.

Spying Aaron near the stage, he waved a hand. "I'm off."

The wry twist to Aaron's mouth stirred Brandon's annoyance. For whatever reason, his best friend found this amusing. For God's sake, it had been Aaron's idea to cozy up to Natalya. He *knew* better than to think this little get together was anything but investigation.

Yeah. Investigation of curves and skin and what all else would make her mewl like she had when he was fucking her.

Brandon squelched the annoying voice in his head. Thoughts like that wouldn't keep his focus any clearer. It was difficult enough to remember she was the lead suspect when he got within five feet of her. When he touched her—he damn sure wasn't thinking. Period.

"Where are you off to, baby?"

Before Brandon could pull back from his thoughts and focus on the woman standing in front of him, Jill shimmied against his body. Still dressed in her short silk robe, the heat of her skin soaked through his lightweight dress shirt. Her thigh slipped between his, and she lifted her leg to rub the length of his cock. Strangely, he found himself completely immune. Though the woman drove him bat-shit crazy, his dick had still been aware of willing woman. Until now.

No. Until yesterday. When Natalya Trubachev arrived wearing power suits and the most enticing, sweet, lilac perfume known to man.

Must find out if it's lotion.

He stepped back, annoyed with the thought and the woman in front of him. "To eat."

One long red fingernail slid over the buttons on his shirt. "I know where there's a buffet." She dipped her chin, set her teeth into her lower lip, and looked up through unnaturally long eyelashes. "We can take turns helping ourselves to dessert."

How had he ever slept with this woman? Good Lord, had he really been that desperate? He set his hands on her shoulders and guided her out of his path. "I want real food."

A shadow fell over her face, reminiscent of the dark cloud he vaguely remembered when she'd caught him staring at Natalya. It struck him then that Jill, when her true colors showed, wasn't the least bit pretty. She looked almost . . . sinister.

Bracing one hand on her hip, she cocked her weight on one tall heel and jerked her chin toward the casino's exit. "Running after a new piece of tail, Brandon? That one wags like all the rest, but it'll cut you to pieces."

He slowed to a stop and gave her a dubious look. "What?"

"She's got money written all over her. If she's working here, it isn't *her* money." A nasty laugh escaped Jill's thinning mouth. "She'll give you a ride. A good hard ride. Then she'll buck you off in the mud."

Too many years of necessary suspicion wrenched Brandon's gut into a knot. Had Natalya lied when she'd said there wasn't anyone else? He'd made the mistake of forgoing all the lessons street life taught him and taken her at her word. If she was their killer, lies would come easy. Hell, he hadn't even been looking at her face when he'd accepted her answer.

But he'd been staring into her eyes when she'd told him she'd never been in a position to consider children. Unless this mysterious man Jill hinted at was in his eighties, or married, if she had a sugar daddy, she'd had plenty of opportunities to *consider* children.

On the other hand, if her blank file indicated witness protection, as the larger part of his conscious suspected, he could relate to her position. If she was on the run, she wouldn't put two thoughts into kids and family.

He frowned, the clamor in his head too much after an already long and eventful night. He gave Jill his best, self-assured smile. "Thanks for the advice. I'll keep it in mind."

With that, he left Fantasia behind and fell into pursuit of the longest legs his hands had ever had the pleasure of touching.

Eighteen

Twenty on red." Natalya set her last four chips on the table. Forty-five minutes at the roulette table, and as odds would have things, she'd lost everything. She ought to give up and go home. Brandon wasn't coming, and she'd be lucky to have a job tomorrow. Which meant she'd have to tell Dmitri that Fantasia wasn't cooperating, and the next person in a body bag would be Brandon Moretti.

Her shoulders slumped.

The press of a warm, hard chest against her back brought her upright. The scent of sweetened spice, combined with a faint touch of smoke, made her belly flutter. She knew that smell. *Brandon.*

Her heart stumbled into her ribs.

His knuckles brushed the undersides of her arms as he slid his hands around her waist to grab the table. He leaned in, aligning his body with hers, pressing his weight against her from shoulders to thighs. His cock nestled between her buttocks. Warm, moist breath caressed the sensitive skin at the base of her ear. "That's a pretty safe bet for a woman who just cracked a man's chest."

A ridiculous heat spread through her body, and she sucked in a shallow gasp. Oh, she wanted to touch him. Wanted to lean back against those corded muscles and draw his arms around her belly. Rub against that hard ridge between her cheeks and feel him deep inside her again. Turn and set her lips on his. He had such a soft, assertive mouth. She could kiss him for hours. Days.

"No more bets."

The croupier's call reminded Natalya of the unseen eyes that filled St. Petersburg's halls. She fastened her attention on the spinning wheel and moved out of the direct heat of Brandon's body.

He stepped up to the table at her left, the padded rail pressing into his loose black dress pants and smoothing the fine fabric against one thick thigh. The hand that had been under her right arm slid around her waist to settle in the small of her back. In his left hand, he held a one hundred dollar bill, which he wagged at the croupier. "One black."

The croupier tossed him a black chip as the ball she'd bet on dropped into the red 16 pocket.

Brandon's grin was instantaneous, as was Natalya's light laugh. She wrinkled her nose. "Safe paid off. I doubled my money." She accepted two, twenty-dollar yellow chips.

"But roulette's no fun without risk."

Brandon's playful wink made it impossible to dwell on all the reasons she shouldn't be standing next to him. She took a sip of the watery margarita she'd been nursing since her arrival and grinned over her straw.

The croupier picked his dolly off her winning number. "Open for bets."

Brandon leaned over the rail and confidently set his solitary chip on the black 35 square.

She'd have sworn when Brandon straightened, he moved closer. His presence warmed her side, and like a heat-seeking missile, her body swayed toward his. She stopped herself from sinking into his chest seconds before her shoulder made contact, and she took another healthy drink.

His thumb stroked the base of her spine. Intentional or just an absent gesture, she couldn't say. But damn, she liked the feel of his fingers moving over her body. If only things weren't so complicated. If they could be simple people. A vacationing couple, like the man and woman across from her, who displayed open affection with a lingering good-luck kiss.

Her own lips tingled, the memory of Brandon's kiss rising to the forefront of her thoughts. With that remembrance came another, one far more earth-shattering—Brandon's body draped across hers, the feel of his cock gliding in and out of her pussy. Electricity arced through her veins, making her shiver.

"I didn't think I'd find you here," Brandon murmured as the croupier spun the wheel. He brought his free hand up to push her hair behind her shoulder. As he lowered his arm, his knuckles trailed down the side of her neck.

Natalya ignored the chill that followed his brief touch. She tightened her fingers around the padded rail and gave him a hesitant smile. "I keep my appointments."

"Appointment?" Humor crinkled the corner of his eyes. "That sounds awfully formal."

Absolutely. That way, if the man to her right, who had developed a habit of watching her, swore allegiance to Dmitri, this would still appear casual. Strictly business. Even if Brandon's hand had slipped lower and that taunting thumb now swept back and forth over the waistband of her skirt. Her awareness honed in on the lazy stroke. Up, to glide over the muscles framing her spine. Bare skin tingled. Down, drawing her focus to the weight of his hand. Her womb tightened. Up. Down. Up . . .

"Figures." Brandon let out a husky laugh. "Never bet your age."

Zapped out of the blissful sensations ebbing through her body, Natalya looked up to find the roulette wheel stopped, the ball resting in the red 1 pocket.

His age. They were the same age. She should've remembered that from his file, but she'd forgotten. Why it mattered escaped her. Nevertheless, a foreign pleasantness crept beneath her skin. Giddiness. She hadn't been giddy since college.

Damn it felt *good*. Like maybe, despite all the darkness surrounding her, hope still remained she could find forgiveness for the girls she'd harmed. The lives she'd ended. Maybe someday, she could still reclaim innocence.

She turned to Brandon, releasing all the lightheartedness with a genuine smile. "Did you still want to get something to eat?"

Hot and laden with suggestion, his gaze raked over her body. The corner of his mouth quirked, and he bent his head to hers, his lips a heartbeat from her shoulder. "Are you on the menu?"

She backed away from the table, grabbed him by the wrist, and headed for the Simple Kitchen where the aroma of maple syrup hung heavy in the air.

He caught up with her in one easy stride. "I'll take that as a no."

Laughing, Natalya glanced at him from the corner of her eye. "I haven't made up my mind. Feed the stomach. Then we'll talk about the rest of me."

His eyes sparked deep gold. A slow sensual smile curved his lips, and he took the lead, slipping his hand into hers and escorting her inside the sparsely populated buffet, where they claimed a booth in the farthest corner from the door.

B randon eyed the way Natalya sipped her orange juice through the straw, imagining how it would feel to have those full, pink lips locked around his dick. The swirl of her tongue. The firm pressure as she sucked.

He shifted in his seat. Spending the rest of the remaining hours of early morning tangled together had morphed from desire to fierce, aching need. Their banter drove him insane, though he was aware she purposefully tried to push him into insanity.

She'd done a good enough job of it. His cock was so swollen it hurt. If he could have gotten away with it, he'd have swiped their empty plates off the table, dragged her on top of it, and fucked her right here.

But he wasn't the only one affected by their conversation that had, to his shame, drifted nowhere near to the purpose he'd convinced himself he sought. He'd come no closer to answers about her childhood, her background, or that devastating knee. Instead, they talked about the mundane. What movies they liked. What books they read—he didn't; neither did she. They both jogged, which explained the strength in her fantastic legs. They both hit the gym when schedules allowed.

They both liked Chinese food. And pancakes. With a double helping of fresh strawberries and one fat dollop of whipped cream.

And they both found sitting at home with a rental far more enjoyable than clubs, crowds, and the blinding lights on the Vegas Strip. A discovery that, for some strange reason, warmed Brandon from the inside out.

"So," he murmured, mesmerized by the deepening color in her eyes and the heavy droop to her long eyelashes. They'd dropped the same way just before he'd kissed her.

"So," she echoed.

They were dancing around the one subject that stood out like a pink elephant—mutual desire. Why the hell couldn't he spit it out? *Come back to my place.* It wasn't like he'd ever had a problem making the suggestion before. But no matter how he worked the thought around, he couldn't get it to slip loose.

Because you're afraid she'll say no.

She had earlier.

He opted for a different topic—one he should have been focused on all along. "That kick. Where'd you learn how to do that?"

For a fleeting instant, something passed across her face. Something he couldn't recognize, but it had surfaced more than once over their short breakfast. As she dropped her gaze to her lap and plucked at her paper napkin, it hit him—shutters. That brief lowering of her eyes, the slight shift in her focus, blocked him out like someone might close shutters over a window.

He'd seen it before too. When he asked about Sergei. When she talked about her parents. It had snapped closed when he brought up the subject of children.

She was hiding something. But what? The history *not* in her file, or something more sinister? Jill's warning rose in his memory: *If she's working here, it isn't her money.* No, not that either.

He sighed inwardly. Whatever the secret, she hid it well. He'd have never noticed if he hadn't been so damned interested in finding out everything he could about this seductive redhead. Another guy, one who hadn't become accustomed to *looking* for lies, would've never given the insignificant tension that touched her soft lips a second thought.

"Self-defense classes," Natalya answered as she reached for her juice.

Not in any self-defense class he'd ever taken. A kick, sure. Not to the chest. Not so precise, and certainly not so deadly. A hair more to the left, and she could have cracked that man's ribs, punctured a lung, or worse, thrown him into cardiac arrest.

He let it slide. He'd find out. Maybe not tonight, but he'd dig out that answer one way or the other. Besides, experience proved he'd have better luck in the bedroom . . . er, on the couch. Or the floor. Or wherever he could have her, so long as his bed didn't enter the game.

Glancing at his watch, he noted it was going on six in the morning. He reached across the table and captured one of her hands in both of his. His thumbs caressed smooth skin. He lifted his gaze to her face, his air strangling in the back of his throat when he observed her expression.

Lips parted, she studied their joined hands. Her long, slow blink told him her thoughts had found the same path his had wandered all night. But it also carried a curious touch of an emotion he couldn't name. Pain? Remorse? Maybe fear? When she dragged her eyes to his, those shutters stood wide open. He gazed into fathomless jade green pools that rippled with a reflection of a woman who resided behind the conservative clothes, the come-get-me heels, and the cool confidence. A dash of vulnerability, a sprinkling of simplicity, and a whole hell of a lot of femininity.

That woman, whoever she was, cast a spell over him. And she only ever surfaced when Natalya forgot whatever she harbored and desire began to dominate her mind.

He cleared his throat to regain control of his voice. But his words still came out hoarse. "Want me to give you a ride home?"

Her fingers trembled against his, and she swallowed with visible difficulty. "Please. I walked to work."

Walked? No, he absolutely wasn't going to ask. More questions would mean sitting here longer, and right now, all he wanted to do was find the remotest, most isolated corner he could claim and feast on those parted lips. Her house suited that need perfectly.

Reluctant to let go of her hand, he slid his own away slowly, allowing their fingers to touch all the way to the tips of her conservative nails. He pulled out his wallet, tossed two twenties on the table, and eased out of the booth. It took all the self control he possessed not to fit his hands on her hips, pull her against his body, and steal the kiss he'd hungered for since the moment his lips left hers earlier that night. Instead, he gently took her by the elbow, and without a word, led her through the exit, out the casino's front doors, and around the corner to where he'd parked his Mustang Shelby—the one luxury he possessed, though some might question the validity of *luxury*.

For Brandon, who'd spent most of his adult life in the same red Chevy pickup he'd purchased at sixteen, the car defined opulence. He'd earned enough in the last several years to purchase it in cash. Not like he had a whole hell of a lot to spend his paycheck on anyway.

He opened the passenger door, and as Natalya slid into the leather seat, he caught a whiff of her sweet perfume. He closed his eyes, breathing it in. The desire flowing in his veins intensified. God, he liked that sweet scent. It made him think of springtime, and he loved spring.

Winter let go. The temperatures climbed. All the shit he waded through in narcotics undercover brightened.

Shutting her door, he fought the anxious hum bubbling in his veins. *Get a grip, man. You're acting like a fourteen-year-old about to get his first blowjob.* At least his hands were shaking like they had on that fateful day.

He slid behind the wheel and started the car. "Where to?"

"Turnberry Towers."

This time he couldn't keep his mouth shut. With an incredulous blink, he asked, "You walked three miles to work?"

"Yes."

"What the hell for?"

"To work some things off my mind."

He gave her a dubious look. "What kind of things take three miles to work off?"

Natalya held his gaze quietly, those curious shutters once more wide open for him to look straight into the depths of her soul. A shiver coursed through him, despite the sudden warming of the air around them. His skin felt tight, his chest too narrow for his lungs. He knew what she would say, before her whisper slipped free.

"You."

Brandon choked back a groan. Swallowing hard, he curled his fingers into the steering wheel, but clutching it in a death grip didn't stop his voice from catching as he asked, "Did it work?"

Her gaze dropped to his mouth. She licked her lips, lowered her eyelashes for a suspended heartbeat. Blood surged to his cock, and the racket behind his ribs intensified. His body coiled tight, a hair trigger ready to discharge with the slightest pressure of a steady hand.

The catastrophic squeeze came with her barely audible answer.

"No."

He didn't know who moved first, who breached the distance between them by leaning over the center console. But their mouths met hungrily. His hands tangled in her hair, hers squeezed into his shoulders. She tasted like heaven. Sweet like the syrup on their pancakes, but beneath that sugary layer was a darker flavor. A tang that branded her as a woman who knew the meaning of passion and wouldn't shy away if things got a little rough. A little out of control.

His teeth pricked her lower lip, testing the theory.

The low moan that rumbled in the back of her throat nearly made him come right there. He sucked in a sharp breath and pulled away. The rasp of their breathing filled his ears. Tightening one hand at the base of her neck, he pressed his forehead to hers and concentrated on returning his heartbeat to a moderate level. "If I don't get inside you soon, Natalya . . ." *I'm going to die.*

He couldn't bring himself to voice the rest of the thought. It had to be an exaggeration. He couldn't have become that desperate for a woman in such a short time. But damned if he could remember wanting someone the way he wanted her. The thought that he might *not* have her constricted his heart and filled him with crazy ideas of carving holes into the man who did.

Her hands shook as she slid them down his arms and slowly retreated into her seat. In the dim lights from the dash, he watched the hard rise and fall of her breasts, taking some relief in the fact she seemed to be as needy for him as he was for her.

"Turnberry," he murmured to fill the quiet with something other than the sound of ragged breathing.

Dropping the car into gear, he navigated out of the parking lot.

Nineteen

Natalya tried like hell to keep the hurry out of her stride as she made her way through Turnberry's lavish lounge to the elevators with Brandon at her heels. The cautious voice of reason screamed what she was about to do was sheer insanity. Sergei, though his remarks had been completely out of line, threw it all in her face with black-and-white terms. Brandon had a right to know what he was getting into. It was his decision whether sex might be worth his life.

If she possessed a shred of human decency, she'd tell him as soon as the doors to the elevator closed. Brandon was a cop. In her gut, she knew Sergei called him straight—he couldn't be anything less than clean. Maybe a little unorthodox in how he resolved his cases, but he damn well didn't work for Dmitri.

She didn't want to believe in Brandon's goodness because believing stripped away all the reasons she shouldn't let desire have control. The truth, however, refused to stay behind her veil of ignorance. Beyond all of Sergei's sound arguments, she'd witnessed the proof in the car, when Brandon had kissed her with wild abandon. Dmitri's goons might have tried to set her up, out of envy for her position, or even because Dmitri asked them to test her loyalty. Yet, no one under his employ who actually *wanted* her, would dare risk his neck by trying. He'd be just as afraid she'd rat him out, as she was afraid of being ratted out.

But the raw hunger in Brandon's kiss wasn't fake. In thirty-five years, she'd never been kissed so recklessly. Nor had she ever returned a kiss with her whole soul, as she had less than ten minutes ago. She'd thrown herself into the heady warmth of his mouth, the velvety caress of his tongue, desperate to return to that place of abandon he created in her office.

She stared at the closed elevator doors, excited and nervous. *It's his choice, not yours.*

Yes. She'd tell him. Give him the choice. If he walked away, it would sting. But maybe they could gain an ally. Lord knew they needed one. If Brandon wanted her to, she'd even confess her security breach to the agency and arrange some way to keep him sheltered, should the assignment go south.

The elevator dinged open. To her immense relief, the wood-paneled cubical stood empty. She took a deep breath, stepped inside, and thumbed the button for the forty-sixth floor.

Brandon hauled her into his arms the second the doors slid shut. Hard and hot, his mouth captured hers. His hands slid around her waist, his fingers splayed over her bottom. Urging her backward, he pressed her into the wall and sank his weight into her. Their bodies aligned perfectly. His hard chest warmed her heavy breasts. Powerful thighs brushed hers. His fingers curled into her bottom, lifting her, guiding her hips into his, and his thick cock fit neatly against her damp pussy.

An electric shock surged through Natalya. *Oh, wow.* That felt good. He felt perfect. The way his fingers kneaded into her buttocks, the firm grip that trapped her exactly where he wanted her and made his intentions perfectly clear. The slight undulation of his hips that stroked her swollen clitoris—he wanted entrance and intended to have it.

She arched her back, which scraped her aroused nipples against his firm pectorals. Her hands slid up his shirt, over the taut sinews of his chest, across intimidating shoulders, and into the cropped hair at the back of his neck. Her nails scraped against his scalp.

"You drive me crazy," he murmured, leaving her mouth to trail his lips down the side of her neck.

Sharing his confession, she turned her head, her breathing hard, and dragged her nails down his back. Clutching at what remained of her senses even as she clutched at him to bring him somehow closer. "We need . . . to talk . . . ," she managed through short, breathless, gasps.

The tip of his tongue traced the line of her V-neck collar and dipped into the valley between her breasts. "Later," he murmured. "Can't think right now." His breath was hot and moist against her flesh. Her nipples tightened so sharply, she let out a soft moan.

"Just want to feel you." He rubbed his erection against her aching center as one hand slid between them to pop the topmost button on her jacket and tug the lace of her bra over her hardened nipple. "Taste you."

A gasp ripped free as Brandon closed his lips over the pert nub, and Natalya's knees threatened to give out. She grabbed at his shoulders to stop the sensation of falling and let her head drop to the wall in surrender. He sucked hard, pulling sensation through the soles of her feet and into the depths of her womb. Her pussy clenched, moisture flooded between her legs.

He was doing it again, taking her to that scary place where she couldn't think, couldn't do much of anything but yield to what he wanted, and that loss of power frightened her just like it had earlier. What would happen if she let go? If she let him creep beneath the pleasure?

No, she couldn't risk it. Not with Brandon—not with anyone. She couldn't yield no matter how she wanted to. She needed to master him if she had any hope of surviving the sexual paradise he'd introduced her to in his office.

Using all her strength, she pushed on his shoulders, dislodging his glorious mouth, and shoved him into the opposite wall. As his breath left his lungs with a grunt, Natalya hit the elevator's stop button. A blaring alarm rang out. Ignoring the ear-splitting buzz, she jerked at his belt and pushed his pants down his hips. She sank to her knees at the same time she took his heavy cock into her hands.

"Natalya," he ground out as his hands slid into her hair.

Merely lifting her lashes to meet his heated gaze, she licked the swollen head of his cock. The desire that flared in his eyes and the line of tension around his mouth pleased her. This was how she wanted him—on the edge, subject to her will, imprisoned by pleasure.

Slowly, she closed her lips around his hard flesh and sucked as her tongue caressed the sensitive skin beneath. Brandon's fingers fisted into her hair. His reaction, the sharp edge of arousal that shadowed his features, intensified the rising need inside her. Her clit was swollen, the rasp of her damp panties sheer agony.

"Christ, Natalya . . ." Brandon guided her head, easing himself deeper into her mouth. When she used her teeth to scrape against his cock, an oath hissed between his teeth. She encouraged his pleasure, suckled harder on the tip, until his head fell against the wall and his hips began to move of their own volition.

Yes, this was what she wanted. Control over Brandon. Control over the crazy desire that had sparked between them. Another thrill rocketed through her, and she let out a moan.

With one hand she gave the base of his erection a firm squeeze. With the other, she cupped his balls, finding satisfaction in the way they pulled into his body. *Take him all the way. Bring him to his knees.*

It was the only way she knew how to confront the all-consuming ache his simple touch ignited.

"Shit, baby. If you don't stop, I'm going to—"

"Is everything okay in there?" a voice blasted through the intercom.

Brandon's body tightened like a ripcord. He pushed his hands into her scalp, urging her mouth away from his wide, thick cock. Desperate to bring him back to where he'd been seconds before, Natalya sucked harder. His groan tore through her, and she felt her own pleasure mounting. If she didn't stop, not only would he come, she would as well.

And Lord, how she wanted to.

"Is everything okay in the elevator?" the voice repeated.

"Yeah," Brandon ground out hoarsely. He surged into the depths of her mouth again, almost touching the back of her throat. Natalya shuddered as a drop of salty flavor saturated her tongue.

"Damn it, no!" Digging his hands into her shoulders, Brandon snatched her to his feet. His mouth crashed into hers, hungry and demanding. She felt his hand fumble at the wall, distantly recognized the sway of the elevator as it began to move once more. As despair launched through her, slowing the rapid beat of her heart, she choked back a whimper.

The assault on her mouth eased, and Brandon broke the kiss. His breath rasped against her cheek as he pressed his forehead to hers. Between their bodies, he fumbled with his pants. "Not like this, baby. I don't want to go off like a rocket. I want to fuck you long and slow. All damn night."

A foreign sensation filtered through her veins, lighting her up from the inside, telling her whatever he had in mind she could survive. *Would.* Unexplainably, Brandon's insistence to hang on to his control strangely pleased her. Disappointment gave way to the slow burn of anticipation, of certain, absolute, pleasure.

The low chime of a bell announced they'd reached the top floor, and Brandon disentangled his body. He held fast to her hand as he led her through the doors, giving her only a brief moment to straighten her jacket before he pulled her close and kissed her once more. This time slower. Sweeter. But beneath the languorous swirl, arousal lingered on his tongue.

As it occurred to her they were necking in the hall with her door only four feet away, a giggle escaped. She edged out of the kiss and his wandering hands. "Let me get my keys."

He flashed a grin that gave him a surprisingly youthful charm. She caught a fleeting image of what he'd looked like before twelve years as a cop hardened his eyes and etched wisdom beyond his years into his handsome features. Her heart clenched. Her belly fluttered. How many women had fallen victim to that young man? Did one of them have something to do with his insistence he wasn't father material?

She resisted the urge to reach out and trace the softened contours of his jaw and opened her purse. A brief rummage produced the simple keychain that held her condo key. Fastening her purse before he could observe the 9mm Sig inside, she beckoned him to follow with a tilt of her head.

Intent on distracting her, Brandon nuzzled the back of her neck as she put her key to the lock. Laughing, she tried to brush him off, but he snagged her around the middle, holding her in place and making it damn near impossible to unlock her door.

"Brandon," she scolded with a laugh.

His chuckle rustled her hair. But he let go, hands held up in mock surrender. His rueful smile played havoc on her senses.

Natalya turned back to the door, touched her key to the lock, and froze. Her gaze riveted on the gap between the doorframe and the heavy metal door. Every bit of heat Brandon had stoked in her blood turned to ice. Someone had been here.

Maybe still inside.

Brandon noticed the breach at the same time. In a heartbeat, a streetwise cop replaced a simple man with one thing on his mind. As he stared at the opening, the playful light in his eyes died. From his shoulders to his toes, all the parts touching her went stiff. He wedged a shoulder between her and the door. "Let me go in, take a look around."

Natalya's head spun. What if Iskatel´ had made contact and left something incriminating behind? Had they been seen together? Was one of Dmitri's thugs waiting in her living room? She needed an excuse, but a housemom who'd taken a few self-defense classes had no reason to argue a perfectly capable man's assistance.

Shit!

At a complete loss, she did the only thing she could think of—she threw herself between him and the entrance, braced her palms on both sides of the doorframe, and shook her head. "That's not necessary."

The harsh line of his jaw revealed his own struggle between his cover and his instincts. He searched her face, as if questioning the very same thing that ran through her mind—confess. But nothing, and no one, would make her reveal her cover now. Or ever. She'd come too close to endangering Brandon. Taken one too many risks, and the reality of her position, the magnitude of subterfuge miring around her, demanded she walk away, no matter how painful.

"Don't be foolish, Natalya." Brandon's eyes turned cold and punishing. "There could be someone inside."

"I can take care of myself, Moretti." She sucked in a deep breath as she slipped her hand to her purse and opened the magnetic flap. "You should go."

Their gazes clashed. At his thigh, he curled one hand into a fist. "You're out of your mind if you think I'm letting you walk in there alone." He lifted his other hand over her shoulder and shoved the unlocked door open. "Get out of the way."

"No." She parted her feet, bracing them also against the doorframe in case he decided to try and physically remove her. As she slipped her hand inside her purse and curled her fingers around her gun, she turned her head toward the blackness at her back. "See. Empty. Now go."

Mentally, she counted off the seconds before she removed his options. *One* . . . Her eyes latched on to his, full of unyielding insistence.

Two . . . His jaw worked as his scowl deepened. Weight planted firmly on both feet, he told her in no uncertain terms he wasn't going to leave.

Three . . .

When Brandon didn't step backward, Natalya pulled out her pistol at the same time she spun into the doorway and kicked the door shut with her heel. It automatically locked behind her. She stared into the shadows, her heart thundering against her ribs.

A heavy hammering rattled her door. "Natalya! God damn it!"

"Sorry, Brandon," she murmured beneath her breath. Ignoring his pounding, she flipped on the light switch. Sig held in front of her, finger on a ready trigger, she slowly turned. Her eyes touched each corner of her living room, then the attached kitchen.

Two dozen red roses situated on her dining table brought her gun to her side. She let out the breath she'd been holding, crossed to the bouquet, and laid her pistol on the polished wood. Picking up the card her intruder had propped against the crystal vase, she scanned the handwriting that bore her name. Nothing she recognized.

But the note inside told her no florist had written the message. Written in all caps, the words were in Russian.

YA BOL', CHTOBY BYT' S VAMI. S LYUBOV'YU, DMITRI.

I ache to be with you. All my love, Dmitri.

As another heavy fist slammed into her door, Natalya crumpled the card. "No one's here, Brandon. Go home!" she hollered, hating the words, knowing no other option. "Before I call security."

It's his *choice, not yours.*

Her hands trembled as she pressed them to her face to stop the sudden rush of tears. She'd ignored Sergei and heedlessly given in to selfish desire, never once stopping to consider what Brandon might want. He saw a housemom. A woman who knew how to dance a man into insanity. She could take off her clothes, but she had no right to strip his life away.

God, Kate had been right when she'd called her a killer. Only a cold-blooded murderer could be so thoughtless.

Distantly, she recognized Brandon had stopped pounding on her door. Silence engulfed her, oppressive and suffocating. The tears she tried to confine broke free. Devastated by the realization of the woman she'd become, Natalya dropped to her knees, curled into a ball, and let them fall.

———

Classical music intruded on blissful unfeeling. Natalya opened her eyes, confused at first as to why she was lying on the floor in front of her door. Bright sunlight streamed through her open blinds, and she blinked at the invading light.

As her bleary vision cleared, the disastrous events that led her to her present position on the carpeting pummeled into her mind. Brandon. Dmitri. Flowers.

Her phone was ringing.

She dove sideways for her purse and yanked out her cell phone. A quick glance at the LCD told her only two hours had passed since she'd collapsed under the weight of her actions. But the increasing volume of Tchaikovsky's *Romeo and Juliet* didn't give her time to think about her breakdown. She punched the CONNECT button. "Hello, darling."

"Did I wake you?"

Pulling herself up off the floor, Natalya smoothly lied, "Yes, but I'm glad you did. I got your flowers."

"Ah, good." Pleasure vibrated in Dmitri's voice. "I wondered if they'd reached you yet. The house is empty without you."

She could picture him, sitting in the front room where they dined each evening before the wide windows that overlooked his beautiful lawns. He'd have his Armagnac beside his untouched plate. Leaning on the rear legs of his chair, one ankle would rest on one knee. His smile radiated through the line.

He loved her. Maybe more than any woman had a right to be loved. If he hadn't killed so many people, if he hadn't spent millions arming terrorists, if he'd flinched *once* at the idea of shipping unwilling women to Dubai, she might have felt guilty. But he hadn't. And his soullessness provoked the same lifeless feelings inside of her.

"I miss you as well." She picked up her gun and put it back into her purse. Then, craving the comfort of her bed, she wandered down the hall, undressing as she walked.

"I've been thinking. There's no reason for me to stay here another week."

Panic fingered at her spine. He couldn't be planning to come earlier. She'd die, just *die*, if she had to face Brandon with Dmitri at her side. "What about the matter with Boris?"

"It's resolved. Boris agreed his nephew couldn't be trusted. The man's been disposed of. We'll see no more trouble from that corner of Moscow."

Her skin crawled at his casual reference to killing a man whose only mistake had been following the law. She swallowed down a shudder. "I see."

"Yes, and since that went so smoothly, my schedule is free. I've decided to join you early. It will take a bit before I'm finished with the negotiations on Dubai, but I'll arrive in three days. We can marry the next morning."

She almost dropped the phone, surprise hit her so hard. Dmitri rarely ever changed his schedules. He must be missing her a lot more than he let on.

Shit! Three days. Oh, God, what the hell was she going to tell Brandon? She'd lied tonight, claiming she belonged to no one else. Now she'd be married, *married*, in a handful of days. Her heart tripped into triple time.

"And," pride blossomed in Dmitri's warm tone, "I've even arranged it so we can leave that evening on our honeymoon."

That could only mean one thing—Kate. As Natalya's stomach bottomed out, she groped for the bedpost. *No . . .*

"Has Iskatel´ ruined my surprise?"

"No," she answered, lowering herself to the mattress's edge. "I haven't been contacted by anyone."

"Good! I wanted to tell you myself. We've accelerated the exchange. Iskatel´ will contact you with the details I shared, but three nights from now you'll deliver this Kate to Yakov at the warehouse on Nellis."

Three nights . . . Her stomach clamped down violently. She was going to be sick. She didn't know any of the players yet, couldn't pin down a name to save her life—and right now, her life was definitely in need of saving. She pressed a hand to her belly to stop the churning.

In a last-ditch effort to make progress on the case, she took a risk she wouldn't normally have attempted. "Darling, who is Yakov?"

Something heavy hit the wood floor on the other end of the phone. Presumably, his front chair legs. "You don't know?"

Surprise was the last thing she'd expected. She blinked, then pulled her phone away from her ear to give it a frown. Of course, she didn't know. He'd never told her. In fact, he'd done everything he could to seemingly keep her in the dark.

Struggling for patience, she returned the phone to her ear. "No, darling, I've heard from no one since I arrived. I can't very well take Kate to Yakov, if I don't know it's him. Or where to find him."

Gravelly laughter filtered through the receiver. "My love, you're priceless. I'm sorry, I thought you already knew. Yakov is Nikolai— we visit his lake house each summer."

Nikolai Botkin. Damn! Now that he'd said it, she *should* have known. They'd openly talked about the project. But the two men did it so comfortably, using all the code words Dmitri insisted on to keep the household staff from overhearing, Natalya had even missed the conversation.

"Nikolai is here?"

"He's been in the States since we returned to Moscow this summer."

"Oh." She forced a light laugh. "Well, I feel silly."

"Don't, my love. It's my fault. I should've told you more."

Gingerly she tested the waters. "And . . . Iskatel'?"

Another round of laughter reverberated in her ear. She sat silent, waiting for his amusement to fade, all the while wanting to reach through the line and choke him to death. When he finally managed to get his humor under control, he coughed.

"It isn't obvious?"

"No," she grumbled.

In Dmitri's classic, twisted sense of humor, he laughed again. She could feel his wide grin. *Damn it, Dmitri, this isn't funny!*

"I'm not going to tell you. The surprise is too good to be true. You'll kick yourself when you make contact . . . and you'll be quite pleased Nikolai chose someone so well."

The urge to scream possessed her. She gripped her phone so tight she feared the plastic casing would crack and bit down on her tongue to stop the belligerent sound.

"Damn," Dmitri muttered. "I'm sorry, my love, I must go. Someone's ringing in. I'll call you tonight, and I'll see you in three days."

"But—"

"I love you, Natalya."

He disconnected, relieving her from uttering the lie.

Natalya stared at her phone, unable to believe the cruel twist of fate. Dmitri was coming to Vegas. She had three days to put the last piece of the puzzle together and stop his despicable human trafficking. Three nights before dawn gave her life or sealed her tomb.

Three days.

Twenty

Not wasting time with looking at the caller ID, Dmitri punched the connect key, switching to the incoming call. Whoever had interrupted the longest conversation he'd had with Natalya in too long, better have a damn good reason for it. He didn't appreciate his plans for an appetizer of jacking off while Natalya purred in his ear being ruined.

"What?" he snapped.

"Sorry to bother you." Iskatel''s tone was suitably apologetic.

A tiny bit of Dmitri's frustration slipped off his shoulders. He huffed out a breath. Iskatel' still had much to learn, but progress couldn't be overlooked. Scolding overmuch would only reverse things. Still, the interruption warranted a correction. He tempered his tone, but left a deliberate edge in his voice. "I was talking with Natalya. What do you need?"

"That's what I was calling about."

"About Natalya, or about what you need?" Slowly, he sat forward, a frown gathering on his brow.

"Natalya. I delivered the flowers as requested. I'd intended to discuss the changes with her then. But she didn't answer her door."

Dmitri rolled his eyes, finding the discussion not worth his time. He'd grown tired of the jealousy within his family, those who couldn't accept that he'd willingly given his fiancée significant power. Everyone wanted the confidences he shared with her. Wanted to be rewarded for loyalty that surpassed hers by years.

He couldn't give it. She was days away from becoming his wife, the mother to his children, and he would not hear another objection about his decision to trust her with the necessary business matters. She'd beyond proven herself as a trustworthy gunman. And she'd beyond proven her loyalty as his lover.

Annoyance crept into his response. "She probably stopped for coffee. You know very well where she was last night. You were with her."

"Yes." A deep breath filtered through the receiver. "I do know where she was last night. She left with Moretti. Who also wasn't at home at six AM."

Dmitri shrugged, his annoyance growing with each accusing utterance. "There's no crime in meeting with a supposed employer. Gaining trust is necessary. She'll do what she needs to." He picked up his Armagnac and took a drink to calm his rising temper.

"Does that include devouring each other from across the room? Anyone in the goddamn club could have read the 'fuck me' in their eyes, Dmitri. I'm telling you she met him last night and it had nothing to do with her job."

A chill invaded Dmitri's blood. He tightened his fingers around the brandy snifter. What Iskatel' suggested . . . No. He refused to believe Natalya would betray him. Her dress hung in their bedroom closet—a fifteen thousand dollar gown that had taken her two months to pick out. Their rings were with his jeweler. She would use seduction as she needed, but she would not cross the line into betrayal.

"I'm sure you've misjudged the situation."

"There's no misjudging the hard-on in his pants. Or the two occasions they've been locked in his office for longer than necessary. You can think what you want, but after she crushed a man's chest tonight with her knee—which in itself ought to tell you she's not thinking about the job—Moretti lit out of here like a dog chasing a bitch in heat. I know *him* well enough to know what's going on."

To Dmitri's surprise, Iskatel''s voice hardened. Confidence emerged. A touch of arrogance as well, which only pissed Dmitri off further. He slugged back another long drink, grimacing against the burn that slid down his throat and pooled in his belly.

Natalya wouldn't be unfaithful.

"I'm not going to listen to you insult Natalya. She's capable, and she knows what she's doing."

"Jesus. I didn't want to have to spell this out for you, Dmitri."

The silence that followed cast a shadow over Dmitri. The hairs on his arms lifted. His skin crawled. The same way it had when he'd learned his brother had betrayed him two years ago.

"I saw them. Kissing in his car. And I tell you, she was as anxious for him to stuff his dick inside her as he was to put it there. I can send you the security video of her sucking him off in the elevator, if you really need proof." Iskatel′ waited a heartbeat before adding in a lower tone. "Now you've got a problem. What do you want me to do about it?"

Visions of Natalya's soft mouth wrapped around another man's cock possessed Dmitri's mind. Not Natalya. He'd given her the world. Offered her the universe. He felt suddenly sick. Violently, desperately ill. His fiancée, the one person he trusted above all others, the woman he loved, had betrayed him.

His fingers closed around the glass so tightly, the stubby stem snapped in half.

He swallowed down the bitter taste of bile. As the pain inside his chest let go enough for him to draw a breath, he gritted out. "I want him dead."

"And her?" Iskatel′ asked quietly.

"I'll take care of her."

Dropping the phone, he stared, unfeeling, at the blood that flowed between his clenched fingers.

Brandon lay wide awake in his bed, hands fisted into the sheet, sunlight streaming in on his naked body. The damn dreams had to stop. After this morning, he never wanted Natalya to touch him again—not in reality, nor in his imagination. A blind man could have seen she was hiding something. *Someone*, his mind corrected. If she didn't want him inside her condo, and she wasn't concerned about an intruder, that could only translate to one meaning—she knew who was inside.

She just hadn't expected *him* to be there. And Brandon didn't doubt for one second the person beyond that door was indeed a *him*. The evidence stared him in the face. She couldn't begin to afford the rent on a Turnberry condominium on what she made at Fantasia. Her clothes screamed money. While she didn't wear jewels, she might as well have been dripping in them.

Above all else, the way she went out of her way to keep their attraction to each other disguised said everything he needed to know. He'd just been determined not to see it.

He didn't share. Wouldn't share. And he damn sure didn't want her in his head when crawled into his bed to lick his wounded pride. He lifted his hips to ease the discomfort of what she'd done to him while he tried to forget her. Instead, the sheet slid across his swollen erection, the feeling not unlike the tickle of her hair. His breath came out in a hiss.

He sat up. Fuck this. She knew something. He'd stake his life on the assumption she was connected to the killer, and he wanted answers. Now.

Snatching his phone off the nightstand, he stared at the blank screen debating who to call. At eight in the morning, Aaron would give him attitude certain to tailspin him into a hell he couldn't crawl out of by the time work rolled around. After two relatively sleepless nights, Brandon needed rest, one way or the other, today. He wouldn't find it by dragging his teammate out of bed this early.

That left only one other person he could discuss the case with, unless he wanted to call his captain, which was out of the question. Joe's top would blow like an M-80 if he discovered Brandon had possibly compromised the investigation by letting his dick lead him around by the nose.

But could Rory handle it? Yeah, he could. He'd probably welcome the opportunity to contribute. Besides, Brandon had promised to call.

He tapped out Rory's number, leaned back against the pillows, and waited as the line rang.

Six tones later, Rory's voice mail answered. Brandon dropped the phone on the mattress. He raked both hands through his hair, then worked his fingers into the tense muscles at the back of his neck.

Everything pointed to Natalya. Each day that passed, he had more reason to suspect her. Hell, Aaron knew half of what he did, and Aaron suspected her enough to suggest Brandon follow through on the insane urge to fuck her silly.

There's no one else.

No matter what he'd seen, what solid fact rose in black and white, his disobedient cock wasn't the only part of him that believed that whispered confession. His mind refused to let it go.

It grabbed on to one insignificant chain of words the same way it had four years ago when Jon Sampson, age fifteen, swore he hadn't killed a rival gang member. Jon had the gun that put two bullets in Ricky Suret's head. His alibi proved false. Hell, they'd found Jon's DNA on Suret's clothes. The department had laughed at Brandon's insistence Jon was telling the truth.

Six months later, after a speedy conviction, Brandon ran into the real murderer. He'd finally landed the critical evidence to prove, and haul in, Suret's California supplier. Turned out he'd made a trip to Vegas that afternoon, bringing Suret a fortune in heroine. He walked in on a fight. Jon brought the gun, intending to erase Suret that afternoon. When the dope showed up, things changed. All three shot up until they were out of their minds high. Jon had passed out. And Suret paid the price for stealing from his supplier when the asshole fitted the gun in Jon's hand and used his limp finger to squeeze the trigger.

Brandon had known then, and he knew now, things weren't cut and dry with Natalya. He saw the goddamn evidence in her eyes. The only time she opened those shutters was when he inadvertently disarmed her with his hands. His mouth. Whatever other part of his body came into contact with hers.

The rest of the time, she kept everything out.

And damned if he didn't understand why. How many times had he locked himself up the same tight way to keep his family's secrets from surfacing? He'd taken one person into confidence, a girl he'd been pretty hooked on when he went to college. A girl whose tongue was as fickle as her body later proved to be.

How many times had he witnessed the same closure on his mother's face?

Sliding out of bed, Brandon made his way to his living room and the picture of his mom. He picked it up, studying her round cheeks for the telltale tension. He looked in her eyes, recognized the same veil that shrouded her emotions. Her smile lighted her face, but that brilliance didn't make it to her eyes.

Faking it.

He set the picture down, brows furrowed in thought. Witness protection had a way of killing people, even if they physically survived. The fear never went away. The constant worry that someone might overhear the wrong words, pick up on a habit despite dyed hair, name changes, and relocation.

There's no one else.

If Natalya's agent had dropped in unannounced, that explained why she wouldn't let Brandon inside.

No way in hell could he believe a woman who showed such compassion to a hysterical stripper could kill another woman. Still, his instincts said Natalya knew something about the killer. Could it be possible she wasn't his accomplice, but his *victim*?

He needed to gain her trust. If he could accomplish that feat, everything else would unravel accordingly.

The sudden erratic barking of his neighbor's dog crashed into his ears, and he swore. While he liked dogs, that particular bundle of fur would push any dog lover into madness. The part shepherd, part elephant had sent their mailman to the hospital last winter when it got off its chain—which it did frequently.

A flash of gray sped past his front window, and Brandon swore again. Good thing the damn dog liked him, as often as he had to catch it. One of these days he was going to get around to building that fence that he'd suggested the single mother of three erect. He just hadn't gotten around to barring her girls from using his swing set.

He dragged on the jeans he'd worn the night before and jogged out the back door in pursuit of the canine escapee. "Opie! Here boy!"

Three houses down, he found the mutt under a tree, barking its infernal head off at an orange tomcat. Probably the culprit who had a habit of digging in his trash. Though he was sorely tempted to let Opie teach it a permanent lesson, Brandon dropped to a squat and clapped his hands. "Opie!"

The dog cocked its head, wagged its tail. In one exuberant, saliva-shaking lunge, it bounded toward his outstretched hand. Brandon braced himself for the impact of a large, slimy tongue. It hit him square in the face.

When he finally managed to get the monster to calm down, he worked his hand under Opie's collar and found the method of escape. Three chain links still dangled from his collar, the snap still intact.

"Breaking that chain are you now? Guess I'll have to bring home something stronger tomorrow." He gave the dog's thick hair an affectionate rumple. "C'mon, boy."

Fifteen minutes later, he had Opie confined in his owner's garage and a note plastered to the door to keep them from opening it without warning. As he made his way back to his front porch, a dark stain at the base of his driveway drew his attention. He bent over the spot and muttered at the iridescent sheen of oil.

It figured. With everything else splitting apart at the seams, why should his engine be immune? Times like these, he'd give his right hand to have his brother around. Over the years, Stefan would've saved him a fortune in mechanics bills.

Grumbling, Brandon retreated to the emptiness of his house. He'd blown his morning to hell, and all he wanted to do was crawl back into bed and get a few hours of shut-eye before he had to open the club. Unfortunately, Derek wouldn't understand that, and if Brandon intended to get him to MGM to help with a cub, a brief nap was out of the question. He had just enough time to take a shower.

He scooped up last night's shirt from the back of his couch, and Natalya's sweet perfume sideswiped him. Lifting the fabric to his nose, he breathed deeply. His body stirred, memories of her even sweeter flavor flooding his mind. In one strong heartbeat, he returned to the place he'd been in dreams. The exotic paradise where Natalya's velvety tongue glided against his cock, and the intoxicating musk of her arousal blended with the springtime scent of lilacs.

His cock filled, and Brandon dropped the shirt to his side with a mutter. Christ. He was damn tired of jacking off in the shower. One way or the other, he'd find his answers. When he did, he'd make sure Natalya understood, very clearly, she'd be spending a lot of time making up for the torture she inflicted.

Twenty-one

Though yearning for a shower, Natalya didn't waste time with the luxury. She dragged on the first pair of shorts she grabbed out of her dresser and yanked a tank top over her head. Two twists of her wrists had her hair pulled back in a ponytail. She glanced in the mirror long enough to make sure her black bra straps didn't show through the lime green tank, and that the gray cotton shorts accomplished the same trick with her thong. Last night's makeup, sparse as it was, would have to do. Kate and Sergei needed to know the changes. Now.

Satisfied she didn't resemble a blue-light Kmart special, she shoved her feet into her running shoes, jogged down the hall, and stopped at her purse for her car keys. She rummaged . . . and rummaged . . . and scowled.

Where the hell were her car keys?

Turning the small satchel upside down, one shake sent the entire contents clattering onto the table. Cell phone, mascara, lip gloss, gas receipt, condo key, Sergei's condo key, Agency condo keys. No car keys.

Natalya let out a groan and hurriedly stuffed everything except Sergei's key back inside, this time adding her Sig to the collection. She needed to stop at Sergei's, anyway—she'd catch a ride to Kate's with him. She'd find her car keys later. Besides the jog to Fantasia would eat up too much time as it was.

Slinging her purse over her shoulder, she dashed into the hall and headed for the elevators. There, one glance at the numbers above the twin cars had her groaning again. Both glowed with Ls for the lobby, and in the five seconds that she ticked off in her head, neither changed.

She made an about-face and headed for the stairs. His condo was only two floors down. Stairs were faster, and she took them two at a time. Barging onto his floor, her pace accelerated, and her body fell into the natural rhythm of a casual run all the way to the end of the long hall, where she knocked on his door.

Silence answered.

"Damn it, don't tell me you left already."

She banged again, a little harder. Okay, a lot harder, just in case she'd caught him in the shower.

No dice. No footsteps moved behind the door, no voice called out demanding she hold her horses. Sergei wasn't home.

She glanced at the door, debating whether to let herself in. If he'd picked up her keys, she knew exactly where she'd find them—in the little box on his dresser that held his extremely out-of-fashion watch. Everything he didn't want to lose, he kept in there.

Instead of fishing for her keys immediately, she grabbed her phone and hit his number on speed dial. They'd exchanged keys, but only with the understanding they could enter only on emergency. While she loathed the idea of jogging four miles to Kate's, not to mention the time it would take, she wasn't entirely certain this qualified as an emergency. Better to ask.

Except, as soon as the phone rang, it flipped to his voice mail, telling her he'd, once again, forgotten to charge it. He never turned off his phone intentionally, not even during sex, but he couldn't seem to remember to plug the damn thing in.

To hell with it. Speed was critical, and with three days to stop Iskatel´, this qualified as emergency enough.

Natalya slid his key into the lock. The door opened to his usual disarray, but even for Sergei, the mess seemed out of place. Dishes in front of the television, newspaper that usually occupied a quarter of the couch covered the floor, and the couch cushions themselves looked like someone had given them a shakedown. One overlapped the other, cockeyed and partially off the seat.

A rustle in the back stopped her forward progress down the hall. At once, the disarray clicked into place. Not his usual state of organized chaos. Someone was here. Looking for something.

Standing still, barely breathing, she listened as she reached into her purse and eased out her gun. Another rustle, followed by a muted thump, as if someone had closed a drawer. A masculine mutter.

Chills coursed up and down her spine. Was it someone with a grudge against Dmitri? Or someone settling a debt with Sergei?

She proceeded slowly, pistol at her side, reflexes primed for confrontation. Another thump; another drawer. Natalya gritted her teeth against a surge of anger. Screwing with Sergei came as close as it could get to screwing with her. They'd been partners too long. If Dmitri was behind this, she'd find a way to inflict physical damage before she locked him up for the rest of his despicable life.

Using her toe, she nudged Sergei's bedroom door open wide enough she could step through. Her gaze flicked to the mirror on the wall at the foot of his bed, its positioning perfect to give her a wide-angle view of the room and the man within. She lifted her gun, prepared to catch him by surprise . . . and froze.

Eyes wide, she stared, not at some intruder digging through his belongings, but at Sergei himself. Rather, his tight, *bare* buttocks, and his sculptured shoulders that bunched and pulled as he strained to hold himself off the equally naked woman beneath him. The thump? Not the drawer—his headboard.

Shit!

Natalya flattened her back against the hall wall and squeezed her eyes shut. She could have gone the rest of her life without that visual. Damn it. She'd spent a torturous morning huddled on her floor, while her partner romped in the sheets. If he'd bothered to charge his damn cell phone, she wouldn't be standing here humiliated.

She took a step toward the door, before abruptly stopping and squinting at the heavy wood. Then, because he *had* embarrassed her beyond all reason with his terrible habit of not charging his cell phone, she changed direction and marched through the door, into his bedroom. Maybe a little mutual mortification would teach him to plug the damn thing in.

Cocking a hip against the dresser, she folded her arms over her chest. "I'm guessing there's no booby-trap there."

Sergei reared off the girl and scrambled to throw the sheet over their nude bodies. He did a double take, before exploding, "Jesus fucking Christ, Natalya! What are you doing here?"

With a surprised squeak, the girl made herself as small as possible. Her eyes peeked over the edge of the sheet.

"Obviously not what you are. I came for my keys. I would've called, but gee, go figure, your phone's dead."

Dragging in a breath that required a significant amount of effort, he lifted a murderous gaze. "I don't have your keys." He speared his fingers through his tousled hair and swore beneath his breath. His gaze dropped to the woman. "Could you give me a minute?"

"That entirely depends on how long a minute you need. If you don't have my keys, and you're going to be a while, I need to get to Kate's." She stopped at the door, adding, "You should probably get yourself to Kate's too."

With a smug smile, she closed his door. In the hall, however, she gave over to threatening giggles. He was going to kill her. But after the morning she'd had, she needed the humor. Dismayed she'd have to either fight for a cab or strike out on foot, Natalya left Sergei to his mid-morning workout and took the elevator down to the lobby.

One look at the already crowded Vegas Strip, and she decided jogging would take her to Kate's faster. If nothing else, the pounding of her feet would work out some of the tension in her body, and she could occupy her mind. Trapped in a slow-moving cab, she'd think herself into a panic.

The blocks passed in a blissful blur. Brandon tried to creep his way into her thoughts, but each time he surfaced, she shoved him back down. She'd spoiled that. No use fantasizing about all the things that *wouldn't* happen between them. She couldn't take the risks.

Twenty-two minutes later, she arrived at Kate's doorstep, sweaty, but wide-awake and relaxed. Her head no longer felt like someone had crammed it full of angry bees. She suspected the fact she'd formulated a solid plan had more to do with her rejuvenation, but she couldn't entirely dismiss the possibility she'd been sorely in need of a good physical work out.

Kate answered the doorbell so promptly, she must have been standing behind the door. She blinked, then stepped outside, closing the door behind her. "Good grief, what are you doing here?"

"We need to talk. Can you send Derek to his room?"

Backing into the house, Kate opened the door, inviting Natalya in. "I'll send him outside. He'll throw a fit if I try to confine him in his room."

Natalya sat on the edge of the couch as Kate corralled Derek into a lightweight jacket and shoes. He fought her every step of the way, anxious to be outdoors, evidently for the first time in several days.

Since I've been here.

She flinched, realizing how her out-of-the-blue appearance had upended her nephew's sense of normalcy. Once more, she vowed when this ended, no matter the outcome, Derek would never worry again. He'd never have to spend another day indoors when the sun shone bright beyond. And Kate . . . Kate would smile again. Laugh like she used to. Natalya's gaze drifted over her sister. Maybe she'd ditch the heavy makeup and take a little time to do something with herself when she wasn't at the club, instead of wearing beat-up sweats all the time. Take pride in herself, like she used to when Erik had been alive.

Her sister took the couch opposite and folded her hands in her lap. "What's wrong?"

She'd always been perceptive. A wry smile tugged at Natalya's mouth. She held it in check, knowing Kate wouldn't appreciate the humor that kept Natalya going when everything else looked bleak. No matter how she answered, her response would send Kate into fits, so she made the swift decision to spit it all out at once, no sugarcoating, no beating around the bush.

"Your kidnapping's been bumped up. We've got three nights."

"What?" Kate's exclamation ended in a soprano shriek.

Before Natalya could say another word, the front door clanged open, and Derek rushed inside. "Mom! Mom! There's a guy in his car in our driveway!"

The remaining color in Kate's face, scant as it was, drained away. Natalya reached for her purse, her instinct to grab her gun. But as Kate's tremulous eyes drifted to her son, Natalya's fingers hovered over the clasp. She couldn't pull a gun out in front of a four-year-old.

Instead, she took her whole purse to the door and poked her head out, investigating the driveway.

Sergei's nondescript black sedan blocked the sidewalk.

She rolled her eyes as she returned to the couch. "It's Sergei." Giving her nephew a pat on the back, she ushered him outside. When he took off for the large ornamental rocks in the front yard, she turned back to Kate. "I asked him to meet me here. I'll warn you though, he's probably not in the best mood."

Kate glanced at her, distracted. The questions she couldn't ask in front of Derek glimmered behind her wide eyes. "Why?"

"I walked in on him this morning."

"Oh." The flat answer gave way to a startled blink as Kate made the connection between Natalya's answer and the meaning. *"Oh,"* she repeated.

The brief change in subject restored the faintest touch of color to Kate's cheeks, and as Sergei walked inside, a dark cloud shadowing his face, she sat down on the couch.

Natalya's partner didn't look at her as he took a seat at Kate's side. She chewed on a smirk, covered it with a cough, and repeated what she'd just informed her twin. "Dmitri phoned me this morning. He's moved everything up. Kate's kidnapping is to take place two nights from tonight."

That drew Sergei's attention on her. His amber eyes sparked with suspicion. "Did he say why?"

"He's moved the wedding up also."

The slow arch of his eyebrow said one word, one very reproachful word: *booby-trapped*. Natalya shifted position, the weight in her chest returning, along with a significant helping of guilt. She stuffed the uncomfortable emotion into an abandoned corner of her mind, refusing to dwell on Brandon and what she'd done. She focused on the only positives she possessed. "I have a plan."

"You've had a plan all along. It hasn't worked." Kate jumped to her feet again and began to pace in front of the counter that separated her kitchen from her living room. Her teeth worked furiously at her lower lip.

"It hasn't worked because Brandon's thwarted me every step of the way."

"Brandon, who you want me to believe is part of this. God, what if he is? What if you've been right all along, and that's why he's been thwarting you?" Her voice rose again as her feet moved faster.

"He's not," Natalya and Sergei answered in unison.

Sergei gave her a surprised blink.

She ignored him.

"How do you know?" Kate cried. "Just yesterday, you were warning me not to trust, explaining things weren't always what they seemed. How do you know your plan will work this time? What if it doesn't, Natalya? What if two nights from tonight, you fail and this Iskatel´ person runs off with me? What happens—"

"Kate," Sergei's smooth voice rose over her rapid-fire questions as he eased to his feet and went to her side. Looping one arm around her shoulder, he guided her back to the couch where he sat, then pulled her down beside him. "I know this is difficult. But you've got to stay calm. Natalya has a plan, let's hear her out."

"I can't stay calm! The man you think is tied to this is spending the afternoon with my son! What if he takes Derek, and everything you think you know is false?"

Brandon? Coming here? Natalya stiffened. He hadn't said anything about Kate. Then again, they hadn't exactly been focused on anything but how quickly they could get out of their clothes. Good-bye hadn't involved pillow talk either.

"He's not going to hurt Derek," Sergei soothed. "He's not part of this."

Kate shoved out from under the weight of his arm and twisted beyond his reach. "You don't know that! Unless you've figured out who Iskatel´ is. You wanted me to be concerned—fine, I am. You're not going to fix this with that smooth, confident tone."

Sergei's brows dove down his nose. He rubbed the back of one hand and rolled his shoulders. "Does it help if I tell you I know him? That I know him so well I'd swear on my life he's not part of this?"

It was Natalya's turn to blink. She gaped at her partner. He *knew* Brandon? Why hadn't he told her? Damn it, they couldn't keep secrets from each other with this hanging over their heads. She had a right to know, particularly when *her* life was at stake, not just Kate's.

He didn't give her the opportunity to vent her anger. Reaching across the couch to grab Kate's hand and hold it tight, he continued to blow holes in all Natalya thought she understood about her partner. "I grew up with him. I know some of the shit he dealt with as a kid. It wasn't pretty. Take my word for it, he'd choose the grave over Dmitri."

Grew. Up. Together. And he was just now sharing this news? Wait. Why hadn't that tidbit shown up in his file? Nothing in the report she'd pulled from the agency matched a single tidbit about what she knew about Sergei's past. Sergei had spent his entire life in Chicago. Brandon, on the other hand, had been born in Kansas City, then moved to Texas under the witness protection program. Last time she'd checked, Chicago and Texas weren't neighbors.

She squinted at Sergei. Someone was lying. Someone's agency report was lying. And she didn't have to look any farther than the man sitting across from her, the man she knew so well she considered him a brother, to guess whose.

When they left here, Sergei Khitrovo owed her one hell of an explanation.

Kate had calmed down, however. Evidently Sergei's little bomb had worked. Her cheeks filled with healthy color, and she turned a frown on Natalya. "What did you have in mind?"

"I'm getting on that stage tonight." Sergei would rebel at what came next, but desperation called for a little risk. She took a deep breath and held his gaze. "You're going to distract Brandon long enough for me to accomplish it. Find something, *anything*, to keep him out of the back of the house from nine thirty until after I leave the stage."

He opened his mouth to protest, but she rushed on before he could utter a sound. "Kate, I need you to find a couple things for me, starting with a bikini that doesn't fit like dental floss, and ending with orange and yellow lighting."

Her sister cocked her head, and Natalya read the turning wheels inside her mind. Something clicked into place, and Kate left the couch, retreating into her bedroom. Five minutes later, she returned with a relatively simple, beaded bra-style bikini top and bottoms that fit like shrunken boy shorts. She held both up, iridescent beads glittering in the bright morning light. "I have heels to match."

"Have you worn it?"

"Nope. I bought it for my first night. Didn't try it on. Got home and discovered Derek made things fit a little different than they used to."

"It's perfect."

"I'll get the shoes."

As Kate disappeared down the hall once more, Natalya avoided Sergei's searching gaze. He could suffer. He'd temporarily lost the privilege of being the first to know what was on her mind. She'd been apart from Kate for three years, but that insignificant span of time couldn't sever bonds of sisterhood, let alone the special understanding twins shared. It was time to depend on Kate, as much as Kate depended on her. And when Brandon discovered she'd gone behind his back and pulled Becca off the stage, she'd need every bit of Kate's familiarity with Brandon to navigate that impending tornado.

He'd understand. Someday. When she was far from here, and he was safe. Alive.

The front door flew open and thirty-six inches of exuberant boy raced down the hall to his mother's bedroom. "Mom! Brandon's here! We're going!"

"Easy there, little guy. Slow down, I need to talk to your mom a minute. We have to ask about—"

Natalya looked up, and Brandon abruptly stopped. Eyes widened by surprise quickly narrowed to rake down the length of her body, then slowly up to her face. Appreciation gleamed beneath coal black eyelashes.

Like lighted pyrotechnics, the temperature in the room spiked.

Twenty-two

I'll be right out, Brandon," Kate called from the back room.

He murmured a muffled response, but his eyes never left Natalya's. Cleanly shaved, dress clothes exchanged for a dark gray T-shirt and faded blue jeans, he commanded every minuscule particle of Natalya's attention. She marveled at the way his shirt pulled tight across his broad shoulders, its loose fit managing to hug just enough skin her imagination could fill in all the blanks. Sharply defined pectorals, corded washboard abs . . . her gaze dipped to the black belt at his waist. Lower. Broad masculine hips, and though the denim was by no means tight, it couldn't hide the distinct bulge behind his fly.

Her cheeks flooded with heat, and she looked away, hoping he hadn't caught her staring. Knowing he had.

"Natalya."

Though he said nothing more than her name, his voice vibrated through her, setting off a wild flutter in her belly. With it came the ache of longing. The knowing she could never have more of this incredible man, but wanting him more than she'd ever wanted anyone. *Anything.*

He moved into the room, easing the door shut behind him. Her skin prickled. She knew, even before he approached the couch, that he'd sit down beside her, and her heart clamored violently. Electrified energy arced through her as he came closer, urging—no begging—her to lean sideways and soothe the tightness of her skin by sliding into his exposed side.

"I didn't expect you two to be here." The cushion shifted as Brandon dropped into the seat at her right.

Why didn't he look mad? He should be furious with her after last night. Sitting as far away as possible, not close enough to drive her crazy but still too far away that touching became impossible unless she moved. She wasn't going to move. Not unless someone held a gun to her head, and even then, if it meant keeping him at a distance that ensured his safety, she'd be hard pressed to scoot closer.

She managed to get her stumbling tongue to behave long enough to murmur, "I came for my keys."

"How are you, Sergei? Great job on those numbers last night, by the way. Meant to tell you that."

"No problem. Glad they worked for you."

"Brandon!" Derek came flying around the corner, carrying a police car the size of a loaf of bread. "Look what Mom got me yesterday."

Natalya watched in fascination as her nephew bounded onto the couch between Brandon's right elbow and the stuffed arm, then crawled onto his lap. As Brandon's muscular arm bent around the boy's sinewy back, Derek hit a button on the car's trunk. Sirens wailed. The light bar flashed. Her nephew turned a cherubic smile up at Brandon, who rumpled his hair.

Damned adorable. Brandon clearly had it wrong—he was absolutely father material. His whole expression softened as a chuckle rumbled in his chest. And his eyes crinkled with so much unspoken affection that Natalya's heart swelled.

He glanced her way, and his grin faltered for a heartbeat, replaced by a staggering flash of something she couldn't define. Whatever it was, it nearly knocked her backward before Kate's emergence from the hall drew his attention.

"Hey, Kate."

"Morning, Bran." Heels in hand, she plucked her glasses from the countertop, slipped them on, and rested a hip on the arm of the opposite couch. "You want something to eat before you guys head out?"

"Nah." Brandon patted Derek's shoulder. "I'll grab him a donut on the way. But we were talking outside."

Derek looked up, his grin full of impishness. His giggle conveyed a secret not yet shared.

"Would you object if I dropped him off with my neighbor's kids for the night? I'll make sure he eats. The girls next door caught me on my way out and asked when he was coming back over. Sue said she didn't mind watching him."

"Please, Mom! Please! I wanna play with Opie!"

"Well . . ." Kate's hands twined together in her lap. She slid Natalya a questioning look, glanced at Sergei, then sought answers from Natalya once more.

Natalya subtly dipped her head. Let the boy have some fun. He wasn't in danger, and Kate wasn't really either, not for another couple of nights.

"I suppose that would be okay." Sliding to her feet, she set the heels on the bar and dusted her hands on her long pajama pants. "I'll go pack a bag real quick. Do you have time to wait?"

"Sure thing."

"I'll help!" Derek scrambled off Brandon's lap and made a beeline down the hall.

"So what are you two up to today?" Brandon asked as Kate disappeared, leaving the three of them to stumble over awkward conversation.

Leaning back against the couch, Sergei stretched his arms across the back. "Not sure. I had plans. But they were changed for me." His gaze fell meaningfully on Natalya.

She'd admit she deserved a scolding. But given the same set of circumstances, she'd do it all over again in a heartbeat. He really needed to learn to keep his cell phone charged. If she really wanted to be honest with herself, she'd admit a certain degree of envy drove her to spoil his morning as well. Honesty, however, wasn't in today's line-up. At least not when it came to internal confessions.

Brandon must have observed Sergei's pointed stare, because he looked right at her as he answered, "Imagine that."

Backed into a corner, the sudden need to defend herself from these two men stiffened her spine. She opened her mouth to object. But what to say? She didn't have any appropriate defenses. None that Brandon could learn anyway. Tell him she'd spoiled her partner's morning because she was sore about spending the night alone? Right. That'd only lead to why she'd forced Brandon away.

She snapped her mouth shut and folded her arms over her breasts. Frowning at the both of them, she chose instead to answer his question. This time though, as her response slid up her throat, shock squelched it. She looked once more at Brandon. At Sergei. Sitting this close to one another in the broad daylight, similarities jumped in front of her face. Their foreheads possessed the same identical slope. Their eyes bore the same bright spark of humor, their unique color of molten gold as the sunlight kissed them.

She quickly inspected the rest of their bodies for likenesses. Brandon was slightly taller than Sergei, and Sergei's shoulders were slightly wider than Brandon's. Their build wasn't identical, but close enough to bear resemblance. Right down to the same way Sergei sat forward, leaned his elbows on his knees, and clasped his hands together. Their hands had the same rough, strong build and identical long fingers.

Sergei's voice echoed dully in her head. *Angelo ordered the murder of his family. I know him so well I'd swear on my life. I grew up with him.*

Holy shit!

No wonder Sergei balked every time she'd mentioned his working at the club. No wonder he'd been incensed about her involvement with Brandon. He'd never particularly given a damn who she slept with, why or where until now . . . because he was looking out for his *brother.*

Her gaze jumped back to Sergei. She cocked her head, mentally cutting off his unruly long hair and dressing him in Brandon's clothes. They fit perfectly, the familial resemblance unmistakable.

His grimace confirmed everything.

Hurt stabbed through her. Why hadn't he trusted her with his secret? Because of Dmitri? Or because he'd become so wary of every human being he encountered, that in some corner of his mind, he genuinely didn't trust her?

Like someone dropped a boulder onto Natalya's chest, the full realization of their circumstances shortened her breath. What had they become, she and Sergei? They couldn't be human. Not anymore. Human beings weren't designed to analyze everything upside down and crosswise. They were supposed to feel. To live. To know laughter as well as they knew sorrow, and while she and her partner might find humor easily enough, they blocked out the rest of the emotions.

They didn't trust a damn soul. Not even the people they not only spent three-quarters of their time with, but also those who were supposed to be true friends. Those willing to take a bullet for the other.

She was the worst of the pair. Sergei might have killed people without a second thought, but he'd never deliberately led innocent victims to their grave. She'd abused every bit of trust *given* to her, manipulated it to an advantage she justified as national security, and while she could weep over her own circumstances, she couldn't find a damn tear for any of those women.

Not even her sister.

She couldn't live like this anymore. Couldn't lie like this. Not to others. Not to herself.

The large front room suddenly became stifling. Brandon was too close. Sergei too distant. Needing escape, she stood. "I think I'm going to go run some more."

"Things to work out, huh?"

Brandon's quiet question stopped her hasty escape. She halted at the door, trapped by his knowing stare. Holding his gaze for a heartbeat, she implored him not to push. Begged him to just let her walk away from this, from *him*, before he pulled out every emotion she didn't know she possessed and broke her into pieces.

When she didn't answer, Brandon's full lips curved with a faint, hesitant smile. "I could use a jog myself."

Shivers coursed up and down her spine so violently she had to close her eyes to find the ability to breathe. Her grip tightened on the doorknob she had yet to turn. She looked to Sergei, silently beseeching his help.

Instead of the stoic strength she needed, his expression tossed her insides upside down. While his features remained motionless, the tightness of his jaw indicated a hint to his own inner turmoil, and his eyes filled with silent apology. For his harsh words the night before. For his failure to share his confidences.

A resigned sigh brought her partner to his feet. He shoved a hand through his long hair, then stuffed both in his back pockets. Agitated— when he couldn't use his hands to work out something, he hid them away. "Kate said on the way home last night, you were taking Derek to feed the cubs at MGM, Brandon. Still on for that?"

"Yeah. He likes Rainforest—thought we'd stop there for lunch. Then I'll take him to Sue's."

Conversation resumed, Natalya turned the knob, intent on leaving.

"Have you seen the lions, Natalya?" Sergei asked.

The suggestion hung in the air, mixing up her mind even more. But despite her riotous thoughts, she recognized what he didn't say. He was giving her back his trust. Or maybe giving it for the first time. He was trusting her to navigate this minefield with his brother.

"Why don't you come with us?" Brandon asked. "I'm sure Derek wouldn't mind."

A full afternoon with both her nephew and the man she couldn't get enough of. Her blood warmed, filling her ears with a pleasant buzz. Kate though—Kate didn't want her around Derek. She shook her head. "I don't think that's a good idea."

In a surprising display of his usual good humor, Sergei, who she depended on for solidity, chuckled. "I think it's a great idea if it keeps you out of my condo the rest of the afternoon." He moved to the hall. "I think I'll help Kate."

Sergei was gone before Natalya could squeak out another protest, leaving her very much aware that she was alone with Brandon.

Brandon stood and wordlessly crossed the three feet between the couch and the front door. She instinctively retreated. Her back flattened against the closed exit. As panic swelled, she furiously tried to turn the knob again.

Brandon reached under her elbow and flipped the deadbolt. He braced his other hand on the wood above her shoulder and leaned in close. Heat rolled off his chest in waves, washing over her, filling her breasts with a heavy weight, and making the downy hairs on her belly stand on end.

He traced a knuckle over the curve of her jaw, beneath her earlobe. His fingers slid into the gathered hair at the base of her ponytail, and gentle pressure from his hand guided her off the door, into the sweltering heat of his body. She closed her eyes as her breasts pressed against his chest. A soft gasp slipped off her lips.

The sound faded under the featherlight touch of his mouth as he dusted it over hers. "I dreamed about you."

Natalya shivered, unable to find words.

"I dream about you every night." His lips captured hers, soft and pliant, warm and intoxicating. "The things I want to do to you." The tip of his tongue slid along the seam of her mouth, nudged her lips apart. "Feel with you." At the back of her head, his fingers tightened. "You make me crazy, Natalya. Fucking crazy."

His tongue touched hers, and her resistance shattered. She lifted to her toes, her arms sliding around his neck, welcoming his kiss. Rich masculine flavor soaked into her veins, stirring the warmth in her blood to intolerable levels. The slow, languorous slide of his tongue against hers lacked the passionate demands of his kisses the previous night, but they stripped her bare just as quickly. Maybe even quicker.

He dropped his hand from the door to her hip, but he didn't haul her in close. The bite of his fingers evidenced the desire to, but he held back, treating her to the singular ecstasy of his mouth. Her heart slammed wildly against her ribs, hammering so hard he must have felt it. Remembrances of the perfect way his body molded into hers filled her head with vivid pictures. He'd felt good then, his cock buried deep inside her, his fingers pressing against her swollen clit. But this . . . this was heaven on earth. His strength supported her weak legs; the taste of him made her dizzy. He surrounded her, body and soul.

She curled her nails into his shoulder and gave in to a low, pleasurable moan.

His chest vibrated with a similar sound, and then he was gone, his moist breath scraping over the side of her face before his cheek grazed hers and he leaned away. The pressure in his hands relaxed.

Hoarse and thick, his voice scraped pleasantly. "You can shut the door in my face, but I have the key." Slowly, deliberately, he pressed his hips into hers. His hardened cock teased her pussy with unspoken promises of ecstasy. "Let me in, Natalya. Come with us today."

She searched his face, taking in the smoldering burn in his tawny eyes, the honesty of his unabashed desire. "You don't know what you're asking."

"I think I do." He touched his lips to hers once more. Lingering. Enticing. "I'm not afraid to learn."

No, she doubted he was afraid of anything. Anything he could comprehend, at least. He'd sized her up. Decided he knew the odds. Placed a bet he intended to win.

He couldn't be more wrong.

The safest answer was no. It rose to the tip of her tongue, waiting. When she opened her mouth to let it escape, something else interfered. Distantly, she heard the soft ring of her voice. "I'll go with you."

Twenty-three

Brandon leaned against the door to the lion handler's containment room, smiling as Derek and Natalya knelt on the ground before one of the playful cubs. As he watched, Derek picked up a large baton-like toy affixed with a prickly, dog-sized rubber ball on a string. He waved it over the little cub's head, giggling when the feline rose up on hind legs to catch the toy between its paws.

The ball slipped free, snapping up to plunk Derek straight in the forehead. Brandon suppressed a chuckle. Natalya's laughter rang out bright and clear.

His smile deepened at the rich melody of her laugh. She didn't do so nearly enough.

As if she sensed his pleasure, she glanced over her shoulder and caught his gaze. A pretty pink blush infused her cheeks. Color that raced straight to Brandon's heart and turned it on end. He felt the pull of her body, the driving need to move up behind her and touch—her shoulder, her hair, he didn't care where. Just so long as he maintained contact. But this was their time. Derek was having the time of his life, Natalya looked it too, and Brandon was content to stay in the background. Watching. Admiring. Trying to read between all the intricate layers and discover the woman who opened those shutters to her soul.

"She's something, Bran. Where'd you find her?" Kaycee Janus, the trainer he'd briefly dated when he first arrived in Vegas, assumed the position on the wall at his left.

"You think?"

"Think?" Kaycee laughed. "Look at Dave over there. His tongue's been hanging out since you two came in the back room."

Brandon's gaze jerked to the other trainer who, like himself, watched Natalya. His ego flared, and a smirk tugged at his mouth. He looked away, his redhead far more interesting than a chubby man openly ogling a woman who had yet to notice his not-so-veiled attempt to get a look down her tight tank top.

"Is she the boy's mom?"

"No. Just a friend."

Kaycee shot him a disbelieving look and let out a soft snort. "Uh-huh."

He blinked, uncertain what he'd said that amused her. "She's not Derek's mom."

"She's not just a friend either." Her eyes laughed at him. "There was a time I'd have cut off limbs to have you look at me the way you're looking at her right now."

A slow, pleasurable burn spread through his body. He didn't know where it came from, or what produced it, but it slid through his veins like warm sunlight. He liked looking at Natalya. Enjoyed the secret knowledge of the things they'd done. The things they would do yet.

Man, she's good with Derek. Natural.

"Like how?" he murmured absently.

"Like that."

He dragged his eyes off Natalya to squint at Kaycee. "You're seeing things."

"Mm-hm. So are you. Tie me down, commitment, sort of things."

His eyes went wide as a nervous stutter took root behind his ribs. Commitment hadn't entered his mind . . . Had it? He shook off the question with a shake of his head. "Wrong. You know that's not my thing."

"Then why's she here?"

Again, he blinked. "Because I asked her to come?"

"Exactly." Satisfaction filled her knowing smile. "*You,* my friend, don't date in the daytime."

"I do too."

"All right." Mirroring his posture, she folded her arms across her chest. "How many lunch dates have you had in the last two months? How many days have you gotten out of bed to do something other than work or get ready for work? And how many times have you taken someone along on your outings with Derek in the past year?"

Brandon's smile slowly faded as he searched his memory. He dug deep, but try as he might, he couldn't come up with a single example to back up his claim.

"Told ya."

So what? He just hadn't had a good excuse to abandon his nocturnal habits or give up his solitude. This was work, anyway. She fit into his case somehow. He frowned at Kaycee and turned his attention back to Natalya, who once again laughed as Derek dragged the ball across the floor, and the cub repeatedly pounced in attempts to catch it.

Lord, that was a beautiful sound.

"You're toast, Bran. She might as well have *Property of Brandon Moretti* stamped across her back."

Perturbed by the sudden increase of his pulse, he grumbled. "Aren't you supposed to be helping Derek feed one of those monsters or something?"

Kaycee's chuckles lingered long after she abandoned her position at his side to take a prepared bottle over to Derek and Natalya. "Here, Derek, he's hungry. You wanna feed him?"

One eager nod accompanied Derek's full-faced grin.

"Come over to this chair." Kaycee picked up the cub with one hand, while she ushered Derek to a bench on the wall. She passed Natalya the bottle, then placed the cub on its back in Derek's scrawny arms. Patiently, she instructed him on how to hold the bottle and the cat.

After a few uncoordinated attempts, Derek dropped the bottle, and the cub wriggled free. He giggled, not at all dismayed by his lack of coordination.

Kaycee offered the bottle to Natalya. "You want to try?"

Though he could see only her profile, Brandon recognized the surprised lift of her eyebrows. Her confidence cracked, replaced by the briefest glimpse of insecurity before she nodded and sat down uncertainly on the bench.

Kaycee placed the cub in the crook of Natalya's arm as she had with Derek, and helped her convince the cub to latch on to the large rubber nipple. When it did, Natalya's expression softened like an angel's. Wonder filled her gaze. Her lips lifted with unabashed adoration.

Brandon's heart skipped several dozen beats before he finally managed to calm it down enough and suck in air. Even then, he wasn't entirely certain the rhythm behind his ribs resembled anything close to normal. The fierce knot that formed in his gut certainly wasn't.

He gritted his teeth against the uncomfortable cramp. He told himself it had nothing to do with Kaycee's suggestion he was considering settling down. That all he wanted from Natalya was an unforgettable fuck, no strings attached. That she was part of his case, nothing more. But deep down in his soul, he knew the ball of lead that rolled around in the pit of his stomach didn't bode well.

Natalya rubbed her index finger beneath the cub's chin, its purr as loud as a lawnmower. Fed and satisfied, the playful cub dozed lightly, content to have her rub its belly, its chin, its rounded ears. As she watched long whiskers twitch, she thought back to the day Kate gave birth to Derek, the last time she'd held anything this close, let alone anything young enough to be considered dependent.

She'd been afraid to touch the red-skinned infant who miraculously just *existed*. Her nephew. When Erik had tucked Derek into her arms, that maternal instinct supposedly every woman owned hadn't flared. She'd felt awkward, incompetent, and definitely detached from the human being in her grasp.

Derek had been the first, and the only, baby of any kind she'd held since she and Kate lugged home two stray kittens when they were eight. While she'd always liked the cat that bonded to her, and accompanied her later to college, unlike her sister, she'd quickly outgrown the desire to dress it in doll clothes and try to convince it to stay in the stroller for a walk around the house. No, Kate had always been mommy material. Natalya, however, had never envisioned it as part of her life.

Yet now, as she cuddled the kitten, a strange, distinctly maternal, sensation tickled in her chest. And though it wasn't uncomfortable, she wasn't certain she cared for it. A ticking biological clock could become a ticking time bomb for her. At the same time, in the last few days— ever since Brandon had asked her that damnable question—she'd begun to question what she might have missed by choosing an operative's life.

She could fault him squarely for that. For this weirdness churning around inside her now. If he hadn't posed the question, if he hadn't kissed her to the point she couldn't think straight and had agreed to come here . . .

Looking up, she caught his stare. His gaze burned, strengthening that unidentifiable pull on her lungs. The sudden, ferocious need to have his mouth on hers and his hands on her body, rose fast and hard. They'd avoided almost all contact since that incredible kiss against Kate's door. Now and again, when their bodies had drifted closer, they'd hooked pinkies. Shared a few intimate smiles, and more than a few laughs at Derek's enthusiasm. But as she held Brandon's unblinking, unsettling stare, she realized the scarce contact wasn't enough. She wanted more. A lot more than she had any business considering, and likely more than he'd care to give.

As if he too shared that intense need for closeness, he moved off the wall, approaching in much the same way the cub had stalked the toy. He hunkered down in front of her, his large hand moving alongside hers in the lion's fur. Behind him, Derek and Kaycee entertained a second cub.

"Pretty cute, huh?" Brandon murmured. Their hands brushed.

"Adorable." She twined her pinkie around his.

Brandon's eyes never left hers as he lifted his hand, raising hers, and slowly slipped his fingers between hers. Taking advantage of the fact all other eyes focused on the laughing little boy and the growling cub, Brandon scooped up the lion in her arms and set it gently on the tiled floor. He leaned in close, his mouth hovering at the base of her ear. "I want you, Natalya. I don't give a damn about what you think I don't realize. I want you."

By sheer force of will, she silenced a whimper. She closed her eyes, swallowed hard.

He leaned away and pulled her to her feet before she could fully recover from the chaotic trembling of her stomach. This time, he didn't let go of her hand. His palm fit snugly against hers, his strong fingers comfortably possessive. "Derek, are you hungry? We've got time to go to Rainforest before I have to go to work."

Derek bounded to his feet. "Can we go to Sue's now?"

"You don't want to go to Rainforest?"

"No. We can go next day."

"You sure, buddy?"

"Yeah."

Brandon extended his free hand to take Derek's. "Okay. We'll go to Sue's. I have to stop at the hardware store and pick up something first though."

Natalya shot him a curious look.

"Chain. Sue's dog is a master at getting off his tie-out."

To Natalya's surprise, Derek turned his nose up at Brandon's offered hand. He passed behind them, appearing on Natalya's opposite side. "Boys hold girls' hands. Mommy says so." Though it was the first time her nephew had reached out to her, Derek fitted his tiny palm against her fingers as if he had been doing it all his life.

Oh!

He had no idea he'd just connected with his aunt, but Natalya reeled under the casual gesture. She didn't know what to do, what to say. If she should say or do anything at all.

Brandon gave her other hand a tight squeeze. "You're right, little man. Boys hold girls' hands. Tell Miss Kaycee thank you."

He peeked around Natalya and waved at Kaycee. "Thank you."

"Anytime, Derek. Come back and see us whenever you want."

"Thanks, Kaycee," Brandon called as they headed for the door. "I owe you one."

"Just send me an invitation."

Invitation? Natalya squinted at Brandon. "Invitation to what?" she asked once the door closed behind them.

Brandon shook his head, but his face told a different story. His color paled, and his gaze held just the faintest touch of . . . fear? No. Couldn't be. Must be something else. Brandon's arrogance didn't know the meaning of fear.

"Nothing," he answered a little too fast.

It was something. Something he didn't want to share. She shrugged it off. In a few days she'd be far from here. Where he went, with who, wasn't her business unless it related to Dmitri, and nothing Dmitri did involved invitations.

Outside the casino, the sun beat down, making Natalya glad she'd worn shorts. She turned her face up to the bright light and basked in the warm rays. Derek exuberantly swung her hand, half-skipping, half-walking as they made their way to Brandon's car.

"What time is it anyway?" she asked as they crossed the street.

"One thirty."

"Ugh. I need to be getting home. I need a shower, and I've got to get ready for work." She needed to check in with Kate and make sure her costume was ready. Not to mention, she needed to beat Brandon to the club, so she could talk to the props department before he had the opportunity to discover her plans.

While Derek crawled into the backseat and buckled himself in, Brandon set both hands on the car's frame, trapping Natalya in place. His eyes spoke intimate promises. "You can use mine."

"No, really, I need to get home."

"Chicken."

She squinted.

A teasing smirk twisted the corner of his mouth. *"Begawk."*

Natalya pushed at his chest, refusing to give in to the laughter that bubbled to the surface. "I'm not chicken. I have a job that's important. Remember?"

"Mm. I remember I'm your boss. I won't fire you for being late." He leaned forward and nuzzled the side of her neck with his lips. "Especially if you're in my shower."

Shivering, she pushed harder, her laughter impossible to contain.

"Brandon, c'mon, I wanna go," Derek complained.

Natalya's tormentor quirked an eyebrow and cocked his head. "Well?"

She gave up, the temptation of Brandon's hardening cock against her thigh too great. Yeah, she wanted that. Wanted him. Shower or otherwise. "Fine. But I'm not staying more than an hour."

"I'll take what I can get." Shrugging, he backed away, giving her room to climb into the car.

She slid inside, buckled her seatbelt, and plucked her cell phone out as Brandon started the car. Sergei was just going to have to give up his little afternoon rendezvous and help her out. He'd have to bring the costume Kate laid out and meet her at her condo early. No way could she ask Brandon for a ride to work.

Brandon glanced at her hand as she tapped out a text message, but he didn't comment. He dropped the car into drive and pulled out of the lot, turning north.

While they waited for the light to turn green, her phone vibrated with the message: **Got it. Go away. Busy.**

Natalya frowned. **Be nice, Sergei Moretti.**

His answer disturbed her sense of normalcy. The screen flashed with the solitary word: **Stefan**.

Light green, Brandon stepped on the gas as he bent to flip on the radio. She quickly deleted the text messages and looked up in time to see a flash of movement beyond his hunched shoulder. Barreling down the east-west street, an older, silver pickup blew through the light. Impact imminent.

"Brandon!"

Her scream snapped him upright. "Son of a bitch!"

He jammed his foot on the brakes. Natalya's seatbelt snapped tight, locking her in place. The truck roared past, clipping the Mustang's driver-side front bumper. They spun. Horns blared. Somewhere glass shattered, and a sickening *thud* echoed.

As their momentum slowed, and they skidded to a halt facing the oncoming traffic, crying broke out in the back seat. Natalya glanced over her shoulder to find Derek's attempt at buckling himself in had failed. His booster chair slid forward, tossing him into the back of Brandon's seat. Blood flowed freely from his nose.

She threw off her seatbelt and lunged over the seats. "Sweetie, it's okay." Clamping her fingers over his nose, she pinched. Solid cartilage beneath her fingertips offered relief. He hadn't broken it. Thank God.

Brandon's muffled curses overpowered Derek's tears. As best Natalya could, given her position over her headrest, she slid her other arm around Derek's shaking shoulders, offering comfort while Brandon navigated them out of the middle of the intersection to the curb.

His door opened, then slammed shut. Natalya hefted herself over the seat a little more, far enough she could push Derek's hair aside to check his head for additional injury. To her immense relief, no red marks identified bruises to come, and no further blood trickled over his face. "It's okay, buddy. You're just fine. Some stupid idiot didn't see the light turn red."

He swiped his fingers over his eyes, curbing the falling tears. An ever-so-slight nod said he understood.

"Let's see if it's stopped?"

"Okay."

Tentatively, she lifted her fingers. Stared at his nose. When nothing happened, she let out a breath she hadn't realized she'd been holding and ruffled Derek's hair the way she'd seen Brandon do countless times throughout the day. "You okay, kiddo?"

He nodded with a sniffle.

"Don't sniff. Breathe through your mouth."

Obediently he opened his mouth and took a deep breath.

Good thing little boys were resilient. Good thing too, that Kate hadn't been sitting beside her son. She'd be in hysterics. Blood had never been her strong point.

Brandon's door opened, and he slid into the seat, storm clouds on his face. He gripped the wheel with both hands, ground his teeth together, then exhaled audibly. "Are you two okay?"

"Yeah, we're fine. How's the car?"

"Banged up, but driveable. Truck bailed. No one else is involved. I'll walk in a report later."

"Okay."

Natalya slid back into her seat, intending to retrieve a Kleenex for Derek, when she noticed blood on Brandon's hand as well. She furrowed her brow and leaned over the console, her fingers investigating the back of his hand.

He turned his palm up, revealing a long gash across the meaty part of his thumb. "Headlight."

"Let me get you a Kleenex."

She reached down for her purse, only to find the contents scattered across the floorboards. Her Sig lay in plain sight. She silently swore, and hurried to shove the gun back into her purse before Brandon could notice. Tissues in hand, she straightened, passing one to Brandon.

The lift of his eyebrows said she was too late.

Twenty-four

Thirty minutes later, chain in hand, Derek bounding merrily off with three pigtailed girls, Brandon escorted Natalya into his house. His temper warred with self-disgust. He'd fucked up. Derek was his responsibility, and he'd been too preoccupied with negotiating a little alone time with Natalya to check Derek's seat belt. He could have been seriously injured. As it was, when Kate found out, she'd chew his ass.

At the same time, if that dickhead had been paying attention to the lights, Derek wouldn't have been hurt, and the Shelby's front end wouldn't look like Swiss cheese.

Then there was the matter of Natalya's gun. He hadn't said anything about it yet, not really wanting to hear the answers. He was pretty damn convinced she couldn't produce a concealed carry license—that would've shown up on her file. Right now, don't ask don't tell sounded damn good.

So did a beer.

While she wandered around his living room, investigating the sparse knickknacks on his shelves, he went to the fridge. "You want a beer?"

"Water would be great."

His hand throbbed as he reached into the fridge and grabbed a cold Corona. He glanced at the cut, disgusted. He knew better than to try to pry loose a bent fender with his bare hand, yet he'd done it anyway, losing his grip and slicing himself open on the shattered headlamp. It'd heal, but it'd hurt like a bitch for the next couple of days. Good thing he'd used his left. He used his right for everything else.

He ran the cut under the water, his annoyance increasing when the long gash refused to stop bleeding. Out of patience, and lacking the initiative to walk to his bathroom for his first aid kit, he ripped off a paper towel, jammed it against the cut, and clamped his fingers closed. With his free hand, he filled Natalya's glass. Beer between his teeth, her glass in hand, he returned to his living room where he set everything on the table and sank into the couch with a heavy sigh.

The first cold swig balmed his annoyance enough his frown smoothed. He leaned back, careful to keep his injured hand away from the cream-colored cushions and hooked his right ankle over his left knee. Natalya milled around the shelves that framed his flat-screen television, her head tipped in curious interest.

"That's quite the baseball collection." She picked up his favorite, an autographed Jose Canseco.

"It's not really anything special. There's not much money in it."

"I don't know much about baseball, but I know this name. How'd you land this one?"

A smile drifted across his face. "I was in a frat at A&M. Bunch of us went out to the Rangers stadium, drunker than skunks, on opening day. I about fell out of the stands jumping after that thing."

Her soft chuckle deepened his smile. The memory of what had happened two weeks later stirred. But it stayed still for once, lulled to sleep by the lift of Natalya's mouth. She put the ball on its tiny wooden stand and picked up the picture of his family.

"Your family?"

The canker that never healed gnawed at his heart. He nodded, seeing his sister's shining face though Natalya's back blocked his view. "Yeah. They're gone now."

This letting her into his personal life reminded him of new shoes. Comfortable at first, but the longer they were worn, they rubbed blisters. He itched to distract her. To start some conversation that would draw her attention off his things, pull her nose out of his past. He didn't talk about this crap with anyone, not even Mayer. Certainly not the women who flitted through his life.

At the same time, while she threatened to rub him raw, a certain mysterious curiosity kept him from doing what instinct directed. Would those blisters form? Or, would taking this leap come with some sort of parachute?

Along with the wondering came his mind's logical reminder that if he intended to pull her secrets forth, he must forge a bridge. So he told himself he was allowing her to get comfortable. With his things. With his space. With *him*. Quietly, he added, "They were killed when I was twenty."

Her profile revealed the slow closing of long eyelashes that touched her cheeks several seconds longer than they should have. "I'm sorry," she whispered.

"So am I." It was the first time he'd allowed the honesty. On the extremely rare occasion he mentioned the tragedy, when he did, invariably someone apologized. For too long he'd dismissed the sympathy with a flippant remark. A benign comment that made a wide circle around his guilt.

She turned around, coming to the table for her water. Her knee jostled his as she bent over to pick up her glass, jarring his hand. He jerked away with a hiss.

"Crap. I'm sorry." Natalya frowned at his makeshift bandage. "You should put a bandage on that. You're still bleeding."

"It's fine. I don't really have the energy to deal with it."

Her delicate eyebrows dove farther down her nose, and she stuffed her fists on her hips. "Well I will then. Tell me where."

"It's really not necessary. Just a scratch. I'll live."

She rolled her eyes. Turning toward his dark hall, she repeated, "Tell me where."

"Second door on the left. There's a first-aid kit under the sink in the bathroom."

The response came so naturally he didn't realize what he'd said until he heard his bedroom door creak open. Panic turned his chest into a vise. His space—he'd just sent her into his sanctuary. Shit. He jerked to the edge of the couch, prepared to intercept her and send her back into the living room. Halfway to his feet, sense shoved him back into the couch.

Chill. It's the fucking bathroom.

Pulling in deep fortifying breaths through his nose, he stared at his door, counting the never-ending seconds that it took her to find the kit and return to the hall. Thirty-eight. It took thirty-eight seconds to recover from a near-death experience.

He exhaled hard.

Natalya rummaged through the plastic case as she walked across the room. A gauze pad dangled from her mouth. Around her finger, she wore the reel of waterproof bandage tape. She carried a bottle of hydrogen peroxide—not found under his sink, but in the medicine cabinet above, he acknowledged with some discomfort—under her arm.

"Okay, gimme your hand." She held out her palm.

He obliged with a tight chuckle.

Her fingers were as gentle as rain. She dabbed a peroxide-saturated cotton pad against the torn flesh, bent closer, and inspected the cut for what he assumed was leftover glass. He watched, fascinated by the focus she gave to the menial task, enchanted by the tenderness in her touch.

How long had it been since he'd allowed someone to see to his needs? Too damn long, if the last person he remembered was his mother. He'd been a scrawny boy the last time he could recall any but his own fingers bandaging his cuts.

Brandon lifted his gaze to study her face. Her brow was smooth, her expression rapt. She chewed on her lower lip as she folded another gauze square just so and laid it over the torn flesh. Winced on his behalf when the tape pulled too tight, widening the gash before she could lift it with her nail and ease the sting.

Beautiful. Not just physical beauty, but something that came from within. That woman she kept behind a shell. This one right in front of him—his chest suddenly felt tight.

"There," she said quietly. Straightening, she closed the first aid kit. "Now you won't bleed all over your couch."

He stared at the tight hem of her shorts that accented the sharp definition of her muscular thighs. She stood less than a foot away, close enough he could smell the sweet flowery fragrance he'd come to associate with her. His gaze flicked up, resting on her narrow waist, her flat stomach. Something fierce and hungry reared in his mind, striking him with the sudden desperate need to possess her. To somehow mark her in such a way no other man would ever want to touch her.

The power of that startling sensation unsettled him. She wasn't an object he could own. No trophy he could display alongside his baseballs. Yet something about her twisted his thoughts into knots. Rationality vanished. Right alongside sensibility.

He reached out and fitted his palms on her hips. Caught by the spell of everything she was, he urged her a step closer. His thumbs pushed up the hem of her tank, exposing creamy skin and the cutest belly button he'd ever laid eyes on. Scarcely aware of his actions, Brandon leaned forward and pressed a kiss to that adorable little dimple.

Natalya gasped at the tickle of Brandon's breath. Warm, soft lips moved across her skin, following the waistband of her shorts. When he reached her side, he scattered the same slow, lingering kisses across her midriff to the opposite hip, only to return once more to center where he dipped the tip of his tongue into her belly button.

Pleasure fragmented through her body. She clamped her hands on his shoulders to keep from stumbling and closed her eyes. He was doing it again. Making her feel. Slowly stripping away her control. She floated to a daunting height, hanging precarious on some unseen ledge. The fear of falling tugged at her mind. But a deeper, wiser voice assuaged that apprehension with a promise of safety.

He traced the circumference of her belly button with his tongue, drawing pinpoints of heat to the surface of her skin. She tightened her fingers against the slow spreading warmth and reveled in the reverent way he worshipped such a benign portion of her body.

"Brandon . . . ," she exhaled.

The nip of his teeth answered. His cheek rubbed against her quivering stomach. Beneath her fingertips, his shoulders expanded as he pulled in a deep breath. His ragged exhale stirred the fine hairs on her skin.

He lifted his mouth for a moment, opening his eyes to look up at her. Their gazes locked for several stuttered heartbeats, and something passed between them Natalya couldn't define. Acceptance maybe. The unspoken acknowledgement they couldn't control what was happening between them, along with the understanding that all the desire they'd toyed with had come to one final, devastating end. No stopping it. No turning back.

His eyelashes lowered, and his lips grazed across her abdomen. She held on, trapped in place by feelings she'd never known, as he lowered the waistband of her shorts. Gradually his mouth inched lower, her clothing giving way with the unhurried tug of his hands. He bared her bit by bit, nudging aside one protective layer after another with each small sliver of skin he unveiled.

Natalya trembled so violently it was all she could do to breathe. But his hands were there to hold her up, to stop her from falling into a limp pool at his feet. Her shorts and underwear tumbled, the last bit of elastic drawn over her legs. They gathered at her ankles, confining her further. She knew she should kick them aside, should do something other than cling helplessly to Brandon's shoulders. Yet no matter how her mind instructed her to move, she couldn't function.

He spanned one large palm over her bottom, supporting her as the other hand ran down the length of her leg. Gently, he cupped her ankle and pulled it free from the gathered cotton. He lifted her leg, cradling her calf as if she was as fragile as a porcelain doll, and set her foot on the cushion. Subtle calluses scraped pleasantly over her thigh, teased the sensitive skin at her hip, and glided around to join the hand holding her up.

Knowing what came next, she gasped before his mouth ever touched her. When it did, when that searing heat nuzzled through downy curls and his tongue slipped between her damp folds, her hips bucked forward. Her fingers bit into his shoulders, and she sagged into his hands. *Oh, God . . . please . . .*

Sparks crackled through her veins.

Brandon held her on her feet effortlessly. His fingers massaged her buttocks as his tongue swirled over her swollen clitoris. He suckled at the hardened nub. Scraped it with his teeth, only to soothe the bite by suckling again. She shuddered violently. Strong thumbs pressed into her hips, guiding her pelvis forward, and his tongue delved lower to lap at her weeping opening.

She waited for words, accustomed to Dmitri's brash and vulgar vocalizations. But Brandon didn't make a sound, as if he sensed saying anything at all would dissolve the magic that engulfed them. Pleasure soaked through her limbs. It stormed down her spine, shot through her womb, and left her aching. She moved against his mouth, countering the languorous stroke of his tongue.

More. Please, Brandon, end the lies. Make me feel.

His tongue slipped inside her, and she let out a moan. Using her elevated foot for leverage, she lifted into the steady, rhythmic thrusts. Ecstasy brimmed, the agonizing in and out adding drop after drop of pleasure, slowly filling her up. He pushed in deep, sliding against her swollen tissues, his mouth hot against her overwarm flesh. One hand slid around the curve of her bottom, in between the thin crevice of her cheeks to massage the tiny hidden entrance there. A brief moment of apprehension slipped into her spine. She should be offended, had been every time Dmitri attempted to touch her there. Yet, at the same time, Brandon moved his masterful mouth to her clit and sucked the nub hard, turning apprehension into something dark and exotic. She pushed against his mouth, pressed back against the pressure of his middle finger.

"Brandon. Oh, God . . ." *What are you doing to me?*

Tearing her into pieces, that's what he was doing. Making her want so badly it had become painful, the need for release, blinding. She shifted against his mouth, aching with pleasure. When he edged his tongue back inside her, her pussy clamped around the glorious intrusion. She didn't know which way to move, which sensation to chase, the ecstasy of his tongue fucking her, or the torment of his finger easing closer, pushing barriers no one had ever breeched before.

She undulated against him, no longer able to control the motion of her body. As pleasure rose, and she struggled to remain upright, Brandon nudged the tip of his finger beyond the tight muscle, delving ever-so-slightly into her forbidden channel, and sparks burst behind her closed eyes. Natalya overflowed, her pussy pulsing around his probing tongue, her body trembling against the unexpected, astounding invasion. She screamed with the force of her release, calling his name.

Floating. Falling. Up or down . . . she didn't know. But if heaven existed on earth, Brandon had taken her there, and she never wanted to return to the world she knew. She clung to his shoulders, trembling as her hips slowed in time with the slide of his tongue. He guided her through her orgasm until he brought her safely to the ground, the landing painless, the journey divine.

As he scattered light kisses to her belly button her death grip on his shoulders relaxed. She opened her eyes to look down into his molten gaze. Something unnamable moved within her then, stilling her heart and squashing her lungs.

"You're beautiful," he whispered.

She swallowed to wet her dysfunctional throat. But before she could dismiss his praise with a laugh, he eased her into his lap and wound his arms around her waist. Despite the confines of his jeans, she felt the insistent press of his swollen cock against the flesh he had loved so thoroughly.

One hand lifted to tug her hair free from the ponytail. "Goddamn mesmerizing, Natalya." A smile touched his mouth as he ran his fingers through her hair. Shifting position, he sprawled onto his side, laying her alongside him. "When your eyes sparkle that way, they do something to me. I don't know what it is, but . . ." He shook his head with a wistful expression. Lowering his voice, he murmured, "It's powerful."

Her cheeks heated, his praise unexpected and wholly unfamiliar in her world of cruel intentions and even crueler minds.

"All I want to do is get lost in you." He dropped his mouth to the thick vein at the side of her neck, his hand sliding beneath her shirt to cup her breast. "You should wear green more often. I like it on you."

With that singular phrase, Brandon shattered Natalya's paradise. The warmth in his hand turned to ice. The comfortable pressure of his body became an unbearable weight. She edged away, unable to see cropped dark hair and captivating tawny eyes. Instead, she stared at Dmitri. Felt his soulless body cover hers.

Every damning aspect of what she was smacked into her. A liar. A manipulator. A killer. And she'd just done the unthinkable with Brandon, she'd given herself to him. Not just physically, she'd allowed that hidden portion of her soul to escape its corral with a man who was real. A man she lied to at every given opportunity and she couldn't stop. She couldn't be . . . Natalya. Not unless she wanted to stand at the edge of his grave and mourn the life she'd taken.

This couldn't continue.

"What time is it?"

His brows dipped, confusion clouding his gaze. He glanced at the wall behind her. "Three. Why?"

"I've got to go. I need to get ready for work."

Sharp and severe, his frown settled into place. But his anger reflected inward, not out through his quiet, speculative stare.

"Let me up," she insisted quietly.

"No." He dragged the word out as if considering whether he should say it at all. Then, more decisively, he repeated, "No." Dragging a knuckle across her cheek, he released his frown and his gaze searched her face. "I said something wrong. Tell me what."

Natalya forced out a laugh. "Don't be silly. That was very nice. I just need to get home and get ready for work."

His head moved side to side in minuscule fractions. "No. You were right here with me when that was incredible. Now you're gone and it's *nice*. What did I say?"

Incredible. No one had ever told her that her solo orgasm had been incredible.

She shoved down the rising pleasure. He could read her, which meant he'd already gotten too close. She turned her head aside. "Please. Take me home, Brandon."

Instead, his lips trailed down the side of her neck. Slowly. Deliberately. At the same time his hand skated over the flat of her belly, drifted lower to the damp curls between her legs. He cupped her pussy, but kept his fingers still, using his mouth alone to tease her flesh back into wakefulness.

His lips tugged at her earlobe. His tongue traced the delicate shell of her ear. "If you really want to go, I will. But I don't think you do." To prove his point he pressed his middle finger against her wet opening and swirled a lazy circle. Her hips automatically lifted into his hand. A soft sigh escaped her lips as all thoughts of Dmitri faded beneath Brandon's gentle touch.

"Do you?" he asked, his voice like gravel against her skin.

No. But she couldn't bring herself to speak. Could barely form the thought. Fire slid back into her veins, and she rotated her hips, silently begging him to push inside her and quell the growing ache.

She nearly whimpered when he withdrew both his hand and his body, leaning back to grasp the hem of her shirt. As he pushed it up her body, Natalya leaned forward, allowing him to remove the last of her clothes. When both her shirt and bra lay on the floor, Brandon gathered her breasts in his hands and placed a chaste kiss on each pert nipple. "Powerful things, sweetheart. I want to fuck you so badly it hurts."

For once, the choice of words didn't send revulsion tripping down her spine. Instead, his raw honesty lit her up like a match. She reached for him, suddenly desperately hungry for all the pleasure Brandon could create.

His chuckle lighted tender warmth in his eyes. "Not so fast this time, sweetheart. We're gonna take it nice and slow, and I get to drive."

Drive her into oblivion? Who was she to object? Obediently she fell back into the cushions, yielding to the questing touch of Brandon's fingertips as he traced her curves. From shoulder to ankles, he explored her flesh, his mouth following the caress of his hands. The touch was so feather-soft she squirmed beneath him, want intensifying into a burning need. "Brandon. Please."

Brandon closed his eyes to the pleading quality of Natalya's voice. If she begged again like that, no matter how much he liked the sound of it, he'd blow. He couldn't remember a time where the mere act of touching a woman had him so on edge. But the more he explored Natalya's body, acquainting himself with all her sensitive spots, the more he struggled to chain his own mounting desire.

He bent over her again, sliding his hands up her long, lithe legs, spreading her thighs until her wet pussy opened to him. He loved the taste of her. The musky flavor that held a hint of something he couldn't define but couldn't get enough of. When she'd come against his tongue he'd lapped as if he'd been denied water.

Drawn to that dewy paradise, he slid his tongue through her folds, suckled at her swollen clitoris. She bucked into him, nearly dislodging his mouth, and beneath his tongue, her flavor erupted. His cock throbbed in answer, equally hungry for the damp heat.

Fuck. He was coming undone already. No way could he bring her back to orgasm without spilling himself right along with her. Forcing desire down, he edged his tongue inside her opening, lapped greedily, then rocked back on his heels and eased from the couch. Her gaze burned into him as he shucked his clothes, devoured his body when he stood before her completely bare. When those green eyes dropped to his cock, and he witnessed the appreciation in her paralyzing stare, his throat cinched closed. He'd kept himself in shape, but no one had ever looked at him that way. *No one.*

"Come here," she whispered, her hand extended.

The quiet request punched through his momentary paralysis, and he slipped his palm into hers, allowing her to draw him back to the couch. He knelt between her legs, bent over and captured her in a heated kiss. Her tongue tangled with his, wild and untamed, until breathing became impossible and he had to tear his mouth away to gasp in much-needed air. The pressure in his balls demanded satisfaction, and Brandon could no longer fight his raging desire. He needed this. Needed the firm grip of her pussy, the hot, wet depths to glove him tight.

Bracing his weight on his elbow, he leaned over her, pulled open his coffee table drawer, and fished out a condom. A smile touched her mouth as he ripped open the packet with his teeth. "May I?"

He nearly choked at the thought of her wicked fingers coming anywhere near his cock. Shaking his head, he chuckled. "If you touch me, it's all over."

She nodded, but the lift of her hips, the slow gyration she made beneath him as he rolled the condom on, teased. Her wet flesh met his throbbing cock, and even through the thin barrier between their skin, he felt her searing heat. Brandon sucked in a sharp breath. Dodged her hands as she reached to guide his cock inside her.

Her eagerness broke him. Never had sex been so absolutely necessary. So imperative. Nor had it been so mandatory that he watch himself slide inside her flesh. But it was, and he gripped her hips, lifting her body until the head of his cock aligned with her slick opening. Her hands locked onto his forearms, nails biting into his skin. Holding his own breath against the cataclysmic pleasure, Brandon eased the tip of him inside her tight, wet heat.

Ecstasy slammed into him. She gripped him hard, her pussy clamping around his rigid length, nudging him closer into headless abandon. So much for taking his time and drawing this out. No way could he wait.

With one prolonged thrust, he slid deep inside her. He watched as her flesh ate him up, as his cock speared into her pussy. Heaven. Goddamn paradise.

Natalya's back came off the couch, her cry as sharp as glass. His cock pulsed against the tightening of her tissues, and it took every bit of self-restraint he possessed to fight down release. He breathed through his nose, counted the hash-marks between the numerals on his wall-hanging clock.

Then, Natalya moved beneath him, bending her knee, shifting so he slid in a hairsbreadth deeper. *Christ!* She was tight. Blisteringly hot.

And he was done for. He pulled back, drawing out the pleasure of sliding through her pussy, then plunged in hard. Her arms laced behind his neck, her legs wrapped around his waist. Her pleas, her muted cries urged him on. The rapture in her expression tore him apart at the seams, and Brandon wasn't sure he'd ever come all the way together again. He thrust again, and she opened her eyes. Fathomless depths of jade bared her soul. He couldn't look away. Lost in that mesmerizing stare, he felt her so deeply he'd swear they'd become one. He knew then. Something had cracked inside him. A permanent rend.

He blocked the unsettling discovery and increased their tempo. Harder, faster, he fucked her until he silenced the yearnings he couldn't name.

"Brandon!"

As his name tore from her lips, her nails scored into his shoulders. She arched her back, lifting into his driving body, and a throaty moan possessed her. Around his cock, her flesh gripped tight. He gave in to ecstasy, feeling his climax rip through his veins. He drove inside her once more, his thoughts a haze of blissful nothingness as he came.

Natalya's legs relaxed around his waist. She slid her hands along his spine, gentle pressure urging Brandon's body down against her sweat-slickened skin. He tumbled into her embrace, his heart beating a frantic rhythm as he dusted kisses across her shoulder. "So beautiful. You are so beautiful when you come, sweetheart."

A faint smile drifted over her lips as she murmured, "So are you."

Twenty-five

Brandon opened his eyes to the late-afternoon sunlight. He blinked, momentarily disoriented. His living room . . . His couch . . .

The warm body sleeping in the crook of his arm brought the memories back in a rush. *Natalya*. She'd drifted off while he tried to make sense of what had happened to him in her arms. He must have fallen asleep as well. Huh. That was a first. Not the nap, but that he'd napped with company. *Feminine* company. In broad daylight as opposed to the middle of the night.

Lying motionless, he took inventory of all the places they touched. Ankles twined. Legs tangled, her knee tucked securely between his. Her hip fit into his groin, the gentle curve of her waist molded against his belly. Soft breasts rose and fell beneath his arm as she breathed, and her hair tickled the side of his neck.

Pleasantly.

Yeah. She felt good. He could relax like this for a long time. Maybe wake her up with his mouth, coax her back to that incredible place where all he could think of was being inside her. But as the idea surfaced, another voice in his head balked at the notion. Why disturb her when this was so satisfying? Maybe he'd just close his eyes a little longer . . .

He let his eyelashes fall. *Yeah.*

The silence settled around him, tugging him back into the contented void of sleep. They'd be late to work, but not by much. His internal clock would have him up at five. Fifteen, twenty minutes max. Still plenty of time to navigate their mutual responsibilities.

A branch scraping against the side of his house opened his eyes once more, and he became aware of why he'd awakened in the first place. The short hairs at the nape of his neck lifted, silent triggers to something out of place. He listened for noises above the hum of his air conditioner.

No sounds, but something. Something out of the ordinary.

The overwhelming feeling they were being watched crawled down his spine. Logic argued against the possibility—his house was in a good neighborhood, a sign in the front yard broadcasted his security system. No one would peep around his windows in the middle of the day. No one had reason.

His wariness must be some kind of reaction to the memories Natalya stirred. Old demons rising to the surface to remind him he was a wanted man.

He closed his eyes again, and a car door slammed beyond his front window. Too close for comfort. He lifted to an elbow, sighting the room for where he'd laid his gun when he'd come home this morning. Spying it behind the planter on the kitchen counter, he disentangled his leg and lifted it over Natalya's.

When he worked his arm from beneath her head, she rolled onto her side, snuggling close to him. One hand clutched reflexively at his chest. A misplaced smile drifted to his lips. He liked that. He suspected if she knew she'd just silently instructed him to stay put, she'd run like the wind. But the primitive part of his brain saw a woman needing protection and was eager to fulfill her subconscious request.

Toast. Officially, he was toast.

An engine roared to life in his driveway, reminding him why he'd lifted to his elbow. He vaulted over Natalya's body and stumbled around the coffee table to the window. Leaning a shoulder into the curtains, he peered through the mini blinds, catching the briefest glimpse of a silver sedan as it sped down his street. License plate obscured.

Son of a bitch! Someone *had* been here. But why? Had the right people finally gotten word of his not-so-subtle invitations for his father's friends to come and find him? He'd spent the better part of the last year dropping hints, making remarks in circles he felt certain would relay the news back to Kansas City and the silent, sleeping mob. Aaron and he had almost gotten into a fistfight when Aaron learned Brandon had openly revealed his parentage.

Had his father finally come to finish what he screwed up the first time?

Brandon moved across the room, habitually seeking out his gun. He checked the magazine, the chamber, then double-checked the safety and set it back down. This was exactly why he didn't take naps on his couch with beautiful women who filled his brain with ridiculous notions that snuggling could be better than sex.

One way or another, she'd suffer if he let her inside. She'd either find disappointment when she learned he'd brought about his family's murder, or she'd find herself staring down the barrel of a loaded gun, bait to draw him out.

If she were lucky, she'd disintegrate in an explosion and she wouldn't feel pain. Or fear. But she'd pay the price for his mistakes.

He turned back to the couch wanting nothing more than to ease back down between the cushions and her body and return to the contentment he'd known minutes ago.

Shaking off the notion, he focused on what he understood—desire and the intense way she responded to him. God, he'd said some foolish things. Pathetic remarks that he vaguely realized he should keep to himself, but his damn tongue refused to stop. *Get lost in you . . .* Brandon softly snorted. Right. So much for letting his dick think for him.

He glanced at the clock, observing it was ten minutes after four. She'd wanted to be home by now. He could almost guarantee when she woke up, no matter how sated she'd been when they fell asleep, she wouldn't be pleased. Better get it over with. Take her home, ask about the gun like he should have an hour ago, and get to work himself. If they left now, he could still get back here in time to deliver Opie's new chain. Sue's girls would be ecstatic. With the heavy-duty links he'd bought, Opie could play with them in the backyard, and they'd never again worry about him breaking free.

And he'd never again have to chase the overzealous elephant down.

Yeah. Wake her up before he could fully remember the way she'd tasted against his tongue.

He went to the couch, bending over to give her shoulder a shake. "Hey, you. It's time to get up. You're going to be late for work."

Her eyes snapped open. Unmoving, she stared at the buttons on the cushions. "What?"

"It's after four. We fell asleep."

Like a rocket, she shot off the couch and to her feet. "You're kidding! After four? Oh, God, I don't have time to get ready." She grabbed her underwear and hastily stuffed a leg inside. "Damn it!"

"You've got plenty of time. The girls aren't there this early."

"Jill is." She tugged on her shorts.

"Well that's because—" He stopped himself seconds away from announcing to the current object of his desire that he'd slept with Jill. Not a good move. Jill possessed enough jealousy for both women.

"Because what?"

"Because Jill's an overachiever."

Natalya lifted an eyebrow. "There's not much to overachieve with stripping."

It sounded lame to his ears too, but he clung to the excuse, not knowing what else to say. "She wants Kate's slot."

"Funny." Natalya shrugged into her shirt and bra, picked up her hair tie, and hastily pulled her long auburn lengths back. "I'd swear she wants my job."

True. But not the job Natalya referenced. More like the one she'd just assumed—ardent lover who came to life in his hands and whispered his name when he put his mouth on her flesh.

Natalya crossed her arms at the door and threw him an impatient look. "Well? Are we leaving? You might as well take me straight to Fantasia. I'll grab a shower there."

Perfect! All he needed to do to make today the day straight from hell was deliver Natalya to the club, in broad daylight, announcing to the entire world—and Jill—he'd spent the day with her. Damned ideal.

Still, he could hardly insist Natalya find her own way to work. Grinding his teeth together, he yanked on his clothes, palmed his keys, and strode outside. His car's crumpled front fender only added to his mounting agitation. Smashed car, peeping tom, jealous ex—life just didn't get any better than this.

He let Natalya inside, then rounded the trunk to climb behind the wheel. He needed to get a grip. Once again, he'd lost an entire day. Where he could have used the five or six hours of her company to dig for information, he'd wasted it on trivial pursuits.

No, that wasn't entirely right. He hadn't wasted it. He'd been trying to draw her out. It hadn't worked. She knew more about him than he could claim to know about her. Still, they'd become closer. Physically, if nothing else.

Patience.

He took a deep breath and started the car. *Take your time. Draw her out.*

And ask about the damn gun. He'd seen the stamped 226 on the grip, branding it as a Sig Sauer—no amateur's gun. She had to know how to shoot to use that beauty.

Backing out of his driveway, he deliberately avoided looking at Natalya. "You wanna tell me about that gun?"

From the corner of his eye, he saw her go still. But she recovered with a quick shrug as he started down the street. "Just a gun. Self-defense. You carry one at the club."

"What's the model?"

For a moment, she chewed on her bottom lip. Then, reclining into her seat, she casually answered, "Tactical operations. I thought it was pretty."

Brandon choked on surprise. Damn pretty. It even sported a ta-clight and reflex site—nothing that came straight out of the box. Professional customizations.

"You thought it was pretty," he repeated. "You realize that's no toy, right?"

"It's not?" She lifted her eyebrows in false, wide-eyed innocence.

"So you can shoot it accurately?"

Again, she shrugged. "Enough. If someone's coming at me, it'll do the trick."

He didn't need psychic abilities to know she wasn't telling him the full truth. For a woman to carry a firearm like that in her purse, she knew more than "enough" about what she had in her possession. No amateur carried around a customized Sig 226 Tactical Operations because it was pretty.

So why did she have a top-of-the line, Navy Seal's pistol in her purse?

The answer tugged at the back of his mind. *Protection.* As in the witness kind. She feared someone enough to seriously learn how to defend herself. But still . . . something didn't ring quite right. She could have chosen a dozen different types of semi-automatic pistols that would fulfill her needs. The average buyer with the same casual flippancy she showed wouldn't know enough to choose that particular gun.

His hackles rose.

He'd bet his Shelby if he looked in her eyes right now those shutters would be firmly locked in place. Another guise. Another block to prevent him from seeing who she really was.

Who the hell was she hiding from?

Fantasia rose before them, forbidding him the opportunity to dig deeper. He pulled into the lot and dropped the Shelby into park. "We're here." And there sat Jill's car, right next to the door, parked alongside Natalya's. She'd know Natalya hadn't come back for hers last night.

He groaned inwardly as another truth hit him. She also hadn't walked to work as she'd claimed the night before. Damn the lies.

"Well, I'll see you after a bit." She flung open the door, setting one foot onto the asphalt.

"Wait."

Again the wide-eyed innocent look as if the entire afternoon together had been insignificant. Damn it, she'd let him in. Why insist on keeping him out now?

His hand snaked across the center console to wrap around her wrist. Against his better judgment, he hauled her back inside the car and firmly planted his lips on hers. He'd force his way inside that protective shell of hers if he must. He was done with the game of back and forth.

Prepared to fight for what he desired, her instantaneous surrender surprised him. Her mouth moved across his, soft and pliant, lacking all traces of her deliberate cool reserve. Slender fingers lifted to his cheek, resting there as her tongue greedily tangled with his.

Pleasure vibrated in his chest, the kiss transforming from languorous and thorough to hungry and needy. He tangled his fingers in her hair, angling her head so he could taste her more deeply. Darkly sexy, her rich feminine flavor soaked into his senses, and his body responded like a whip. His heart pumped hard. His cock filled.

Before desire could take command of his body and subject him to an agonized state, he abruptly terminated the kiss. With one chaste brush of his lips against her cheek, he settled back into his seat. "I'll see you in a bit."

"Yeah," she whispered. She gave him a long look, full of meaning he couldn't decipher, then slid from the car.

Brandon watched the gentle sway of her hips as she walked to the door. Smiled at the way she touched her fingertips to her swollen lips. He'd caught her off guard, but he'd succeeded. For one fleeting moment, he'd made contact with the woman she kept hidden.

The door closed, blocking her from his sight. Dimly, it occurred to him he'd just kissed Natalya in public, something he never did. But he pushed the thought aside before it could breach his full awareness. He pulled out of the lot, struck by a nonsensical urge to do something else he'd never done for any woman.

Turning left, he fell into pursuit for a gift. He told himself it was all part of the game. Spoil her a little. Crack her resolve. Draw her in and learn her secrets. After all, it was just a little money spent on something trivial. That his pulse kicked up a notch had absolutely nothing to do with the absurd notion of keeping her around.

Twenty-six

M istake.

Natalya rifled through the papers on her desk, intent on finding her keys. The whole damn afternoon had been one big mistake. If she'd stood her ground and refused to see the lions, none of this would have happened. She wouldn't have ended up naked in Brandon's living room, wouldn't have fucked him until she was delirious, wouldn't have fallen asleep, and wouldn't have kissed him outside Fantasia. Dmitri's Fantasia. Where God only knew who might have witnessed them.

She scooped up a handful of junk and dumped it in the trashcan. Just seeing the clutter reminded her of the way her breasts had crinkled the papers as Brandon slammed into her from behind. The way she'd willingly submitted . . . the confounding power he had over her. He treated her like a woman, and by God, she liked it—but she absolutely didn't care for the realization.

Damn it, where the hell were her keys? Annoyed with the debris she'd inherited, she swiped the full surface contents of her desk into the trash. She didn't need the litter. It only added to the chaotic state of her office and stoked her temper. Disorganization made her twitchy.

Just like Brandon.

What was it about that man that turned her common sense to mush?

She yanked open the narrow center drawer and dug through an ocean of pens, safety-pins, pasties, tampons, Little Debbie chocolate cakes, and more scribbled notes on torn scraps of paper. Everything she could want to survive a full week of living in her office, but no keys. She slammed the drawer shut, rattling a plastic cup full of more pens.

Planting her hands on her hips, she surveyed her office and walked through the last time she'd driven her car. She'd come straight here, sat down, and navigated Becca's crisis. Her gaze pulled to the chair where the hysterical dancer had sat. The mountain of piled bikini tops and other assorted costume parts looked promising.

She attacked it with a vengeance, tossing article after article of clothing over her shoulder onto the floor in front of the door.

"Missing something?" Sergei's low voice rumbled with amusement.

Natalya turned to find her partner lounging on the doorframe, humor turning up one corner of his mouth. She threw up her hands in exasperation. "I can't find my damn keys. They've got to be around here somewhere."

"I'm sure they'll turn up. You better check these over and make sure I brought what you wanted. I've got to hit the floor." He extended his arm, offering the plastic bag that dangled off his index finger.

Her spirits lifted at the sight of her costume, keys temporarily forgotten. She snatched the bag, and opening it, rummaged quickly through. Shoes, bikini top and bottom, body glitter . . . Perfect. "Looks good." She set the bag in her chair, then folded her arms over her chest, pinning Sergei with a hard look. "I think you need to do some explaining."

He gave her a shake of his head. "Not here. Not until we've accomplished what we came to Vegas for."

Natalya's gaze narrowed. "You're going to leave without saying anything?"

"I haven't decided yet."

That hardly seemed fair. Brandon should know his brother lived. Then again, she had her own fair share of secrets she held from Brandon, and she hadn't decided whether to tell him before she moved on to her next assignment, or whether to keep him in the dark. She couldn't very well lecture Sergei on the ethics of lying.

Kate didn't give her opportunity, anyway. She breezed past Sergei into Natalya's room, panting. "Oh, good." She sucked in a short breath. "He's not back here." Sagging, she leaned on the edge of the desk. "When I didn't see him in the front of the house, I thought for sure he'd be with you."

Natalya rolled her eyes as she turned around to pick through the rest of the clothes on the chair. "Just because I went to see the lions with him and Derek doesn't mean we're attached at the hip." Having reached the bottom of the clothing stack and finding nothing, she scooped the clothes off the floor and piled them all back on the metal seat. "Did either of you see Harvey on your way in? I've got to talk to him about props."

"I'm right here. Just finished hauling up Sapphire's trunks. Whatcha need?"

Peeking around Sergei's shoulder, Natalya spied the shorter, stick-thin man in the hall. He wrinkled a freckled nose and shoved thick black glasses up his nose.

Sergei twisted into the hall. "I gotta get out front. Talk to you both later."

"Come in, Harvey," Natalya beckoned with a wag of her hand. "Shut the door."

He did as requested, the constant fidgeting of his hands indicating discomfort. While his gaze flicked between Natalya's and his untied combat boots, he avoided eye contact with Kate at all costs.

"Hey, Harv," Kate greeted as she took Natalya's chair.

The man's face turned three shades of red, gradually increasing in depth until he glowed like he'd spent three weeks under the desert sun. "H-H-Hi, Kate." He shuffled his feet.

Natalya chuckled to herself. A crush had never been more obvious.

Poor kid. He couldn't be much older than twenty-one, and she'd lay odds on the fact he didn't have the first clue what to do with a woman. Certainly not Kate, Fantasia's gem.

"I need to talk about an act with you."

He snapped to attention, his back straighter, his expression all business. "Is there a problem? I know Ben's new, and he's screwed up a couple things, but I think we've covered pretty smoothly."

"No, it's not about Ben. You're crew's doing a good job. It's a new act for tonight."

"Oh, whose?"

A slow smile crept over Natalya's face. "Mine."

An hour later, considerably later for work than he'd been in a good two years, Brandon sat in Fantasia's parking lot and stared at the one-eyed reflection of his Mustang's front end. The accident still pissed him off. But playing the Good Samaritan for his neighbor, even if securing Opie's chain had delayed him, eased the burn of his damaged car. One headlight also gave him good reason to ask Natalya for a lift home. If she agreed, knowing he'd have time with her later would give him the ability to focus on the case while he worked tonight.

He stared at the door, loathing the idea of what came next. Most prominently, Jill. If she witnessed that earlier kiss, she'd be in viper form. He really needed to sit the woman down and spell it out in black-and-white lettering again. Yet, he couldn't bring himself to stomach the short time alone with her that conversation required.

Hell, he wasn't entirely certain the talk would do any good. He'd already told her as plainly as he could they were done. There hadn't even been a *they* to be done. Just a couple of nights—which he'd also gone into with his cards face-up on the table.

His gaze dropped to the small green bag on his passenger seat. Tufts of a chocolate mane poked through the plastic handles, and he smiled. He'd wanted to give Natalya something significant. Something worthy of her natural class and elegance. Jewelry, however, implied a hell of a lot more than he wanted to say.

Clothes were also too personal, and he didn't want to offend her by accidentally picking out the wrong size. Candy—way too impersonal. He'd been seconds away from giving up altogether when he'd walked past the MGM Grand's gift store and spied the stuffed lion. Impulse handled the rest.

He grabbed for the bag, feeling more than a little foolish. What if she laughed?

Why did he care?

As his fingers looped through the plastic, something metallic on the floorboard glinted in the light of Fantasia's neon sign. He bent over to inspect the object peeking out from under his passenger seat. A phone. Natalya's phone.

Sitting slowly upright, he ran his thumb across the darkened face. The touch screen lit up, date and time stamped against a dark blue background. Beneath, where his phone displayed the factory-issued welcome greeting, newsprint Russian crawled across the screen. The tiny words he couldn't decipher brought the mystery of Natalya front and center.

He knew so little about her. The file gave him nothing. Their conversations even less. The only hard fact he knew came from Sergei, who swore they had no deeper involvement, and even with that, Brandon had to rely on a stranger's words.

His thumb accidentally brushed the screen again, changing the display to a menu of icons, all labeled in Russian. He stared at the picture of a sealed envelope. What if she, like the rest of his teammates, kept her life in this little gadget? He'd never become that dependent on technology, but Aaron was constantly plugging some little tidbit into his phone. A hot girl's number, a quick text to someone on the team, video games on the web—Aaron couldn't function without his phone.

What if Natalya's secrets were crammed inside this little rectangular box?

The detective inside him refused to let go of the possibility. What if she had something inside this electronic toy that helped with the case?

He punched the envelope button. The screen flashed. A little triangle in the middle slowly rotated 360 degrees as the page loaded. When it stopped, a text box prompted him to input something. Likely a password. He squinted at the background, recognizing the generic layout of an e-mail system.

Not text messages. He pressed the back arrow until the menu screen flashed once more. This time he touched an icon that resembled a torn-off piece of notebook paper. Damn it. He couldn't read the three little folders that flashed into view.

Frustrated, he punched each one, one after another, all taking him to blank screens. Brandon muttered under his breath and scrolled back to the menu page. He piddled with several other buttons, landing on similarly useless pages of white space and title bars he couldn't decipher.

He should have known better. For a woman who took such pains to keep things out of her expression, she wouldn't carry her life in something anyone could get their hands on. Just like he was doing now, too much risk came in the chance someone might pry.

Giving luck one last shot, he tapped the icon bearing a silhouetted head.

A list of names flashed on the screen, along with two smaller icons, both arrows, one pointing left, the other pointing right.

Incoming. Outgoing.

Sweet!

Triumph spread through his veins. Maybe he wasn't such a technological idiot after all. He dragged the scrollbar down, exposing her address book. To his dismay, however, only six names resided, all of them Russian. Sergei, Dmitri, Alexei, Vladimir, Ivan, and Petyr. No Kate. Odd.

He ignored the uncomfortable twist in his gut that came with the acknowledgement all six names belonged to men and tapped the incoming call icon. A quick scroll through the list showed Sergei had phoned once in the last week, and Dmitri, whoever he was, daily for the last four days, always at the same five o'clock time. Except today, when he'd phoned shortly before eight this morning.

Brandon's mind ran through the numbers, calculating what time it had been when a phone call interrupted his thorough enjoyment of Natalya's arousal in his office. The knot in his stomach wound down tighter as his memory supplied the intimate tone of her voice.

Another recollection slammed into his head. She'd said her parents had phoned. According to her paperwork, she still bore her adoptive parents' name. But the last names here didn't come close to Trubachev.

Lie.

The word surfaced swiftly. It sounded vile, and with it came a bitter taste. She wasn't just hiding information from him, or beating around the bush as she had with her gun, never saying anything that cemented her to something she couldn't explain. She'd flat out looked him in the eye and lied.

Why, damn it?

You know why. How many times did you do the same thing in college?

Closing his eyes, he gripped the phone more tightly. When his family had interrupted him, he'd lied to his friends, claiming someone else phoned to keep them out of the limelight. When Stefan had repeatedly asked to visit A&M, Brandon had lied through his teeth to create reasons why his little brother should stay home where it was safe—studying, dates, anything he could think of.

He'd lied left and right to protect his family and to protect himself. It hadn't been until after his family's murder that he'd started to tell the truth to those he was closest to. By then, he'd lost every reason to keep the secrets, and like now, he no longer cared if his father's thugs tracked him down. He welcomed discovery.

Still, Natalya's lies dampened his budding good spirits. He'd put himself out there, even if unwittingly, and in exchange, she threw up barriers every step of the way. Hell, he'd even been foolish enough to believe the kiss they'd parted with would keep those damn shutters cracked.

He frowned at the stuffed lion, his earlier enthusiasm now flat. If he were smart, he'd give the toy to Derek, someone who'd honestly appreciate the gift. He wouldn't feel so foolish about buying a grown woman a stuffed animal either.

Sighing, he closed his hand around the sack. Fuck it. When it came to her, he hadn't done a sensible thing yet. He'd bought it for her, not Derek. He'd leave it on her desk when she stepped out of her office, then he wouldn't have to be present to witness her reaction.

Later tonight, when she took him home, he'd discover the truth about whether she genuinely appreciated the toy or not. He knew one way, and one way only, to open those damn shutters. If he died trying, he'd pry them open wide. Then he'd convince her that whatever she feared, whatever kept her running, she could trust with him.

Thank God he'd gone with his instinct to refuse to let her dance. He might not be able to offer her much protection until he knew her full situation, but he could keep the asshole who'd locked her into an emotional prison from discovering her onstage. He'd ask later—if she needed the money that came with stripping, he'd give her a raise. Not to mention, the less anyone knew about her, the less apt his own ghosts could harm her.

Nothing would happen on his watch that would put her in greater jeopardy, and as far as he was concerned, his watch encompassed twenty-four, out of twenty-four hours in the day. He'd already exposed her to too much. Duty demanded he do everything he could to negate those risks. He damn sure couldn't guarantee her safety, or gain her trust, by staying clear of her. Distance left too much room for someone to inflict damage. He'd let down his guard with Rachel. Took her training for granted and left her wide open for attack. He'd failed his family by staying away.

Not this time.

Grimacing, Brandon shoved Natalya's phone into his pocket and exited the car. Protecting her had just become a close second to solving his case. This time, he wouldn't fuck it up.

Twenty-seven

Under the guise of refilling Kate's second, and final, allotted drink for the night, Natalya hurried through the dancers' lounge, empty glass in one hand. With Kate taking the stage in twenty minutes, and another ten for the props guys to overhaul the stage, time had come for Sergei to implement whatever diversion he'd concocted. Although she began to doubt the necessity of her ploy. Gossip put Brandon at the club over four hours ago, and he'd not made an appearance backstage. Maybe he'd stay away.

She shook her head as she reached for the door. Better safe than sorry. One screw up here tonight, one tiny assumption that backfired, and she'd never find an opportunity again. Brandon would lock her in his office if he got wind of her plan to take the stage. She and Kate had worked too hard coordinating music, planning a brief script, and coaching Harvey, to ruin everything.

A firm push sent the door swinging outward. False smile in place to cover up the nervous quiver in her belly, Natalya entered the dark, smoky main house. She glanced at the stage, looked to the bar. Where had Aaron stuffed Sergei?

"Hey, you."

The warm wash of air against the base of her ear accompanied a voice she'd begun to know too well. Rich and husky, full of assertive masculine confidence, Brandon's low murmur kick-started her heart. That sound was all it took to filter arousal through her veins. God, what was wrong with her? She couldn't get enough of this potent man.

She turned as his strong fingers closed around her bent elbow. He inclined his head toward his closed office door. "Got a second?"

Natalya glanced up at Brandon, her brows drawn into a tight line. Thirty minutes—she didn't have time to spend a single one chatting with him. "Is something wrong?"

His slow, sensual smile amped up the intolerable racket behind her ribs. "Just wanted to say hello, beautiful."

Oh, Lord, the endearment stirred memories of the fantastic way he fit inside her. She swallowed, knowing she should refuse, unable to stop from nodding. "I've got a minute."

He steered her through the crowd, his grip on her arm firm yet comfortably familiar. "Sorry I've been tied up most of the night."

She managed to loosen her tight throat. "That's okay. The girls have kept me busy." More aptly, his absence backstage gave her time to step through her routine. An act she now had twenty-nine minutes to prepare for. She looked over his shoulder, scouring the room for Sergei's unruly dark hair. Instead, she found Jill not more than five feet away, rooted in place as if she'd stopped mid-trajectory. Narrowed eyes glinted with sheer malice.

Natalya glanced back at Brandon. "Ms. Overachiever is throwing daggers at the back of your head. Any particular reason why?"

His smile vanished. With a mutter, he released Natalya's arm and shoved his fingers through his short hair. "Just a disagreement on job description."

Uh-huh. Brandon could dance around the subject all he wanted— Jill wanted *him*. Natalya couldn't help but grin at his obvious attempt to keep the truth disguised. "Let me guess, she wants benefits."

The instantaneous widening of Brandon's eyes turned educated guess into solid proof. Natalya laughed, the surprise on his face priceless.

"Yeah, well . . ." He shifted his weight and opened his office door, gesturing for her to enter. When she did, he shut the barrier, the snick of the lock ominous and, damn it, exciting. Desire hit her like a fist to the gut, making her forget everything except how incredibly hot he looked in dress pants and a tailored shirt.

She cleared her throat, uncomfortable with her body's inability to behave. "I just have a few minutes."

He closed the distance between them, his arms winding around her waist, his mouth nuzzling at her neck. "I think we can make do with a few minutes." His voice had assumed a husky tone, and he palmed her breast, squeezing as he rolled her nipple beneath his thumb. "Sit on the desk."

This was insanity at its finest. But God help her, she couldn't say no. Her body was already humming, the promise of what came next an aphrodisiac she couldn't resist. Natalya perched on the edge of Brandon's desk. As he stepped between her thighs, he tugged her tank top over her head and dropped it on the floor. Those large, fantastic hands of his slipped beneath the sheer fabric and cupped her breasts. Talented fingers knew just how to squeeze to elicit enough pleasure-pain that desire arced through her body, filling her with the sudden need to touch him as he touched her.

She yanked at his shirttail, pulling it free from his pants, and slid her hands over the corrugated muscle beneath.

"Damn, I love it when you touch me," he murmured against her lips. His kiss branded her, the wild tangle of his tongue as addictive as the rest of him. She scooted closer to the edge of the desk and wrapped her legs around his waist, yearning for the feel of his cock aligning with her softness.

Lifting her hips to stroke that hard ridge, she smiled. "I'm pretty fond of your hands on me too."

He grunted softly. Seduction was over, replaced by ferocious, mutual need. Brandon hauled her off the desk and eased her shorts and panties down her legs. When they caught on her heel, she kicked them aside. His mouth kept her busy, searing a path of ecstasy down her throat, across the swell of her breasts, and his fingers worked magic between her legs. She let out a groan and reached for his belt.

Natalya couldn't get him undressed fast enough to satisfy the deep hunger that awakened as he flicked his thumb over her clitoris. The jangle of his belt as his pants dropped to his knees clanged over the music that drifted through the locked door. She ran her hands around his waist, dipped her fingers into his firm buttocks, and urged him closer.

He hesitated only long enough to grab a condom from his desk drawer and slide it on. Then Brandon fastened his hands on her hips, lifted her onto the desk again, and holding her in place, edged past her damp folds to slide easily into her slick sheath. His chest expanded as he dragged in a deep breath. Eyes flashing with dark intensity, he held her gaze. "You feel so fucking good. That's it beautiful, squeeze me tight." His fingers bit into her hips and he inhaled sharply. "*Damn*. Just like that."

Natalya couldn't have controlled her reaction if she wanted to—her body moved of its own accord, her vaginal walls clamping around the thick intrusion, needing to feel him deeper. Needing the slide of his flesh against hers. "Tell me you want me." She didn't know why, but it was suddenly imperative Brandon say the words.

"God, yes," he ground out roughly. "I want you. Like this. Every time I turn around I think of it. Of how I can't get enough of you."

"I do too," she murmured, awestruck.

"Close your eyes," he whispered. "Feel, sweetheart. Feel the bliss."

Natalya leaned on her hands and let her head fall back. She lifted her hips higher, taking him deeper. But his firm hold on her forbid her to do much more. He held her in place, pistoning in and out of her body like a well-oiled machine. The sound of their slapping skin blended with his soft grunts and her even softer moans. Passion funneled through them, ebbing off him, into her, then out of her and into him until they knew nothing but the dance, the pleasant, thought-stealing friction.

Ecstasy slammed into Natalya, carrying her to that strange, un-identifiable place Brandon created. The haven where feeling ruled, and for one brief moment in time she was nothing but a simple woman being loved by a powerful man. She arced forward, desperate to ground herself against Brandon's solid body. He guided her legs around his waist, crushed her against his chest, and pumped once more. His groan filled her ears as his cock filled her body. Deep inside, she felt him pulse, felt the hot wash of his seed beneath the condom barrier.

Gently, Brandon lowered her to the desk and eased himself from within her sensitive tissues. His gaze flicked to hers, darker and more intense than it had been before passion claimed them. Yet he remained silent, one corner of his mouth upturned with a touch of arrogance as he tied the condom off and dropped it in the trash.

He brushed a kiss against her cheek and tucked a stray lock of her hair behind her ear. "Beautiful," he whispered. "I could do that all night long." Backing off, he righted his pants.

So could she, but she didn't dare admit it. Instead, she nodded as she slid to her feet and reached for her clothes. As she dressed, Brandon dropped a small green sack on the desk near her elbow. "Found your phone in my car. You got a text message about an hour ago. I'd pass it along if I could read Russian."

He'd answered her phone. Well, almost, at least. Where did he get off? Her phone belonged to *her*. He might have made her come, but damn it, that didn't give him grounds to go poking through her stuff.

As anger ignited in her veins, a glimpse of dark brown fuzz poking out of the bag stopped the slow spread through her limbs. She pulled the handles apart, revealing a small stuffed lion. Bewildered, she arched an eyebrow. "This isn't my phone."

Brandon shifted his weight again. Shoving his hands into his pockets, he looked to the floor. "It's in there."

Hell, he felt as awkward as she did. Gifts, no matter the nature, always carried meaning. A trinket to seduce, a token of thanks, an apology—no man gave presents without subtly implying something else. Damn it, the lion would have to be adorable. If it'd been ugly, or hadn't brought the stark reminder of the memorable hours they'd spent at MGM, she'd have shoved it back at him with a refusal to accept.

This, however, took her back to days at the circus with her family. Afternoons spent cheering her teenage boyfriends on as they tried to knock over milk bottles for a prize at the summer fairs. Days her mind had forgotten, but her heart kept the memories alive. Back before she'd known how it felt to watch a man die.

"Um. Thank you," she mumbled, unsettled by the suffocating warmth that spread all the way down to her toes. Innocence. He'd given her a glimpse of innocence. A ball of emotion lodged in the base of her throat. *Oh, God.*

As awkwardness spread between them, leaving them staring at each other, both clearly wanting to escape. A knock at the door broke the budding tension. She'd never seen Brandon look more relieved as he answered. Sergei's shadow descended in the entryway. His gaze caught Natalya's for a fleeting moment, long enough she could give him an affirmative nod to go ahead.

"Hey, boss. I think you better come listen to this guy against the wall."

Quick as lightning, Brandon's demeanor changed. Confidence replaced the shy downcast of his eyes. He stiffened his shoulders, at immediate attention. "Problems?"

"Maybe. He's been getting handsy with the girls. I'd hate to have Natalya step in."

She shot Sergei a frown. Seeing her moment of escape, however, she gave her sack a shake. "I'm going to go back to my office. Night's almost over."

"Wait a minute." Brandon swiveled around to face her. "I had a point in seeking you out. I need to know if you could give me a lift home. I've got one headlight—"

"Sure." She'd have promised him the moon if it let her escape faster. As it was, she doubted he'd hold her to her word once he witnessed her betrayal. Aaron could give him a lift home.

They departed his office, and Natalya took another look at the stage as Kate's routine concluded with an uproar. Brandon and Sergei disappeared into the crowd. She backed through the heavy metal door in one giant stride. No more fooling around—time to locate Iskatel´.

Avoiding the curious glances from the dancers who occupied the lounge, she jogged to her office and set the bag on the desk. Whimsy claimed her for a heartbeat as she pulled the lion out of the sack and smoothed its wild, fuzzy mane. A soft smile floated over her face. In a hundred years, she'd never admit how this little stuffed animal touched her. All the priceless jewelry Dmitri had given her didn't compare to Brandon's far simpler gift.

She buried her nose in the soft fur, closed her eyes, and reveled in the memory of Brandon's awkwardness. That momentary lack of confidence, the first she'd witnessed from the hardened cop, touched her deeply as well. He'd been nervous—and for him that said a lot.

Namely that he was getting too close.

Sighing, Natalya set the lion in the middle of her desk and fished inside the bag, producing her cell phone. A touch of her fingertip brought the Russian text message into view. It was labeled, **Private.**

Her heart jumped to her throat, beating hard and fast. There'd only be one person not already in her contact list who'd communicate with her in Russian—Iskatel´. Dmitri had said to expect contact.

She tapped the touch screen to open the message, and her heart skidded to a halt.

Like the student observes the master teacher . . . I'm watching you.

The phone slipped from her fingers, clattering to the floor. She gripped the corner of her desk and pulled in short breaths to ease the constriction of her chest. Watching her. In all the times she'd coordinated with Alexei on targets, though their communications were often cryptic, this went beyond. No suggestion they meet. No implication they should discuss the plans or her role in them. Instead, he delivered a veiled warning.

A warning that she'd screwed up.

She clutched the desk tighter and fiercely shook her head. No, she was imagining things. Dmitri sent her here to *teach* Iskatel´ how to manipulate the women so the killing would end. She was just being paranoid. Nothing she'd done with Brandon in public could be construed as anything but an attempt to forge the necessary relationship with her employer that would give her the ability to do the things Dmitri desired.

Except that kiss.

Her stomach balled into a knot.

She dragged in another deep breath and straightened to peel off her clothes. Iskatel´ would make contact again. Regardless of the meaning to his message, he'd armed her with one solid, unavoidable fact: If he could see her, then she could see him.

She pulled on her bikini bottoms, more committed to her pole dance than ever.

S tupid.

Brandon chastised himself as he followed behind Sergei to a row of plush chairs and polished wooden tables near the front of the stage. He'd thought of a dozen ways to casually present his gift, all of which eluded his grasp as he nearly shoved the stuffed animal into Natalya's hands with the lame excuse he'd found her phone.

Her reaction hadn't been comforting either. No, that hesitancy, the wavering before laughter or sincerity, downright had him questioning why he'd bought the toy in the first place. A toy, for God's sake. Who bought a grown woman a toy?

He ordered the nonsense in his head to stop as Sergei brought him to a halt behind a balding man wearing a thick gold chain around his neck. Sapphire wagged her ass in his face, but the rhythm of her hips was interrupted by her constant attempts to slap off the man's wandering hands.

Brandon eyed the clunky gold wedding ring on the man's pudgy left hand as he once again fitted a palm around the curve of Sapphire's smooth cheek and gave her ass a firm squeeze. She jumped forward, whipped around. "Damn it, Paul! How many—"

Her gaze jumped up to Brandon's scowl. Eyes wide, she took a step backward. Paul's head swiveled around, his ample size making it impossible to twist his body more than a half an inch or so.

More than happy to give this client the full picture of his displeasure, Brandon stepped into Paul's line of sight. "Problem here?"

"Uh." Beads of perspiration broke out over Paul's glossy forehead. "I paid her to dance. One hundred fifty dollars. I want my damn money's worth."

Brandon's gaze skidded to Sapphire, her trembling eyes questioning whether her new boss would stand behind her or throw her to the wolves for the sake of pleasing wealthy clientele. "Did she tell you her rules?"

As Sapphire nodded, Paul answered, "I don't remember anything but her stuffing my money in that scrap of red." He thrust an angry hand toward Sapphire's string-tied top.

The slight widening of Sapphire's eyes, followed by their abrupt narrowing, spoke anger she wouldn't dare confess in front of the clients. Too many years on the Strip had taught her tips didn't come from pissing off the men. Nor did job security. But the unspoken fury she wielded toward her customer told Brandon all he needed to know.

He shifted his stare back to the double chins beneath Paul's arrogant smirk. "Let's get this straight, *Paul*. Like your *wife* sets the rules in your house, the girls set the rules in mine." Bracing both hands on the arms of Paul's chair, he leaned down until his face was inches from the smirk that now faltered. "If they tell you paws off, you keep your fucking paws off. Got it?"

"Y-Yeah."

"Good. Now apologize to Sapphire before I change my mind and have Sergei escort you out."

Brandon stood, hating the disbelief that reflected in Sapphire's startled stare. Damn it. Whoever had taught her strippers didn't have rights in Vegas needed a good beating. Sadie's had been that way too before he'd taken it over—pretty girls terrified if they stood up for their bodies they'd find their asses on the street. The whole scene disgusted Brandon on so many levels he couldn't name them all.

He gave her a supportive nod and turned away. Now, to finish his conversation with Natalya.

When he reached the edge of the stage, the house lights went dark, preparing for the next girl. Becca, who was filling Chablis' spot damn well.

"Now, gentlemen, we have something new for you," the DJ droned through the speakers.

Brandon paused. Cocking his head, he looked toward the glass-encased booth where Eddie addressed the crowd. New? Becca couldn't have developed a new routine so soon. When the girls switched up, they practiced for countless hours before opening. He'd spent a lot of time here with the former management during those events, witnessed the meticulous way they analyzed their costumes' functionality and the coordination of props and lights.

Two orange floor lights blinked on, crisscrossing each other and illuminating a thin screen that shimmied and gave the simple lighting life. Behind the veil, another set of lights blended into the action, creating the effect of fire.

"We all have secrets. Desires, passions, sins," Eddie intoned. "She's there inside you all. That being who wants nothing more than escape. Wanting freedom." The low resonating beat of drums filtered through the speakers, adding mystique to the DJ's voice. "Wanting pleasure."

A third light faded in, illuminating a mock fire pit in the center of the stage, and with it, a silhouetted woman.

"She is, the Shadow."

Drums exploded, and the silhouette came to life. Slowly, she gyrated around the stacked logs, her hips a matched rhythm to the pulsing beat. A hush descended over the crowd. Brandon stood transfixed, along with every other man in the room, his gaze riveted on the slow undulation of smooth hips, firm breasts. The sensual cadence of a woman who knew true seduction involved the imagination.

The elegance of something more than skin and jiggling tits.

It can't be.

Arms raised over her head, she turned a hypnotic circle, then flattened her breasts to her thighs and slid outstretched fingertips all the way down to her toes. Rising, she uncoiled like a flower opening to sunlight, only to once again shimmy hips that knew no restraint. Belly dancing. But more . . . something . . . Brandon's heart thumped hard. *Enchanting.*

A collective murmur rumbled through the crowd.

The drums increased tempo, pounding with more intensity, and the dancer's cadence increased. Driving. Gyrating. Slender hands, made more so by the trick of lights, skimmed up her ribs, cupped her breasts. She tipped her head back, as if she arched her back in silent ecstasy, and long hair tumbled to the backs of her knees. Hair she gathered into her hands as she swiveled her lithe body upright. She piled it on the top of her head, only to let it fall as she glided those tempting hands down supple curves once more.

Brandon's body tightened, his own imagination replacing her hands with his. He might have only known Natalya for a handful of days, but he recognized the natural grace in a heartbeat. Hell, she'd just arched her back the same way less than five minutes ago.

Natalya.

His hand clenched into a slow fist. God damn, when he should be so furious arousal couldn't find a place to spark, let alone ignite, his body was attuned to the stage like she'd cast a magnetic field around him. She gyrated, her silhouetted form in profile, and his cock pulsed with the motion of her hips. Her whisper echoed in his head. *Brandon* . . .

Primitive drums supercharged the smoky air with an undercurrent of electricity. Taking full advantage of her mesmerized audience, Natalya turned her backside to the crowd. Spiked heels spread two feet apart, she undulated her torso, lowering her shoulders level to her waist. Dainty hands fanned out straight, gracefully arced to the back of her thighs. Only the outline of her fingertips marred the smooth lines of her silhouette as she bent in slow motion, until one-by-one, she closed her fingers around her ankles, her hair touching the stage between her legs.

Brandon's body recoiled. The image came unbidden—a glimpse of moist swollen flesh, seconds before her honeyed flavor soaked into his tongue. He could smell the sweet musk of her arousal and swallowed hard. Shut his eyes to block out dewy skin even the lack of lights couldn't hide from his mind.

When he looked again, she moved around the fire pit, a snake dance of the deadliest kind. He swore. She was fantasy. Every man's Jezebel. Alluring. Beckoning. Daring him and every other bastard in the room to indulge in what they wanted to see. The secret forbidden pleasure of chimera.

On one heart-stopping crescendo of bass and tams, the stage went dark. His temper surged to the surface. She'd defied him. Natalya had ignored his insistence she stay off the stage and exposed herself to danger.

Son of a bitch!

Driving an open palm against the stage, he blocked out the bellows of protest, angry men taken to the brink and left unfulfilled. He shoved past one who'd surged to his feet as if he sought to climb on to the stage after Natalya and stormed toward the backstage door.

Halfway across the room, one solitary blue light broke through the blackness, illuminating Fantasia's seventeen-foot-tall brass pole. Brandon froze and slowly turned around. Every instinct he possessed warned him to escape backstage where he could remain ignorant of what was about to happen. He had a better chance of surviving a bullet than what came next.

Instead, like the other lemmings in the room, he gravitated closer to the stage, his eyes riveted on the upside-down dancer at the top.

Twenty-eight

Natalya dangled from the top of the pole, legs stretched in vertical splits, the one at her head crisscrossed to secure her in place. The other stretched out behind her body. As she waited for the opening chord to 007's *The World Is Not Enough*, she scanned the crowd, looking for the man who assessed from a distance, his stare unseeing, his mind focused on potential, not what lay before his eyes. Her song choice, one Sergei would surely appreciate, gave her the slow rhythm necessary to both perform and observe.

At the opening crescendo, she loosened her leg grip, pushed into a slow spin, and descended head-first, rotating around the pole like a diamond on display. Three feet from the bottom, she smiled at the collective silence, hooked her right knee around the pole, and elongated into a swanlike backbend. Her hand caught the heel of her black stiletto and pulled it to her forehead. The other stretched above her dangling hair. As her muscles stretched, a slow burn spread across her belly.

It felt good to push herself beyond the half-assed entertainment she gave Dmitri. This came from her soul, an exercise in unrestrained freedom. She'd defied Brandon. Defied Dmitri. Right now, in these few precious moments she could be herself. Not a CIA agent. No man's lover. Just Natalya, the same girl who'd danced for tips because she loved to do so and thrived on pushing her body to abnormal limits.

The spin came to a gradual stop, and she gripped the pole with both hands, gracefully arcing her feet to the floor. Sultry vocals kicked in, and Natalya threw her weight into a ground move, wrapping her body around the brass in synchronized time with the sensual rhythm. As the chorus emerged, and the bright strings built in strength, she gripped the cool metal in both hands, hooked her ankles, and undulated her way up the solid shaft.

Halfway to the top, she tucked her left foot behind tight, elongated her right until it was perpendicular to her waist. Holding the pole in her right hand, she leaned back until her fingers touched, then nothing. She lowered her arms slowly, using only her abdomen muscles to drop her upper body into another tight backbend.

This one she held only for a beat before she grabbed the metal shaft at her cheek and kicked both legs off, extending her body horizontally. She turned her smile to the crowd, looking over the faces once more as she held the position, widening her legs into splits, easing them closed over the scope of several musical bars.

Nothing in the crowd. Only wide eyes and slack jaws. She shifted her position, bringing her breasts to the pole, one hand over, one hand under, horizontal for a heartbeat before she propelled her legs skyward and latched her ankles around the brass. Hands free, she crossed her arms over her chest and dangled in a painstakingly motionless crunch.

Then, as the music infiltrated her veins, she threw herself into the dance, Iskatel' forgotten as she resumed her artful ballet. Curling into her body, she grabbed on with both hands and flung herself into a sit-spin. Her toes pointed in a *V* toward the ceiling, head back, she focused on an extinguished light to keep from losing her equilibrium. The spiral ended as she planted her heels vertically on the pole and lowered herself into the splits, the insides of her thighs flat against the smooth brass.

Without losing a beat, she eased out of the trick, caught the pole under her arm, cocked one knee around the metal, and shimmied all the way to the top. Beneath the heat of the solitary blue light, she wedged herself by armpit and hipbone and kicked her feet to her head.

She grabbed the tops of her ankles, arched her back, and touched the very tips of her four-inch heels to the crown of her head.

A collective murmur rumbled through the crowd. Exhilarated by the dance, Natalya smiled as she lengthened her legs and reached one arm toward the sky. Hand-over-hand, she inched upside down. She spread her legs, eased them together again with a graceful back-stroke kick. Adrenaline pumped through her veins as she prepared for her second freefall.

Taking her legs away from the pole, she dropped into a pike, then snaked in a half circle, winding her left leg around the length of metal. Natalya pushed her upper body skyward, locked her ankles around the brass, and let herself plummet toward the stage below.

Her palms connected, her ankles tightening to slow her fall and ease her body to the ground with an undulation from shoulder to toes. She looked up into the crowd as she let go completely to roll onto her back and gyrate against the floor. Her gaze fell on Brandon, his tawny eyes stormy, his expression a maelstrom of fury.

Brandon didn't know whether to drag Natalya offstage and threaten her within an inch of her life, or whether to stand transfixed and indulge in the magic of her body. Half of him wanted to kill her. The other half wanted to yank off that sequined scrap of a bikini, bend those long legs toward her head, and ride her into orgasm.

A taunting smile danced upon her lips as she sashayed around the pole, her gaze never leaving his. Damn her! She was playing him. She knew good and well he was seconds away from exploding both physi-cally and verbally, and she was goading him.

And then she was upside down again, palms and heels braced on the floor, a backbend that filled his head with erotic images of all the things he could do to her in that position. Split her down the center with his tongue. Stand between her thighs, slide into her tight body as her rosy-tipped nipples stared him in the face.

He choked down a groan. God, he wanted to fuck her. No. Not fuck her. Every man in the room wanted to slam home inside that supple body, and he'd already done that. Brandon wanted something the rest of them couldn't have. He wanted that woman who made a brief appearance when she'd come apart against his mouth. When he'd spontaneously kissed her in the car. The fragile glimpse of innocent femininity that peeked from behind tight shutters when she held a lion cub in the crook of her arm.

His chest tightened to painful limits. If she didn't scramble off that stage soon, he'd suffocate in this smoke-filled room.

In slow motion, she lifted one leg, curled an elegant calf around the pole, and crept her hands toward the base. Inch by inch she caterpillared her way up the long metal shaft. No wonder she'd cracked a man's chest in half—the strength in her thighs rippled with every gravity-defying extension. Part ballet, part gymnastics, part striptease, all combined into one erotic *cirque du soliel* that outclassed every pole routine he'd ever witnessed.

Kate had said Natalya was good. This routine didn't even come close to that simplified description. If he possessed half the management skills he was supposed to, he'd force Natalya to take the stage nightly. That is, if he wasn't so busy falling for her.

And damn it, he was. With each elegant spin, every upside-down and sideways twist, the realization sank in further. Whoever she was, *whatever* she was, he was falling hard. Fast.

Fucking terrifying.

He glanced sideways, making the mistake of noticing the pained grimace on the man's face at his left. The sudden urge to backhand that look of bittersweet pleasure gripped Brandon's mind. Though Natalya's bikini covered more skin than the swimsuits he'd find at a family-friendly pool, he couldn't tolerate the devouring eyes. She belonged to him.

He stepped aside before reflex could overrule his sense. A strong hand clamped onto his shoulder, stopping his single-minded trajectory toward the backstage door. Aaron's voice rumbled with laughter that didn't cross his face. "Too much for you to handle?"

Brandon glowered at his best friend. He shrugged off Aaron's hand. "Screw you, Mayer."

The laughter broke free. "You should see your face. I've seen starving wolves that look more approachable."

Aaron's jab brought home all the sound, logical reasons Brandon had been angry with Natalya. Not because she exposed her body, but because she exposed *herself.* If Mayer could read his reaction to the auburn-haired vixen onstage, Brandon would put money on it someone else could too. Like the someone else who'd been peeking through his window. The assholes who'd finally accepted his thrown gauntlet.

He went ramrod straight and scowled at the stage. Damn her. She hadn't just defied him, she'd pulled things inside him out into the open and marked herself as a target.

At the top of the pole once more, Natalya twisted her body into a knot. Upside down, sideways, upside down again. One arm linked around the metal, her toe touched her head, stealing his breath. His gut ground down like a vise. Beneath his loose dress pants, his cock swelled to painful limits. So graceful. So limber.

She caught the pole beneath her arm, extended her body horizontally, and held the position, spinning as the chorus repeated to a strong, abrupt end. As the vocals faded, the bass guitar thrummed twice. Natalya let loose, plummeting down the pole so fast, Brandon was certain she'd hit the ground and break a leg.

At the last chord, she tucked into a tight ball, stopping her rapid descent less than three inches from the floor. The stage went dark. The crowd burst into riotous noise. Aaron lunged for a drunken buffoon who was stupid enough to climb onstage, leaving Brandon to storm through the backstage doors.

He needed a beer first. Just to take off the edge so he didn't follow through with the fleeting idea of strangling Natalya.

Confined within the shadows, Natalya took one last look at the mutinous crowd. She'd done all she could to draw her routine out to muscle-cramping limits so she could get a good glimpse of the men. The act gave her ample time, no question there. But she'd recognized nothing, other than Sergei's amused expression and Brandon's murderous scowl.

Of course, the rapt faces caught her eye, stroking her ego, but she'd seen nothing of significance. Not a single flinch that might indicate one of the suits stretched out in a chair might be Iskatel´. Jill had disappeared as well. More reason to suspect Iskatel´ wasn't a man at all. A suspicion that gained more evidence with each passing hour.

Natalya lifted to her toes and looked sideways to the bar where three security guards restrained four red-faced, struggling men. She laughed quietly. It had been a long time since she could claim she'd started a brawl.

Her gaze settled on Brandon, ten feet away from the backstage doors and heading for a beer tub. She grimaced inwardly. The man was downright furious. Standing that close to the dressing rooms, he snuffed out her brief hope that she'd danced him out of his anger. Natalya shrugged. He'd get over it once he stopped to listen to the throaty demands for an encore. Favorite dancers brought in more money. Influential clients brought the drug ring he'd been tracking closer. His narcotics team would reap the rewards while Fantasia reaped the financial benefits.

A flitting shadow caught her attention. Beyond Brandon's shoulder. Closer to the door. She rose to tiptoe, waiting for Scott to stop the figure.

But Scott wasn't there. Preoccupied with the fistfight closer to the bar, no one stood at the door.

She frowned as the door opened and a distinctly masculine form slipped inside.

Natalya bolted down the long hall. A glimpse inside the lounge revealed only empty couches, the dancers having poured into the main house to use their talents in soothing the boisterous crowd. She stood still, head cocked, listening for noises. Props guy maybe? Harvey?

The closing of a door further down the hallway indicated her suspicion was correct. But Harvey and his crew weren't allowed to exit through the girls' door. They had a separate entrance that opened up behind the bar. The same exit the barbacks used to haul up beer and bottles from the basement cooler.

Natalya followed the noise to the askance stairwell door. She pushed it open quietly, again listening for footsteps on the stairs.

Silence reigned.

Strange. She'd have sworn someone had passed through here. The air even felt agitated. As if it had been disturbed from its usual dormant stagnation.

"Harvey?"

"Yes, ma'am?" His voice rang up the stairwell. In seconds, his carrot-red head popped over the banister.

"Did you just come through here?"

Harvey blinked. "No. Me and the guys are closing up down here. Organizing for tomorrow."

"So everyone's there then? No one came downstairs? The door was open."

"No, ma'am. We've all been down here since we brought up the last round of trunks. Sorry to give you a scare—someone musta left it open."

Natalya's frown deepened. "Yeah. Okay."

She'd *heard* the door open. Someone had been through here. There were only four doors. Her office, this one, the wide-open dressing room with nowhere to hide, and the back exit, which threw an alarm when opened.

Fighting off an uneasy chill, she turned to investigate the dancers' lounge. Maybe she'd heard the backstage door, and whoever had come back here had discovered this wasn't the bathroom, thus making a speedy exit.

Halfway through the room, Brandon stormed inside. His intimidating size became more imposing under the influence of his malevolent scowl. Angrier than she could ever recall seeing him, his chest heaved with the effort of restraining his temper. The tiny scar on his chin pulled tight as he worked his jaw, and his scalding gaze swept down the length of her half-clothed body.

Alarm bells buzzed inside Natalya's head. She'd known she would piss him off. She'd expected a little temper, a lot of yelling. Not the heat that rolled off him in waves and the searing way his narrowed gaze pierced into her. Instinct kicked in, along with a shiver. She fought down the reflex to run and hide. Ordered her legs not to shake.

She gulped, realizing a far more frightening fact. She stared at a man who could actually intimidate her.

He jabbed a finger at the door behind her. "Your office. *Now.*"

With calm that belied the nervous trip of her heart, she back stepped through her door. She wasn't afraid, just off-center. With Dmitri, she knew what to expect. Knew which buttons would soothe his annoyance. Sergei and she fought like brother and sister, but while he possessed the skills of an agent, she could still outshoot him if she needed to. The rest of the people she encountered, she treated with polite mistrust. The less she *expected* from them, the more she anticipated the worst.

Brandon, however, was as unpredictable as the weather. She trusted him to a degree—her first mistake. That trust wanted to please. But the deep-rooted need for self-protection made trying to diffuse the situation with an honest conversation more frightening than confessing her betrayal to Dmitri.

Her office door closed heavily. Natalya's knees hit the back of her chair, stopping her retreat. She clasped her hands in front of her waist and squelched an apology behind pursed lips. She wouldn't apologize.

Not when she wasn't sorry for doing what was necessary to see her mission completed.

Brandon met her level stare for several heartbeats, his jaw clenching and unclenching. Color rose to his cheeks. He took a short breath, then exploded, "What the fuck was that all about?"

Forcing herself not to give in to guilt, Natalya summoned a light-hearted laugh. "What? The dance? Didn't sit well with you, huh?"

"Didn't *sit well* with me?" His voice rose by several decibels.

"No, I suppose not." She let out a false sigh and casually crossed her legs. "I should have expected this afternoon would give you the wrong idea. Jealousy isn't a pretty thing for you, Brandon." Willpower stopped the wince that threatened to creep across her face. Cattiness had never been her forte. Worse, a secret part of her soul *wanted* this afternoon to give him the wrong idea. Backed into a corner, however, with no way to protect herself from the blows of guilt and the weight of deceiving this incredible man, she had no choice but to turn the tables.

Instead of the shocked surprise she expected, his tawny eyes flashed with hot color, pinning her to the chair.

Twenty-nine

Natalya's flippancy shredded Brandon's control. In his years on the force, having seen the cruelty drugs could inflict and more dead bodies than any human being could ever want to witness, he'd never experienced the violent, unrestrained anger that her light laugh provoked.

Gave him the wrong fucking idea? She'd been right there with him as caught up by what was happening between them as he was. Hell, she'd screamed in pleasure. Nothing would convince him she didn't share the same enormity of feeling.

He slammed the ball of his fist down on her desk. A box of chocolate-covered cherries jumped. He glanced at the white and red carton briefly, then dismissed it, locking his gaze with Natalya's once more. "I'll tell you about wrong ideas. Let's start with how your *boss* told you *not* to dance, and you decided to do so anyway."

"My boss?" Natalya laughed again. "Make up your mind which role you want to play, Brandon. You're only my boss when it's convenient. Otherwise you're too busy fucking me."

He clamped his teeth down on the stream of oaths that choked off his air. He couldn't argue with the truth. Moreover, he caught the flat glint of her eyes. The unfeeling stare that told him the words were real enough, but the woman who said them wasn't. For a moment, in the dancers' lounge, he'd glimpsed that mesmerizing Natalya who drove him to maddening limits. While this shell made him every bit as crazy, he ached for the woman who prompted him into foolishness. *She* had been on the stage. *She* deserved the fight.

"Damn it, where are you?" Frustrated beyond all means, he swiped his arm across the desk, sending the chocolates flying into the wall.

She blinked. But not at him, he realized, as he followed the trajectory of her gaze. She stared at the floor where the box had broken open. Smashed chocolate-covered cherries coated the floor, sugary ooze pouring from a squashed corner.

Brandon straightened. Unease filtered through his angry haze. He'd hit the box hard. But not hard enough to smash two entire trays of candies, each held in egg-shaped cups. Those chocolates were already crushed, long before he'd hit them. And to accomplish that, while keeping the flimsy plastic cups from collapsing, someone had done it piece by piece.

"Who gave you that?" His gaze flicked back to hers, and he took a small measure of satisfaction at witnessing the truth behind her eyes before she once again snapped the shutters closed.

"I told you jealousy wasn't a pretty color for you."

He pursed his lips, ground his teeth together. With patience that defied his years of training, he gritted out, "No games. Who gave you the chocolates, Natalya?"

Defiance radiated in the proud jut of her chin. Sparkled behind her challenging stare. Then, as she blinked, the facade crumbled. She shook her head. "It wasn't here when I left for the stage."

In the next heartbeat, the color drained from her face. He knew then, she'd made a connection. Associated the candy with someone else. Someone who had the capacity to strike fear into her fearless little heart.

His arms ached to draw her close. To offer comfort and reassurances. But he'd come to realize enough about Natalya that he also knew the moment he attempted to soothe those deep-rooted fears, she'd clam up and block him out.

Damn it. He didn't know which to be more concerned about—the person who she was running from, or the people chasing him. They couldn't be the same. The mafia didn't work with subtle insinuations, and they wouldn't want to intimidate *her*. If they had a message to deliver, it would come to him. They might use her as the vessel of delivery, but threatening Natalya accomplished nothing.

On the other hand, whoever erased her past on paper had resurfaced. Or something made her believe such, at least.

"Get your things," he murmured. "We're leaving. We'll talk about this at my place." Sighting her keys on the corner of her desk, he swiped them up and dangled them in front of her nose. "I'll wait in the hall while you dress."

Without giving her opportunity to object, he yanked open the door, stepped into the hall, and firmly pulled it shut. Standing in front of it, he looked up to find Jill seated on a chair in the lounge, a smug smirk tugging at her thin mouth. Unnaturally high eyebrows arched even higher. She mouthed, *Told you.*

Brandon bit back a low growl. He didn't have the patience for her antics. Closing his eyes, he dropped his head against the doorframe and blocked out everything but the nagging voice that insisted Natalya was in danger.

Natalya shivered, unable to tear her gaze off the sugary goo on her floor and her mind away from the keys Brandon had swiped off her desk. For three years, she'd forced herself to swallow down the thick syrupy candy. Each time Dmitri went away for more than four days, he brought chocolate-covered cherries back. She'd eaten the first box only out of politeness, in hopes that enthusiasm over his thoughtfulness would bring her that much closer to the formidable *Bratva* leader. Over time, he'd just assumed she liked them.

Now they were here. Smashed in the box. Like someone had picked each one up and squeezed it between thumb and forefinger.

Jill's warning. The strange text message from Iskatel'. Smashed cherries and keys that miraculously appeared when she left her office to assume the stage—all messages. Now, Brandon wanted her to take him home. Expected to finish this argument inside his house, with her car parked in his driveway, broadcasting for anyone who might be tailing her, that she was inside.

She might as well stand him in front of his bay window and paint a bull's-eye on his back.

Damn it! What she wouldn't give to have Sergei outside her door. But that wouldn't happen. As enraged as Brandon was, she didn't stand a chance at convincing him to give her more time before they left. Certainly not to have a personal conversation with her friend.

Natalya picked up her phone instead. Flipping to Sergei's name, she quickly sent a cautionary message: **I'm in trouble. Must see you in the AM. Don't reply.**

Deleting it just as quickly, she shoved the phone inside her purse. Her fingers touched the cool metal of her gun, offering her a modicum of relief. As she withdrew her hand, her phone vibrated. She fished it out, scowled at Sergei's name, and punched the answer button, lecturing in Russian, "I told you not to reply."

"You also told me you're in trouble. I'm not going to ignore that. Given the circumstances, morning might very well be too late."

Her gaze pulled to the smeared mess on her floor. Shaky fingers tightened around her phone. "I think I've been made."

"Made? What? How?"

"There's chocolate-covered cherries all over my floor. I got a cryptic message from Iskatel', I think—it was a private number—saying he was watching me."

A muffled oath drifted through the phone.

"And Brandon wants to talk about *stuff* at his place tonight."

"Stuff like your dance."

"Mm-hm."

At Sergei's heavy sigh, she pictured the way he raked his fingers through his long hair. A gesture so similar to Brandon's self-conscious habit, it made the familial link impossible to ignore.

"What do you want to do, Natalya?"

She couldn't help but chuckle. "What I want to do is selfish and wrong. I need to get far away from Brandon. From this mess."

"Can you hold it together for two more days?"

"I think so. I'm worried about him though."

"C'mon, babe, if anyone can keep him safe, it's you."

Frowning, Natalya scratched at a dried smear of fingernail polish on her desktop. "I don't understand why you're suddenly encouraging me to pursue your brother when less than a day ago you went to great pains to make me acknowledge the danger."

"Look at who we are, Natalya. Any minute, you or I could cease to exist. You said it yourself—you've spent three years unfeeling. Maybe you made me realize lying to ourselves only makes everything worse."

"But he's your brother, which you still owe me an explanation for."

He skipped over her not-so-subtle hint. "Yeah, he is, and if there's a man in this world who can pull you out of this hellhole and keep you out of it, it's him."

She snapped her mouth shut, stiffening in her chair. Pull her out? Had Sergei recognized that she'd cracked? What if she didn't want to be pulled out? She didn't need to leave the agency and the Opals, she needed to leave this assignment. A few weeks from now, with Dmitri locked up and Brandon far away, she'd be fine. The blissful world of non-feeling would be a welcome relief to the chaos raging inside her now. She could once again look at her reflection in the mirror without cringing.

"Go on, babe. I'll stay close."

With that, Sergei terminated the call.

For several moments, Natalya cradled her phone and stared at the back of her door. Pull her out . . . Her own partner thought she couldn't take the life anymore. Maybe he had a point. Maybe agents didn't come back from falling apart. But she didn't know how to live a normal life. Wasn't sure she wanted *normal*. What if she tried and failed? What if she'd gone so far beyond innocence, she'd never be able to find it again?

A stiff knock reminded her Brandon waited. She dropped her phone into her purse and quickly stripped off her bikini. Sliding back into her clothes, she blocked the frightening questions Sergei stoked and focused on what plausible lies she'd tell Brandon this time.

In an otherwise dark room, Dmitri sat beneath the glow of the Vegas Strip. From his position in the far corner, he possessed the perfect view of Natalya's door. He glanced at his watch, smiling as he noted she would soon be home. Would she be surprised to find him here?

Or had her traitorous heart come to expect he'd arrive?

He ground his teeth together, leaned forward, and picked up the black-and-white photograph of his beloved tucked beneath another man, fast asleep, her bare legs twined intimately with Moretti's.

Unfaithful bitch.

He ripped the picture in half. Then in half again and again and again . . . until all he held were tiny pieces. Opening his fingers, he let the scraps scatter to the floor.

He crossed one ankle over his knee and settled into the thick stuffing of his leather chair. Even if Natalya didn't know about Moretti's near-collision with Iskatel' this afternoon, the chocolates would send the clear message he'd arrived. When she came through the door, she'd grovel. Like the blind, besotted lover he'd allowed himself to become, he'd accept her apologies.

Hold her close. Breathe in the flowery scent of her hair. Fuck her in this chair, then carry her to the bed and make her come again. Cradle her close. Shower her in love.

And then, while his dick was still inside her, he'd wrap his fingers around her delicate neck and choke the life out of her unfaithful body.

The last thing Natalya Trubachev would know in this world was how it felt to have him possess her. Not her lover, *him*, the man she'd vowed to marry. The man she had sworn eternal devotion.

The temptation to keep her alive, to watch as the drugs claimed her senses and led her into a delirious haze, ran deep. He could still travel to Dubai and enjoy her as he wished. Make her his slave. Listen to her beg. Laugh when she shed tears over the future they could have had together. But the fleeting concern she might *enjoy* one of her Johns kept him from committing her to the same fate that she'd bestowed upon two dozen women.

His lip curled at the bitter taste of bile that rose to the back of his throat. How long had she fucking misled him? How many other men had fucked her when he'd left her at home, convinced she loved him as deeply as he loved her?

Dmitri shoved the vivid images aside and clenched his jaw as his hands curled into tight fists. He glanced down at his watch again. Four fifteen. Any moment now, her keys would rattle in the lock. Maybe he'd get lucky enough to find Moretti at her side. From this angle, he had a clear shot. What pleasure it would be to watch the bastard fall at her feet.

No, Natalya wouldn't be foolish enough to bring her lover home after receiving the warnings. Moretti wouldn't die tonight, but his time was limited. Dmitri's perfect princess would unwittingly lead her lover to his death.

At the thought, warmth overtook the chill in his veins. Maybe he'd keep Natalya alive long enough to deliver the news.

Or maybe, he'd have Iskatel´ fuck with Moretti until Natalya was dead and gone. Watching that man suffer would be almost as satisfying as ensuring Natalya would never again betray him.

Yes. His smile broadened. He'd keep Natalya here tonight. Enjoy her in ways he'd only dreamed of, ways only a whore could be enjoyed. Tomorrow he'd drug her into silence. Wait until she awakened and take his fill of her again. Moretti would worry. His concern would make him careless. Recklessness Iskatel´ could use to make Moretti disappear. But before that bastard took his last breath, he would lie beside Natalya's lifeless body. The last thing he'd see was her vacant stare.

Nice. Tidy.

Just the way Dmitri preferred things.

Thirty

With Natalya's hand firmly trapped in his, Brandon stalked through Fantasia's empty front room. His singular purpose remained on ushering her as fast as he could to his house, where he intended to finish their argument.

He shoved open the heavy glass doors and half-dragged her into the cool night air. She didn't particularly protest, but her resistance came with the slowness of her step. The occasional shake of her arm as she tried to dislodge his admittedly too-harsh hold. But he was done with the games. Whatever happened tonight, whether they launched into some sort of unchartered future, or whether they tailspun into solid finality, the games were over.

No more shutters, no more excuses, no more lies.

Or so he told himself as he opened her car door and waited for her to climb inside. Deep down, fingers of ice clawed at his insides, making the prospect of unveiling all his secrets to Natalya slim. He couldn't tell her about his father, about the danger that surrounded his existence. She already feared one threat—he'd rather lie his ass off than give her reason to worry about another.

He sighed as he pushed her passenger door shut. His brain felt like mush. Too much to process. Not the least of which, this crazy turbulent feeling that pitched him off one end of the emotional scales, only to have the side he landed on toss him high in the air. A goddamned teeter-totter. Not a roller coaster—no those were smooth rides with exhilarating highs and lows and loop-de-loops. This was the teeter-totter from hell. Every time he thought he found the point of balance and things would level out, some little thing Natalya did shoved him off-center.

He could firmly say he now understood the junkies who claimed they'd crashed and burned.

If he wasn't careful, he predicted the same end for himself. For God's sake, he'd put her name and *children* in the same damn thought earlier. Within an hour of leaving Kaycee, he'd found himself admitting her claims that he was toast. He hadn't put too much protest into Kaycee's subtle hint of permanency either. Sure, his insides had turned to ice, and his throat had closed. His brain, however, actually formed the picture of tuxedos and white dresses. Natalya—a woman he'd known for three days!

Just like the addicts he'd locked up, he knew the warning signs, understood the risk. And he couldn't stop. Couldn't back away from Natalya and just let her be. Treat her like the suspect she *ought* to be, not the victim he suspected.

He let himself in and keyed the engine. Holding both hands on the wheel, he stared at Fantasia's concrete wall, hating the tension that crackled between them. He'd created it. While she might deserve every bit of his anger, he hadn't given her the ability to understand where it came from. He'd kept that from her, and from the outside, he looked like a class-A jerk.

He licked his lips and rested his hand on the gearshift between the seats. "I'm going to get this out of the way here, but it isn't going to change the fact we're having a conversation when we get to my place." Edging his gaze sideways, he met her quiet stare. "I'm sorry."

She nodded, and Brandon mentally kicked himself. So much for smoothing things over. The hours ahead only looked more rocky.

The brush of her fingertips against the back of his hand was so faint he almost took it for accident, until he looked down and saw the deliberate way she'd positioned her hand next to his, the tip of her index finger resting on his pinkie. He curled his pinkie around her finger, smiling when she lightly squeezed. Returning the subtle affection, hope brimmed.

Maybe he could salvage some of his decency yet. She just had a way of provoking him to extremes.

He breathed a little easier as he released her finger and slung his arm over the back of her seat, twisting to back out of the parking slot. As he turned, his foot hit the brake, and anger blistered all over again.

"Son of a bitch," he muttered as he threw the car into park and kicked open his door.

N atalya blinked as the dome light came on. What was his problem now? She swiveled in her seat, curious what he'd seen that set him off again. Her stare riveted on a dark red heart, painted on the inside of her window. Sloppily crafted, rivulets of crimson dripped down the smooth glass.

Her eyes followed one long drip down the topmost curve, onto the top of her rental's velour seat, and all the way into the crease where the seatbelt protruded. Several more splatters slashed the interior, the paint obvious, but the effect clearly intended to resemble blood.

Her mind raced—Dmitri? Iskatel′? Which one now?

The driver's seat sprang forward, and Brandon ducked his head into the backseat. "Guess this explains why you couldn't find your keys."

"Yeah," Natalya murmured. If Dmitri knew about Brandon, it explained the bloody heart. At the same time, something about the symbol didn't fit. It wasn't crude enough. Too . . . cheesy for her murderous fiancé. He'd be more inclined to draw the thing in actual blood, not red paint.

Which took her back to Iskatel′. Only . . . Her gaze moved with Brandon's hand as he reached for something metallic in the seat. Swearing beneath his breath, he tossed aside a condom packet that had been neatly cut in half. Natalya blinked. Iskatel′ wouldn't cut up condoms. That rang personal.

She pulled herself out of the seat and leaned over to inspect what was behind her back. Brandon's mutterings increased in volume, his oaths sharp and bitter as he picked up a distinctly used rubber.

Natalya's gag reflex kicked in, and she wrinkled her face in disgust. A third condom lay in a wadded-up ball, smeared with the same paint, evidently the artist's paintbrush of choice.

"Well. This is . . . certainly interesting."

Brandon shot her a look that said he didn't appreciate her attempt at humor. Judging by the seriousness of his expression, maybe she should be more concerned about the graffiti. Her stomach rolled in on itself. Maybe Dmitri had run out of fresh bodies. He normally didn't kill without a reason. And if he weren't convinced she'd betrayed him, he might try something less gruesome to bring her running into his arms. Then again, if her suspicion Jill and Iskatel´ were one in the same, the heart made even more sense. It carried the distinct touch of catty femininity. Iskatel´ didn't do violence, which explained the paint even more.

"Do you have something in your purse I can put these in?"

"Um. No."

"Anything in the glove box?"

"It's a rental—what do you think?"

"I think someone's trying to express their displeasure about you and me."

Obviously. What other message did three mangled condoms, one obviously used—recently at that—and a bloody heart convey? She slid back into her seat and let out an exasperated sigh. "Just leave it. I want to go home."

No sooner than the words popped out, did her eyes fly open wide. *Home?* Holy crap, she'd just equated Brandon's house with hers. She held her tongue, praying he'd slide behind the wheel and shut the door, allowing the darkness to disguise her mortification.

Muttering again, he extracted himself from the backseat, wiped his hand on his pants, and climbed behind the wheel. "Yeah. Home sounds good."

Natalya had to admit, a certain peacefulness descended around her shoulders at his reference to home. How long had it been since she'd felt comfortable within four walls? Like she might actually *enjoy* staying awhile? The closest she'd come in as many years as she could count had been the brief excursion at Alexei's rat-hole apartment. Even then, that had only come from the escape of Dmitri's, not from some sense that she wanted to stay in the roach pit. Or with Alexei. He made for a good time, but the man never cracked a smile.

Her thoughts inched back to Dmitri, now more convinced than ever that Brandon was in danger. As misplaced as it might seem, no one else had reason to vandalize her car. She pulled her purse into her lap, her hands seeking security in the firm outline of her gun.

"Hey," Brandon murmured as he eased to a stop at the edge of the parking lot. His strong fingers closed over the back of her hand, pulled it off her weapon, and tucked it firmly into his lap, where he covered it with his large palm. "You're safe with me."

She closed her eyes, wishing beyond all reason she could take comfort in his gentle assurance. If the circumstances were different, if she wasn't trapped in a deadly game of espionage, she'd believe his assertive claim. Any girl would feel safe and protected with Brandon Moretti at her side. Just not her. She was in too deep. Over her head.

And if she didn't find a way to extricate herself from Brandon, he'd pay for her crimes.

The way Natalya had reached for her gun twisted Brandon's heart so painfully he wasn't sure it would ever unwind. His thoughts cycled back to his mother, the sound of her tears when she awakened from nightmares. The muffled sobs had awakened him more than once through his teenage years. Sometimes he still heard them now, when his house was quiet and dreams he couldn't remember jolted him awake.

He tightened his grip around Natalya's hand, wanting nothing more than to absorb her fear and free her from that prison. Instead, he opened her to more danger. The painting in her backseat evidenced that clear enough. Smashed chocolates might have been directed at her, but this was a message to him. A personal message. One that made him question how anyone might know he'd be inside *her* car, and why that person hadn't vandalized his.

The obvious answer lay in the supposition the mess happened sometime last night, when he'd taken her home. She'd lost her keys that night. She'd probably left them at Fantasia. Sometime between when they left through the casino and when he dropped her off at the club this evening, the culprit had seen an opportunity.

The other obvious answer screamed like a siren. *Jill.* It was beyond time to talk to her. He should've sucked it up and dealt with her jealousy at the first symptoms. Now, he'd let it go too far, and once again, someone paid the price for his failures.

Another reason he and Natalya couldn't just pretend *I'm sorry* fixed everything.

He weaved through the Vegas traffic and headed west, toward his neighborhood. The silence they shared lacked the earlier tension, but it was still a far cry from comfortable. Too many things needed to be said, none of which could be resolved in the short distance to his house. So he drove, lightly holding on to her hand, willing her to find faith in him. Faith he, himself, had begun to doubt.

When they pulled into his driveway, Opie sounded the alarm, barking his infernal head off and lunging at the end of his new, improved chain. Brandon took a moment to observe the dog's enthusiastic attempts to break free, smirked when the thick links held and jerked Opie back each time. Exactly what the elephant had needed from the get go.

Natalya hesitated at his front porch steps. "Maybe you should park the car in the street."

He glanced at her, trying to ascertain if he'd heard sarcasm in her voice. The worried tug to her eyebrows, however, revealed seriousness.

"Why?"

She shrugged. "In case anyone else gets any bright ideas about screwing with my car."

He squinted at her. "So we'll park it farther away?"

"So if it, I don't know, blows up or something it can't do any damage?"

He almost laughed. Until he remembered one particular explosion that struck too close to home. Glancing over Natalya's shoulder, he considered her car. Parking it a block away had merit. Parking it in the garage, however, held even more. He'd hear the door open if anyone tried to tamper with the Accord.

Brandon returned down the short walkway and punched the keycode opener on the side of his garage. As the panel lifted, he jogged to Natalya's car and moved it inside. She met him at the interior door.

"Better?" he asked with a grin.

"Better."

Fitting his key in the door, and his free hand into the small of her back, he escorted her inside his kitchen where the light over his island stove illuminated the tiled floor and walnut cabinets. Natalya gravitated to the drop-in convection oven. "You cook?"

"Not much. You?" Brandon shoved his hands under the faucet, anxious to scrub.

"I used to when Kate and I were in college. Not so much now. That's some dog next door."

She was stalling, and he wasn't terribly inclined to hurry her up. The more she relaxed, the more likely he'd get something meaningful out of her. Specifically who she feared and why.

"Opie's a nut ball. If he likes you, he *loves* you. If he doesn't like you, you better run and hope the chain holds."

"Sounds like the perfect kind of dog." Natalya meandered to his refrigerator and pulled open the door.

"He's not so bad. Can I get you something?"

"Mind if I have some of this orange juice?"

Brandon pulled a glass from the dishwasher. Before he could turn fully around, Natalya plucked it from his hands. "You don't have to wait on me. I can get it."

As she poured, he admired her thighs. Until tonight, when he'd watched her use those damning legs to hold herself onto a metal pole, he'd never realized just how much strength they contained. Now, as he traced the contours of well-formed muscle, he wondered how he'd never noticed. Pretty legs. Deadly legs.

He cleared his throat as the familiar stirring of desire prickled his skin. "Listen, Natalya, back at Fantasia—"

"Oh, that." Natalya drank deeply from her glass. "Don't worry about it."

"No. It isn't that simple."

Delicate eyebrows arched. "It's not? Looked that way to me. You told me not to, I did it anyway, and you didn't like it."

Brandon's frown returned in an instant. Put that way, the summary did sound simple. But she glossed over the real concerns. Some of which she understood. Some of which she couldn't begin to comprehend. He crossed to her and braced both hands on the countertop, framing her between his arms. "No, it's not that simple."

Time for some bold honesty. If he intended to gain hers, he'd have to surrender some of his. He took a shallow breath and another step closer. Her body heat rolled into him, making him painfully aware of her nearness. His pulse kicked up a notch. "You said some other things."

"Right. Like you're jealous." Over the rim of her glass, her eyes twinkled. "Are you?"

Avoiding the question, Brandon plucked the glass from her hands and set it on the counter near her hip. "Why are you here?"

She blinked. For a nanosecond, her cool facade faltered, and those jade green eyes failed to cloak momentary surprise. But on her next blink, the mask of indifference settled firmly into place. "Because you needed a ride home."

"And you have yet to ask me for your keys to leave."

Come on, baby. Where are you? He pressed his thigh between hers, searching for contact with the truth the only way he knew how. A lift of his heel brushed the top of his thigh against her pussy. Slowly. Deliberately. He left his leg there, adding a little weight to tease her clitoris as her lashes fluttered and her lips parted. Lowering his voice to a near whisper, he asked again, "Why are you here, Natalya?"

"Because . . ." She licked her lips and swallowed. Her composure threatened to break again, evidenced by the hitch in her breathing. With her next breath, however, control slid over her expression once more. "I haven't asked to leave yet."

Damn it.

His gaze searched hers, his own heart thumping, his cock hard. She was like a safe, locked up tight and impossible to open without the right code. There had to be a way, other than using her body against her. At this rate, by the time she yielded, he'd be so turned on he'd forget what he'd set out to accomplish.

He lifted his knee again, stroking her clit a second time. Turning his head a fraction, he brushed his lips across her cheek. "Why not?" Determined on victory, Brandon bent his elbows and grazed his chest against her breasts. Her hardened nipples stabbed through the light fabric of his shirt. His cock pulsed, the urge to satisfy her body's silent requests, instinctive and fierce. She was primed and ready. But damn it, so was he.

Summoning every last ounce of his willpower, he straightened his arms and withdrew his upper body. Heavy-lidded, her gaze latched onto his, but her eyes remained impassive. *Where are you, Natalya? Where, damn it?*

"I just haven't," she murmured.

Brandon's body screamed for contact. His skin felt too tight, his pulse much too fast. The hollowness in his gut corresponded with the throbbing of his cock, and he gave into temptation for a fleeting heart-beat. He dropped his body full into hers, lowered his mouth to the side of her neck. A teasing nip was all he could risk, and even that had him swallowing back a groan when she tipped her head sideways inviting him to more.

Lifting his head, his eyes tracked the delicate line of her jaw to her full, soft lips, the bump at the bridge of her nose. She hadn't always been so elegant. A tomboy once? Had she broken it climbing a tree? He couldn't help but grin.

Yet as his eyes locked with hers, his grin vanished. His heart clanged into his ribs. She was here. *Right fucking here.*

"Why?" he whispered.

"Because I want to stay," she answered just as quietly.

Now they were getting somewhere.

Thirty-one

ecause you want to feel me inside you?" Brandon whispered against
Natalya's shoulder. Her skin turned to gooseflesh beneath the light
caress of his lips. He glanced up, certain to keep his eyes on hers with
every response. His voice was hoarse, even to his own ears. "Because
you can't wait to fuck me?"

She flattened a palm against his chest. Fingertips curled into his
shirt. The breath she drew shuddered. "Yes."

Truth. He closed his eyes and breathed in the sweet scent of springtime lilacs. Forcing himself not to get caught up in the heavenly aroma,
he steered his mind back on course. This was about answers. Quenching
desire came later.

He trailed the tip of his tongue along her prominent collarbone.
"Because what happened this afternoon wasn't just casual?"

Her nails scraped against his chest as her fingers curled tighter. He
felt the tenseness in her shoulders as she held her breath. She closed her
eyes, and Brandon swore silently. Retreat. She'd retreat before he could
ever reach through, grab on, and hold her near. Damn, damn, *damn*!

But when Natalya's lashes lifted, to his complete surprise, nothing
had changed. He could still read through to the depths of her soul and
witness the unguarded truths she continually locked out of sight. Her
breath came out in a shaky rush, arousal claiming her as quickly as it
claimed him. "Right."

His stomach pitched a somersault, and his cock filled to capacity.
Holy shit. He'd suspected. But he hadn't expected her to *admit* it.

Caught up by a wave of unexpected feeling, he gave himself permission to indulge and wound his arms around her waist, urging her body into alignment with his. She came willingly, her hips molding into his, her arms sliding around his neck. Brandon caught her lower lip between his teeth, tugging her mouth closer. Their kiss was fleeting, the brief touch of their tongues insignificant. Intoxicating all the same.

He surrendered her mouth and rested his forehead against hers, praying he could hold out long enough to accomplish answers. "Did you defy me to provoke me?"

Natalya shook her head, but her eyes never left his.

Truth.

"Because you need the money?"

"Yes," she murmured, her blink lasting longer than necessary.

Lie. He frowned and dropped one hand to the gentle curve of her bottom. He'd let the lie slide, but under no circumstance would he allow those shutters to snap closed. Holding her firmly in place, he rubbed his swollen erection against the sensitive flesh he knew would be wet. Her hoarse moan gave him victory.

Slipping his other hand between their bodies, he tugged at her tank top, bunching it into his hands until the warmth of her skin met his knuckles. He slid his fingers over her ribs, higher to the thin satin that covered her breasts. Cupping his palm around the weighty flesh, he rolled his thumb over one hard, distended nipple. He played with her lips, kissed her slow and easy, tasting the desire that burned within her. Her breath came hard and fast, beckoning to him, and Brandon let down his guard to sink his body into hers and kiss her with all the ferocious need that boiled in his blood.

At her moan, he drew back. Not yet. He couldn't get lost in her until he understood. Aware what he intended to ask next possessed the ability to repel her away, he took his time, keeping his forehead against hers, holding her gaze steadily. A union far more intimate than anything he'd ever experienced. Looking into her eyes, touching her body, *watching* the honest way she responded to him—Brandon's head felt dizzy.

She arched her back into his palm, her lashes threatening to close. When he gave that aroused nipple a deliberate pinch, her lashes lifted, and she let out a gasp. The sound ricocheted into him, vibrating down his spine to take root in his groin. His cock throbbed in answer.

He swallowed to wet his drying throat, but his words still came out harsh and unsteady. "Do you carry that gun because you're afraid of someone?"

"No."

He'd made the mistake of letting his gaze drop to her mouth, and at her answer he jerked it swiftly back to her eyes, expecting to find the veil barring him from the truth. Instead, it shocked him to find once again, she'd spoken the truth. She wasn't afraid? How the hell was that possible?

A frown pulled at his brow as he searched through all the logical explanations he could come up with. He took his best guess. "For someone?"

Biting down on her lower lip, she wriggled her body against his with a faint, but distinct nod. "Please, Brandon, no more talking." Her nails raked down his back as she dragged her hips firmly against his. A shudder rolled down her spine, and she let out a soft moan.

Damnation, he ached to give her the relief she wanted. It would be so easy to yield and lift her onto the countertop. Peel off her shorts, unfasten his pants . . . He bit back a groan and squeezed his eyes shut tight. He still had things to say, and once they crossed that bridge, he didn't know what might happen. She could very well lock herself away so tightly he might never get through again.

He brought his other hand between their bodies and pushed her shirt all the way up. Withdrawing from her long enough to pull it over her head, he dropped it on the floor and dipped his mouth to the deep valley between her breasts. Cupping her breasts with both hands, he massaged the soft, warm flesh and trailed his lips over the high swell. Working his way lower, he paused above one dusky nipple and looked back up to her face. "Would it be so bad if I were jealous?"

Natalya's fingers slid into his hair as she arched her back, urging her nipple closer to his mouth. "No."

Truth.

Brandon swirled his tongue around the erect bud. "Would you believe me if I told you I wanted you off stage to protect you?"

"Yes."

Lie. What the fuck?

He closed his mouth around her nipple and sucked hard. Her gasp cut through the relative quiet, and her nails dug into his scalp. He ignored the pressure of her hands that demanded he stay put and let the slippery flesh slide from his lips. The undulation of her body sent spasms of pleasure rolling through him. Good Lord, he wanted to be inside her. He didn't know how much longer he could suffer the torment of desire and the conflicting need to know what made her tick. The need to understand just how she viewed this *thing* between them.

Releasing her breasts, he brought both hands to her waist and dipped his fingers beneath the tight elastic of her shorts. He pushed the cotton down, taking her thong underwear with it, and cupped the smooth contour of her firm cheeks. Bringing her softness closer to his aching cock. So close he could feel her moist heat despite the barrier of his pants. Brandon shuddered.

His teeth scored into her shoulder before he closed his lips and planted a soft kiss against her creamy skin. "I do, Natalya," he murmured. "I want to protect you."

Natalya's hands slid over his shoulders. Nimble fingers found the buttons along the front of his shirt, slowly popping them free. When she pushed the loose material to the edge of his shoulders and her smooth palms glided over his chest, he sucked in a sharp breath. Brandon swayed under the staggering sensation. He hadn't realized how much he'd been craving the feel of her hands on him. Not until now, when he'd pushed so hard to make contact with her that he'd opened himself as well.

She moved her leg, and her clothing tumbled to her ankles.

Brandon splayed one hand over her tailbone, the other he moved around in front to cup her pussy. Moisture met his seeking fingertips. He slid his index finger through her damp folds and pressed the heel of his palm against her sensitive nub.

Natalya trembled. Her nails dug into his bare shoulders as she leaned against the countertop and curled a slender calf around his leg. Eyes closed, head tipped back, she moaned, "Brandon . . ."

He had to know. Had to hear her say it. Leaning his bare chest into hers, he eased his finger inside her slick sheath. His voice rang thick and hoarse. "Do you want to come, beautiful?"

Her inner muscles contracted. "God . . . yes . . ."

Brandon pushed in deep as his body coiled tight. *Fuck.* The simple utterance was enough to hurtle him to the brink. He sucked in deep breaths to temper the shock of ecstasy. "Go ahead. I want you to, sweetheart. I want you to feel me. Know me."

"Not without you," she rasped.

Oh, *holy crap*. That was no way to stop him from coming. And damned if he could fight the pleas of her body any longer. The time for answers had come and gone. He stepped back, yielding to the questing of her hands at his belt. She tugged it loose, the jangle of metal like a gunshot to his frayed nerves. He held absolutely still, scarcely able to breathe as she released the solitary button, then his zipper.

He glanced over his shoulder at the couch—no way would he make it there. Stepping out of the material pooled at his ankles, he grabbed her by the hipbones and set her on the countertop. Her legs wound around his waist. Her mouth found his, hungry and demanding. His low moan mingled with hers, and his erection pressed against her slick opening. A rock of her body urged him to bring them together. To take them both to that delirious place where desire bound them tight and carried them away.

On a shaky breath, Brandon pulled his hips back and pushed through her soft tissues, sliding in deep. She surrounded him. Her hot flesh gripped and squeezed. Her nails scored down the length of his back. *Fuck*. He couldn't move. Couldn't think. She was warm, wet, and perfect. The needy tangle of her tongue fringed with an innocence he couldn't define. Like a calming breeze before a thunderstorm rolled in. "God, you feel good."

She leaned back to brace her hands on the countertop behind her and lifted her body into his. Sensation surged down his spine. His cock swelled. Bliss threatened to drag him into oblivion. Robbed of the ability to breathe, he tore his mouth from hers to whisper against her cheek, "I'm not going to last long. But I'll make it up to you."

A faint smile crossed her beautiful face as she lifted her eyes to his. Her leg tightened, drawing his body closer as she glided along his hard length. "Me neither."

He resisted the driving need to slam inside her, determined to let her find pleasure first. Holding on to her waist, he guided her slowly and bit down on the inside of his cheek. Jesus, this was heaven. Unlike anything he'd ever experienced. His body strained with the effort of controlling himself, his arms shook, his thighs bunched tight.

Up and down, she lifted, taking him in deep, then withdrawing until he thought he'd lose his mind if she released him all the way. But just as he felt certain he'd fall from that sweet, hot haven, she pushed forward again, bringing him home.

He made the mistake of looking between them and witnessing the way he moved in and out of her body. Swearing beneath his breath, he dug his fingers into her hips. "Natalya," he ground out between clenched teeth.

"Feel me."

Her response came so softly he had to strain to hear her. It's effect, however, brought him to his knees. In one thunderous heartbeat, she engulfed his senses. Her perfume carried him away to the naivety of youth, and the rasp of her breath erased a decade of guilt. The warmth of her body sliding against his soothed something restless and untamed.

His arms wrapped around her waist, his mouth crashed into hers, savage and hard. Unraveled and exposed, he drove in and out of her in wild abandon, oblivious to all but the ecstasy building at the base of his spine.

"Brandon. Oh, God. Brandon . . ." Her words gave way to a throaty groan.

Brandon felt her flesh quiver around him. Her ragged cry crashed into his awareness, and sent him surging over a high cliff edge. Pinpoints of light burst behind his eyes as release stormed through him. He groaned against the spasming of his body, his breath catching as he came unendingly.

Spent beyond all means, he dropped his head to her shoulder and gasped for air. The last of her orgasm pulsed around his softening erection, and he gave in to a soft smile. He brushed a kiss to her damp shoulder. "I don't think I can move."

Natalya's chuckle danced down the side of his neck. Light fingertips trailed over his ribs. "Me neither, but you're going to have to. I can't sleep on this countertop."

Summoning the last of his remaining strength, Brandon scooped her into his arms and eased her to her feet. The separation of their bodies filled him with a strange sense of disappointment, but it also explained why their lovemaking seemed so much different than anything he'd experienced. As he reached to the floor for their clothing, he glimpsed the sheen of moisture along his sagging cock.

Panic kicked his heart into overdrive. In countless entanglements, not once, not *fucking* once, had he been dumb enough to forget a condom.

He balled their clothes into his fist and struggled to swallow. He was clean, no question about that. He sincerely doubted she didn't look after herself as well. But there were other repercussions. Long-term ramifications that always had exceptions.

Trying to keep the terror out of his voice, he extended her clothes and suggested, "How about we curl up on the couch?"

"How 'bout we go to bed? It's after five."

It was his turn to lie. He hated doing it, but he hated spoiling the magic by explaining his hang-up with beds more. "I'm not ready to crash yet. I'll put a movie in. You can doze in my lap." For emphasis, he gave her a meaningful look and added, "I don't want to let you go just yet."

At least that was truth. He took her hand in his unsteady one and led her to the couch where he stretched out and drew her into his embrace. Picking up the remote, he clicked on the television. Then, he dragged the afghan on the back of the couch over their bare bodies. Natalya snuggled close, her chin tucked into his chest.

For several moments, they enjoyed the silence. But try as he might, Brandon couldn't let go of the unprotected sex issue. Fully aware he was making a bigger deal out of it than perhaps he should—obviously if she were concerned she'd have said something by now—he pulled his fingers through her long, silken hair and let out a heavy sigh.

"So. I'm kinda concerned."

"Oh?" She tipped her head back, looking up at him with the brightest green eyes he'd ever seen.

He frowned, feeling suddenly very childish. If he didn't ask, however, he'd never sleep. "I just had the orgasm of my life without a rubber glove."

"Of your life, huh?" Grinning, she trailed a nail down his chest.

To his consternation, his cheeks flushed hot. He tightened the arm about her shoulders, pulling her closer so she couldn't see his blush. "Yeah."

"Relax, Moretti." Natalya pressed a kiss to the center of his chest. "I've had an IUD since college and my job requires quarterly testing."

He raised an eyebrow. "Your job?"

"Well, my former job, I guess."

A law secretary? He frowned. No law firm he knew of required employees to test for STDs every three months. Setting two fingertips beneath her chin, he tipped her head up to look into her eyes. *Truth.*

Weird.

To cover the searching of his gaze, he dipped his head and drew her into a languorous kiss.

As he eased it to a close, her palm settled against his cheek. "Tell me more about this *of your life* part."

Chuckling, he dragged a knuckle over the bump on the bridge of her nose. "How about you tell me how you did this?"

"That?" Natalya laughed softly. "Someone hit me."

"Hit you?" His voice escalated.

"Yeah. He broke it in three places. I had two black eyes for almost two months."

"He?" Brandon lifted to his elbow, possessed by the sudden urge to slam the bastard's teeth into the back of his head.

Natalya looped her arms around his neck and dragged him back into the couch. Eyes twinkling, she brushed the tip of her nose against his. "I broke his jaw."

He couldn't help but laugh. Winding his arms around her tight, he hauled her atop his chest. "Listen, there's something you should know. The graffiti on your car . . ." Trailing off, he pondered the wisdom of telling her he'd been involved with Jill. She might leap out of his arms and run. On the other hand, she deserved to know why she'd been made a target. At least in that respect. He steeled himself for the worst. "I'm pretty sure Jill's responsible. I made the mistake of going home with her, and I haven't been able to get rid of her since."

"I figured it was Jill," she answered a bit too quietly.

"It's not what you think."

"I'm not thinking anything."

"And this isn't the same sort of thing."

"It's not?"

He trailed his hands down the sloping length of her spine and cupped her bottom. "No. I like you."

"I should hope so." She chuckled again.

Though he'd had his fill of her moments before, the stirring of her warm flesh against his cock sent desire hurtling through his veins. He felt himself rise against her abdomen.

She noticed the intrusion and ground her hips against his swelling length. "I like you too."

"Tell me what I have to do to keep you offstage."

Natalya lifted to her hands and dragged her body down his hardening cock. The damp folds of her pussy enveloped him, taunting with a promise of paradise. Seeking to return her teasing, he fitted a hand between their bodies and pressed his thumb to the hard little nub between her legs.

She closed her eyes and gyrated her hips against his hand. "That's not . . . possible."

"It's not, huh?" he murmured as he slipped his finger lower, sliding through her moist flesh to swirl around her slickened opening.

Natalya refused to yield so easily. She took him into her hand and closed her fingers around his swollen cock. As she slowly pumped him, the color of her eyes darkened to deep emerald, and she shook her head.

Christ, the woman knew how to manipulate him. He gritted his teeth against the pressure of her fingers, determined to resist. His body, however, refused to comply. Unbidden, his hips lifted into her hand, the pleasant friction nothing less than addicting.

Before she could coerce him into blissful oblivion again, he elbowed her hand aside and caught her by the waist. Lifting her where he wanted her, he brought her body down against his mouth and speared her weeping pussy with his tongue. She bucked forward, her gasp as sharp as breaking glass.

Several thorough minutes and two intense orgasms later, Brandon's own raging need threatened to break him into bits. He rolled her over into the cushions and positioned himself between her thighs. Taking her without a condom had been exquisite—no way was he going back to barriers between them. As he thrust high and sank into her ready depths, her gaze locked with his, baring her vulnerable soul. Her soft cry echoed through him.

Brandon knew then, he had one choice, and one choice only. She'd never agree to leaving the stage. For some reason it was important to her. He, however, couldn't accept that risk. Jill might have painted Natalya's back window, but someone else left her smashed chocolates, and despite what she said, that gun symbolized her fear. Maybe she didn't recognize it as fear, but she recognized the threat.

As he lifted up into her, stroking that spot of pleasure few women knew how to enjoy, he whispered, "You're fired."

Whether she heard him or not, he couldn't say. Rapture washed across her face, and closing her eyes, she surrendered to the motion of their bodies. He gave up thinking, caught her hands in his, and let his eyelids fall. As pleasure swept him away, he dimly recognized the flash of headlights that brightened his front room. Attributing it to a passing car, Brandon lost himself to the incredible feeling of Natalya.

Thirty-two

Natalya woke to the sound of a barking dog and Brandon's comfortable weight trapping her between his body and the back of the couch. Puzzled by the bright light, she glanced at the clock. Ten after nine? Crap! Sergei would be at the agency's condo by now.

She pushed at Brandon's shoulder. He mumbled something, tightened the arm he held at her waist, and pulled her deeper into his embrace. She sighed, torn between spending the energy to struggle free and laying here a while longer.

The low coo of a nearby dove convinced her to wait. Tracing one firm biceps with her fingertip, she admired the man who had loved her so thoroughly throughout the wee hours of morning. It seemed his appetite was insatiable. Then again, the same could be said for hers. No matter how many times he took her to the brink of ecstasy, or whether he did it with his mouth, his hands, his cock, she couldn't get enough.

He'd fired her too, and in her bleary haze, she'd welcomed the opportunity to be nothing but woman. Fleeting pleasure she'd known would end come dawn. It must. Tomorrow night, Iskatel' would move on Kate. While Brandon might have barred her from the stage, he couldn't keep her from Fantasia. He couldn't protect her either, not when she had to risk her life to save Kate's.

But for a few hours, she'd known absolute freedom. He'd given her a part of him. Exposed himself in the way he made love to her. And in so doing, he'd pulled unimaginable feeling from deep within her soul. She liked him. Respected him. Admired him.

If things were different, it would be so easy to fall in love with Brandon Moretti.

The dove cooed again, and Natalya dusted a light kiss over Brandon's mouth. He'd made her laugh. She couldn't remember the last time she'd laughed so freely. Not even the playful banter she shared with Sergei satisfied the way she'd laughed hours ago.

Together they'd built bridges. Burned a few as well. Last night changed them, but no amount of lovemaking could change who she was, and who she was jeopardized Brandon's life.

She could enjoy him for now. Maybe even through tomorrow. After that, the fantasy must end. She'd leave; he'd go on solving cases and spending his nights with beautiful women. Their paths might cross briefly, but they weren't meant to intertwine.

The dove had to stop. That eerie sound of mourning made her nerves stand on end. She pushed at Brandon's shoulder, intending to shoo the thing away from his front porch. "Hey, I gotta get up," she insisted quietly.

"Mm." Light kisses fluttered over her breast. "Stay right here."

"Brandon," she protested with a laugh. Humor drained away as he captured her nipple between his lips and her flesh pulled with the suckling of his mouth. She threaded her fingers through his short dark hair, pressing his head deeper to her breast. A satisfied murmur rumbled in the back of her throat. "You're going to break me."

He lifted his head to turn molten gold eyes on her. "Are you sore?" he whispered, his voice husky.

"A little."

Brushing her hair away from her face, he gave her a tender smile. "How about some coffee then?"

The reality that their night together had come to an end crashed into Natalya like waves against a rocky shore. She shriveled under the bitter disappointment and summoned a wistful smile. "I really need to be getting home. I have plans with Sergei and Kate today."

He dropped his head once more, this time capturing her mouth. Slowly, he kissed her, the velvety brush of his tongue a vibrant reminder of the thorough way he'd explored each inch of her body time and again. Warmth filtered into her veins, along with the craving to forget about Sergei, dismiss the tenderness in her body, and surrender to the arousal Brandon's mouth stoked. But as his cock stiffened against her thigh, he brought the kiss to a leisurely close and gave her a playful grin.

"I'll take you to Kate's in a little bit. I have to take Derek back. Mind if I borrow your car today?"

The dove's soulful call distracted her, and she frowned as a chill spread over her skin.

"Never mind, I can ask Aaron," Brandon added quickly.

"No, no." She shook her head, dismissing the stupid bird. "You can borrow my car. That's fine. You have pigeons."

"You sure?"

"You can't hear them?"

"No, about the car."

"Yeah, that's fine."

Chuckling, Brandon rolled off the couch and extended his hand. She slid her palm into his, following him to her feet. A glance at her shirt had her wrinkling her nose at the prospect of putting it on. With it came a vivid memory of the last time Brandon had carried her to the heights of passion and how he'd used it to dry her body off as she drifted between sleep and wakefulness. His hands had been gentle, his touch laden with tenderness.

As if he sensed her hesitation, he bent over and picked up the tank top. "I'll wash this. You wanna borrow one of mine?"

"Please."

A short nod, punctuated with a chaste kiss to the tip of her nose, left her wanting to reach out and stop his retreat down the hall. Some-where in the middle of the night, hardened cop became gallant. And sweet. No wonder Jill refused to let go. If he'd treated her with half of the affection Natalya had experienced in the last six hours, she could understand the graffiti.

This isn't the same sort of thing.

His voice echoed in Natalya's mind. If it wasn't the same sort of thing, then just what was it? Had he been telling her he wanted more? Things she couldn't give? Natalya chewed on her lower lip and gravi-tated to the picture of his family that sat on his shelves. He looked so young and carefree. Sergei too.

"Here you go." Brandon appeared at her side, one hand on her shoulder, the other at her belly and holding a white T-shirt branded with *Sadie's*.

She shrugged it on and followed him into the kitchen, dismayed he'd donned a pair of cotton boxers that thwarted her view of his tight butt. While drinking coffee in the nude might be unconven-tional, she hadn't considered she'd lose the ability to admire one of his best features.

The dove cooed again, and Natalya grimaced. That sound made fingernails on chalkboards pleasant. "That bird has to go." Leaving Brandon to the coffee, she picked up a magazine, rolled it into a tube, and followed the sound to his front door.

The chain lock rattled against the striker plate as she pulled the heavy wooden door open. Eyes trained to the porch rafters, she scanned the overhang for a nesting bird.

Ooo—wah-hoo.

Natalya glanced down, and a scream rose to the back of her throat. She backed up rapidly, tripping in the process. Landing on her butt, she squeezed her eyes against the sight. But the image had already scalded into her mind. Trapped in a white wicker cage, a white dove cooed from where it stood in a puddle of sticky blood. Its mate lay on the cage floor, bright crimson covering its pristine breast. Its heart had been cut out. The lifeless muscle dangled from the bloody cavity, still attached by one thick vein.

The heavy *thump* from the front hall made Brandon cock his head. "Natalya? You okay?"

When she didn't answer, he set down the coffeepot and darted around the corner. His door stood open. Natalya sat on the floor, facing the porch, one arm thrown over her eyes to block out something he couldn't see. "Sweetheart?" he asked cautiously.

"Get it out of there!"

Her hysterical cry set off blaring sirens in his head. He took a step closer, moving so he could see around her. The shock made him recoil. He'd seen death. Was no stranger to blood. But witnessing the dead bird on his doorstop pitched his stomach violently. That the other bird had been left to grieve its lifemate, twisted something deep inside his gut.

He shut the door on the massacre. When he had Natalya settled down he'd dispose of the dead bird and set the other free. Bending, he fitted his hands beneath her arms and helped her to her feet.

The dove cooed, low and mournful.

"Get it out of there," Natalya screamed again. "Get it out! Oh, God, get it out." Turning her face into his chest, her shoulders shuddered, and she let out a sob. She brought one hand up to his chest and beat a futile fist against his ribs. "Get it out," she choked through her tears.

"Okay. Shh." He smoothed her hair. "I'll get the bird out. Come sit down."

He guided her back to the couch where minutes ago they'd known perfect peace. She huddled into the corner, her unfocused stare riveted on the dark television. Tears streamed down her cheeks, clawing at Brandon's heart.

When he found out who'd done this, he'd rip the bastard into pieces. If it came from his father's *family*, even more so. This was too much. Too cruel. The implication too chilling.

Grinding his teeth together, he stalked down the hall for a towel, then stormed to the front door once more. As he opened it, the poor dove cooed again. It bent its head and nudged its dead companion. Brandon let out a hiss.

He jerked open the cage door and shoved his hand inside, fitting his fingers around the mourning bird's wings. It offered no struggle as he pulled it out of the cage and carefully wrapped it up in the towel. He kicked the cage behind the bushes. Until he could clean up the mess, he didn't want the neighbors seeing it.

Now what to do with a bird? Somewhere in the recesses of his mind, he recalled his mother telling him hand-reared birds didn't possess the ability to fend for themselves in the wild. This one sure didn't seem afraid of him. Not like he'd expect a wild bird to be. Hell, it hadn't moved except to cock its head and fix a dark soulful eye on his face.

He went back inside and approached Natalya, who also hadn't moved. "Natalya?"

Like the sound of his voice was a physical line thrown to draw her back, she slowly focused on his face and retreated from her thoughts. Returning to the present. "Yes?" she asked, eerily calm.

Brandon sank into the cushion next to her. Setting the bird in his lap, he slid his arm around her shoulders and drew her into his side. His lips moved through her hair as he fought off his own grief. Sorrow that he'd brought this to her. "I'm so sorry," he whispered. Sorry that he'd coaxed her into admitting her desire. That he'd let her stay the night. That he'd exposed her to this nightmare.

She curled into his embrace, collapsing against him. All the strength he knew she possessed, the courage he'd witnessed and admired on countless occasions, vanished in the desperate clutch of her hands. The tremble of her shoulders.

He tightened his embrace and tucked her head beneath his chin. The bastard would die. He'd sacrifice his badge, his career, his life if it meant Natalya would never again know this kind of fear.

Natalya didn't know how long she soaked up the warmth from Brandon's body. But gradually the ice in her veins thawed and the vise around her throat let go enough she could swallow without gagging.

Other truths sank in the longer he held her. She'd finally cracked one-hundred percent. She'd stood toe-to-toe with men and pulled the trigger. Even the unforgettable way a person's eyes slowly turned cold as death stole over them had never brought her to collapse. She'd mopped up blood, and no crimson pool had ever made her want to vomit the way that poor bird's had.

She'd lost her grip, and all she could think about was that dove grieving its butchered companion. It had been calling for help, *mourning*, and she'd been annoyed.

A bird shouldn't possess the ability to turn her inside out. Shouldn't be able to bring her to her knees. And it damn sure shouldn't make her afraid.

Yet, she was. She'd become a liability to everyone—Brandon, Sergei, Kate. Herself. Without the ability to block out emotion and focus on the objective, she was a risk. After the warnings last night, she should have been on guard, anticipating something more would come. But no. She'd let it slide into the back of her mind and became careless.

Worse, if she'd had any doubt at all about Dmitri knowing her involvement with Brandon, she'd just become convinced. They'd planned doves for their wedding. He found their ability to choose a mate for life fascinating. *As it should be,* he'd remarked. *The perfect symbol of love.*

Sniffling, she dropped her hand and stroked the top of the dove's head.

Dmitri knew, and Dmitri meant for one of them to die. The other was meant to suffer.

Fear trickled down her spine. She had to talk to Sergei. To Kate. Make it clear she'd screwed up and there was only one way this could end. She had to disappear.

Eternally.

Thirty-three

"I'm coming back to get you when I pick up Derek." Brandon caught Natalya's elbow as she reached for the car door, his grip gentle, but firm enough to communicate he wasn't letting go until she agreed. "In the meantime," he said as he inclined his head toward the Accord's rear window, "I'll get that cleaned up."

That would give her approximately two hours to do the things she needed to do, and him time enough to call a brief meeting with Mayer. Other than that, he didn't intend to let Natalya out of his sight.

Her quiet gaze reflected worry, and he released her arm to cup the side of her face. "Hey, you're going to be fine."

"It's not me I'm worried about."

"*We're* going to be fine." We. There—he'd said it. He'd equated the both of them together. Damned if it didn't feel good too. After an incredible morning in Natalya's arms, he was done fighting that as well. He cared for her, and he didn't intend to set her aside any time soon.

Especially not with someone threatening her.

Her smile struggled for freedom, and he stroked her cheek with the pad of his thumb. Adding pressure to the back of her head, he urged her to lean across the center console so he could kiss those swollen lips. "I promise," he whispered against her mouth.

As she nodded, she closed her eyes, and her lips moved against his. Softly. Gently. He reveled in the simplicity of their embrace, the warmth that invaded his veins. Arousal tugged at the back of his mind, but it stayed there, dormant. Surprisingly satisfied by just the silken feel of her mouth beneath his and the sweet honeyed flavor of complacent woman.

Brandon eased the kiss to a close and gave her free hand a squeeze. "I'll see you in a little bit."

"Okay."

With one last meaningful look over her shoulder, she climbed out of the car and hurried to Kate's front door. He frowned at Sergei's car as he backed out of the driveway, not at all pleased Natalya had turned to him. Brandon couldn't particularly blame her—their deep-rooted friendship was obvious. Still, it burned that he couldn't fill that need.

Patience.

She'd come around. He'd make it impossible not to.

He stepped on the gas and headed for his house once more. Thirty minutes ago, he'd snuck in a phone call to Mayer while he was dressing. Mayer ought to be there by now.

Sure enough, the red Volkswagen sat in Brandon's driveway, and Aaron lounged against the driver's door, legs stretched out, ankles crossed. He straightened as Brandon pulled in beside him and turned off the Accord.

"Sharing cars now, huh?"

Brandon gave him a stern frown. "The Shelby's at the club. I got hit yesterday—gotta take it in to repair the headlight."

"Uh-huh. Those headlights are so important during the day."

"Shut up, Mayer." Brandon unlocked his front door and ushered his best friend inside.

"So what's the big problem you mentioned this morning?"

"Close the door and meet me in the kitchen."

He headed for his bedroom and the bird he'd put in an old crate he found in the corner of his garage. Opening the door carefully, he glanced around to make sure it hadn't flown out before entering. It sat in the crate, head cocked, watching his approach. So far, so good. It hadn't keeled over yet. He didn't know what kind of stress a dead companion could create, but he imagined it couldn't be good. The bird, however, seemed resilient.

Brandon checked the dish of water they'd set inside, then for good measure covered the crate with a towel. His neighbor had a cockatiel; he'd consult her later.

Convinced the dove wouldn't fall over dead any time in the immediate future, he headed for his kitchen, where he found Mayer at the island table, coffee in hand. In front of him sat a stack of papers Brandon didn't recognize.

"What's that?" He gestured at the paperwork as he picked up his earlier mug.

"While you've been playing in the sand box, I've been working."

Brandon grunted.

"I dug up some names in Kate's history. I figured if nothing's standing out about the people around her, then we ought to see where she came from. Natalya and she knew each other in college. Natalya's file is too clean. Someone surely remembers the both of them."

Interest piqued. The one thing Brandon craved was information about Natalya. After this morning, nothing would convince him that she wasn't somehow associated with the murders. She'd said she was afraid for someone. Repeated it in Kate's driveway. To Brandon's knowledge, Kate and Sergei were the only people in this damn town Natalya knew. She'd shown up coincidentally when all signs pointed to Kate being the next target?

Nuh-huh. Not buying it. If Mayer found a common link in Kate's background, someone *else* they could investigate, answers might come faster.

Overnight would suit Brandon just fine. Preferably before Natalya stumbled onto another dead bird. Before things escalated, and he had to confess the danger he posed to her. When that time occurred, he wanted to be in position to get away for a little while. Escape he couldn't indulge in with this case hanging over his head.

"Did you find anything useful?"

"Well, I did find Kate's former sister-in-law. She and her husband have a house over in Newberry Springs. I gave her a call."

"And?"

"*And*, when I told her I had reason to believe Kate and Derek might be in danger, she was more than happy to agree to meet me. I'm going there this afternoon."

"Sounds good." Two and a half hours to Newberry—Brandon just might get overnight answers. He took a long swig of his coffee and rolled it around his mouth, debating how much to tell Mayer. Hell, there wasn't much Mayer didn't know about Brandon's life as it was. No use keeping stuff back now.

"Be careful would you? I'm pretty sure a few enemies of mine have decided to finish what they started fifteen years ago."

Aaron's expression turned serious, his arrogant smirk fading into a speculative squint. "Good old Dad?"

"Yep." Brandon pushed a hand through his short hair and leaned back on his stool. "Natalya found an eviscerated bird on my porch this morning. In a cage. It's companion very much alive."

"No shit."

"She took it pretty hard."

Lifting an eyebrow, Aaron shrugged a shoulder, as if to say, *not surprising.*

"Jill vandalized her car. And the other day, I'd swear someone was snooping around outside the house."

"Shit, Bran, why didn't you say something?"

Brandon shrugged. He'd been too concerned with Natalya in general to really give much thought to the situation. "Just keep an eye open. If they're following me, chances are they're following you. Don't open somebody else to trouble."

"I already called Rory. Thought he might want to get out of town for a little bit."

"He hasn't left for his mom's?"

Shaking his head, Aaron took another swig. "He might have. I left him a message. Told him I thought we had a lead. Gave him two hours to get his shit together and go with me."

A moment of silence passed before Aaron's steely gaze locked with Brandon's. "I think you better distance yourself from Natalya. I know I pushed you, and now you don't want to believe it, but I'll put money on it that I come back with things you don't want to hear. Stuff that's going to make her empty file point right to these murders. There's too many coincidences, Bran." He ticked off points on his fingers. "We know the clubs hired a new dancer right before each girl disappeared. Natalya shows up to fit that. She danced after you told her not to— maybe it's a sign of some sort. Her file makes her an angel, and you and I both know that's not true. And her friend Sergei's too damn good at his job."

Splaying his hands on the countertop, Aaron leaned in closer. "Now you're telling me people are dicking with you? An accident. A dead bird. Someone snooping around your house? C'mon, pull your head out of your ass. She might be a good fuck, but she's playing you."

Fierce banging at Brandon's front door brought the conversation to an abrupt halt. Cautiously he rose and retrieved his gun from behind the planter. Keeping it hidden at the small of his back, he went to the door.

Derek stood on the other side, bouncing from foot to foot. His little face lit up like a Christmas tree when Brandon opened the door. "Brandon! There's clowns at the park! And rides! Sue said I could go with them—can I? Can I?"

He blinked, the stream of joined together words too much for his already sluggish brain. Behind his back, his finger slid off the trigger. He tucked his pistol into his waistband, then hunkered down, eye level with Derek. "Whoa, slow down there, buddy. What?"

Feminine laughter drifted up his driveway seconds before Sue emerged. "Sorry, Brandon. There's a carnival of some sort down at the park. Heard about it during cartoons this morning. I'm going to take the girls. If you think Kate wouldn't mind . . ." She inclined her head at Derek.

"Oh. Well." Brandon straightened to his full height and braced a shoulder against the doorframe. "No. I don't think that'd be a problem. I've got some errands to run today. I'll pick him up from the park and spare Kate the trouble. What time?"

Derek bounced higher, the tap of his sneakered feet accented by high-pitched squeals of glee. "We're going to the clowns, going to the clowns."

Brandon watched the little boy's enthusiastic display. Oh, to be young again and know the magic of clowns, balloons, and corn dogs. He met Sue's dark gaze, her smile saying the same thing.

"How about three?"

"I'll be there."

Sue lifted on tiptoe and looked around Brandon, down his front hall. "Is that Aaron's car in the drive?"

A laugh burst from Brandon's gut, and he stepped out on his porch. Ever since she'd run into Aaron one afternoon when the girls were playing in the backyard, she made subtle hints that she'd like to meet Brandon's partner. Knowing Mayer as he did, Brandon couldn't tolerate the thought of sweet Sue joining the ranks of throw-away women that piled around Aaron's feet. She was a *mom* for God's sake. Moms deserved respect. A concept Aaron had yet to grasp.

Setting both hands on Sue's shoulders, he guided her around the opposite direction. "Yes. I'll tell you again, he's more trouble than you want."

Chuckling, Sue shrugged free of his hold and reached her hand out for Derek's. "One of these days, Brandon, you're not going to be here to babysit."

"Uh-huh." He grinned down at Derek. "Be good, buddy. I'll see you after a bit."

As the little boy waved, Brandon closed the door. Now, to get

Mayer's help in cleaning up Natalya's car and bagging the evidence. He wanted DNA off that condom. Solid evidence Jill was behind the vandalism. When he had that, he'd think about the facts Aaron wanted him to see.

W hat the hell are you talking about?" Sergei shot to his feet, his face a mask of hot angry color. He glared down at Natalya, fists clenched as if he fought the urge to shake her. "You can't put yourself in that position!"

Ignoring the way Kate furiously fidgeted with her glasses, Natalya straightened her back and held Sergei's furious glower. Contrary to the way Brandon's anger intimidated her, Sergei's only fueled her resolve. "It's not about can or can't. I *must*. Tomorrow's the night. We know *nothing*. Dmitri, however, knows everything. If you think he's going to link me with Iskatel′ now, you've lost every bit of sense you've ever possessed."

His fingers relaxed. Clenched again. Unblinking, she waited for him to accept the full measure of their circumstances. A switch-up was their only alternative. Take Kate out of the picture, insert herself, and play the part accordingly.

"What if you fail?"

Sergei's quiet question hung in the air, ominous and heavy. Slowly, he lowered himself into the seat beside Kate and leaned forward, elbows on his knees. "What if you fail, Natalya, and the *Bratva* kills you? Then where are we? Dmitri's still free. Iskatel′'s still operating. Kate's *still* in danger, and all the intelligence we've gathered is as worthless as the dust on that shelf." He thrust his hand toward the shelf above Kate's couch.

"I won't fail." Natalya absorbed the assertion, gaining confidence from hearing the words. Failure wasn't an option. "It's the only chance we have, Sergei. If I don't go, Kate's lost. I'm dead anyway if we don't crack this case in twenty-four hours. And Brandon might be too. You might get out of it. The agency can bury you. But you'll always be looking over your shoulder."

"Would you two quit talking about me like I'm not sitting here." Exasperated, Kate stood up and began to pace. "I'm not going to let you kill yourself, sis."

"What are you going to do?" Natalya challenged. "Go to Dubai? Wait for us to squirrel you out of there? Do you have any idea how long that would take? Derek needs you!"

Kate threw her hands in the air. "Don't you have some sort of tracking device I can eat or something? You're the CIA, damn it!"

"No, Kate, that crap's for the movies. This is real life. You of all people should know how easy it is for you and I to swap places." Natalya rolled her eyes. "We haven't done it, oh, but all through college."

"How am *I* going to become *you*?" Kate cried. "You can become me, easy enough. But damn it, Natalya, you're involved with Brandon. The people who want me know you. How am I supposed to play those parts? Brandon would be the first person to notice." She hugged her arms around her waist and huddled into her oversize sweatshirt. "If I have to get cozy with him, I'll puke."

At the thought of Brandon with her sister, with anyone for that matter, the same sense of revulsion churned Natalya's stomach. She couldn't keep him, but she loathed the idea of Brandon's mouth on anyone but hers.

Forcing the distasteful reality aside, Natalya took a deep breath and focused on Sergei. "That's why I'm going to disappear. When it's over, you'll tell him *everything*."

He flinched. Unobtrusively, but a flinch all the same. Good. He understood the lies stopped once Dmitri was behind bars.

The low mellow tones of Russian washed over Natalya as Sergei asked, "What if he still wants you then?"

A chill drifted over Natalya. It would be nice if Brandon would accept what she was, the ugly truth of the lies she lived and the people she'd killed. But it was a fantasy that would never happen. She'd always be a liability.

Shaking her head, she answered, "He won't."

She tucked her hands between her knees, relieved Sergei had stopped arguing and finally understood the severity of their situation. "So we're agreed? Make the arrangements tonight. Tomorrow, I'll wait for your call. Nikolai will never know the difference."

"Who?" Kate asked with sudden interest.

"Nikolai," Natalya repeated. "Why?"

"While you were onstage, Jill was bragging about her VIP tip. *Nikolai* gave her five hundred dollars. He and another guy she didn't name."

In a heartbeat, Natalya's hands turned clammy. Nikolai had been in the club. There could only be one person capable of dragging Nikolai out of his hideaway and into the public—*Dmitri*. The warnings weren't just from Dmitri, he'd delivered them personally. *Shit*.

"Who's Nikolai?"

At the demanding, rough baritone, Natalya turned to find Brandon in the doorway, his stormy eyes locked on her.

Thirty-four

Brandon didn't need an answer as much as he wanted to hear Natalya's confession. Her ashen face, coupled with the sudden hush that descended on the room was enough to tell him Nikolai was the ghost from her past. Whoever he was, he'd caused the blank pages in her file.

"One of Jill's VIP customers." Kate's smile was bright and cheery.

Nice try, Kate. She couldn't lie to save her ass. Brandon pushed the door shut and joined the small crowd gathered in Kate's living room. He stood at the end of the couch nearest Natalya. She glanced up, also giving him a false smile.

He groaned inwardly. Time for another game of truth and lies. Why the hell wouldn't she just take a leap of faith and trust him? They weren't exactly strangers anymore. Not after some of the things they'd done on his couch, and certainly not after someone left them bloody birds for breakfast.

"Where's Derek?" Kate asked.

"Sue took him over to the carnival." Reaching down, he grabbed Natalya's hand and pulled her to her feet. "We're going to get him now."

She balked, tugging her arm. "Really. I need to shower. Need clothes."

"We'll stop by your place after we drop Derek off here."

Her eyes went wide for a fraction of a second before she latched onto her reserved mask and furrowed her brows. Maybe not her place.

She looked like she'd rather run a marathon than go by her condo. Dipping his mouth to the delicate shell of her ear, he whispered, "You can shower with me."

Drawing away, she arched an eyebrow, but a glimmer of emerald slipped in to darken her jade green gaze. She liked that, did she? Well, he'd be more than happy to lather every inch of her body once he found out who Nikolai was and why his name had turned her ghost white.

She turned to Kate, denying him the opportunity to taunt her further. "Kate, can I borrow something to wear?"

"Closet's there." She pointed down the dim hall to her open bedroom door.

Surprising Brandon, Natalya gave his hand a tug and started down the hall. He followed, ignoring Kate's knowing smirk and the deliberate way Sergei suddenly found an issue of *Woman's World* interesting.

Natalya barred them inside Kate's room by closing the door and leaning against it. "What do you think you're doing?"

"I think the better question is, what are *you* doing?" He moved closer and set his hands on her hips. Nodding at the closed door, he leaned his weight into her and murmured, "This seems vaguely familiar."

"Mm. It does." Though her voice mirrored the purr of arousal, her pursed lips spoiled the effect. So did the palm she flattened against his chest and the push that distanced their bodies. "I can't spend all day playing with you."

"But you want to."

She scolded him with a frown.

Undaunted, Brandon stepped close again, fastening his hands on her hips. He dropped his head and trailed his lips down the length of her neck. "Admit it, Natalya, you'd like nothing more than to get rid of these clothes and feel my body against yours. My mouth on you, my hands on you." He lowered his voice, whispering at the base of her ear. "To have me so deep inside you that you make me tremble."

At the catch of her breath, he tugged on her earlobe with his teeth. "I'm not going to lie about how much I want you. But we're in Kate's room, and we've got to pick up Derek."

The hand on his chest relaxed, slid down to his abdomen. A soft sigh escaped her parted lips. "What do you want from me, Brandon?"

He traced the tip of his tongue around the hollow beneath her ear. "I want to know what you're afraid of." Fitting a hand into the slight distance that separated them, he palmed her breast and gently squeezed. "I want to know where you go when you're hiding behind this infuriating indifferent attitude."

Abruptly withdrawing, he placed a soft kiss against her lips. "And I want you to stay in my shirt."

As he'd expected, she latched on to the least intimidating confession and grinned. "Your shirt? I think that's manageable." Her gaze dropped to his groin along with her hand. As she stroked a finger down the length of his flagging erection, wry humor danced in her eyes. "That is, if you can control yourself enough to let me change the rest of my clothes."

Brandon grunted and stepped away. He sat down on the edge of the bed, all too aware of the intimate setting. Kate's bed, the comfortable pillows, the closed door, Natalya's desire bright in her laughing eyes. It held a strange appeal. Lacked the usual discomfort bedrooms brought. He could almost feel what it would be like to lay Natalya on the down comforter, the way her body would pillow his, the way the mattress would support their joined weight. The linens would be clean and crisp, her body as soft as the feathers behind her head.

He stood up, certain if he stayed another minute he'd suffocate. "I'll wait in the other room."

Without so much as a backward glance, he swiftly exited. No bedrooms. No beds. He might be falling for her, but not that hard.

Kate appraised him with a single glance that said she knew exactly what he'd done the night before and all the dirty thoughts that flooded his mind. He focused on Sergei, in need of some male support. But he found none in the face that watched him with the same wisdom in his quiet stare. A face that Brandon again felt certain he'd seen somewhere before. Maybe without the long hair.

Impossible. He'd never spent time in any of the places listed on Sergei's file.

Natalya exited the distant bedroom, wearing a pair of Kate's tiny jeans shorts and his shirt. Beneath her arm, she carried a flimsy turquoise top. A pair of low-heeled matching sandals dangled from her fingers.

Good. She was planning on staying a while. The night—if he had his way.

"Hey, Moretti," Sergei called as Brandon made for the door.

"Yeah?"

"Natalya said you got sideswiped yesterday. You want me to take a look at your car this afternoon?"

"You know cars?" Brandon asked with a touch of surprise. He'd have never pegged the guy as a grease monkey.

"I can find my way around them. Done a little body work here and there."

"Sure, if you don't mind. It'd save me the trouble of taking it in."

Sergei answered with a long, slow nod.

"I'll call you later," Natalya told Kate as she opened the front door.

"Bring my son back in one piece. No more bloody noses!"

Despite the very real reference, Brandon chuckled. "Not a problem."

Now that he had Natalya alone, he intended to find some answers before they picked up Derek. It was two—that left him a full hour to dig before Sue expected him. He slid into the car, Natalya having beat him inside, and turned the key. "Do you have any siblings?"

Puzzlement shadowed her face. "Yes. Why?"

"Just curious." *Truth. Good start.* "Are you close?"

"Never met her."

Lie. He sighed inwardly. Before he could reclaim the lost ground, however, Natalya turned the tables. Swiveling in her seat, she said, "Tell me about your brother."

Shit. Not the subject he wanted to discuss.

The tightening of Brandon's hands on the steering wheel evidenced his discomfort. As Natalya observed the way his knuckles whitened, a wave of guilt lapped at her conscious. He didn't like talking about his family. She'd witnessed the same closed body language when she'd mentioned the picture in his front room. This time, however, she didn't intend to let him clam up. He'd pulled enough of her secrets free since his arrival at Kate's. She needed to regroup.

"Were you close?" she pressed.

"Yeah." A heavy sigh preceded several drawn-out moments of silence where he did nothing more than stare at the road and navigate around two corners. Then, as the car straightened out on a flat stretch, he sighed again. "The little shit used to tag around with me and my friends every chance he could. Couple of times, when I first turned sixteen, I had to haul him out of the backseat so I could go on a date."

Picturing confident Sergei lapping at Brandon's heels brought a smile to Natalya's face. He'd kill her if he knew she was learning this kind of dirt.

"How many years apart were you?"

"Two." A wistful smile lifted one corner of his mouth. "I remember when we were real little I used to beat the crap out of him. I was jealous as hell. Couldn't stand it when Mom made a fuss over him. I bit him so many times that going to my room became part of my morning routine."

She laughed softly, the image of Brandon and Sergei wrestling on a carpeted floor, Brandon emerging the victor with some coveted toy, taking root in her mind.

"God, I miss him," Brandon whispered.

Struck by the raw emotion in his quiet confession, Natalya reached between the console and slid her palm over his thigh. He dropped his hand, wrapped his fingers around hers, and squeezed.

Twenty-four hours. You'll see him again in twenty-four hours.

"And your sister?" she asked hesitantly.

Brandon shook his head, swallowed visibly. "I can't talk about her. She was too young. Just an innocent kid. I let her—" Another fierce shake of his head silenced whatever he'd intended to say.

Natalya's heart twisted. She closed her eyes, wishing she could absorb his pain. "I'm sorry. I shouldn't have asked."

The tightening of his fingers around hers said it was okay.

"Stefan was Mom's golden son. He did real well at school, had an easier time than I did—but he tried to hide it. I think he bombed a few classes just so no one would know how smart he was. Always thought he'd end up someplace like NASA."

Natalya turned her hand over and laced her fingers through his, sensing Brandon needed to talk.

"He'd wanted to come visit me at A&M that weekend. I had a date with this sorority girl, and I didn't want my little brother hanging around. Told him he could come down the next weekend." Brandon gave a sad shake of his head. "Last time I saw him," he chuckled, a forced sound that lacked true amusement, "I think his last words to me were, *Fuck you, Bran.*"

That she could believe. Sergei had an inordinate way with words. But the fact that Brandon believed his brother had died angry with him tore her to pieces. The words sat on the tip of her tongue—*He's not dead. He's at Kate's.* She clamped her teeth, forbidding the truth to escape. He'd been gone fifteen years, and while making Brandon wait longer bordered on cruelty, twenty-four more hours wouldn't make much difference.

Brandon pulled into a parking space before the brightly colored carnival rides and shut off the car. Struck by the sudden need to ease his loss, Natalya did the only thing she could think of. She leaned across the console as he reached for the door, caught his shoulder, and turned him around with a tug. Then, she settled her mouth on his, and kissed him with all the topsy-turvy feeling that his overwhelming presence provoked.

Their tongues tangled hungrily. His greedy murmurs sent ripples of indescribable pleasure shooting through her nerve endings. The pull of her hair as he tangled his hand through the long lengths sent shivers coursing down her spine. And as his heart drummed hard against her breast, Natalya's opened wide. It let him in where he didn't belong. This man felt. He grieved. He was *real* in so many ways. When he touched her, when he barged his way inside and demanded that she feel, she wanted nothing more than to be the innocent woman he believed her to be. A simple female, in need of his strength, his protection . . . Maybe even his love. Someone who hadn't manipulated everyone she'd known in her adult life, except perhaps Sergei, to satisfy someone else's agenda.

Someone who possessed very real needs. Very real emotion.

Brandon pulled on her hair, tipping her head back and terminating the kiss. His breath rasped in harmony with hers. He nudged her mouth with his, caught her lips again, then turned his head and rubbed his cheek against hers. "I want you to forget I said this," he whispered as he increased the pressure on the back of her scalp and urged her forehead to his shoulder. "I don't even know what I mean by it."

His mouth dusted over the crown of her head. "But I think I need you, Natalya."

Her breath caught, the sudden overflow of emotion bringing unbidden moisture to her eyes. He'd reached right in and pulled the words out of her very soul. If anyone needed the other, *she* needed him. Needed the way he made it impossible to hide.

As her heart soared, however, sorrow dragged it back down. He might think he needed her, but that would change. When he realized she'd lied to him, that she'd played a prominent part in Rachel's death, and he learned all the terrible things she'd done over the course of her career, he'd despise her.

Nevertheless, this one moment was hers to cherish. She might have lied about her past, and a whole bunch of other things he'd hate, but she refused to lie about *him*. The words slipped off her lips, shaky and hesitant. "I think I need you too."

Thirty-five

Bright peals of laughter helped to soothe the unsteady hammering behind Brandon's ribs as he held Natalya's hand and led her to a bench across from the row of food vendor trailers. Need her—yeah. Crazy as it sounded, she woke him up in ways he'd never imagined. She drew him out of the shell he'd built fifteen years ago when he'd lost everything that ever meant anything. Hell, he'd just talked about Stefan for the first time in he didn't know how long, and it hadn't hurt. Hadn't come with the immense guilt that threatened to squeeze the life out of him. Not like it had before Natalya.

He doubted he'd ever get to the point where talking about his sister didn't clog him up. But he would in time, and he also suspected when that time came, it would be okay if he broke down in front of Natalya. He just couldn't deal with that collapse yet. When he could be certain Natalya was safe, and his best friend wasn't trying to mark her as a killer, he could let Gina live again through words.

Sitting down, Brandon watched the kids play and absorbed the comfortable silence he shared with this woman he'd known only a few days. He sighted Derek behind the slide talking to a clown with a puffy green nose. The clown twisted a yellow balloon as Derek watched in fascination.

"I'm going to get a snow cone—you want one?" Natalya slid off the bench.

"No thanks."

Brandon watched her walk away, admiring the sway of slender hips and waist-length auburn hair. As she stepped up to the window, he looked back at Derek. Sue caught sight of Brandon, bent to Derek's shoulder, and pointed Brandon's way. Derek's face lit up. In seconds, he was bounding across the short grass, waving good-bye to Sue and her girls. Under his scrawny arm, a yellow balloon animal's tail bobbed with the pounding of his feet. In his hand, he clutched a crumpled piece of paper.

"Brandon! Brandon! Look!" Breathless and panting, he skidded to a stop near Brandon's knee and held up his little raccoon-bear-cat shaped balloon. "It's a panda!"

A panda with a possum's tail. Brandon chuckled. "That's quite a panda. What's that?" He pointed at the wad of paper in Derek's hand.

"This? It's a fortune-teller's game. You put your fingers in here, like this." He fitted his fingers into the folded flaps and opened and shut them, in a complicated Pac-Man way. "And you pick a color. Then a number. Then it says something. But I can't read it."

Instantly, Brandon recognized the origami fortune-tellers from grade school. Nostalgia warmed his soul. "Here, I can help you with that." He plucked the folded toy off Derek's hand and fitted the tips of his fingers into the paper pleats. "Okay, pick."

"Blue."

Brandon moved the paper in and out, spelling out, "B-L-U-E." With the points closed, he asked, "Number?"

"Six."

Diligently, Brandon moved the paper six times. "Pick your last number, little man."

"Okay! Three."

Catching Derek's enthusiasm, Brandon grinned. "Let's see what this says." He pried up the number three flap, anticipating the usual children's predictions. Something along the lines of "You'll be rich." What he read, however, made him do a double take. He scanned the flap again, his gut wrenching down tight.

You will have an accident very soon. What kind of sick joke was this? Sue's kids wouldn't have teased so morbidly.

"What's it say, Brandon? What's it say?"

Brandon cleared his voice. "Nothing good, buddy."

"Do it again."

They went through the motions a second time, and Brandon peeled back the flap.

Death will be slow and painful.

Brandon ripped open the rest of the flaps, his temper escalating with each one. The last number he lifted, number 8, skyrocketed his anger. *Did you like the bird?*

He grabbed Derek by the shoulders, his heart kicking double-time. "Where'd you get this, Derek? Who gave it to you?"

Derek's little eyes went wide as saucers, and he squeaked something unintelligible.

Willing himself to calm down, Brandon eased his grip and urged, "C'mon, buddy, you're not in trouble. Who gave it to you?"

"T-The clown."

"With the green nose?"

Derek nodded.

"Did he say anything else?"

"Just that it was a game for you and me."

Glancing over Derek's head to where he'd last seen the clown, Brandon silently swore. A shadow descended on them, signifying Natalya's return. He took one look at her and jumped to his feet. "Watch him for a minute."

His blood boiled as he jogged toward the tall slide where the green-nosed clown had fashioned Derek's balloon. Who the hell left threats with kids? What if Derek hadn't shown it to him, and had tried the thing out with one of Sue's girls? Damn it! Terrorizing a four-year-old who couldn't read accomplished nothing. All it did was make Brandon that much more determined to see his father's thugs to the grave.

Passing an open trash can, a shock of candy-apple red caught his eye. He glanced inside at a fuzzy red wig topped with one foam green nose.

"Son of a bitch," he muttered.

He scanned the grounds. A young blonde mother bounced a chubby baby near the merry-go-round. To Brandon's left, a man knelt before a crying boy, offering comfort. Near the pair, a heavy-set man with a dark mustache hawked a cardboard flat of cotton candy. Further out, the crowd was too thick.

Damn it. The bastards were here. Right beneath his fucking nose.

Catching Natalya's curious stare from across the way, he forked his fingers through his hair and swore again. She was too exposed. They'd gotten to Derek in the middle of a carnival in broad daylight. They could get to her just as easily.

Brandon shoved the wadded paper into his hind pocket and willed himself to walk, not run, back to Natalya and Derek. The seconds that it took to travel the fifty feet or so spanned out to intolerable limits, every one of which he visualized a stranger coming up behind her and dragging her away.

Finally arriving at her side, he brushed off the curious lift of her eyebrows with a slight shake of his head. "I think we should get him back to his mom now." He set a hand on Derek's shoulder, more to reassure himself the little boy hadn't been harmed than for any real necessity. "What do you say, buddy?"

"I'm hungry. I want a snow cone."

Natalya laughed, and the tenseness in Brandon's spine ebbed. He caught both her hand and Derek's and pulled them toward the vendor's trailer. "One snow cone, coming up. What flavor?"

"Grape."

"Ah, good choice." He winked at Natalya and her purple ball of flavored ice.

He needed to call Aaron and make sure he'd taken the samples in.

Maybe they could find some answers there. Although, in Brandon's heart, he knew his father's hired guns weren't stupid enough to leave a trail behind.

No, the best thing he could do right now was enlist Mayer's help. Two pairs of eyes could watch over Natalya better than one. But before Mayer would agree, Brandon had to clear her name. To accomplish that, he had to get her talking.

Not easy when the only way he knew how to open her up made it near impossible to focus on conversation.

"You okay?" Natalya whispered at his shoulder.

"Yeah. Just thinking."

Denying her the opportunity to say anything further, he stepped to the window. "One grape snow cone please."

A re you going to tell me what happened at the park, or keep pretending you didn't shoot off the bench like a bottle rocket?" Natalya slid onto Brandon's island stool, set her elbows on the counter, and rested her chin in her hands.

They'd danced around the incident for an hour. Each time the silence fell too heavily, Brandon found a way to fill it with the mundane. They'd talked about a lot of nothing since they left the park.

Standing in front of the open refrigerator, Brandon's hand tightened on the door. His lack of immediate response left her wondering if he'd heard her. Then, as he leaned in to pull out a Corona, he replied, "I'll tell you if you'll tell me about Nikolai."

Like someone had shoved a rod down her spine, Natalya sat upright. Nikolai again. How the hell had he picked up on Nikolai from the little bit he'd overheard at Kate's?

"There's not much to say."

"Then nothing happened at the park."

She gritted her teeth against the desire to scream. Their gazes clashed, a stalemate of wills. This time, he wasn't going to win. Pushing away from the island, she scooted off the stool. "I'm going to take that shower now. Why don't you think about what we're going to do for dinner. Unless . . ." She stopped between the kitchen and the front room and glanced over her shoulder. "Unless you want to take me back to Kate's so you can go on into the club."

"Not a chance."

"I didn't think so."

Determined not to let him get under her skin, she headed for his bathroom and the shower. No longer concerned about his association with Dmitri, her reasons for keeping the secrets dwindled to one. One very poignant justification—his life. The less Brandon knew, the better his chance for survival. Dmitri might be after him now, but if she and Sergei succeeded, that threat would end tomorrow. If they failed however, there still remained a chance that if she disappeared, she could protect Brandon by keeping him ignorant of the *Bratva*.

All of which meant, no matter how she might want to confide in him, she couldn't answer his questions.

The water splashed against closed glass doors, and she peeled out of her clothes. Her wrist brushed against her knee, reminding her she hadn't shaved in three days. Wrinkling her nose, she pulled open a drawer near the sink in search of a disposable razor. Toothpaste, toothbrush, floss, hairbrush—no razor.

She tried the drawer on the opposite side of the sink, finding aftershave, deodorant, condoms, and an electric razor still in a sealed box. The man had to shave—where in the world was his razor?

Natalya pulled open the mirrored medicine cabinet above the toilet. Neatly stacked bottles of aspirin, Tylenol, and Aleve sat amongst an expired prescription for Amoxicillin and a couple of Band-Aid boxes. She stuck her head out the door. "Brandon?"

Over the fall of running water, his footsteps echoed down the hall. "Yeah?" Stopping abruptly in the middle of his bedroom, he looked over her head at something behind her. In one passing heartbeat, the light in his tawny eyes turned to molten gold.

Curious, Natalya peeked over her shoulder to find her backside fully exposed in the mirror. His gaze riveted there, taking her in from shoulder to mid thigh, the shifting color of his eyes a change she'd become all too familiar with. A thrill shot all the way down to her toes.

"Where's your razor? All I can find is this electric one."

He blinked, as if her question jarred him. Though his gaze still burned hot, his dark eyebrows furrowed. "It's in the shower."

"Oh. Okay." Turning around, she padded across the cool tile floor and pushed open the shower stall door.

Behind her, the bathroom door opened wider. Brandon leaned inside, his gaze holding hers through the mirror's reflection. "You were in my drawers?"

Natalya couldn't help herself—she laughed. Batting her eyelashes, she answered in the most serious voice she could find, "Yes, baby, I've been in your drawers."

Annoyance flicked over his features. He dragged his eyes from her hips back up to her face. "That's not what—" His stare slipped downward again, resting on the reflection of her bare breasts. Under the heat of his gaze, her nipples pebbled.

She loved the way he looked at her. Appreciative. Admirable. And though his stark desire was evident, a degree of respect lingered in those beautiful eyes.

"Aw, hell," Brandon muttered. He entered the bathroom fully and pushed the door shut. "Why not? You were heading there anyway."

Natalya blinked. "What?"

With a shake of his head, he pulled his shirt over his head. "Nothing. Just talking to myself." He took three steps forward and looped his arms around her waist. "Mind if I join you?"

As the warmth of his skin met hers, Natalya's insides turned to liquid. She flattened her palms over the tight planes of muscle across his back and arched into his embrace. Their bodies merged from collarbone to abdomen. Pure heaven.

She turned her face into his shoulder and inhaled the cinnamon-spice of his cologne. "I don't know how much showering we'll get accomplished." Sliding her hands around the broad expanse of his ribs, she ran the back of her knuckles across his abdomen. Washboard muscles jumped in time with the sudden catch of his breath.

"I think we can manage." Brandon leaned forward to drop his mouth onto her shoulder and one large palm covered her breast.

Natalya dipped her fingers lower, slipping beneath the tight waistband of his jeans. Her middle finger touched the erect, smooth head of his cock and Brandon's body jerked. He let out a hiss. The sound scalded through her skin, spreading heat through her veins and crackling through her pussy. One small, insignificant—maybe not so insignificant—reaction from him, and she was wet and ready.

Good Lord, she should be ashamed at how easily her body responded to Brandon Moretti.

Instead, she felt utterly at ease. As if this were the most natural thing in the world. However, while the act itself might be, all the things Brandon did to her insides, the parts he couldn't physically touch, were as unnatural as snow in the Sahara. But it was this freakish feeling that made everything so innate.

She popped the solitary brass button on his jeans and lowered his zipper. His cock jutted forth arrogantly. Just like the man. All dominance. Yet nothing like the control-freak Dmitri had been.

Brandon moved away from her inquisitive fingers before she could savor the heat of his cock against her palms. Smiling that sensual smile that always made her heart trip, he peeled off his jeans and gestured at the open shower door. "We're getting water all over my floor."

With a laugh, she stepped under the hot spray. He joined her, shutting the door behind him. Water ran in rivulets over his hard chest and trickled down his abdomen. She traced a nail along the path of one roaming droplet, over a defined pectoral, around a puckered nipple, lower to the trail of dark hair beneath his navel. Lower still to the base of his erection.

Brandon's body tightened visibly. Natalya took full advantage of his anticipation and slowly closed her fingers around the swollen length of his cock. She gave him a firm squeeze.

He slapped an open palm on the slick tile wall and sucked in a sharp breath.

"You like that?" she whispered thickly.

"Do you have to ask?"

His voice was low and hoarse, and it scraped pleasantly over the aroused nerve endings on her skin. She shivered, despite the steady stream of hot water. No, she didn't have to ask. The tight bunch of his buttocks and the rigid nature of his muscular thighs revealed more than words. She released her fingers just enough to slide her palm down the hard length of him. His hips followed the retreat of her hand, his erection pushing through her fingers as he closed his eyes and exhaled long and slow.

"You took care of me last night." Her hand worked a steady rhythm as she spoke. "But you didn't give me much chance to do the same."

"Ah, sweetheart, you have no idea—" A low groan rumbled in his throat as she slipped her free hand between his thighs to gently cup his balls. "Shit, Natalya, this isn't . . ." He sucked in another harsh breath, his jaw tightening. "Showering."

"No, it isn't."

Wanting to give him the same ecstasy he'd so willingly given her in the wee hours of morning, she eased to her knees and swirled the tip of her tongue around the smooth head in her hand. His hips jerked, and a bead of salty moisture touched her tongue. Her womb constricted instinctively. The tingling between her legs became a gnawing ache. Emboldened by his primitive reaction, she closed her lips around his cock's wide head.

"Natalya." Brandon ground out with difficulty. His fingers pushed her wet hair out of her face, then curled into her scalp. None too gently, he tugged on her hair, urging her to stand. "Not . . . a good . . . idea."

Ignoring his protests, she suckled at the tip, lapped with her tongue. Guided him with the push and slide of her hand. She wouldn't take him all the way, but she wanted him like he'd been in the kitchen the night before. Lacking control. Reservations abandoned. Not the gentle, consummate lover he'd been the many times after.

Her wish came true as she increased the pressure of her fingers and ran her tongue across the sensitive ridge on the underside of his swollen tip. She felt his desire begin to rise. His hand tightened painfully on her hair, forcing her to either stand up or loose a thick fistful. The instant her feet touched the floor, Brandon slid an arm around her waist and backed her to the wall. His other hand curved around her thigh, lifting it, urging her to wrap her legs around his waist.

Natalya obliged. Hot and hard, his cock pressed against her inner thigh, making it impossible to resist the urge to wiggle against him. Her body throbbed with want of him.

He hoisted her higher and thrust in deep. Their combined groans echoed off the walls. Feet braced wide to keep from slipping, he held her with ease. She caught his mouth, as hungry for her kiss as she was for the rest of him. He gave it to her, but only for an instant before he withdrew, his body retreating as well.

"No," he murmured as he bent forward to catch a droplet of water with his lips. "Look at me. No barriers. Let me in, Natalya." His scalding gaze latched onto hers as he thrust in high.

He filled her to perfection. His body, slickened with water, heated from desire, merged with hers. The innumerable pressure points of contact overwhelmed her. He was there. Everywhere. Forcing her to be right there with him, and dear God, she didn't want to resist. She couldn't imagine making love to Brandon any other way but with every portion of her being. Pleasure pulsed through her veins, and her vagina clamped around his thick length.

She angled her hips and fastened her hands on his shoulders to stop the sudden dizzying pitch of the shower floor. He pushed in again, rolled his hips to stroke her clitoris, and a pleasured cry slipped off her lips. She blinked, only for an instant, unable to stop the reflexive action, then locked onto his soulful stare once more. In those tawny eyes, emotion glinted bright, and she knew instinctively, he'd managed to unveil the same unfettered feeling in hers. How could he not? She was completely, devastatingly susceptible to this man.

"Brandon," she exhaled as a tidal wave of bliss built to a slow rise.

"I'm here," he whispered. He hit her hard and deep, his breathing matching the velocity of hers. "Always." For one brief moment, he broke their spellbinding eye contact to plant a firm kiss on her mouth. "Always."

Natalya curled her nails into his shoulders as he increased the tempo. His promise, something she was certain he hadn't intended to say, combined with the staggering intimacy of looking into his eyes when they were as close as two people could be, sent her crashing over the edge. Ecstasy stormed through her body. She cried out with the force of it, dimly aware of his hoarse shout.

Thirty-six

Brandon gathered the long thick lengths of Natalya's hair in a fluffy towel and squeezed the water out. He held it there, admiring the gentle slope to her creamy shoulder before flicking his gaze to the mirror and meeting her turbulent green eyes. Something had happened to him, to them, in the shower. He couldn't put a name to it, wasn't sure he wanted to, but he knew he had changed the moment he'd surged into orgasm while staring into the depths of her soul.

Stepping away, he tossed the towel onto the toilet and gave her a smile that disguised his internal quaking. "How about Chinese for dinner?"

"That sounds good." Her fingertips dragged down his arm, as if she too shared the need to maintain contact.

Right now, though, Brandon needed distance to digest how easily and unexpectedly a man could fall in love. Even when he'd sworn never to do so. When he didn't *want* to.

Only, as he left the bathroom and tugged on clean clothes, he realized it was no longer a question of want, or intentions. It was damn well happening, and he wasn't certain he wanted to cut off this flowing channel of emotion.

No. No, he didn't. It was the most frightening experience he'd ever known—worse than any narcotics sting gone bad. Yet thrilling all the same.

The sensible thing would be to take her back to her condo, drop off her car, walk to Fantasia, and let her go before he couldn't. He'd fired her; they'd identify the killer, and he'd have no cause to see Natalya again. Further, he didn't need any more reminders of the danger he'd dragged her into. If he walked away now, the mafia couldn't use her as a tool to get to him.

Yet, he couldn't. He could tell himself day and night all the reasons that he *should*, but he couldn't shake the instinctive awareness that cutting her out meant carving off a piece of him he wasn't ready to sacrifice.

"Holy shit," he exhaled as he stepped into the hall and pulled the bedroom door shut behind him. "This isn't real."

Any minute, he'd wake up on the couch, Natalya still in his arms, and discover everything that had happened today was all just part of a wicked nightmare. His ability to love had died with his family. Fifteen years of cold, unfeeling existence didn't just change in a mere four days. Unlike Rory, he couldn't see himself behind a desk, taking the safe approach and settling into a *family man*. While he couldn't see himself doing undercover work the rest of his life, either, desk jobs were just too boring and the department had made it clear he wasn't likely to make it into organized crime in this lifetime.

Maybe homicide. Yeah. If he solved this chain of murders and dragged in a serial killer, he might well convince Joe to let him stay on homicide. That'd keep him out of the station and relatively clear of bullets. Long hours, but still enough time in the day to come home and—

Shit! He squeezed his temples with the base of his palms. No. He was *not* going to start down those paths. Allowing her to rummage through his bathroom drawers did not equivocate to *giving* her one of her own.

Though a second razor was a necessity. No way in hell would he allow her to use his. He'd seen what could happen to an unsuspecting man's face. Vaguely he remembered carving up his own when his twelve-year-old sister had gotten her hands on his razor the summer between his freshman and sophomore years at college. Hell, he'd prided himself on his ability to outsmart that female instinct by keeping them *out* of his bathroom. He refused to join the ranks of men who jumped into their cars with tiny pieces of toilet paper stuck to their chins.

A wry smirk twisted the corner of his mouth as his unease settled, and he began to find humor in his predicament. On the positive side of things, he'd definitely found a way to dissuade her from stealing his razor, and it hadn't even provoked an argument.

A thump drifted through the walls as she rummaged around in his bathroom, doing God only knew what. He liked her there. Really, truly, liked her there.

"You about ready to go? I'm starving," he hollered.

"Coming. Just finishing up."

His blissful little reverie shattered at the sound of an engine's roar. He glanced up, looking out the window as a car rushed by. Like snapshot images, the warnings of danger flashed in his memory: the Peeping Tom, smashed chocolates, vandalized car, massacred bird, and one little boy used as a message bearer. Chills invaded his blood. Natalya was in very real danger. He didn't dare leave her at Kate's or her condo or anywhere alone tonight. And he didn't want her at the club where she could get herself into more trouble.

He fished his phone off the island and dialed Aaron.

"Yeah?"

"I need you to handle the club tonight."

"What the fuck? I'm stuck in California, man. I'm going to be late myself."

"Stuck?"

Aaron's harassed sigh drifted through the line. "Blame it on Rory. I told him to meet me, and I sat around and waited on his ass. He didn't show. I'm just now getting to Newberry. I'll be another three hours, easy. If I can catch up with him when I get back, he's evidently got something from Russia for us."

From Russia? Who the fuck did Rory know in Russia? Brandon

dismissed the oddity and glanced at the clock above his couch. "It's just shy of five now. Give Jill a call, have her handle the back of the house. Have Sergei handle the front till you get in."

"What are you going to be up to? Or do I want to ask?"

As Natalya stepped into the kitchen, Brandon's gaze wandered appreciatively over the short hem of her jeans shorts and the loose, linen top that dipped daringly low across her breasts. "Probably not. I'll talk to you tomorrow."

"Yeah, whatever, *Lieutenant*."

Brandon disconnected and shoved his phone in his back pocket. He passed Natalya her purse, grateful that at least one of them would have a gun on hand if things got worse. He didn't dare bring his without a jacket to hide it in, and the muggy weather made jackets ridiculous. That sixth sense so integral to a cop's survival, warned him things weren't as calm as they seemed.

The cool desert breeze sifted through Natalya's hair, soothing and tranquil. Hands braced behind her on the large, flat rock, she tipped her head back and gazed up at the star-filled sky. Beside her, Brandon sat with his elbows looped around his knees, staring off at the long line of sandstone rocks that fringed the horizon.

"It's beautiful out here," she murmured, afraid the sound of her voice might disrupt the serenity.

"It's better than the flash and bang of the Strip, that's for sure." He tipped his head to take in the full moon. "I get sick of all that, to tell you the truth."

Leaning sideways, she touched her shoulder to his. "Kate and I camped on the California side when we were in college. We went in the spring and the fall. Right after classes let out and right before they began." A wistful smile lifted the corner of her mouth. "Been a long time."

"What did you think the first time you saw the Canyon?"

She shook her head, still awed by the magnanimity of standing on the rim and looking down on the mighty Colorado. Even after fifteen years, she could remember the moment a naïve, Old Believer girl from Nikolaevsk, Alaska, had looked out over the terracotta cliffs and realized how vast the world was.

"Yeah," Brandon whispered as if he could hear her thoughts. He glanced at her, the light behind his eyes soft and intimate. "Maybe I could convince you to come camping again with me. Last time I went, Stefan was still alive."

Her heart stumbled into her ribs. Throughout the night, little comments here and there had given her the impression Brandon was hinting at permanency. Nothing she could concretely identify as a long-term outlook on their involvement, but subtleties that left her wondering if he'd shared the same soul-shattering experience she'd encountered in his shower.

What she'd give for a normal life and the ability to indulge in possibilities. Her answer came in a whisper even she had to strain to hear. "Maybe."

"What was it like in Russia?"

Natalya shivered, despite the temperate air. The truth tumbled free without hesitation. "I hate Russia."

"There's nothing you like about it?"

"We have beautiful buildings."

They fell into silence, and Brandon leaned back, covering her hand with his. After several moments, he broke the quiet with another question. "If you could go anywhere in the world, no limitations, where would you go?"

She chuckled to herself. She'd been to most of the major cities throughout the world. A few days here, a few months there—most recently three years in Moscow. But as the Eiffel Tower and the Great China Wall surfaced in her mind's eye, the answer resonated in her heart. *Home.* She missed her family. Missed the quaint old-world ways, though she and Kate had long departed from the Old Believer Orthodox teachings. A few days in the village might just be the thing to restore her spirits when she left Vegas.

"Alaska," she answered as she squinted at the high North Star. "I'd like to go to Alaska and watch the Northern Lights over the glaciers." Her gaze skimmed sideways to meet Brandon's. "You?"

"I've never seen the Northern Lights."

"You'd like them, if you like this." She gestured at the bright illumination on the horizon. "They make that neon glow flat-out ugly."

Brandon twisted to face her more fully. He brought one hand up to the side of her face, his expression sedate and meaningful. His thumb caressed her cheek. He said nothing, merely searched her face for something Natalya couldn't comprehend. Answers? Another attempt at breaking into the depths of her soul?

Before she could ask, his mouth feathered across hers. Their breaths mingled for a prolonged heartbeat that stood Natalya's nerves on end. Then, offering fulfillment she hadn't even realized she'd been craving, he slid his tongue along the inside edge of her lower lip and touched his tongue to hers.

She melted into his arms, sitting up to loop her wrists around his neck. His hands dropped to her waist, and the firm press of strong fingers conveyed a deeper passion than his possessive kiss. That strange, unnamable sensation surfaced again, hungry for undefined fulfillment. Something more than sex. More than the ecstasy his body gave to hers.

Pulling away, just as she began to drift on the tide of rising emotion his gentleness provoked, Brandon's mouth hovered over hers. "I need to make love to you."

Make love. Since when had they moved beyond fucking? *The shower.* He'd felt it too. *Oh, God.*

"Now?" she asked, overwhelmed.

"Right now." Emphasizing his insistence, he tilted her hips into his so she felt the firm press of his cock. His breath scraped along the side of her neck, his words a low murmur. "With the wind in your hair, and your eyes twinkling like the stars."

Excitement danced in her belly. It was truly shameful how easily he lit her up. But instead of fighting the call of arousal, she embraced it and looped her arms around Brandon's neck as she eased into his lap. He plucked open the buttons on her blouse, teasing each inch of flesh he exposed with a nip, a lick, a nuzzle. When his lips grazed the thin satin of her bra, he pushed the cup down and drew her nipple into his mouth.

Natalya arched her back, lifting her breasts closer to the magic of his tongue. Her hands plied at his shirt, tugging it free from his jeans, and pushing it up so she could explore the tight contours of his body. She loved touching him almost as much as she loved his hands on her.

Brandon rubbed his cheek against her breast and lifted his eyes to hers. "You're so damned beautiful. I don't know what's wrong with me. This ache for you won't stop."

She felt it too—the constant need to be as close as humanly possible. And she told him so by rolling her hips forward and grazing her damp center against the bulge behind his fly.

"I touch you, Natalya, and I have to be inside you."

Her mouth curved with a tender smile. "I'm not stopping you."

That was all the encouragement Brandon needed. His mouth latched onto hers, his kiss as feral as the coyotes howling in the distance. He did away with the last of her pesky buttons by giving the opened panels of her blouse a tug and popping the chips of pearl. As her hands dipped to his waist to free his impatient cock from the confines of his jeans, Brandon dragged her body flush with his. The press of his bare skin intoxicated her. Her womb contracted, and she let out a soft moan. "Brandon, God I lo—" She pressed her lips to his to stop the sudden rush of words. *Love you.* She'd almost said it. *Holy shit.* Covering up her nearly fatal confession, she whispered, "Love the feel of you." To further distract him, she nipped hard on his lower lip. "Take me."

A possessive growl rumbled in the back of his throat. She didn't know how her shorts ended up on the rock beside them, but in the next heartbeat they were, and Brandon was lifting her body, aligning her wet opening with the wide head of his cock. He lowered her slowly, easing inside her narrow channel, stretching her bit-by-bit and sending shocks of pleasure surging through her veins.

"Brandon. *God.*" She clutched his shoulders, feeling very much like she'd just plummeted off the canyon rim.

He moved inside her, pulling back, slowly filling her up again. "Come for me, beautiful," he whispered against the hollow of her throat. "Let me feel you hold on to me."

It wouldn't take much at this rate. A few more slow strokes like that and she'd—*Oh!* Brandon pressed his thumb against her clitoris, his lazy stroke as powerful as the deep thrust that hit the mouth of her womb. She tried to move against the fantastic pressure, but his other hand held her hips in place, subjecting her to the blissful agony of his masterful possession. A whimper bubbled in the back of her throat.

"Oh, please . . ." Her vagina clenched, and against her inner walls she felt his cock twitch.

"Like that," he rasped. "Just like that." Again, he tapped her clitoris, again he pushed high into her slick sheath, the pressure on her hips pushing her down as he lifted up.

Another wave of pleasure hit her hard, and Natalya clung to his shoulders, scarcely able to breathe. She managed a few jerky gasps, found the ability to somehow swallow. But when she lifted her lowered lashes, his smoldering gaze seared past the last of her crumbled defenses. In those tawny depths emotion reigned. Feeling so foreign to her she couldn't be certain she translated correctly. But her heart recognized the language—the same words she'd nearly spilled gleamed in his turbulent stare.

Just like that she soared, his name tearing from her lips as ecstasy crashed through her body. Brandon groaned long and low, and clutched her hips with both hands as his body spasmed into hers. Deep inside, she felt the pulse of his cock, the heat of his ejaculation spilling against her needy flesh.

He held her still, his breath hard and heavy against her shoulder. Natalya trembled in his arms, the feeling running through her so powerfully frightening. She didn't know what to say, what to do . . . and she damn sure didn't want to move.

Brandon solved the dilemma with a feather-soft kiss to her cheek and whispered, "I'd like to see the Northern Lights with you."

"With me?" To her shame disbelief clung to her dry throat.

"Yes. With you." He captured her lower lip with his teeth and teased her mouth open once more. But his kiss ended too soon. "I meant it when I said you did powerful things to me."

Afraid he'd say more than her heart could withstand, Natalya pressed her fingertips to his parted lips. "There's things you don't know, Brandon."

He turned his head, easing himself out of her. "I'm not stupid. I know that. Trust me, this scares the shit out of me. But I'm not going to be ruled by fear." He took his hand in hers and added more quietly, "Not anymore."

That damnable emotion welled once more, and Natalya felt the salty prick of tears. She dipped her chin to hide her welling eyes.

Unwilling to let her hide, Brandon framed her face between his hands and turned her gaze to his. "I'm falling for you, Natalya. If you don't want me, you need to tell me now, so I can walk away."

Her throat clogged, forbidding her reply. She swallowed once. Twice. Felt the hot splash trickle down her cheeks. Ashamed, she tried to twist her head. He denied her the ability by dusting his mouth over her damp skin and kissing away the tears.

"I know you've got a secret you don't want me to know yet. I'm okay with that. For now."

"Brandon—" The twisting of her heart was too much. Did she want him? God, yes, she wanted him. If she could find a way to save Kate, protect Sergei, and drag Brandon to a corner of the world where Dmitri could never find him, and know that Brandon would be *happy*, she'd do it in a heartbeat. But she couldn't. She was leaving tomorrow night.

Feeling her heart breaking already, she twisted away from his soul-searching gaze and pulled on her shorts. A passing car jerked his attention to the road. She looked after him, observing the snail-like pace of the approaching vehicle. It slowed more as it cruised past the Accord they'd parked on the highway's shoulder.

Brandon eyed the silver sedan, instincts on high alert. A flash of his memory painted the picture of a similar car shooting past his window. He stiffened as the sedan drove thirty yards past the Accord, then nosed into the shoulder. It turned perpendicular to the highway, headlights shining across the dark landscape.

He sat taller, and his heart rate accelerated. Taking his eyes off the vehicle long enough to glance at Natalya's hip, he ensured she'd brought her purse. She already had it in her lap.

The buzz of warning shifted into a high-pitched alarm as the sedan pulled a U-turn, then backed into the opposite shoulder. Bright light splashed across the rock he and Natalya shared. The sedan sat no more than fifty yards away.

"Give me your gun." He opened his palm, but made no other move.

"What?"

More firmly, he repeated, "Give me your gun."

"Like hell. I'm not giving you my gun."

"Damn it, Natalya," he said as he glanced at her stubborn expression.

A car door opened. Slammed shut. The echo drummed through the barren landscape.

He let out a controlled breath, his jaw tight. His order came out in a venomous hiss. "I'm a fucking cop, give me the goddamn gun!"

Across the highway, a shadow passed before the headlights. It stopped on the passenger side, lifted bulky arms.

Brandon reacted on reflex. He grabbed the back of Natalya's hair and dragged her to the ground. As her cheek made contact with the rock's rough surface, two crisp, rapid-fire shots cracked through the air. They pinged off a rock to his left.

"Son of a bitch!" Brandon outstretched a hand and dragged Natalya's purse beneath his nose. "Remind me next time I blow my cover to make sure I have my badge so I can prove it. Where the hell's your gun?"

He scowled at Natalya in the same instant she confidently rose to one knee. Right arm stretched toward the vehicle, he caught the brief glow of the Sig's night sights. Shit! She made a perfect, motionless target. He grabbed for her ankle, intending to knock her back to the ground, but as his fingertips grazed her skin, she returned fire with two identical trigger pulls.

Brandon jerked his hand away and snapped his head up, a string of curses on the tip of his tongue.

Across the highway, a tire popped. A tinny *ping* announced the second bullet sped home a breath away from the first. The shadow dove over the sedan's hood. Brief light glimmered as the interior dome flashed on. Then, on three good tires, the sedan pealed off the shoulder, flat tire thumping. It vanished into the desert landscape, leaving them, and Vegas behind.

Brandon glanced at Natalya, suspicion creeping in to replace his stunned surprise. "Lucky shot?"

Natalya's stone-cold expression told him luck didn't have anything to do with her dead-on shot.

Her purse still clutched in one tight fist, he snapped his opposite hand around her wrist and struck off for the car. "I've just stopped being okay with not knowing your secrets."

Thirty-seven

elf-defense.

S Brandon ground the word between his teeth, resisting the urge to snort at the ludicrous claim. No self-defense student learned how to hit a target at fifty yards like Natalya had. It just didn't happen. Not unless she'd practiced every day, for hours at a time. Highly unlikely— even *he* didn't have that many hours at the range under his belt, and he was a consistently accurate marksman.

Yet she clung to the explanation no matter how many times he asked during their drive back to his house.

She hadn't reacted to his confession either, which made him more uneasy. Either she knew, she suspected, or she hadn't heard him, which he didn't buy in the least.

He groaned inwardly. What if she was some Internal Affairs piss ant sent to hawk over him? That would certainly explain her blank file. IA would expect him to run a background check, and they'd cover anything that might give him a glimmer of the truth.

What had he done to piss off Joe?

Searching the banks of his memory for something worthy of an IA investigation, he pulled into his driveway and slammed the Accord into park. He pinned her with a squint. "Are you IA?"

Natalya laughed. "Hardly."

Truth. Okay. So if she wasn't from Internal Affairs then what?

Mayer's voice echoed in his head. *I think you better distance yourself.* As the engine *tick-ticked* against the cooling night air, Brandon stared at his unopened garage door. What if he'd been wrong and she was somehow associated with these murders? *No.* He banished the thought as quickly as it came. Just because she could aim well didn't make her a murderer. Or even an accomplice.

He sighed. "Natalya, damn it, talk to me. Who's Nikolai? I know you're afraid of him. How does he relate to that gun?"

Natalya wrapped her hands around the bulky pistol hidden in her purse. "He's nobody. Would you just drop the subject?"

"No, damn it, I won't!" His temper spiked. "I just blew my cover. Twelve years of narcotics work might very well be shot down the drain. All I want is a straight answer from you. Who the hell is Nikolai, and why did his name turn you ghost white?"

She looked out the window, her expression far away. So softly he had to strain to hear her, she answered, "Your cover's safe. I knew you were a cop."

"You what?" he asked slowly.

Her chest heaved as she took a deep breath. "Can we go inside?"

"Fine. Whatever." He shoved open the door and climbed outside. Too frustrated to wait for her, he started up the porch steps and unlocked the door in the dark. Her heels clacked on the pavestones behind him.

Inside, Brandon flipped on the light and stalked into the kitchen. He spun on her when she entered and set her purse on the island. "How the hell did you know?"

She made a production of withdrawing her gun and taking it apart. He waited, his pulse notching up another degree with every drawn-out second, while she pulled a paper towel off the dispenser and wiped down the slide. "You're right, Nikolai is from my past, and I'm very afraid of what he's capable of doing."

The air left his lungs in a rush. She'd rather tell him about her past than explain how she knew he was a detective? Something didn't feel right. The sneaking suspicion that he wasn't going to like what she would say next crawled down his spine.

Her hands moved automatically over the metal parts, meticulously cleaning what two rounds couldn't have possibly dirtied. "Protecting myself is a necessity. I made it a habit to train with this gun. When you aren't sure if each morning you wake up might be your last, it becomes habit."

At the brittle edge to her voice, his heart shifted sideways. A portion of his anger ebbed into sympathy. She was hiding from Nikolai, and it was all Brandon could do to not go to her and offer comfort. But he sensed, if he interrupted her now, he'd never hear the full explanation.

He stayed at the opposite end of the bar, his hands curled into the countertop, gritting his teeth against the desire to rip this Nikolai into pieces.

"I . . . spent a lot of time with him in Russia. He's affiliated with the St. Petersburg casino, silent partner if you will. He was in the club last night. Jill danced for him. Which means he saw me dancing as well."

Ah. The lightbulb clicked on. All the threats led her to the logical conclusion, this Nikolai was after her. She'd misconstrued the truth—then again, he hadn't *given* her the truth to help her over the fear. Something he needed to amend right now.

"Natalya." He rounded the corner of the island and captured one busy hand. "First things first—give me his last name, and whatever he's done to you, we'll make sure he pays the price." Bringing her hand to his mouth, he dusted a kiss over her knuckles and held her gaze. "I won't let him hurt you. It wasn't him who shot at us either. I'll stake my life on it."

Her eyes widened in disbelief.

"Brandon?"

The female voice in his front hall made him jump. He instinctively moved in front of the island to hide Natalya's gun.

Sue poked her head around the entryway. "I'm sorry to bother you. I saw you come in earlier than normal—I didn't realize you had company." A fierce blush colored her face crimson as she ducked her head.

"It's okay. Sue, this is Natalya. Natalya, my neighbor, Sue." Still possessively holding on to Natalya's hand, he gestured at the both of them in turn.

"Nice to meet you, Natalya." Sue's blush deepened. "I'm really sorry. I can wait till morning."

"No, what did you need?"

Stepping fully into the room, Sue wrung her hands together. "It's Opie. I haven't seen him since I let him out three hours ago. The girls are upset. He got off his chain, and you know he usually wanders back home once he trees the cat down the street."

A dog. Not just any dog, but the bane of his dog-loving existence was ruining the most revealing conversation he'd ever had with Natalya. Tomorrow he was taking the whole damn day off and building that fence.

"Did you check the cat's yard?"

"Yeah. I can't find him. He won't answer. I'm afraid he wandered over to the main road and got hit." She wrung her hands harder, and her voice caught. "I don't want to find him that way. I don't think I could handle it."

The question reflected in her hopeful expression. *Would you look, please?*

Brandon slowly let out a long breath. He couldn't tell Sue no, even if Opie's timing sucked. They were too good of friends for him to force her into stumbling onto her dog, splattered across the road. She'd fall apart. And if she left her house, she'd have to take her girls with her—they were too young to stay in unattended. Under no circumstances, would he risk exposing one of those precious little girls to seeing their beloved pet in a bloody mess.

How the hell had Opie gotten off his chain? Those links were a quarter-inch thick.

"Okay. I'll go look. If I find him, what do you want me to do?"

"I'll call animal control."

Brandon gave her an understanding nod and let go of Natalya's hand. Bending his head, he kissed her cheek. "I'll be back in a few minutes."

"I'm going with you."

"I don't think—" Conscious of both their audience and what had transpired in the desert, he snapped his mouth shut. Diverting Sue's attention off Natalya so she could finish putting her pistol back together, he crossed the room and looped an arm around his neighbor's shoulder. "Go on back to the girls. I'll let you know what I find, if anything. If he doesn't turn up, chances are the pound picked him up. It was bound to happen sooner or later."

Sniffling, she answered, "Thanks, Brandon."

"Sure thing." He eased the door closed as Natalya appeared at his shoulder. "Let's go out the back. It's quicker."

While Natalya followed Brandon across his yard to his neighbor's flimsy doghouse, she stepped through the story she intended to spin. Enough of the truth to make it plausible, but nothing close enough to reveal her duty, or the *Bratva*. He believed Nikolai had hurt her in the past. He didn't need to know they'd been partners in crime. He also didn't need to know about Dmitri or Iskatel'. The fewer names he learned, the less exposure he risked, and his dedication to the law would make it near impossible to dissuade him from going after other members of the Brotherhood.

Yes, definitely, the fewer names he knew the better.

Besides, Dmitri and Iskatel' would cease to exist tomorrow. She just needed to make sure no one else tried to take a pot shot at Brandon's head before Kate and she executed the switch.

One of the reasons she'd decided to accompany him on this hunt for the dog. Two rapid shots, usually aimed in the middle of the forehead, were *Bratva* signature. If they caught her, they'd deal with her privately. Betrayal never ended quick and painless. But Brandon was a hindrance. Someone who was meddling in their business. True to *Bratva* design, he'd vanish overnight.

And just because she'd been with him didn't mean Iskatel´ pulled the trigger. Any one of Dmitri's goons could have taken on the job of trash disposal.

Brandon bent over a metal stake driven into the ground, then drew back with a violent oath. Glancing in his outstretched palm, she observed three thick links of chain, the last in the length broken open. Clean serrations identified a deliberate cut.

Apprehension balled her stomach into a tight knot. Careful to keep her head still, she moved her eyes around the lawns, scanned the trees that divided one row of backyards from another row of lawns on the street over. Dogs were complications to tidy murders. More than once, she'd freed a barking alarm so she could slip inside unnoticed.

As Brandon struck off across his backyard, she followed behind. Her gaze remained on his house, searching the windows for shadows, for any sign the missing dog might be a diversion.

Nothing moved inside. No figures hulked beside the overgrown shrubs.

Goose bumps pricked her arms. This reeked of Dmitri.

"Aw, hell."

Four houses down, a mere two from the busy intersection, Brandon came to an abrupt stop. He shoved his fingers through his short hair, and his shoulders slumped. "Damn it. I liked that dog."

She gave him a quizzical look.

He struck off for a long row of short trees. Four foot away, she caught the sight of gray and black fur lying motionless at the thick base of an Arizona Ash.

"How can somebody hit a dog that big? He's an elephant for God's sake." Brandon hunkered down and stroked a hand over the dog's short coat.

It came away bloody.

With another nervous glance around the premises, Natalya stepped to Brandon's left to get a better view of the dog.

"Stupid dog. He's still warm." Grimacing with the effort of containing his own upset over the dog's death, Brandon grabbed both front legs and pulled the oversize canine out of the trees' dark shadows. "What the . . ." Brandon lifted Opie's head.

Two close-range entrance wounds disfigured a wide muzzle and a kind face. The bloody cavity at the back of the dog's square-shaped head marked where bullets passed through brain matter and shattered thick bone.

Natalya's blood ran cold. This was a message meant for her. A deliberate, unnecessary execution that the gunman knew she'd recognize. She could accept the danger of disloyalty, for that punishment would come to her alone. However, she didn't dare say a word and risk exposing her agency roots. Personal deception was one thing. If Dmitri discovered she worked for the CIA, everyone involved would die.

Including Kate.

One other obvious fact settled around her as she stared at Opie's remains. No dog would allow a stranger to hold a gun that close, not even the stupidest of canines. Whoever had shot Opie, knew him. Which meant Iskatel´ didn't know just her, Iskatel´ knew Brandon as well.

And in leaving a clear warning that Brandon's life hung in the balance, Iskatel´ had just identified herself. Everything pointed to Jill. She'd been here. Natalya would wager everything she possessed, she was still close by.

Thirty-eight

Two hours later, Brandon had talked with Sue—carefully omitting the fact her dog had been shot—and buried Opie near the swing set with the promise he'd pick up some landscaping bricks and help the girls plant flowers. Weary in both body and spirit, he trudged through his garage, rested the shovel on the wall, and hesitated at the door, knowing what he must do, yet not at all certain he could stomach the outcome.

The threats had escalated to a point where keeping Natalya in the dark about his past was no longer an option. If he didn't tell her, he left her defenseless, and he'd never survive the guilt if something happened to her. Above and beyond all personal reasons, the decision to stay with him and confront this continual terror was hers and hers alone.

He pushed the door open and entered his house on leaden legs. She sat at the island, ankles tucked around her stool, bent over a cup of hot tea. Exactly where he'd left her. Regret punched him in the gut. He could feel her pulling away already.

God, he hated this. It was exactly why he'd sworn never to get involved.

After scrubbing the dirt off his hands, he pulled a stool beside her, resigned to loss. "Hey."

Natalya looked up as if he'd dragged her from her thoughts. "Hm?"

He clasped his hands together on the countertop and stared at his thumbs. Thoughts ran in a discombobulated mess. Sighting a hangnail, he picked at the sliver of loose skin. "I've been harping at you to tell me things, and I haven't been fair about my own secrets."

Her brows drew together a fraction.

"I'm the reason for the bird. For Opie. For the gunshots earlier." He took a breath. Let it out slowly. "My dad was some big shot in Chicago's mafia—Angelo Mancuso. Mom came over from Sicily on an arranged marriage, and when we came along I guess it got to be too much."

He dug at the loose flap of skin near the bed of his thumb a little harder. "I was nine when Mom went out with some of the other wives one night and Angelo stayed home with us kids. I remember hearing him argue with a man. Later that night, when Gina was asleep, he decided it was time for Stefan and me to learn the family business."

The long-ago night surfaced in his memory, giving him pause. He saw the concrete block walls, the hanging fluorescent light with its green-yellow glow, and the frightening calm on his father's face with crystal clarity.

"He had a guy in our basement. Someone who'd stolen from Angelo. A measly hundred dollars, though that was a fortune to me and Stefan then. Anyway, he made us stand at the bottom of the stairs so we could learn how to deal with folks who betrayed *the family*. Angelo proceeded to unload a full magazine in this guy's chest."

Brandon flinched at the echo of gunshots. Shaking off the memory, he focused on his hands, unable to witness the shock on Natalya's face. "The next morning, Mom and Gina picked Stefan and me up from school and went straight to the Feds. They put us in witness protection, changed our names to Moretti, and moved us to Texas. Mom hardly spoke English at all, so they couldn't alter too much without it becoming obvious. . . . And she didn't fit in well at all."

Natalya's hand crept into his vision, then settled over his. She tucked her fingers between his palms and gently squeezed.

Brandon's heart seized. He didn't deserve her sympathy.

"When I went off to college my sophomore year, I made a stupid mistake. I went out with that girl I mentioned, and we got to drinking. Cheap beer led to one of those spill-your-guts conversations. I told her about my family. The next weekend, Mom's house blew up."

Natalya's fingers tightened, and the heat of her body soaked into his side as she leaned closer.

Guilt rose fast, bringing with it the bitter taste of bile. He swallowed hard, choking it down. "I should have seen it coming. She was Italian, like we were. Ventimiglio—Maria Ventimiglio. She'd even said she suspected her family had connections. I fucking told her everything."

He clenched his fist around Natalya's hand. The last part came out in a rough whisper as his voice cracked. "I killed my family."

"No." Natalya's free hand slid soothingly down his shoulder, across his back. "No, Brandon, you didn't."

He blinked once, clearing away the moisture in his eyes. "Yeah. I did. I put my sweet baby sister in the ground." Shaking his head, he drew on acceptance of his mistake to find the courage to continue the conversation. "I'd told Maria I was going home that weekend. At the last minute, though, I went to Houston with a frat brother."

On a heavy sigh, Brandon skipped over the depression, the thoughts of suicide, and the anger he'd carried around until a cop took pity on him the night he'd decided to drink into oblivion and drive off a ravine. He'd been pulled over for weaving all over the highway. That cop, Joe Cavelli, had saved Brandon's life in more ways than one.

"Anyway, about a year later I decided to get even by going into the police academy and finding Angelo. I've been in narcotics under-cover since—until seven dead strippers linked to my investigation. My captain offered me the chance to move into homicide, and here I am. Only, a week into the trial position, I managed to get my partner killed."

He saw her flinch out of the corner of his eye and refused to look up to see the judgment in her expression. He'd screwed up. He knew that. But this conversation wasn't about offloading his mistakes. He had to make Natalya understand the danger he presented, along with his absolute conviction he would *not* let her be harmed. Still, the decision was hers. She couldn't make it half-informed.

"For the last few years I've made it clear if Angelo wants me, I'm not hiding. I threw a gauntlet, and you're stuck in the middle of it. I didn't mean for this to happen—any of it." Sitting forward, he shrugged off the affectionate hand he didn't deserve and shifted his weight. "I don't have a right to ask you to stay, but damn it, Natalya . . ." He found the courage to look her in the eye. "I swear I won't let anything happen to you."

Silence hung between them as she held his gaze, her eyes bright with unshed tears. He yearned to reach out to her, to dissolve the intolerable space between them though they sat so close their knees touched. What was she thinking? Did she hate him? Worse, did she *pity* him?

Natalya swallowed visibly and slid off her stool. He braced himself for the emptiness of her inevitable departure. No woman in her right mind would stick around for his kind of baggage. Especially not someone with nightmares of her own.

One slender hand touched his thigh. He looked down to where her fingertips rested, his chest so tight he could only pull in shallow breaths. She nudged his leg. Before Brandon could realize her intent was to spread his knees, she'd ducked under his arm and wedged her hips between his thighs. Her arms looped around his neck. Soft lips feathered over his.

Why didn't matter. In that moment, he needed Natalya's kiss more than he had ever needed anything. He crushed her against his chest, and his mouth crashed into hers. Desperate. Aching.

The physical was so much easier to understand than the pain behind his ribs that built with each hungry stroke of her tongue. He didn't know what caused it, or how to make it stop. Just that it went on and on, gnawing away at his heart until he became certain the next fierce beat would make it burst.

Though he'd had her mere hours ago, he was suddenly starved for the feel of her silken skin gliding against his body. He wanted his cock inside her where he could comprehend the cause of the sweet pain that crept into his veins. Where he was part of this woman who possessed the ability to turn his world upside down.

As if she sensed his thoughts, she pulled on the hem of his collared T-shirt and slipped her cool hands beneath. Their lips parted long enough for him to yank off the barriers that thwarted him from what he wanted most. Their clothes fell in a jumbled heap on the floor, then their bodies merged together, hands seeking, mouths questing. Chasing after the desire that flowed like live current through the countless places they touched.

Her kisses rained over his bare shoulder, searing through his skin to add another drop of agonizing emotion into his heart. "Make love to me, Brandon," she whispered urgently. "Make me innocent again."

Brandon didn't comprehend her words; their effect was too monumental. As he shifted his hands to her waist, preparing to hoist her onto the countertop, that weakened muscle behind his ribs ruptured open, filling him with unspeakable emotion. Everything crashed into place, what he'd been trying to tell her on the rock, why it was so important she take a risk on him and stay. *Love.* He wasn't falling in love with her . . . he was already there.

The realization stirred a soul-deep groan, and the countertop suddenly became cold and unfeeling. He scooped her into his arms, cradling her against his chest. Holding her like the priceless treasure she was, he softened the assault of his mouth and kissed her long and slow. A whole new sweetness met the tip of his tongue. He drank it down like expensive champagne, the urgency in his blood ebbing.

Sliding his lips down the length of her neck, he scattered kisses as he carried her down the hall, into his bedroom, and laid her on his bed. He allowed himself a precious moment to admire the way her long lithe body sank into the heavy comforter and how her hair fanned across his pillow. No woman had ever lain in his bed before, and in one glimpse, he knew she belonged right here.

Kneeling over her thighs, he lowered himself into her waiting arms. The swollen tip of his cock brushed through feminine curls, slid through her moist folds. His body constricted.

"Brandon . . . please. I need this." Natalya opened her thighs, lifted her hips.

At that ragged whisper, all thoughts of drawing out their joining vanished. He lifted himself on his hands, latched on to her beseeching gaze, and thrust into her hot, wet pussy.

Rapture washed over her delicate features. Her fingers dug into his buttocks as she slid down his cock, taking him even deeper.

Pleasure hit him so hard it ripped the air from Brandon's lungs. He felt the instantaneous rise of his seed and ground his teeth, halting it. It was all he could do to manage a few short breaths through flared nostrils as she wriggled beneath him, moving up and down his throbbing erection. His body shook with the effort of restraint.

"Come with me," Natalya whispered against his shoulder.

Groaning, Brandon surrendered. He pulled back, then surged in hard. At her cry, he questioned whether he might have hurt her. But in the next moment, as her body rocked against his, his worry subsided. She met his thrusts with the same wild abandon. His fleeting kisses with the same clingy recklessness. His body battered into hers, and at the clench of her pussy, ecstasy knifed through him. Their cries intermingled, his hoarse and rough, hers sharp and sweet.

Gradually, their bodies slowed, and Brandon lowered himself into her languid embrace. She kissed his shoulder, his neck, his cheek. He turned his head to offer his mouth, and she planted a soft kiss there as well.

"I—" He stopped, uncertain whether she'd welcome his confession of love. Deciding he'd rather not spoil the beauty of what had begun as a terrible night, he chose to wait. He shook his head and teasingly nipped at the tip of her nose. "I didn't scare you off?"

She glided her hands over his shoulders, down his back. "No."

Knowing he must be crushing her with his weight, he found strength enough to lift himself off her chest. But to his surprise, she pulled at his shoulders, urging him back down. "Stay put."

"I don't want to squash you."

"I'm fine. This feels good. I like how you feel inside me." A smile drifted over her face as she closed her eyes and hugged him tight.

Content, exhausted, and more sated than he could ever remember being, Brandon rested his head on her shoulder. Several moments later, Natalya's breathing evened out as sleep stole over her. He closed his eyes to the soothing fragrance of his shampoo that clung to her hair.

Natalya woke to sunlight streaming through Brandon's bedroom window. The quiet of the house surrounded her. She turned her head sideways to look at his handsome face. Brandon Moretti was everything she had ever wanted and hadn't realized she needed. In his arms, her sins disappeared. In his kiss, her soul found forgiveness. His love restored her innocence.

Love that she'd read in his eyes seconds before he'd stopped the words from slipping free. Love she would destroy.

As heartache constricted her chest, she eased from beneath the heavy bank of covers and leaned over the bed to give him a farewell kiss. Leaving Brandon would cut her to pieces. Losing him forever, however, would kill her.

Before her courage fled, she quietly left his bedroom and dressed in the kitchen where they'd left their clothes. At the end of the island, she stopped beside a small pad of paper and a coffee mug full of pens.

One more lie. One more necessary story to protect the case, then she'd never say another. When this was over, when Dmitri was behind bars, she'd go home to Nikolaevsk. No one would ever find her in the Old Believer village. There, she might be able to forget.

She picked up a pen and hastily scrawled a note.

Have errands to run. Will see you tonight.

It wasn't a complete falsehood. She would see him. When she took the stage as "Kate," she'd say good-bye.

Thirty-nine

The brittle tones of electronica yanked Brandon from blissful dreams of fucking Natalya atop the flat rock where they'd watched the sun set the night before. He sat up, in search of his phone. A barren spot in the bed instantly prompted a frown. Wasn't one of the joys of taking a woman to bed supposed to be waking up with her?

His phone started in again, and he tossed the covers back and grumbled to his feet. "Sweetheart, can you grab that?"

He hated nothing more than waking up to phone calls. Ringtones meant work, and he was in no mood to work before his first cup of coffee.

The cooing of the bird on his dresser hastened his pace. Dragging on a pair of clean boxers, he half-ran half-stumbled down the hall. Where the hell was Natalya?

At the next techno chord, his phone vibrated on the island. He snatched it up, grimacing at the display. No caller ID. Because he hadn't programmed anyone in yet. Damn it. He thumbed the call button. "Yeah?"

"Brandon? It's Jill."

Oh, God. Anger rose again, the mere sound of her voice setting him off.

"I'm sorry to call, but I tried last night and couldn't reach your voice mail."

Because he hadn't set that up yet either. Damn it. He could have avoided talking to her all together.

"I didn't make it in to work last night. I won't be able to come in tonight either. I'm having some . . . female problems." The hesitancy in her voice slipped through with her flimsy excuse.

Brandon didn't care. Fantasia had obviously survived without her; it would survive tonight as well. "Whatever."

"I can give you an excuse from the ER."

"It's not necessary, Jill." *I don't fucking care.* "Let me know when you'll be back in."

A heavy pause, then, "I don't know if I will be."

He spied the coffeepot, full of yesterday's coffee, and the need for caffeine possessed him. He went to the cabinet for a mug. "What are you saying? Are you quitting?"

"I really don't know. I need some time off. Can I come in before shift and talk to you in person in a few days?"

"That's fine." By then, he ought to have the DNA results back and could fire her for the stupid stunt with Natalya's car.

He poured a stale cup of coffee and popped it in the microwave.

"Okay. Thanks. I'll talk to you soon."

"Yep." Brandon disconnected. Now where was Natalya? Her clothes were gone, along with her purse. He frowned, noticing the piece of paper.

Ignoring the microwave's ding, he returned to the island, a smile crossing his face as he read her handwriting. Worry tugged at him, the realization he wouldn't have contact with her for almost twelve hours taking root. Too much time for a target to go unprotected.

He sighed, shook his head. No. He'd seen her talent with the Sig. If he intended to keep her around, he couldn't smother her with overprotectiveness. She was beyond capable of defending herself. Time to give her a little room to build trust.

And to be honest, much as he'd like to have stayed in bed with her until the early afternoon, he needed to devote some time to his case. Mayer would have updates.

Brandon picked up his phone and his coffee and wandered to the couch. Updates came after coffee and the noon news. He tossed his phone on the table in favor of the remote and flicked the television on. Leaning back, he prepared to wake up with his normal routine.

Next on News 8 Now, breaking information on this morning's fatal collision on the Beltway that killed one motorist and critically injured another.

Brandon sank into the cushions, nonplussed. Vegas traffic was becoming ridiculous. He spaced out through the commercials, then stood to refill his empty mug. Halfway to the kitchen, he caught sight of his reflection and the excessive stubble on his chin. He made an about face, turned up the volume on the news, and wandered to his bathroom where he turned on the sink and fetched his razor from the shower.

The splash of lukewarm water jolted him the rest of the way into wakefulness. With shaving cream liberally applied, he tipped his chin up and dragged his razor over his bristly skin.

It caught, halfway down his cheek. He jerked his hand away, astonished by the slow-growing crimson stain on his face. Slowly, he shifted a glare to the razor. Damn it. She'd gotten a hold of it.

The rest of the venture proved painstaking. By the time he finished, he was swearing blue streaks, but miraculously clean-shaven with only two small cuts. The one on his cheek, and one near the scar on his chin.

He eyed the toilet paper as the newscaster's voice drifted down the hall.

Not in a million years.

Turning, he left the bathroom. Tonight, before he went into work, he was buying Natalya a razor—along with new blades for his.

And now more on that devastating wreck this morning. Authorities have confirmed one man dead and another critically injured. Tom Cunningham reportedly lost control of his car after swerving to avoid an object in the road. He collided with the white Honda Accord, causing it to spin headlong into traffic, where a third, unnamed driver struck it head on.

Brandon stopped in the doorway, frozen in place at the mention of a white Accord.

We've learned Natalya Trubachev was taken to Sunrise Hospital in critical condition. The extent of her injuries are unknown at this time.

His heart dropped through the floor.

Natalya?

As dread seized his lungs, he ran down the hall and snatched his phone off the coffee table. Kate. Kate would know. Fuck! They'd never let him in to see her. He wasn't family. Shit! He didn't have a car.

Halfway through dialing Kate's number, his front door banged open. "Moretti!"

"Thank fucking God." Grateful to find Mayer in the entryway, Brandon dropped his phone on the table. "I need a ride to my car. Natalya's been in a wreck."

"I'll give you a lift, but you need to see this first." He tapped a manila envelope in his hand.

"I don't have time for that. I've got to go now." Brandon shoved his feet into his shoes.

"No."

The firm decisiveness in Aaron's voice gave Brandon the distinct urge to knock him on his ass and confiscate his keys. He balled a fist, seconds away from lunging at his best friend.

Aaron lifted the envelope like a white flag of surrender. "Easy man. I'm not trying to be an ass. I know you've got feelings for her. But before you go rushing off to save your injured princess, you need to decide which side of the law you're on."

Brandon blinked, long and slow. "What the fuck?"

Sidestepping around Brandon, Aaron entered his living room. "I found out things you aren't going to like. And I can't let you go in unarmed."

Brandon ground his teeth together. If Mayer had more of his flimsy excuses and circumstantial evidence against Natalya, he'd choke the life out of him. God only knew how badly she was injured. He needed to be there.

In other news, a gas line explosion destroyed one house and damaged four others in a quiet residential community in California. Neighbors say—

Aaron picked up the remote, flipped off the television, and dumped the contents of his folder, along with his phone, onto the coffee table. "Sit down, Bran."

With no other choice but to listen to Mayer's suspicious drivel, Brandon dropped into the couch. "Make it quick."

"Okay." He picked up an upside-down photograph and a folded news clipping. "You want this the easy way?" Aaron slid the picture in front of Brandon's nose.

Brandon glanced down at two women easily in their twenties. Despite a complete lack of makeup, he identified Kate in a heartbeat—long blonde hair, perky smile. It was the first time he'd seen her wearing something other than ragged sweats or her stripping outfits. It was also the first time he'd witnessed her eyes free from glasses and without the dark liner that gave them an exaggerated cat-like shape.

The woman beside her, however, made him do a double take. She sported the same blonde hair, the same jade green eyes. Her bright smile he knew by heart. Natalya? It couldn't be. Good God, they looked like twins.

He picked it up, peering more closely at the face he recognized, his stomach knotting. The all-too-familiar bump on the bridge of her nose stuttered his heart.

"Or you want it the hard way?"

The newspaper clipping floated in front of him. He swiped it off the coffee table, and his heart slowly came to a standstill. Framed between Sergei and a man he didn't recognize, Natalya looked beyond the camera, as if she hadn't realized her photo was being taken. Long red hair glinted in bright sunshine. Fingers he had come to adore tightly clasped the stranger's hand.

His gaze dropped to the Russian caption that someone had translated by hand. He squinted at the ant-sized capital letters.

JURY FINDS ALLEGED SOLNTSEVSKAYA BRATVA LEADER, DMI-
TRI GAVRIKOV (PICTURED WITH ALLEGED BODYGUARD SER-
GEI KHITROVO AND FIANCÉE NATALYA TRUBACHEV), NOT
GUILTY ON THREE COUNTS OF MURDER AND ASSAULT WITH
DEADLY FORCE.

Brandon felt suddenly, violently ill. He threw the paper aside. "What the fuck is this?"

Aaron let out a heavy sigh. Compassion filled his gaze. "Kelly, Kate's sister-in-law, said her brother Erik never talked much about how he met Kate. She's never met Natalya, and she didn't know her name. But she knew Kate had a fraternal twin sister that Kate evidently didn't talk to any more."

The churning in Brandon's gut intensified as two cups of coffee threatened to make a reappearance.

"After Erik's death, Kelly found that picture in a box of his things from college. She was saving them for Kate."

Twin sister. They didn't look a damn thing alike until he'd seen that picture of Natalya with blond hair.

Though that alone was enough to make him nauseous, the *fiancée* part concerned him more. He gestured where the newspaper had landed, thankfully, facedown. "And that?"

Aaron produced a sheet of paper typed in English. "You can read it, but it's a translation of that article. Rory made a contact over in Russia. This stuff is from her adoptive parents."

Out of patience, Brandon snapped, "What the fuck does it say?"

"The highlights are—the *Bratva* is the mafia. Dmitri there, he's like your old man. Bodyguard translates to hit man, and Natalya belongs to him. The article insinuates she moved up from a position similar to Sergei's."

Her ease with a gun slapped Brandon in the face. It overpowered *belongs to* and *fiancée* with titanic force. Son of a bitch! He'd been sleeping with the same kind of killer who'd murdered his family.

"I think we've stumbled onto our murderer, Bran. Russian mafia sure as hell explains a lot of the ends we couldn't tie up. It explains Rachel's death, if Natalya works for them. They'd need an in. We fell right into it."

Not quite. Brandon heard what Aaron would never say. He'd been on guard. *Brandon* had fallen right into the plan. He'd bought into Natalya's long legs and her half-truths, right up to the point he'd fallen in love with her.

But a sister leading the other to death? Did Kate know? Was she part of this sick plan too? She'd asked him to hire Natalya. She'd never said a damn word about being sisters.

He bolted to his feet and swiped up his phone. Shoving it into his pocket, he snatched his pistol off the counter and started for the door. "Come on. I need my fucking car."

Fifteen minutes later, as Brandon approached his car, he barely noticed his front bumper no longer drooped, and the headlight had been repaired. He slid behind the wheel, gunned the Shelby in reverse, and drove like a bat out of hell toward Kate's. If she wasn't there, he'd chase her down at the goddamned hospital. One way or another, he was getting answers.

———

Natalya toweled off her hair and flipped it behind her head. She stared in the mirror, appraising the long blonde lengths and the odd paint around her eyes.

They'd staged the accident and supplied the necessary information to the press. Stories that put her in the hospital, where Kate now lay unharmed and guarded by three nurses who were more deadly than any terminal disease. She'd "die" in a few days, when the heat from the case cooled off and the accident could be forgotten.

Meanwhile, Kate was safe, and Natalya could accomplish her job. With an hour before Fantasia opened, she'd like nothing more than to collapse on the floor and grieve for her aching heart. She missed Brandon already. Seeing him tonight, yearning to touch him, unable to follow through, would tear her into pieces. Maybe—though the thought of his worrying about her made her want to retch—her false accident would keep him at the hospital.

If there was any luck in this world, it would.

A thunderous knock on the door had her reaching behind her back to check for her gun. The feel of the cool metal against her waist soothed her agitated nerves, and she went to the door, prepared to play the part of sweet, genuine, Kate.

She answered with a bright smile.

Brandon barged inside. "What the fuck is going on, Kate?"

Forty

Oh, shit.

Natalya backed up a step, giving Brandon's temper a wide berth. She reached down deep for the lies she'd rehearsed all morning. "I can't stay and talk, I've got to get to the hospital. I sent Derek next door. Do you want to ride with me?"

"No." He took two steps closer and grabbed her by the upper arms. "I want the truth now. Why didn't you tell me you were her fucking sister?"

Sister? Uh-oh. That one wasn't planned. How had he found out? Smile firmly lodged in place, she twisted to free her arms. "I don't know what you're talking about."

He squinted at her, his gaze searching her face. Slowly, he ground out, "I. Have. A. Picture."

Natalya struggled to keep her mind on explanations, not the soft contours of Brandon's mouth that hovered inches from hers.

"From college? We used to get that all that time. Once, when Natalya had trouble in chemistry, we even swapped places so I could take her test for her." Truth. It hadn't worked, but at least she wasn't lying to Brandon. "I don't know who's feeding you stories, but I've got to go. If she wakes up, there's no one there."

Way to play the guilt card.

He flinched, but it didn't last. He did, however, release her. Backing up, the angry color returned to his face. "I know who's feeding me stories, Natalya. You think I don't recognize the face I fell in love with? Damn it, what kind of idiot do you think I am?"

In love. *Oh, God.* He'd said it. Out loud. As real as the fury burning in his eyes. Speechless, she stared at the tight line of white beneath his chin.

"You're engaged to a Russian mobster. You show up in my club, in the middle of a string of murders, and you've been lying to me since the day we met." He pounded a fist on the couch's high back. "I want the goddamn truth for once!"

She shook her head. "I'm sorry, Brandon. I've got to go. I have a job to finish."

Natalya took two steps toward the door and saw him reach behind his back. She moved faster, spinning on her heel, pistol drawn and level with his.

"Put it down, Natalya. I've got grounds to arrest you for murder. I'm not going to let you kill another girl or help someone else do it."

The hard set to his features and the dull glint in his eyes told her the man who loved had stepped aside. A cop stood in his place, one who wouldn't hesitate to fire. She might get off the first shot, but at this close range, she wouldn't leave unscathed. She'd lost Brandon Moretti. If she'd ever truly had him.

And now, if she intended to salvage anything from this disastrous assignment, she had no choice but to tell him everything.

"I'm not the person you want. Jill is. Yes, I've lied to you. But not because I'm a serial killer. I'm a Black Opal, an elite CIA operative, and if you don't let me go now, I can't stop her."

"Bullshit. Jill's at home with female problems. She called this morning."

"How convenient." She let out a wry chuckle. "Kate said she wasn't at the club last night either." Her gun trained on Brandon, as his was on her, she moved across the room to the coffee table and her purse. With one hand, she fished inside for her phone and lobbed it through the air.

It landed at his feet.

"Dial pound fifty-six. When they answer, ask for Romanov. Ask him about the third frond on the palm. It's the code name for a human trafficking ring with Dubai as the destination country. He'll verify everything I have to say."

His glance flicked to the phone, his conviction faltering. He jerked his gaze back to her face and shook his head. "Probably staged. Put the gun down. I'm taking you in. Your *agency* can come drag your ass out."

"Oh, for God's sake, Brandon! Why the hell would I make that up? You obviously know about Dmitri. You think I *like* the fact I've been fucking an international killer for the last three years?"

A cold, calloused smirk twisted his mouth. "Which begs the question, why were you fucking me? Another job? Just part of the game, huh? At least you got a good ride."

"No," she whispered as her heart cracked from the strain of all the deception. Emotion rose to choke her, blinding her with tears. She lowered her gun, no longer caring about the case or whether Brandon jumped across the five feet that separated them and wrested the pistol from her fingers.

His pain broke her. She'd caused every bit of it. From Rachel to this . . . With a shaky hand, she set her Sig on the table at her back and covered her face with her hands to hide the tears she couldn't stop. "No, Brandon, you were real." She choked back an ugly sob. "*Are* real. And this is breaking my heart."

Brandon's hold on his pistol slipped at the sound of Natalya's cracked voice. He lowered it a fraction, not yet convinced her tears were genuine, but disturbed by them all the same. The detective inside him sidestepped to the rear, and against his better judgment, he began to let her claims sink in.

"CIA?" he asked quietly.

She nodded on a prolonged sniffle. "Black Opals are undocumented. We don't exist on paper."

"What happened to Rachel?"

"Dmitri had her killed." She dragged her hands down her face and watery eyes held his. "There's a chain—Iskatel´ is the finder. He sights the girls and handles the capture. He delivers them to a warehouse on Nellis where Nikolai holds them until a private boat arrives in San Francisco. They're fed meager meals, water, and heroin. When they get to Dubai they're totally dependent on the drug."

"And there?" Brandon asked, already knowing the answer.

"Sex slaves for wealthy businessmen and sheikhs."

"Why did Rachel have to die?" Just knowing Natalya had been associated with Rachel's death made him ache all over. But he had to hear what role Natalya played in that murder.

"She didn't have to. I tried to talk him out of it, but Dmitri wouldn't listen."

As incoherency attacked Natalya, her words linked together with a chain of gut-wrenching sobs, making it impossible to convince himself this was staged theatrics. Her shoulders shook violently, and her face twisted with so much pain, her suffering thumped him hard in the chest. He set his gun on the back of the couch and did the only thing he could think of. He took her into his arms and held her tight.

"Sweetheart," he whispered as he smoothed her hair. "Baby, shh. It's okay." Fists beat ineffectually against his chest, until, in defeat, her hand curled into his shirt, and she sagged into his embrace.

He didn't know how long he held her. Seconds spanned into minutes. Minutes dragged on until he couldn't gauge the passing of time. Her crying cut him to pieces. That he couldn't stop it made him bleed. Strong, confident Natalya wasn't supposed to fall apart. But somehow, the fact that she had, that she'd allowed him to see this vulnerability, swelled his heart to painful limits.

"Natalya." Brandon captured her face between his hands and tipped her head up. His earnest gaze willed her to believe how sorry he was. "It's okay, beautiful." The salty flavor of her tears touched his lips as he bent to kiss her. Her response was faint, a mere flutter of her lips. It encouraged him. "Come on. Let's sit down. Is Kate okay?"

She nodded. "She's under surveillance in the hospital."

"And Derek's next door?"

Natalya shook her head. "He's with another Opal. He's upset, but he knows his mom's okay."

"All right. Then tell me everything."

"You'll hate me." Fresh tears spilled down her cheeks once more.

Brandon sank onto the couch and pulled her into his lap. "Doubtful." Using the pad of his thumb, he brushed her tears away. "Just talk."

For the next three hours, Natalya told Brandon everything she could think of about her job, her life with Dmitri, and the crimes she'd committed in the name of US Intelligence. The sun faded lower, casting them in shadows, telling her she'd missed arriving at Fantasia at Kate's usual time. But the truths wouldn't stop flowing. Her role with the women, Dmitri's insistence she take Iskatel''s place.

His expression remained impassive, giving her no clue as to what he might be thinking. He asked questions, digested her answers, pulled out confessions she'd never even considered. She revealed her plans for the switch, her intention to take Kate's place and have Iskatel' capture her, and her intention to corner Jill who wasn't physically capable of overpowering Natalya. She gave Brandon every opportunity to shove her out of his lap, but he never took his hands off her. Never physically withdrew no matter what direction his mind might have taken.

When she finished, she let out an exhausted breath. Brandon studied her for several quiet seconds before he finally spit out, "I don't like it."

Natalya blinked. "Don't like what?"

"I don't like you using yourself as bait."

"I have to."

"I want to shadow you."

Horrified by the thought of Brandon putting himself in harm's way, she vigorously shook her head. "You can't. You don't know these people. Dmitri is here somewhere."

"That's exactly why I want to shadow you. If he's onto you, he's going to suspect something, and the plan you knew isn't going to be the one he executes." He took her chin between thumb and forefinger and lifted her face. "If something goes wrong, I'll never forgive myself for letting you go in alone."

Steely determination reflected in his tawny eyes. He was so confident. So unshakeable. He just couldn't comprehend the *Bratva* blew all the things he'd learned as a narcotics undercover into meaningless fluff. Hired guns were nothing like junkies with pistols. She'd been trained for these situations. Brandon didn't possess the background.

Yet, she also realized nothing she said would deter him. They could fight until she gave up and let him win, or she could save the effort and concede now, but slow him down. If she arrived at Fantasia before he did, the very training he believed made him qualified to stand alongside Sergei, would stop him from doing anything that might blow her cover.

Better yet, if she could slow him down significantly, he might not make it to Fantasia until after she'd been taken.

"Okay." A shudder rolled down her spine. He might not hate her now, but he would after that particular lie.

He gave her one last lingering kiss before pushing her to her feet.

No longer in need of her phone, she left it lying on the floor. She slung her purse over her shoulder and picked up her gun as Brandon tucked his into the back of his jeans. Beating him to the door, she looked over her shoulder with a soft, wistful smile.

He gave her a look filled with so much affection she nearly dropped her to her knees. "Go on. I've got your back."

"*Ya tebya lyublyu,*" she whispered thickly.

Then, she aimed and fired.

D mitri strolled down the sterile white hallway casually, as if he weren't on the way to view his injured fiancée and snuff the rest of her life from her body. Good thing she hadn't died in the collision. He'd have hated for her to go without seeing his face one last time.

A nurse skittered out of his way as he pushed open the private ICU room door. One of his contacts, perhaps? He shrugged. It made little difference. When he'd heard of Natalya's accident, he'd made an immediate phone call. The contacts he possessed in Vegas quickly supplied the details, including the number of her private room. No one had asked questions. No one offered complaint.

As it should be.

As it would be when he left her lifeless body behind.

He glanced at the collection of tubes and wires connecting her to machines that beeped and whirred, then looked to her beautiful face. Her auburn hair tangled about her shoulders, long lashes barred the eyes he could recall at will. On seeing the purple bruises and fresh scrapes that covered her skin, something deep in his gut did a long, hard roll. *His Natalya*.

He should have been sitting in that wooden chair no one occupied. Holding her hand and talking for however long it took to draw her back from the recesses of her mind. In a moment of sheer remorse, he kicked the chair near her bed and sat down. Taking her limp hand in his, he ran his thumb over hers.

Such a beautiful woman.

Dmitri closed his eyes to the sound of her laughter, picturing her vibrant smile. The lump in his belly worked its way up his esophagus to lodge between his lungs. Her only fault was that she hadn't loved him.

No, not even that she hadn't loved him—that she'd betrayed the love he couldn't restrain. He couldn't forget that fact. Wouldn't. Others, far closer to him than even her, had paid the price for such disloyalty.

He would not allow her to continue to make a mockery of him. She, like his brother, would pay the according price.

Now. Before the nurses returned to check the machines.

Reaching over her fragile body, he pushed the hair away from her face as he stood. He drew back, willing her eyes to open and radiate with genuine feeling, knowing they never would. Quietly, he slipped his hand inside his lapel pocket and withdrew a syringe filled with a colorless substance. Though her suffering would be short-lived, her accident ironically provided the same neatness he preferred. Death could be attributed to her injuries. No one would think to schedule an autopsy. Besides, he was the only family she had. He'd claim he wanted her burial over with so he could grieve.

A shadow in the corner of his eye gave him pause. He closed his fingers around the syringe, hiding it in his palm, as the door to her room opened.

A petite blonde nurse strolled in. She pinned him in place with a frown. "Excuse me, are you family?"

Damn. His contacts had promised he'd have the time he required without interruption. Clearly this nurse hadn't been informed.

"I am her fiancé."

"Then you're not family. I'm sorry, but you'll have to leave."

Dmitri choked down a maddening rush of outrage. He would not have this final glory taken from him. He searched for a charming smile, did his best to keep his fury beneath the smoothness of his voice. "You would not force her to wake alone, would you? She would be terrified."

Smug satisfaction radiated through him as the nurse's hard frown softened. She glanced to Natalya, hesitatingly looked back at him. Her indecision was as obvious as the beeping machines. Dmitri landed the crippling blow, the words that would push her into sympathy. "Hasn't she already been through enough?"

"I—I . . ." She pursed her lips and looked over her shoulder at the partly open door. "I suppose it would be okay for a few minutes. Just while I check her vitals. Then I'm sorry, but you'll have to leave. We can put a chair outside the door."

He wouldn't need the chair.

The nurse approached the bed, her hands fluttering over the lightweight quilt, straightening it. She hummed a soft tune, her actions bringing her closer to where he stood. So close the next sweep of her palm came near his thigh. Too close. She had no cause to stand on this side of Natalya—the machines were on the other side.

Instinct set off alarm bells in his head, the same sixth sense that had saved his ass on more than one occasion when a contact he'd been expecting didn't show on time. This nurse was taking too long. Accomplishing nothing. She hadn't even checked the IV tubes or taken Natalya's pulse. Yet she'd delayed Dmitri by precious minutes. Time he didn't have and didn't risk in places where he didn't hold absolute control.

Nervously, he glanced to the partly open door and the hallway beyond. It was too quiet. Too still. Where were the beeping alerts? The bustling attendants?

As the nurse bent over Natalya once more, Dmitri's gaze fastened on an unnatural bulge in the small of the woman's back. Hard. L-shaped . . .

He reared back, his entire body tight. His gaze scampered once more to the hallway in time to see a shadow he hadn't noticed before move. They weren't alone. Someone else was out there.

Someone who didn't want their presence known.

Son of a bitch—he'd been set up!

As everything clanged into place, he snatched the nurse's arm, drew her back against his chest, and thrust the deadly needle at her neck. "Call off the man outside. You'll take me out of here. Then, we'll forget about this little incident."

For now at least. When he was free, he'd make damn sure no one forgot anything.

Before Dmitri could shuffle a step to the door, the woman in his arms drove the flat of her foot into his knee, wrenching it backward. A sickening *pop* accompanied the sudden explosion of pain. He stumbled, the syringe clattering to the floor. Blocking out the agony that ravaged his body, he thrust a hand inside his coat for his gun.

An all too recognizable *click* ricocheted through his ears as the cold, hard press of steel met the side of his temple. "Not so fast, Dmitri. Time's up. I'm afraid you won't be leaving after all."

As a string of oaths poured free, another woman burst into the room, wearing the same light yellow scrubs and false hospital identification badge. Her gun was trained on him as well. She smiled. "Hope you've enjoyed Vegas. Why don't you stick around a while."

With no choice but to comply, he withdrew his empty hand. Barely containing the venom that roiled in his veins, he held his arms in front of him and offered his wrists. This wasn't over by any means, but he wasn't stupid. He wouldn't sacrifice his life. Someone would deal. He possessed too much information to sit uselessly behind bars.

The first nurse looked to the second. "Did you make the call?"

For the first time since she'd entered the room, the second woman's composure faltered. Apprehension passed behind her eyes. "No one's answering."

"What about the other?"

"Voicemail, first ring."

A small degree of satisfaction blossomed in Dmitri's chest. They might have dropped him, but something in their scheme wasn't working as designed. He resisted the urge to smile.

Forty-one

Brandon lay on the floor, staring at the ceiling. It took a moment for reality to sink in and for his brain to pick up on the message that the stinging in his shoulder wasn't make-believe. When it did, fury boiled through his veins. She'd fucking shot him! Natalya had turned around, aimed, and without a blink pulled the trigger.

He sat up, clutching at the bleeding wound. She'd played him again. Good God, when did the lies stop? He'd held her for three hours, absorbed her tears, soothed her upset—and it was fake! Again! He *ought* to have been shot for his sheer stupidity.

Yanking his collar sideways, he squinted at his left shoulder, inspecting the wound. Just a scratch. Close enough to rip through several layers of skin and require a couple stitches, but a scratch all the same. When he got his hands on her again, *if* he got his hands on her again, that woman was going to jail. No excuses. No chance for tears. Straight to jail.

Like he should have done when he'd discovered he wasn't talking to Kate.

His ego kicked in as he grabbed for his phone. She wasn't such a good shot after all if she couldn't manage more than a graze at close distance.

The door thumped open before he could punch in Mayer's number, and Brandon jerked in surprise. Pain lanced down his arm. He hissed as he eyed the intruder.

Gun drawn, Sergei filled the doorway.

Brandon shook his head in disbelief. First Natalya, now the hit man. Just fucking great. His days were numbered after all. Only he'd been too focused in the wrong direction to recognize the real threat.

"I suppose you're here to finish me off?" Inching one hand behind his back, he reached for his gun. He might lose this one, but damn it, he refused to roll over and die.

"No." Sergei released the chamber and set his pistol on the table by the door. "I came to see how much of you she left behind." He extended a hand.

Warily, Brandon accepted the offered aid and allowed Sergei to hoist him to his feet. Movement sent another rush of white-hot fire shooting down to his fingertips, and he grimaced.

"I've been tailing her since she decided to follow through on this hair-brained plan this morning. Heard the shot, saw her leave, figured you'd tried to talk her out of the idea."

Brandon heard the words, but his mind couldn't process their meaning. Tailing Natalya? Helping him? He took a seat on the couch, pinched the bridge of his nose between thumb and index finger, and tried to stop the racket in his head. "Who's side are you on?"

Sitting on the couch opposite, Sergei shrugged. "Hers, I guess. Which puts me on yours. A little tip—don't try to talk her out of something she's got her mind set on. Work *around* her." He gestured at Brandon's shoulder. "It'll save you skin in the long haul. She's too damn good with guns."

At the jest, Brandon's mind conjured a picture of the silver sedan's flat tire. Fifty yards at least. Two bullets. Luck couldn't be that accurate.

He glanced at his elbow, where blood pooled in the crease between bicep and forearm. She could have killed him. If she'd wanted to, she could have aimed a little lower and stopped his heart.

Brandon groaned as understanding settled in. She'd hit him exactly where she'd meant to. An insignificant wound designed to slow him down.

"*Now* you believe. Funny how bullets can do that." Sergei smirked. "So what did she tell you?"

"Everything. I think." He pushed his right hand through his hair.

"Good. How about I patch that up for you real quick, and we go over to Jill's and put this to an end before Natalya does something else she's going to regret." He barked a short laugh. "That'll really piss her off, but it's a great way to get even."

Brandon frowned. Something didn't feel right. Sergei was her partner, and partners didn't let one member of the team go in without backup. He shouldn't be here. He should be at Fantasia with his eye on Natalya.

A chill invaded his veins. What if Natalya had it all wrong? What if the threat was sitting right in front of him? Sergei knew where Brandon lived, had access to the back rooms, and if he'd been Dmitri's bodyguard, he could easily be last night's gunman. Further, Brandon couldn't bring himself to believe Jill was capable of shooting a gun at all, much less a dog. She was . . . *Jill*.

He regarded Sergei with a lifted brow. "Why are you here? Why aren't you with her?"

The humor drained from Sergei's expression. He sat forward, suddenly deadpan serious. "First, because Natalya's in no danger until ten after ten when she finishes Kate's dance, receives the message, and leaves the building."

"Second?"

Sergei's stare held Brandon's as if he struggled to find the right words. He opened his mouth. Closed it. Let out a sigh. Then, his smile returned to restore the glint of humor in his eyes. "I figure Ma would claw her way out of the grave and kick my butt if I let you walk away from the one woman who can keep your ass in line."

Before the words could fully penetrate Brandon's brain, Sergei stood and pulled his shirt up, exposing a long scar that began near his waistband and curved around his right side. "You didn't kill me,

Bran. Agent Kramer stopped by the shop and pulled me out before he tried to tell Ma and Gina. Fact is, Ma made us. She stood out a little too much."

Dumbstruck, Brandon could only stare at the remaining evidence of the day his brother, Stefan, had run through the glass patio door.

I t was a dream. Maybe a nightmare—Brandon couldn't decide which. He'd fallen in love with a CIA agent, and his brother sat in the seat beside him, navigating the Vegas traffic as they headed for Jill's apartment on the west side of town. He'd been shot. Stitched up with dental floss, no less, and the woman he *had* been fucking was a serial killer.

Just how fucked up could one day get?

He glanced sideways at Stefan's shaggy hair. Brandon had worn his long through junior high, but Golden Boy Moretti wouldn't have been caught dead with long hair. They'd switched places somehow in life.

Shaking off the strange sense of disorientation, he trained his thoughts on the situation. He had time to navigate Stefan's return and the unbelievable news that their mother had brought about the murders, not his loose tongue. Right now, Natalya took priority, and Brandon couldn't shake the feeling they were on the wrong track.

Something she'd said. But she'd said so much. He'd been so angry too. He drummed his fingers on the armrest, feeling the answer on the tip of his tongue but unable to put it into words.

"This it?" Stefan pointed at a small stucco house with turquoise trim.

"Yeah."

They pulled into Jill's driveway and climbed out of the car. The house looked empty. No television flashing in the front room, windows and doors closed—no hint Jill might be at home. More evidence to support Natalya's theory that Jill was Iskatel´.

Damn it, what had Natalya said?

"You go to the door. I'll stay back here and come in behind you." Stefan urged Brandon toward the stoop with a jerk of his head.

"It's not Jill. We're working the wrong angle."

"You know she vandalized the car, right?"

"Yeah, but . . ."

"How much more evidence do you need, Bran?"

"Fine." Brandon bounded up the two stairs in one stride and rang Jill's doorbell. As he waited for her to answer, he glanced at her mailbox, noting several envelopes poked from beneath the metal flap. She hadn't retrieved her mail in weeks.

Odd. He pushed the bell again.

From deep within the house a faint voice rang out, "Coming."

A few seconds later, she cracked open the door and stuck her head out. Puffy red eyes widened. "Brandon. What are you doing here? I said I'd come in and talk to you later this week."

As she closed the door, Brandon braced against it. A stronger push opened it wide enough he could see into her dark house. No lights on anywhere. In one sweeping glance, he took in her disheveled dark hair, terry cloth robe, and bare feet. "I need to talk to you."

"About?" She pulled her robe tighter across her breasts.

"Can I come in?"

"This isn't a good time."

"Come off it, Jill. It's not like I haven't seen it all before. We need to talk now." Not giving her room to argue, he gave the door another push and stepped inside. Taking her by the elbow, he escorted her into her living room and flipped on a lamp. The clutter of her usually tidy place took him by surprise. Dishes sat on the table, half-eaten food left to rot. A pile of rumpled blankets covered the couch. On the floor, he spotted an empty bottle of tequila.

Stefan's appearance in the entryway stopped Brandon from commenting on the disarray. "How's Nikolai, Jill?"

"What?"

The shaky way Jill's hand lifted to pull her robe even tighter bothered Brandon. She either knew exactly why they were here, or as he suspected, she had nothing to do with Iskatel´ and something else was the cause. He took command of the conversation. "I'm going to cut to the chase. I want to know about the car, the birds, and Iskatel´."

Her eyes went wide, and her ashen complexion grayed even more. "The car?"

"Yes, the car."

She sank into a nearby chair. "I wanted you. But that's insignificant now. I'm sorry. Tell Natalya that too. I won't be seeing her again, I don't think."

Apologies? From Jill? Something definitely wasn't right. What had Natalya said? He gritted his teeth, searching for the out-of-place memory.

"See, told you, Bran." Stefan braced his hands on the armrests and brought his face close to Jill's. "It's not just the car, is it? You couldn't stand the fact Brandon chose Natalya so you ratted her out. You told Dmitri. And you've been terrorizing her since. You even shot at her last night. Was screwing up kidnapping seven women not enough? Did Dmitri give you the orders, or did you take it upon yourself?"

"Shot?" Jill scooted into the back of her chair as if she thought she could crawl out the other side. "I didn't shoot anyone last night! I've been sick. I told Brandon that on the phone."

With a derisive chuckle, Stefan pushed away from the chair. "Great act. Not buying it. Last night you felt good enough to take a drive in the desert *and* shoot a dog. You've got plans tonight. We know about them, Jill. Or would you prefer *Iskatel´*?"

"I don't know what you're talking about!" Her voice rose an octave as she shot to the edge of her seat, her usual vigor restored with a burst of anger. "I haven't gone anywhere since yesterday morning when I found out I have ovarian cancer. Stage four. *That's* why I'm not coming in to work! You don't believe me, the file's on the counter in the kitchen."

Brandon recoiled like he'd been kicked in the gut. Cancer? Guilt crashed around his shoulders, and he swore. He was standing here drilling someone he knew wasn't responsible while she was clearly falling apart.

"That's also pretty convenient," Stefan countered. "Dmitri could have any one of his doctors fabricate a report."

Convenient. Brandon's mind locked on Stefan's remark. He'd said the same thing to Natalya when she accused Jill the first time. Later, amidst the tears, she cited what had led her to the conclusion. One of which was Opie—Opie had to know who'd killed him, or Opie would have ripped off the gunman's arm.

Jill had never set foot in Brandon's house. Never met Opie.

"She's telling the truth." He grabbed Stefan by the shoulder and propelled him to the door. "Jill, I'm sorry." It was all he could think to say, given the circumstances. Later, when he could process everything, when Natalya was out of danger, he'd come by and see if he could do anything.

"What the fuck?" Stefan jerked his shoulder free.

"She's never been at my house to meet Opie. Natalya did tell you how the dog was shot, right?"

Stefan's expression turned as hard as stone. "Then who the hell is it?"

"Hell if I know. Let's get Aaron in on this. He can keep an eye on Natalya in the club."

At Stefan's nod, Brandon pulled his phone out of his pocket. Out of habit, he punched the button to access his address book. A screen full of names and addresses flashed in front of his face. "Damn it."

"What?"

"I picked up Mayer's phone by accident. I can't call him. He's probably figured it out, and he won't answer mine."

"Try anyway."

Brandon struck off for the car, waiting for the ringing in his ear to flip to his voice mail. As predicted, the generic voice answered, announcing the mailbox wasn't established. He hung up and slid into the passenger seat. Mayer might not answer, but he'd see a text message. The incoming messages overrode the interface and displayed automatically. A feature Brandon hadn't given second thought, since he rarely ever received or sent texts.

He typed out, **Call me. Natalya in Fantasia as Kate. Needs your protection. She's not the killer, she's CIA.**

When Stefan shut the driver's-side door, Brandon voiced his thoughts. "Natalya's going in blind. We've got to get to Fantasia. We can pull in Mayer, and we'll be another man strong. He knows all the exits and who's guarded them on what shift of what night. It'll be—"

The phone in his hand vibrated with an incoming text message from Rory. Rory who'd supplied Mayer with Natalya's Russian background information. Brandon's heart skipped several beats. Rory had been gone last night. Hell, no one had heard from him since Brandon insisted he take a few days.

Brandon read the message to call and pressed the connect key.

Rory answered on the second ring. "Hey, I got your message from yesterday morning. Sorry man, I'd have gone with you, but I've been with Rachel's mom. I think that house you were at blew up last night, by the way."

Brandon nearly choked. "This is Moretti. What do you mean you think it blew up?"

"I heard it on the noon news. Right after I heard about that girl you interviewed being hit by a car. Gas main leak took out a couple houses in that neighborhood."

Brandon grimaced as his stomach took a nosedive to the floor. "Rory, when's the last time you talked to Mayer?"

"I haven't talked to him since you took me off the case. Why?"

The churning in Brandon's gut rose to violent levels. He clenched a hand around the door handle. "So you didn't give him a bunch of translated Russian documents about Natalya?"

"Huh?" Rory laughed. "Hello? I barely passed English. Where'd you get the idea I could translate Russian?"

"Son of a bitch!" Brandon slammed his fist into the armrest before thrusting his index finger at the road. "Drive!"

"Bran?" Rory asked in his ear.

"I'll explain later." Brandon hung up and took a deep breath to stop the racing of his heart. Eyes riveted on the road, he didn't dare look at his brother for fear he'd read his failures in Stefan's expression. "It's Mayer. And he knows she's CIA."

"How?"

Brandon gritted his teeth against a mountain of self-loathing. "I fucking told him."

Forty-two

Natalya sat in the dressing room, fiddling with her hair. She'd survived an hour as Kate. She had three more to accomplish before she took the stage. Any time after that she could expect Jill to fulfill her role and make contact. If Jill chose the same methods Natalya had used, the request would come as an opportunity to earn extra money, with no house cut, for a wealthy client. And it would be made in private, so no one could hear the message and relay it to the authorities when the dancer turned up missing. Or in Jill's case, often dead.

Sapphire sauntered in and plopped down at the mirror beside Natalya. "Where's your friend?"

"Hm?" She fastened Kate's bright smile onto her face and willed the tension out of her voice. "Who?"

"Natalya. This is the second night she and Brandon haven't been in on time. I think there's something going on there." She smacked her gum and reclined in the chair, throwing one long leg over the other. "Lucky girl. I bet he can make a girl come for hours."

Definitely. Natalya rummaged through a drawer full of hair accessories to hide the heat that leapt to her face. "How's the crowd tonight?"

"Eh, I've seen better."

"Kate?" Aaron's voice echoed in the girls' lounge. "You back here?"

Natalya resumed fiddling with her hair. "I'm back here."

Sapphire gave Natalya a wink and lowered her voice. "I tried that one out the other night. Let me tell ya, he ain't nothing to complain about."

"Hey." Aaron leaned in the doorway. "Oh, hi, Sapphire." His gaze roamed appreciatively down the waist-deep gap in Sapphire's robe before meeting Natalya's eyes through the mirror. "Have you seen Becca?"

"Not since you sent her down to props for toilet paper a little while ago."

He let out a harassed sigh. "Would you get her? She's probably down there flirting with Harvey. I've got guys asking for her in VIP, a problem with the waitresses, and I can't leave the floor too long. Have you heard from Brandon?"

"No. He doesn't usually make it a habit to check in with me." She set her hairbrush down and stood up, glad for an excuse to be free of Sapphire's company. "I'll go fetch Becca."

Ducking under Aaron's arm, she made her way to the back stairs. Her heels clicked against the metal stairs, a hollow metallic sound that echoed through the concrete stairwell. At the bottom, the door blew inward as she reached for the handle, nearly knocking her backward. Harvey and two other men bustled through, their arms laden with the heavy black trunks Mercury used for her stage set.

"Oh, sorry, Kate," Harvey mumbled. His immediate blush stained the tips of his ears.

Natalya chuckled. "It's okay. Is Becca down here?"

"She was." He set down a box to scratch his head. "She might still be in the storeroom. I've been so busy I haven't paid attention."

"Okay. VIP wants her. I'll go look."

Mumbling something Natalya couldn't understand, Harvey picked up his boxes and followed the other two up the stairs.

She entered the vast maze of storage shelves, doorways, and corridors that comprised Fantasia's basement. As Kate, she couldn't ask for directions, so she chose the hall on her right. The first door she encountered opened into Harvey's kingdom of colored cardboard, fabrics, and hunks of metal that somehow became the fantastic sets Fantasia was known for.

Becca hadn't been sent for props though. She closed the door and continued down the hall toward the glowing EXIT sign at the end. "Becca? Hey, are you down here?"

Her lack of response didn't surprise Natalya, given the heavy doors. It'd be amazing if Becca could even hear someone call. She opened the next, closed it when she discovered more props.

The next three proved the same. On the fourth, however, Natalya found a room twice as wide as the others and stacked from floor to ceiling with metal shelves full of paper products. She stepped inside, examining the aisles, working her way to the far back corner. From toilet paper to plastic cups to the promotional coasters that advertised different alcohols, each shelf was jam packed with everything a bar could need to operate for several months without having to restock.

But no Becca.

A thump near the door made Natalya cock her head. A prickling sensation lifted the hair at the nape of her neck. "Becca?"

"Yes?" she answered.

Waves of relief washed over Natalya, and she let out a breath she hadn't realized she'd been holding. She wove her way back to the first row, where she found Becca climbing on the shelves, trying to reach the toilet paper near the ceiling.

"What are you doing? You're going to break your neck in those heels. Here, let me." Natalya kicked off her shoes and set her toes on the edge of the bottommost shelf.

Becca gave her a shy smile as she inched back to the floor. "Thanks."

Natalya snagged a package with her nails and pulled, allowing it to fall behind her. She muttered as it thumped her in the back before landing, then hopped easily off the shelf. As Becca bent for the toilet paper, Natalya bent to retrieve her shoes.

Straightening, one foot in her heels, the other bare, Natalya glimpsed Becca's wide, frightened eyes. Ice flooded Natalya's blood. Her heart skidded to a stop. She didn't need to look—she already knew.

In the next instant, something sharp pierced her neck. She turned her head as a heavy arm banded around her waist. Before everything went dark, Aaron Mayer gave her a sinister smile.

Brandon charged through Fantasia's doors with Stefan on his heels. They made a beeline for the backstage dressing room, stopping only long enough to demand from Scott, "Where's Mayer?"

Scott shook his head. "No idea, boss. Ain't seen him in a good hour."

A fucking hour. Christ! They were too late. They'd driven as fast as they could, but a clog-up on the Interstate set them back twenty minutes. Not that they'd have made it on time anyway, according to Scott, but they might have been able to catch Aaron before he left the club.

"You better go on back though," Scott suggested. "You've been gone, Aaron's not around, Jill's not here, Natalya's not here, and now Kate and Becca can't be found either. We got a mess, and the girls are falling apart."

"You're going to have to handle it," Brandon called over his shoulder as he wheeled around and ran out the doors he'd just entered. He yanked open the Shelby's passenger door and jumped inside, barely getting his foot in before Stefan started to back out of the lot.

"Shit!" Brandon thumped the armrest with his fist once more. He'd put Natalya in this position. The one thing he'd sworn to do—protect her—he'd failed. If they didn't find her, or worse, if they found her dead . . .

He shook off the thought before it could become poison. "You know where the warehouse is, right?"

"Yup. We knew all that coming in."

"No chance they've changed it?"

"Better hope they haven't."

Not what Brandon needed to hear. To keep himself from going crazy as they sped across town, he busied his hands with checking his gun and making sure he had a full magazine. If Natalya hadn't shot him, if she'd just given him the chance . . . He squeezed his eyes shut and willed the horrific visions away. "Hey, Stefan?" he asked quietly.

"Yeah?"

"What does *Ya tebya lyublyu* mean?"

His brother was quiet for several seconds, his hands gripping and loosening on the wheel. Then, he let out a harsh breath. "It means, *I love you.*"

The fist that punched Brandon in the gut knocked the wind from his lungs. She loved him. His throat clogged with so much emotion, carrying on a conversation became impossible. He watched the streetlights pass in a blur, ordered himself not to break down. *She loved him.*

Stefan slowed his frantic speed as they approached the long row of warehouses on Nellis. Under his breath, he counted off numbers, then cut off his headlights and nosed into a vast parking lot. Two black sedans sat in front of the dark building. Stefan parked two spaces down from the one closest to the door.

Like mice in a cat's house, they exited the car and hugged the shadows as they moved around the brick building. Stefan came to an abrupt halt, halfway down the north side. He held up his hand, then motioned Brandon toward a dingy window.

Inside, a solitary lightbulb glowed, illuminating a dark corner where Natalya lay on the floor, unmoving.

Rage seized Brandon. If Mayer had hurt a single hair on her head, he'd kill him. No asking questions, no hesitation—he'd kill him the minute he laid eyes on that bastard's face.

Natalya's hands moved, a faint twitch of her fingers, but movement nonetheless. Brandon's breath rushed out, and his heart kick-started. Alive. *Thank God.*

It took every bit of his training to resist the urge to leap through the window and instead follow Stefan to the door that sat ajar ten feet away. Stopping behind it, they listened. When a door banged shut within, Stefan pulled his phone out of his pocket and punched something in.

Brandon lifted an eyebrow.

Stefan mouthed, *Back up.*

Nodding, Brandon took the lead and eased the door open onto a set of descending stairs. The scent of cigar smoke blended with the dust of disuse, guiding them into the musty dungeon. Voices carried through the long corridor. One female? He couldn't be certain, but it came from behind the closest door, thick and indistinguishable. Two masculine laughs erupted closer to the room they'd glimpsed Natalya in, and then a door barged open.

Brandon and Stefan flattened their backs to the wall, hidden by the unlit hall's deep shadows. Brandon watched as Mayer pulled open a heavy insulated door and stepped inside. His hand shot out near the base, wedging something into the frame to presumably keep it from locking him in.

"Ah, Natalya, you look good blond."

Brandon's blood boiled. His fingers tightened around his pistol, and he forced himself to breathe.

"Dmitri was a fool to hire you."

A smile threatened as Natalya's voice rang down the hallway. It sounded off, as if her words took more work than normal, but she was talking, and her courage shone through.

Stefan pointed at himself, then pointed at the door Aaron had come through. He then pointed to Brandon and indicated he should take Natalya's door.

Fine with him. He had a score to settle with his partner.

Natalya glared at Aaron, doing her best to keep him from observing the grogginess that clung to her body. "Where's Becca?"

"She'll be taking Kate's place." He pulled a wooden stool under the light and took a seat. "It's sad what strippers will do for a little extra cash. I gave her two hundred dollars to get toilet paper and wait for me to come downstairs."

"You have to bribe the girls?" She forced a laugh through her dry throat. "Pitiful. What did they do, fight a little too much? Or were you just that incapable of getting the dosage right? I see you screwed up mine. I shouldn't be awake until tomorrow."

Her barb landed on target. Aaron's face colored crimson, and he jerked forward to grab the gun on the table beside him. His hand stopped just over the grip, fingers slowly closed, and he dropped onto the stool once more. "No. I'm not going to make it that painless."

"Judging from your shot last night, you might miss."

Fury blazed in his dark eyes. "You're as fucking arrogant as Moretti."

She pushed herself further up the wall and flexed her fingers. The tingling in her extremities and the ice-cold feel of her skin had ebbed. "I'd say with good reason, since I was sent here to do your job for you. Why'd you kill the girls?" *Keep him talking.* Soon enough she could use her limbs and claim that gun for herself.

Before she could make a move, however, she needed to know the odds. If he knew she was Natalya, then chances were he knew who she worked for. Which meant Dmitri knew. And Nikolai. And while she could take out Aaron, if those two were nearby, she couldn't overcome all three.

"Where's Dmitri?"

Aaron let out a derisive snort. "That pitiful fool? He's gone. Turns out you *were* his greatest weakness. He swore he'd deal with you. Told me to kill Brandon, and he couldn't manage to do more than send you a box of chocolates." Laughter racked his shoulders as he sadly shook his head. "The little trap you set for him in the hospital—he was too dumb to see it for what it was."

She couldn't stop the surprised blink. Aaron knew about the hospital? She hadn't expected that. It certainly explained why Aaron was here, however, and Dmitri was nowhere in sight.

A sneer pulled across Aaron's face. "You didn't know your operatives locked him up, did you? I guess that means no one knows how to contact you." The wicked gleam in his eyes intensified. "I guess that also means I get to do whatever I want with you now." He picked up the syringe that lay next to his gun. "I intend to remind this *family* what happens to those who betray us. Meanwhile, I'm going to enjoy watching you die."

Instinct snapped into place. "You did it on purpose, didn't you? You killed those girls on purpose."

His smile radiated unspoken praise. "I wondered when you'd figure that out. Very good, Agent Trubachev. Very good indeed." He tapped his finger against the syringe, knocking the air bubbles to the needled end.

Behind him, the door slowly eased open. Natalya's heartbeat tripled as Brandon crept into the shadows. Oh, God, he was here. He couldn't hate her if he'd come after her. But damn it, he was walking into a game he didn't know how to play. She quickly averted her eyes, focusing once more on Mayer. *Keep him talking.* "And the pranks? Why didn't you just kill Brandon the minute you got the order? You were *afraid* of me, weren't you?"

He laughed again, a hauntingly hollow sound that bounced through the concrete-encased room. "What fun is there in that? Shoot him when he's not looking?" He shrugged. "Play with your heads a little before? Watch you fall inside the doorway when you received my pretty present? Much more enjoyable."

"That was you."

Everything suddenly clicked into place. It had all been a game. Jill had nothing to do with the Dubai Project—she'd simply been jealous. Aaron already confessed the chocolates came from Dmitri. But everything else had been one big psychological game.

"Besides, he pissed me off by avoiding my red-light run. Don't worry. His day will come. I'll make sure you get to watch him die before you join him."

Brandon moved closer, his gun trained on the back of Aaron's head. She breathed deeply, willing her heart to stop its infernal racket and offering up a silent prayer for Brandon's safety. She kept the flow of words going to cover any sound his footsteps might make.

"And what did you intend to do with me when you heard I was coming? Did you plan to kill me all along?"

She didn't like the way Aaron set down the syringe and slowly picked up his gun. Her instincts shifted to high alert. Then she saw it. The reason why Aaron had exchanged weapons. Caught by a streetlamp outside, Brandon's approaching shadow inched down the wall.

Aaron bolted to his feet and leapt beside her. He aimed his pistol at her head. His gaze locked on Brandon. "Looks like you're going to get to see him die sooner than later." He cocked the hammer. "Put the fucking gun down, Moretti, or I'm putting a hole in her head."

Forty-three

Brandon's eyes locked with Natalya's. Her courage had snapped, replaced now by evident fear. His heart twisted. She'd been fine before she'd seen him. That fear had nothing to do with the gun pointed at her head and everything to do with him. She worried for him.

Damn it.

A larger fear took root in his veins as he took in the hard set to Aaron's features. Determination. *Commitment.* He'd kill her in a heartbeat.

Aaron's finger tightened around the trigger. "Put it down, Moretti."

A slight shake of Natalya's head ordered him to refuse. He understood her reasoning. He'd fought it a dozen times or more himself. Even if she died, she could still succeed with the case. He could take Aaron down and wrap up the job. The difference this time—he didn't give a damn about anything in the world except the woman at the end of that barrel.

Bending over, he set his pistol on the floor at his feet.

"Get rid of it," Aaron instructed.

Brandon obediently kicked it aside. Metal scraped against concrete as it scuttled toward the wall.

"Now have a seat. Over there." Aaron used his gun to indicate a spot beyond Natalya.

Natalya threw herself at Aaron before Brandon could take a step. Her hands locked onto the pistol, wedging it over her head as she used his locked arm for leverage and hauled herself to her feet. She brought her knee up, driving it solidly into his thigh.

Aaron let out a grunt, but his strength overpowered Natalya. The downward press of his arms doubled her forward, limiting her ability to attack with her legs.

The gun discharged. Brandon froze. For one never-ending heartbeat he stared, certain she'd crumple to the floor. Everything moved in slow motion. Her hands slipped. Regained their grip. She dropped to her knees, and Brandon realized what she was doing. The more she leaned into Aaron's body, the more weight she put on his arms. Miraculously, she'd wedged the gun so it pointed to the floor.

Aaron brought his foot back and kicked her in the gut.

A whole new sense of fury possessed Brandon at the sound of her pained cry. She flew backward, landing sprawled out on her stomach. The gun rested just beyond her outstretched fingertips.

Brandon dove for the weapon at the same time Mayer did. They collided in a flurry of flying fists. Aaron was strong, quite possibly stronger than Brandon. But he lacked discipline. Always had. He fought with adrenaline and left thought behind. Like a wild animal that only knew one instinct—survival.

Adrenaline also pumped through Brandon's veins, enough to override the pain in his left shoulder, but something greater gave him caution—Natalya. He *would not* fail her again. Wouldn't let Mayer lay another finger on her so long as there was breath in Brandon's body.

Raising his forearm, he blocked a fist to his temple, but the backward swing caught him in the side of his face. Fire lanced through his cheek as it split open. The hot, sticky flow of blood wet his skin. He ducked in time to evade another shot at his nose.

Brandon threw his weight upward, driving his knuckles into the underside of Mayer's jaw. A *crack* resounded, and Mayer staggered backward. He recovered quickly. Shaking his head, he charged again. He landed another solid punch to Brandon's already bleeding cheek.

Agony threatened to blind Brandon. Sparks shot in front of his eyes, blackness encroached. He raised both forearms in front of his face and willed his knees into cooperation. The blows came hard and fast, pounding into bone. He flinched with each jarring concussion, backing up, biding his time. Waiting for Aaron to exhaust himself and make a mistake.

An opening arrived, and Brandon took the shot. He summoned his strength and focused on Aaron's Adam's apple. Launching his arm forward, he envisioned it connecting with the wall at Aaron's back and shoved his fist into his former partner's throat.

Aaron's sideways duck prevented the death blow, but Brandon's hit connected with Aaron's vagus nerve. Aaron dropped to his knees. He wobbled in a heavy daze.

Behind Brandon, an angry stream of Russian filled the adjacent hall. Equally charged words spewed from Stefan's mouth. Brandon glanced over his shoulder and caught sight of Stefan shoving a man twice his size down the hall.

"Not . . . going . . . to have her," Aaron rasped out.

Brandon whipped around at the sound of metal table legs scraping against the floor. Arm lifted over his head, syringe in hand, Aaron lunged across the short distance between them. Brandon caught Aaron's wrist seconds before the needle sank into the soft skin between his neck and shoulder.

A shot cracked through the air.

Aaron's eyes went wide with shock. His fingers opened, and the syringe clattered to the floor. All six foot fell onto his face as Brandon let go of his arm. Blood pooled beneath his chest.

Stunned, Brandon swung his gaze to Natalya, and a slow smile spread over his face. She lay on her belly, pistol poised in both hands, her chin mere inches off the cold concrete. As she watched Aaron topple, her fingers let go. Eyes closed, she dropped her cheek to the floor.

Natalya groaned as cool air hit her face. She opened her eyes to find herself in Brandon's lap, wrapped in a blanket, and sitting on a pavement retaining wall outside the warehouse. Twenty feet away, operatives rushed in and out of the building in a steady stream. Red, blue, and white ambulance lights lit up the side of the warehouse. Another four sets of police lights joined the colorful display.

She looked up at Brandon and tried for a smile. "Hey, you." The pain in her chest twisted her effort into a grimace.

Tenderness filled his tawny eyes as he pushed a shank of her hair away from the side of her face. "It's over, beautiful. You did good."

Natalya's heart melted. He'd come after her. Stayed with her. She'd shot him, and he didn't hate her.

She could still feel the pull of absolute terror as Mayer had lunged at him with the syringe. For a moment, she'd thought she might never see Brandon again. That after all this, she'd never get the chance to apologize. To tell him what he meant to her. The case became unimportant. The only thing that mattered was keeping Brandon alive.

Tears welled in her eyes. He was here.

"Shh. Don't cry," he whispered. His thumb brushed across her cheek, wiping a stray tear away. "Kate's safe, so is Becca. We'll take you to the hospital as soon as Stefan's done seeing Nikolai off in cuffs."

"You know." This time she found the ability to hold her smile.

"Yeah. I know a lot of things." Ever so gently, he shifted her position so her face came closer to his. He brushed his mouth across hers, lingering for a heartbeat before he pulled away and gazed into her eyes. "I was scared to death I'd lose you."

Warmth infused her blood, and her heart slowed to the delightful rhythm of complete contentment. The pain in her ribs ebbed. "Don't take me to the hospital. Take me home, Brandon."

"No can do, beautiful. You're not setting another foot inside my house until we come to an agreement about some things."

Surprised, she jerked back, setting off the gnawing ache in her chest. With a grimace, she curled back into his embrace. "Things like?"

His lips moved across her hair. "Like no more lies."

Shivers darted down her spine. That sounded delightful. She'd never utter another lie in her life. "Agreed."

"And you're never allowed to hold a gun while I'm in the same room with you."

She couldn't help herself, she laughed. Mistake. Fire lit her insides. She pressed a hand to her ribs, wheezing. "Don't make . . . me . . . laugh."

Brandon's chest rumbled with amusement. "Swear it, or you're on the street homeless."

"I swear." Lifting her hand, she settled it over his heart and rubbed her cheek against the hard muscle of his chest.

"And . . ." Tightening his embrace, he rested his chin on the crown of her head. "I want to go on vacation. For a long time. Just you and me. No jobs. Some Northern Lights. When we come back, it's consulting for you and a desk job for me."

Nothing sounded better. She nodded, the tightness in her chest now an overflowing of soul-deep feeling. He was offering her a return to the life she'd once known. No fighting. No looking over her shoulder. No need to create stories and the simple ability to just *live*.

And love.

"Anything else?" she whispered.

"Yes." Brandon set two fingers under her chin and tipped her face up to gaze into her eyes. "Tell me what *Ya tebya lyublyu* means."

The husky rasp of his voice sent goose bumps rushing down her arms. Her throat, however, closed around the translation. Tell him? No way in this world could she utter the meaning. She could feel, but she wasn't anywhere near ready to talk about feeling. Certainly not the depth of that one. It might bring pain. Particularly if he couldn't respond the same way.

She stared at his nose as she answered, "It means I like you a lot."

He pursed his lips. "I said no lies."

Natalya blinked. "You know?"

"I also said I know a lot of things."

"If you know, then why are you asking?"

His lips fluttered against hers. "Because I want to hear you say it."

Oh, God. Everything inside Natalya welled up and overflowed. Tears spilled down her face unfettered, and for the first time in her life, they didn't embarrass her. She reached up to touch his uninjured cheek. "It means I love you."

His smile lifted the corners of his mouth and eyes. "I love you too, beautiful."

Long lashes veiled his eyes, and he caught her mouth with his. His tongue glided over hers, slowly, languorously, as if he sought to savor the moment for eternity. She moved into his kiss, deepening it, the pain in her body giving way to the slow burn of arousal. In the darkest moments of her life, she'd stumbled onto something more beautiful than the sunset on the glaciers. Brandon Moretti had led her to innocence, and she'd spend the rest of her life showing him exactly how much she cherished that priceless gift.

Brandon threaded his fingers through her hair and rested his forehead against hers. "Now that I've told you what I want, is there anything you want from me?"

"Yes."

"Name it, sweetheart."

Well, here's to no more lies. She took a deep breath. "Children."

His chuckle washed over her cheek, seconds before his lips touched hers and he murmured, "How soon?"

Natalya didn't have time to respond. He captured her mouth, his eagerness evident in his hungry kiss.

About the Author

TORI ST. CLAIRE grew up writing. Hobby quickly turned into passion, and when she discovered the world of romance as a teen, poems and short stories gave way to full-length novels with sexy heroes and heroines waiting to be swept off their feet. She wrote her first romance novel at seventeen.

While that manuscript gathered dust bunnies beneath the bed, she went on to establish herself as a contemporary, historical, and paranormal author under the pen name Claire Ashgrove. Her writing, however, skirted a fine line between hot and steamy, and motivated by authors she admired, she pushed her boundaries and made the leap into erotica, using the darker side of human nature and on-the-edge suspense to drive grittier, sexier stories.

Her erotic romantic suspense novels are searingly sensual experiences that unite passion with true emotion and the all-consuming tie that binds—love.